CW01513289

'*Vivian Dies Again* is perfect for fans of *Groundhog Day* and *Russian Doll*. It's big, bold, beautifully bonkers, with heaps of heart and a family tree of killer characters. It's time to get ready for the smart, sassy crime caper of the year'
Janice Hallett, author of *The Appeal*

'I loved this book … The perfect blend of bathos and pathos with the most sympathetic unsympathetic character I've read in a very long time. Not to mention the fact that it's really clever, too'
Harriet Tyce, author of *Blood Orange*

'Sharp, funny and well observed, *Vivian Dies Again* made me properly laugh out loud. I absolutely loved it'
Laura Marshall, author of *Friend Request*

'Wickedly clever and properly funny – a time-loop whodunnit that truly kills'
Lesley Kara, author of *The Rumour*

'Hulse skilfully marries together a great hot-mess protagonist, a complex murder mystery, and an abundance of laugh-out-loud moments. *Vivian Dies Again* is brilliantly clever, unique and hilarious. I loved every minute'
Charlotte Levin, author of *If I Can't Have You*

'Move over, Fleabag, there's a new hot mess in town: C.E. Hulse's razor-sharp, witty and original Vivian. If you enjoy your time-loop thrillers dark, deadly and with plenty of bite, you won't want to miss this'
Lizzy Barber, author of *Out of Her Depth*

'Original, funny and sharply observant of what it means to belong. Throw in a murder and it's got everything'
L.V. Matthews, author of *The Twins*

'*Vivian Dies Again is* absolutely fabulous ... Witty, modern, surprising and endlessly enjoyable, this twists in ways you really won't expect, and you'll tear through it in one sitting. Pick this book up – you won't regret it'
Alice Bell, author of *Grave Expectations*

'I snort laughed; I cackled with glee; I couldn't put it down ... Utterly propulsive'
Sam Holland, author of *The Puppet Master*

'Fabulously funny and devilishly dark, *Vivian Dies Again* takes the classic murder mystery and drops it on its head – repeatedly ... Compelling characters, clever twists and moving realisations abound. I fell head over heels for this hapless heroine'
Heather Critchlow, author of *Unsolved*

'Fiendishly well plotted, insightfully observed and just downright hilarious – *Vivian Dies Again* is the most unique crime novel you will read all year. Hulse is an incredibly clever writer and this book is a real treat'
Charlotte Duckworth, author of *The Sanctuary*

'A riotous time-glitch murder mystery with a very funny anti-heroine and lots of family secrets'
Tina Baker, author of *Call Me Mummy*

'Hulse at her very best … An exceptional time-loop murder mystery that explores themes of family, loyalty, responsibility and how to be a good person when it would be much easier to be bad – and it's also hilarious. I couldn't put it down'
Nicci Cloke, author of *Her Many Faces*

'Hilariously quirky. *Vivian Dies Again* is a clever twist on the classic murder mystery … Witty and compelling'
Guy Morpuss, author of *Black Lake Manor*

'A hugely entertaining, conceptually original murder mystery and family drama rolled into one … Darkly humorous and supremely well plotted'
Louise Fein, author of *People Like Us*

'Different, quirky but also full of emotional depth, a brilliantly plotted murder mystery where the victim turns detective'
Alison Stockham, author of *The Cuckoo Sister*

'*Vivian Dies Again* is funny and twisty, and Viv is a wicked character … Tremendous'
J.B. Mylet, author of *The Homes*

'Spit-your-tea-out funny, original and an intriguing mystery to boot; if you're looking for fresh and quirky crime writing, look no further than *Vivian Dies Again*. It's pure delight from start to finish'
Lisa Timoney, author of *Her Daughter's Secret*

Vivian Dies AGAIN

Vivian Dies AGAIN

C.E. HULSE

First published in Great Britain in 2026 by Viper,
an imprint of Profile Books Ltd
29 Cloth Fair
London
EC1A 7JQ
www.viperbooks.co.uk

Copyright © C.E. Hulse, 2026

1 3 5 7 9 10 8 6 4 2

Typeset in Plantin by MacGuru Ltd

Printed and bound in Great Britain by
CPI Group (UK) Ltd, Croydon CR0 4YY

A CIP catalogue record for this book is available
from the British Library.

Our product safety representative in the EU is BGC
Sustainability & Compliance, 7 avenue du Général Leclerc,
Paris, 75014, France. https://baldwinglobalconsulting.com

Hardback ISBN 978 1 80522 626 0
Trade paperback ISBN 978 1 80522 627 7
eISBN 978 1 80522 628 4

For Molly, who made me laugh so much

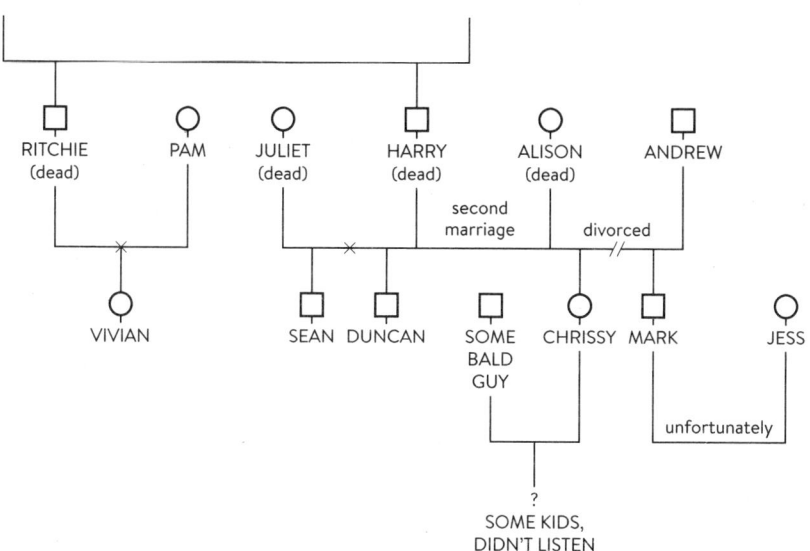

RITCHIE (dead) — PAM
JULIET (dead) — HARRY (dead)
ALISON (dead) — ANDREW

second marriage
divorced

VIVIAN

SEAN DUNCAN SOME BALD GUY CHRISSY MARK JESS

unfortunately

?
SOME KIDS, DIDN'T LISTEN

all the best ones are dead

PART ONE

Harry and Alison's Memorial (New) WhatsApp Group

Pam

Hi everyone. I've just got an email from Chrissy. She's inviting us to a memorial party in April for her mum and Harry.

Angela

???

Pam

Don't be mean.

Angela

Didn't we have perfectly good funerals for Alison and Harry a year ago?

Pam

This message has been deleted.

Angela

What was that? Pam?

Pam

I said I wondered whether Chrissy is having some kind of breakdown, but pretend I didn't say anything.
Chrissy's arranging the memorial at the rooftop bar above the science museum.

Angela

Just attach the email so we can read for ourselves.

Pam

I'm doing a warm handover, like I was taught to.

Angela

But you've not worked in that call centre for twenty years.

Frank

I've always wanted to take a look at that rooftop bar. It's fancy. I heard they charge a tenner a pint.

Angela

Now we know why you haven't been there, Frankie.

Pam

Chrissy says we should wear bright clothes on the day.

Angela

PLEASE just attach the email, Pam.

Pam

I'm never going to be able to attach it if I keep having to stop to read your messages, am I?

Angela

You can attach it as a PDF. You do know how to attach a PDF?

Angela

Pam?

Frank

Give the woman space, Angela.

Pam

I can't work out how to attach it, so I've forwarded it to all of you by email.

From chrissy@cateringdelights.com to pam. slade66@gmail.com

Dear friends,

I can't believe it's been nearly a year since my wonderful mum and her husband, Harry, died. Still, when I watch a new TV programme she'd love, I have a moment where I reach for my phone to tell her.

I am writing to invite you to a memorial party. The details are in the attachment.

I know this might sound strange to some of you. Why a memorial? Why now, when they died a year ago?

Because I want to celebrate their lives properly.

There were so many horrible things about their car accident, and one was the timing. Mum hanging on for those extra weeks meant we were distracted at Harry's funeral. And Mum's funeral felt unsatisfactory in its own way, like we'd pre-grieved her at Harry's.

They deserved so much better.

We're holding the memorial on the rooftop bar above the science museum where they met at their retirement jobs. They both loved that place all their lives – Mum dragged

Mark and I there often when we were kids, and I know Harry did the same with Sean and Duncan.

So let us raise a glass to Mum and Harry one more time. Let's wear bright colours and remember Harry's alarming victory dances when he won at darts. Let's remember Mum's legendary nineties haircut that made her look like a chaffinch, and the time she fell off that banana boat in Fuerteventura.

I bet you all have so many stories. I can't wait to hear them.

All my love,

Chrissy

Harry and Alison's Memorial (New) WhatsApp Group

Angela
Wow.

Pam
I know.

Angela
Do you think Chrissy's in touch with her GP?

Pam
We just need to make sure she has a really nice time on the day.

Angela

I hope she's spoken to Harry's lads about this. She will have done. Surely?

Pam

She's spoken to Harry's lads, but she asked me to invite his friends and other family.

Angela

That's the problem when people only have boys – the extra admin. I feel so sad for people who don't have a daughter.

Angela

Sorry, Pam, that was tactless. I know not all daughters are a gift.

Angela

And please tell me you're not inviting Amy Winehouse.

Pam is typing

Angela

Pam?

Pam is typing

Angela

It's a simple question.

Pam is typing

Angela

Oh, no.

Pam is typing

Angela

Remember that podcast I sent you. Self-care and boundaries! A mother can only do so much. She's thirty-six!

Pam is typing

Angela

Please, Pam! It's you I'm thinking of. Please don't invite Viv!

1

Now

'Fuck me,' Viv says into her sour cocktail, taking in the garden in the Cheshire countryside.

It's the little things: the way the sweeping gravel crunches expensively underfoot. The fact there's been a marquee hired for this non-event, commissioned with a bespoke neon lightboard reading *Francine and Al's Pre-Baby Spectacular*. The way there's no raspberry or pineapple in these cocktails, just the disappointing taste of class, all soil and leather.

Viv stares at the stone-walled house. 'Francine lives *here*?'

Bethan keeps her voice low. 'Don't make it a thing.'

Viv looks around. 'They have hedges in the garden. Not *around* the garden. *In* the garden.'

'They have paddocks too,' Bethan says.

Viv nods. She doesn't know what a paddock is, what makes it different from a field. She's never needed to know.

Guests walk past, mainly thirty-somethings like Viv, just better. She takes in the good teeth, the knee-length dresses.

It should all be so impressive: the paddocks, the soil-and-leather drinks, the dentistry. Yet it's disconcerting. Viv's in a throwback *Daily Telegraph* Stepford utopia, and it makes her want to shiver.

'*How* do Francine and Al have paddocks?' Viv tugs her minidress down. 'Are they wizards?'

'She's a barrister. He's in private equity.'

'But we were the same!' Viv had met Francine a few times in bars in their twenties. Maybe Francine had a better haircut, more expensive lipstick. Maybe she didn't glance down to check the numbers on the bill before throwing her card onto the tray. Maybe she always got a taxi home after a night out – even a decade before, it was only Viv doing the 3 a.m. solo scare-walks along city streets that were eerily silent but for the *tat-a-tat* of her own footsteps and the odd squeal of a fox fighting a cat.

But they were mid-twenties then. Mid-thirties is a different planet. Mid-thirties is when the chickens come home to roost.

And Viv, it turns out, has no chickens.

She swigs her drink. She wishes someone had told her she was peaking in her mid-twenties; she would have made sure she'd enjoyed it more. Still, she's here now, and rich acquaintances mean free drinks. There'll probably be a buffet, and not even a brown one – it'll have vegetables and garnish and actual plates. 'It's nice of Francine to invite me. Especially now she's a paddock person.'

Bethan sips her sparkling water and looks at Viv's feet. 'Are those my shoes?'

'Ah.' Viv looks down at Bethan's suede mules. 'Thing is, they go perfectly with this dress.'

'I *told you* to stop nicking my stuff!' That Bethan has the same size feet as Viv is her personal tragedy. 'I *told you* my moisturiser was the last straw!'

Viv keeps her smile fixed. Right now, Bethan's moisturiser is, again, on Viv's bedside table. She'll sneak it back when Bethan's asleep.

'You're a *parasite*!'

Viv was about to swig her cocktail; she coughs in fumes. 'That's just rude.'

'Oh, go home.' Bethan shakes her head. 'This isn't your kind of party.'

'It's not your kind of party either! And Francine told you to invite me!'

'Only to make up the numbers. You don't know her!'

'I can't leave – you're driving.'

'Leave anyway.' Bethan stalks away over the marquee floor.

Viv watches her go. She would never borrow *those* shoes. They look like great big pies on Bethan's feet.

Viv looks around, sipping her soil-and-leather cocktail, taking in the people around, none of whom she knows. She could always go over to the buffet table, but she's allergic to peanuts. While she is not averse to taking risks with her long-term health, canapé roulette feels just a bit too immediately lethal. She's never had to test the effectiveness of the EpiPen she always carries, and really doesn't want to. Even for Viv, excitement has its limits.

She walks towards the nearest group.

'There comes a point you have to make a trade-off.' The woman talking barely moves her mouth. 'Knees or fees.'

'So our decision was clear.' The man next to her pauses and grins. '*Kum ba yah.*'

The group laugh.

Viv swigs her sour cocktail. She scans the marquee.

It's fine, it's all fine. She can feel another Classic Viv anecdote coming on. *The night I got stuck in a paddock with a bunch of rahs.* Someone famous once said *life is copy* and no one tops Viv when it comes to acquiring material. This night will turn good soon and, if not, it can be buffed up and shorn of its dull bits, made into an anecdote and brought out at an appropriate time to entertain friends at a bar.

Or if no friends are around – strangers.

Viv walks towards another cluster of people.

'You can pay someone to do it, of course.' A shiny woman beams at her listeners. 'But there's no feeling like when you've cleaned the oven. You feel like you've cleaned your whole life!'

Viv heads out of the marquee, the April evening air crisp on her bare arms. She stands under a sprawling oak tree and pulls her phone from her bag.

Maybe Mark can come and get her?

She dials his number. Sometimes Viv likes to play this game with herself, pretend she has a partner she can see any night of the week. Someone who doesn't have her number saved in his phone under *Craig (work)*. Someone who doesn't only message back when his wife's trussed up like a hot corpse at Reformer Pilates.

Mark doesn't answer. Obviously.

Viv's stomach thuds, and she judges herself for it. There's no point knowing something can't possibly happen, yet still being disappointed. That's not good logic. That's not good *living*.

Onwards.

Viv scrolls through the names on her phone, copying and pasting, throwing the net wide.

> Funny story – I've got accidentally stuck in a marquee in Cheshire! Fancy rescuing me? I'll send you a pin and we can go on a mission.

She gets one reply.

> Ha ha, no problem, Viv. Just give me five mins to wake up Autumn and wrestle her into her car seat!

The sarcasm only becomes apparent on second reading. Viv narrows her eyes.

The ticks against her messages turn double blue, but there are no more replies. No triple dots. None of her friends are even typing.

Viv lets her phone hand fall against her leg.

She doesn't know when it happened – slowly, slowly, then *bam* – but it's clear no one she knows plans to leave the house after 8 p.m. ever again.

It's fine. She's only messaged actual mates so far; she has emergency numbers left. She's still a long way off calling

Last Resort Steve. No need to scrape the bottom of that particularly needy barrel just yet.

She can sleep at a bus shelter. She can beg one of Francine's friends for their spare room. The great thing is, whichever way tonight ends, she will make this another *Classic Viv* gasp-anecdote – one to make people laugh in shining-eyed horror.

Viv's smile will only fade when she is sober and alone.

And Viv tries to avoid being sober and alone.

'Hey, V!' Francine beckons from inside the marquee, the sequins of her bodycon maternity dress shimmering like scales. 'So pleased you could make it!'

'Hi!' Viv walks into Francine's embrace until she's stopped by the tidy, solid bump. 'You live like a princess!'

Francine laughs, like Viv is joking. 'I know, right?'

Viv smiles at the rest of the group. It's unsettling, looking from the women to the men: that immediate hit of aesthetic unbalance, like she's watching Afghan hounds from Crufts prance between rusty car parts in a scrap-metal yard. The men are wallpaper-men, identikit and out-of-shape, yet the women glow with built-in ring lights, their silky hair all caramel shades of money-blonde. These are women about which people use the word *sashay*. They look the same age as Viv, but with centuries more evolution.

It's the skincare. And the triceps. Every single one of these women could beat their husbands in an arm-wrestle.

'Viv knows how to get a party started.' Francine's eyes gleam. 'Tell them about the time you woke up to find a kebab in your handbag!'

'Ah.' Viv looks from Francine to her friends in their sensible-length midis. 'That's an old story.'

Francine gives Viv an encouraging nod. 'I can't remember, did you eat the kebab in the end?'

Viv pauses. 'Meat after twelve hours at room temperature? I gave it a swerve.'

'Viv thought she'd cleaned up her bag, but when she got her comb out at work the next day, she combed herself with chilli sauce!' Francine laughs with her mouth open: it makes no sound. 'And, Viv, remember when you woke up to see that guy sleep-urinating into your wardrobe? And that other guy, the one who started clucking after too much coke?'

Viv frowns. 'He was actually mentally ill. That was properly unfortunate.'

'No' – Francine grabs Viv's arm in excitement – 'tell them about the Cheese Man! The one you found eating Bethan's brie at 3 a.m., straight from the packet!'

Viv takes a second. 'Fun times.' *Now* it's clear why she's been invited to this party. 'Excuse me.'

She walks out of the marquee, her smile fading. Once, *just once*, she'd like to be invited to a party because someone thinks she'd add a bit of class. And it's not true, what Francine said: Viv's not a party-starter. She just stops parties ending. Around her, bar staff wipe tables and blow out candles, flicking on lights with a prison-break glare, while Viv is stumbling, waving and coaxing. *Tomorrow's tomorrow! There'll be somewhere still open!*

When people find out she's a classroom assistant, they pause.

From the marquee, someone heads in Viv's direction – a

late-middle-aged vision in triple-teal. Teal dress, teal sling-backs, teal clutch bag. This teal apparition belongs at this party even less than Viv does.

Viv frowns. *'Angela?'*

Three things about Angela:

1. She has type one diabetes. She always says it like that – type one diabetes. Having to say just diabetes would kill her faster than any amount of sugar.
2. She loathes Camilla Parker Bowles. Loathes her, mallow-deep, like Diana was her ride-or-die soulmate, not a tall stranger she once watched get married on the telly. Hating Camilla is like a religion for Angela, and Angela still calls her that – Camilla Parker Bowles – though the woman's been divorced for three decades.
3. There's only one person in the world Angela hates more than Camilla.

'Hasn't Francine done well?' Angela makes a show of studying the surroundings. 'They're thinking of getting alpacas. How about you? Still in the same place?'

Viv narrows her eyes. 'Same place.'

'No paddocks for you?'

Viv makes her voice airy. 'I've never been into paddocks.' She gives her sweetest smile. 'How's your Anthony doing? Did he ever get his shoes back from the nick?'

Angela's eyes flare.

'What did they charge him with in the end?'

'You *know* that was a case of mistaken identity.'

Viv sips her drink, victorious.

'The sergeant offered Anthony a full apology. You *know* that.'

'I'm surprised to see you here.' Viv indicates the stone house. 'Not our circles.'

'Francine's mother and I were at Slimming World together when the Berlin Wall came down. It was so thoughtful of Francine to invite her mother's friend to the party.' Angela pauses. 'In case you're wondering, I don't want to be invited to any of *your* parties.'

Viv laughs into her martini glass.

'I'm going to give you some advice, Viv. As your godmother.'

'I'm thirty-six, Angela. None of us believe in God.' Viv pats Angela's arm. 'But fun catching up.'

Viv walks away, arms goosepimpling. Soon, probably within seconds of seeing the countryside whip by from a passenger seat, she will find this exchange funny. Angela's dislike is bracing, like taking a dip in an emotional plunge pool. The honesty is refreshing.

Angela raises her voice. 'Such a shame your mother had to get a taxi home alone after her op.'

Viv stops walking.

'I would never have let her go on her own, but I'd booked a cottage in Devon that week. It was unrefundable, and your mum refused to let me cancel. She's thoughtful like that. Frugal.'

Viv turns back to Angela. 'What operation?'

'It's not my place to say.'

'But you *have* said.'

17

'There's such a thing as medical confidentiality.'

'But you're not a doctor.'

Angela looks to the sky, as if she didn't deliberately dangle this bait to have this impact.

'Angela.' Viv takes a step closer. 'You've made your point.' She doesn't mind sparring with Angela – a nemesis keeps the mind sharp – but this particular bout feels gloves-off.

Angela shakes her head in pseudo-disappointment. 'Your mother had a tumour.' She lowers her voice. 'Down there.'

Viv's eyebrows hunch. 'But she's OK?'

Angela raises her face to the sky.

'Angela?'

'You know the state of the NHS right now.' Angela looks over Viv's shoulder. 'Results can take months.'

'I would have taken Mum to hospital if I'd known. Yes, *in a taxi.*' Viv gets it in before Angela can point out she's failed her driving test twice. 'I'll phone her right now.'

Viv walks back underneath the oak tree to make the call.

She gets voicemail. 'Mum, I've just heard about your op. I'm so sorry. Please call me.' She pauses. 'It's Viv.'

Viv wishes she hadn't added that bit, what with her being an only child.

She heads back into the marquee, looking for a group to weave herself into. In every direction, there's hard-bodied women and puffed-up men. The dancing has started, and the men's faces are red, though it's only the women dancing. One woman in a floaty dress shows off impressive quads, crouching low and bouncing up in what, if Viv was doing it, would be called a *slut drop.*

Viv tries to sip from her glass. It's empty.

18

She heads to the bar – soil cocktails being shit, but better than no cocktails – and passes a woman in a floral maxi dress leaving a curtained-off area. There's a sign on the curtain.

Astro Audrey. Tarot and Palm Reading.

Viv sniffs. It's bullshit, obviously.

She walks round the edge of the curtain and looks at the woman shuffling a deck of cards at the table. The woman's younger than Viv expected, with a dusting of freckles and a simple black dress. No jangly coins or swathes of purple fabric here, just a clean, corporate vibe. This is a fortune-teller for the after-dinner circuit.

'Do I have to pay?' Viv asks.

Astro Audrey shakes her head. She waves a hand towards the empty chair.

'Because I just walked past,' Viv slides into the seat, 'and I thought – *yeah.*'

Astro Audrey takes Viv's hands. She stares into Viv's eyes for a long time.

Viv's cheeks prickle.

Audrey doesn't blink.

Viv shifts in her chair and tries to hold Audrey's gaze.

Audrey lets Viv's hands go. 'I shouldn't give you a reading today.'

'Why?'

'It's only meant to be a bit of fun.'

Viv frowns. 'Am I going to die?'

Astro Audrey smiles. 'I don't do that kind of reading.'

'Then why won't you do me?'

Audrey makes her voice softer. 'Because you're deeply unhappy.'

'What? No. I'm having fun!' Viv waves an arm. 'So much fun!'

The empathy in Audrey's eyes is unbearable.

'I'm not *unhappy*.' Viv stares her truth into this ludicrous woman. 'I'm at a party in a marquee. There's free cocktails! There's *paddocks*! I'm living the fucking dream!'

Viv's hands start to tremble.

Both women look down.

'I've had some bad news, that's all.' Viv presses one hand lightly with the other. 'And there's a ton of caffeine in those cocktails.' She shoves her palms out. 'Do me. Please.'

Astro Audrey shakes her head.

'Fine.' Viv stands. 'Your job's bollocks anyway.'

She walks out of the tent, her handbag buzzing.

Viv answers the phone. 'Mum! Are you OK?'

'The tumour was benign.'

'Benign's good, right?'

'Benign's perfect.'

'Thank God.' Viv closes her eyes and lets the relief wash through. 'Why didn't you say?'

Mum says nothing.

Viv watches a gesturing reveller slosh sour cocktail over himself. 'I could have been there. Moral support.'

From the marquee, there's a screech of mic feedback. '*One, two.*'

'How did you know?' Mum says finally.

'I just bumped into Angela.'

'And she didn't tell you the tumour was benign?'

Viv narrows her eyes. 'No.' She whirls round, searching for *that bastard*. 'I could have taken you to hospital. Kept your spirits up, bought you Bakewell tarts. You didn't have to be alone.'

Mum doesn't say anything.

'I know we don't always …' Viv stares at the oak tree. 'But I care. You know I care. Surely?'

There's a long pause.

'Mum? I love you. You know that, right?'

'I love you too.'

'I do care. About you. About family.'

Mum leaves a long minute.

'Mum?'

'There's a memorial for Alison and Harry next Saturday.'

Viv places one hand lightly on the tree. 'Right.' Bark scratches the delicate skin of her palm. 'Would you have told me if I hadn't rung?'

'*One, two. One, two.*'

'I know I'm not always great with this stuff' – Viv's voice thickens – 'but when it comes to the important things, I'm here. You *do* know that, Mum. Don't you?'

From the other end of the phone, more silence.

Viv presses her palm into the bark. 'Send me the details of the memorial. I'll be there.'

Still, only silence.

'Send me the details.' Viv makes her voice firm. 'And I'll see you on Saturday.'

2

Now

By 2 a.m., all the paddock party guests are gone – except one.

Even Last Resort Steve doesn't pick up every time.

Viv follows Francine into the spare room, head bowed, a housemaid trailing the lady of the manor. 'I'm so sorry. Again.'

The room is the size of Bethan's whole ground floor, with huge windows and a shedload of visible carpet. The king-size guest bed is flanked by three laundry airers, all draped with drying shirts and socks.

Francine starts stripping washing from the airers.

Viv puts her hand on Francine's wrist. 'It's fine.'

Francine scoops a line of pants into the crook of her arm.

'Leave it. Please!' Viv positions herself between Francine and the airer. 'I thought there'd be a station nearby.' She pauses. 'Or taxis.'

It's not true. Viv doesn't have the cash for a taxi.

'You have to book taxis round here in advance. The other guests did.' Francine can't keep the edge from her voice. 'Shame Bethan left without you.'

Viv watches Francine swipe more lines of washing. 'She must have forgotten I was here.'

Francine turns, the pile of laundry crushed between her folded arms and her rainbow-sequinned chest. One sock escapes to the floor.

Viv squats for the sock and places it back on Francine's bump-pile, not meeting her gaze. Francine's expression is so different now from the one she wore when she introduced Viv at the party. Viv's shitshow of a life is only funny if it's someone else's problem.

Viv swallows. 'Again, thank you for having me.'

'I'll find you a toothbrush.'

'I'll clean my teeth when I get home. I'm no Gwyneth Paltrow.'

Francine starts gathering washing again. 'You'll need pyjamas.'

'No need. *Please* leave that, Francine. Your washing's meant to be here, it's me that isn't.' Viv makes her voice forceful. '*Please.*'

Francine takes a second. She heads for the door, gathered clothes held to her chest. 'I hope you'll be comfortable.'

'How could I not be?' Viv indicates the room, her arms wide. 'Thank you.'

Francine nods. She doesn't say *you're welcome*.

In all the desperate taxi phoning of the hour before, when Viv asked tentatively if there was a cash machine nearby, Francine had snap-insisted she'd pay. *That's* how much she wanted Viv out of her house.

Francine's fault. You invite a circus monkey, you shouldn't be surprised when it starts to dance.

Francine leaves the room and Viv sits on the bed, bursting for a piss. She'll let Francine go first, then tiptoe in carefully when it's quiet. She'll even wash her face afterwards. While Viv is, as she told Francine, not Gwyneth Paltrow, Gwyneth probably isn't this heavy-handed with a smoky eye. And Francine, of course, has the white pillowcases of a domestic psychopath.

Viv strains to listen. Is that the sound of a bathroom door? She rubs her goosepimpling arms.

Tonight was disconcerting in so many ways. Francine told Viv's stories like they were from the past – and they were. Yet it was only last year Viv brought home a guy who necked all her benzos while she was in the toilet. He ate part of a plant, crashed out on her bed, and left her with no choice but to lie next to him till morning, unfucked and wired with outrage, staring at the bitten silhouette of her aloe vera.

How long since any of the people at this party have had a story like that?

Viv doesn't want to know. It's starting to feel less funny, especially now she has to scroll those online forms for the alarming extra seconds to reach her year of birth. When those years are segmented, she's reached the blunt 36–45 bracket.

Though, really, it's a win she's still here. She could have been dead by now.

Her phone beeps. She doesn't rush to pick it up – *too late, Last Resort Steve* – but it's not Steve. It's Mum.

And it isn't quite a message, just an empty capsule shape on the message thread.

There's another beep. Another capsule.

Viv frowns. She hasn't seen Mum for a while, but mid-sixties feels too early for dementia. Besides, Angela would have sprinted over a field of landmines for the chance to shout that information at Viv.

The thought that Mum can't sleep, probably because of their call, makes Viv scratch the back of her neck.

Eventually, a message arrives. I've sent Chrissy's message by email.

Viv checks her inbox.

Dear friends,
I can't believe it's been nearly a year since my wonderful mum and her husband, Harry, died. Still, when I watch a new TV programme she'd love, I have a moment where I reach for my phone to tell her.
I am writing to …

Viv reads the email twice. She taps out a reply on the message thread, overthinking. She types and deletes, types and deletes.

She presses *send*.

Thanks Mum.

She types again.

You're up late?

There's the sound of swilling water. A piss and a flush. Viv's pelvic floor throbs.

Those people who advise to drink water at the end of a party must have elephant-sized bladders. It's never worked for her anyway. Any water she drinks is fruitless, always three hours and eight drinks too late. It's like chasing a blue whale with a kid's fishing net.

Viv stares at the screen, waiting for a reply that doesn't come.

She continues to stare, long after the screen goes black.

Two hours later, Viv wakes, gasping. Is this death?

This is way beyond the usual hangover. It's gone beyond the physical, and turned existential.

Viv is *wizened.*

She switches on the bedside lamp. She takes in the slow blinking light in the corner of the room.

A dehumidifier.

Because of course Francine wouldn't just let the damp from the washing evaporate and seep into the walls, like a normal person.

Viv switches off the dehumidifier. She climbs on the desk and reaches to the high window. It's locked.

She looks for a key, lifting curtains, scouring surfaces, opening desk drawers and pulling out papers.

No key.

Viv pushes documents back into the drawer, glancing at the top paper. *Your Annual Pension Statement.*

She shoves the drawer shut, catching sight of the skin on the back of her hands.

It must be dehydration, but her hands look like her nana's did, right before the last stroke.

Viv needs water – now.

She pulls down her minidress and heads for the bathroom. She sticks her head in the sink, but can't get her mouth at the right angle to drink. She tries different positions, straining her lips, carp-like. No good.

She gropes for the banister, tiptoeing downstairs. She steps onto the cold hall tiles.

Whooping alarm bells shriek into the silence, sudden and aggressive.

From above, there are confused voices. An opening door. A light.

Viv arranges her expression into an apologetic smile. She turns to face the top of the stairs.

Francine's husband sprints round the corner, hand skidding along the top of the banister, sleep-hair pointing at all angles. He's naked but for a pair of creased candy-striped boxers. A line of fox-brown hair runs up the tiniest of paunches.

Viv looks away. 'Hi.' She steps to the side so he can reach the control box.

He taps in a number and the shrieking alarm stops. There's silence, but for faint barking in the distance.

'Sorry.' Viv keeps looking away, his near-nakedness too intimate, too sudden. She's seen a lot of naked men, but it usually feels more consensual. 'I really needed some water.'

Francine's husband gives a curt nod. He heads back up the stairs.

Viv hovers, looking at the alarm box. Has he reset the alarm, or switched it off? She wants to call after this man, but she doesn't know his name.

She thinks of the neon script on the lightbox in the marquee. 'Al?'

Upstairs, a door slams.

Viv bounces her hand lightly on the banister. She looks through the kitchen door.

She can't. Can she?

No. She can't.

She walks back up, into the bathroom. She climbs into the claw-footed bath and readies her face under the tap, opening wide. She switches the tap on.

Cold water overflows her mouth, spilling down her dress, freezing her chest. She gasps and gulps.

'*What the hell?*'

Viv pulls away from the tap, water soaking her hair.

She sees herself through Francine's husband's eyes: a stranger in his bath, her minidress ruched up, gulping bathwater like a feral animal at a broken hose. A feral animal with its pubis evident through semi-transparent pants.

Viv bucks, pulling her dress down. The ceramic stabs her shoulder blades. 'I didn't realise you'd hear.' She switches off the tap. 'Sorry.'

She squeezes her hair, wringing out water. She glances up to make a joke.

The man has gone.

★

At eight o'clock the next morning, Viv turns to the man in the driver's seat. 'I can't thank you enough.'

Francine's husband keeps his engine running.

'Sorry again about … everything.'

He taps his hand lightly against the mocha steering wheel.

Viv scrambles out of the car. 'And congratulations again on the baby. Wonderful news.'

She shuts the car door, giving the husband – Al – her cheeriest wave. She keeps smiling till the car is out of sight.

She hitches her handbag higher up her shoulder, taking in the deserted station approach. She steps slowly down in her walk-of-shame minidress, smiling as she passes a woman pushing a goggle-eyed toddler on a tricycle, a puffa-sleep-suited baby starfished to her chest.

When the woman doesn't smile back, Viv smiles wider. It's fine.

Just as long as Viv has her credit card with her.

And she hasn't already hit its limit.

And – *please, God I don't believe in* – that trains run from this arse end of the Stepford world on a Sunday.

3

Now

On Wednesday evening, Viv drops her new dress on the bed. The cellophane packaging detaches itself from her jumper with a series of static crackles.

She can't put off the RSVP any longer.

She's only met Chrissy three times, but that's enough to know this woman won't have a live-and-let-live approach to party attendance. Chrissy is a woman of preventative physio and 6 a.m. alarms: she is a woman who follows dosage instructions and replicates serving suggestions. She probably has a filing cabinet for the instruction manuals of her household appliances, and Viv suspects she even washes her duvets. Chrissy will expect RSVPs and write the answers on a spreadsheet – and one that is colour-coded, with built-in formulas.

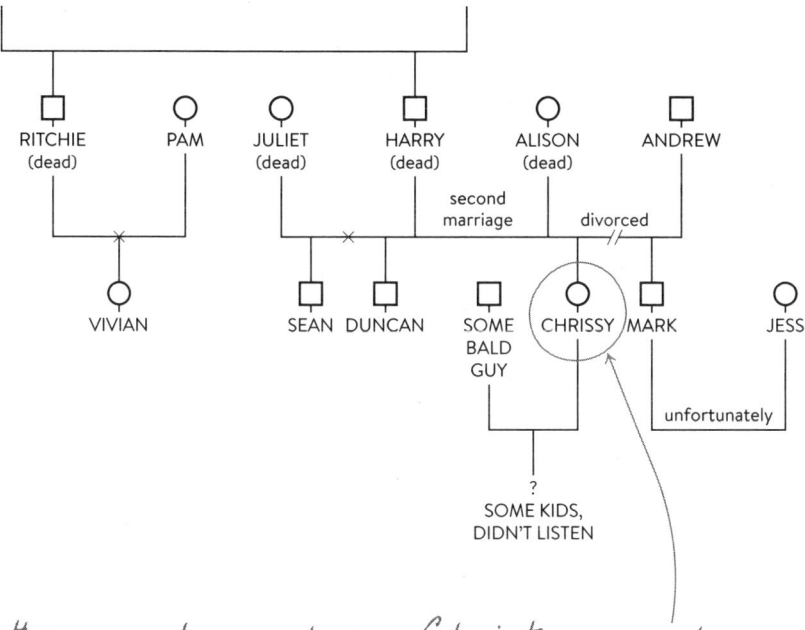

RITCHIE (dead) PAM JULIET (dead) HARRY (dead) ALISON (dead) ANDREW

second marriage   divorced

VIVIAN   SEAN DUNCAN   SOME BALD GUY CHRISSY MARK   JESS

unfortunately

?
SOME KIDS, DIDN'T LISTEN

the one who sends me Christmas cards

In her head, Viv calls Chrissy 'Captain Clipboard'.

Viv sits on the bed, the dress's cellophane seeking her work skirt, reclinging. She glances around her room: around Bethan's spare room. The two used to live in house-shares with several others, but now the only person who needs to share is Viv, straining a once-uncomplicated friendship, inviting pass-agg comments about *the state of the grill pan* and *are all the forks in your bedroom again?* and, at the sight of Viv's bag of knock-off diazepam on her dressing table – *if you shit the bed in your Fucked Girl Summer, you're buying me a new mattress.*

Viv glances at the pills. She won't take any to the memorial on Saturday, and she's not planning to get drunk either. This is a new dawn, a new day, a new life for Viv, etc., etc.

31

She is about to message Chrissy but rethinks. She dials instead. Chrissy gives off a Boomer air and, besides, Viv knows from Harry's funeral that the woman hadn't muted her keypad tones. Viv can't be responsible for any distress caused to the wider community.

'Hello?'

'It's Viv Slade. Harry's niece.'

Viv decides to think of the pause that follows as *contemplative*.

'Mum's told me about the memorial on Saturday. What a lovely idea.'

There's another pause.

Chrissy gets to be superior because she has her own catering business, and kids she made with her own body, and a Nutribullet, and keeps sunflowers seeds in that little pocket of her handbag where Viv keeps internet diazepam.

'I'd like to come on Saturday.' Viv raises her chin higher. 'If that's OK.'

A beat. 'Of course.'

'I wouldn't miss it. I adored Harry.'

It's a perfect gap for Chrissy to say *he adored you too*, but no one in Viv's extended family ever feels like throwing her an emotional bone.

'I can't wait to catch up.' Viv hears herself, as peppy as a cheerleader. The self-hate is strong. 'It will be lovely to see you and …'

Too ambitious. Viv can't remember the names of Chrissy's kids.

'I'd better go,' Chrissy says. 'I'm making dinner.'

Viv tries on her just-bought dress. She watches herself

turn in the mirror of her wardrobe, the full tulle skirts floating round at knee height.

Viv's going to sort her life out. Starting with the memorial on Saturday.

She turns again, looking only at her reflection, trying to ignore the dirty cups on the dressing table, the open bag of knock-off pills, the plate encrusted with congealed rice. She focuses on her cobweb sleeves instead and sees they are perfect: see-through sexy, not *sexy* sexy. Grace Kelly, not Madonna. She looks demure: not like Viv, at all.

Which is ideal: it's crucial Viv comes to this memorial dressed as someone else. Only she will know the price tag's still attached and digging into her shoulder, that she'll be returning the dress the next day to get her money back.

There's a name for the person who turns up unwanted at a party: *the bad fairy*.

But Viv doesn't want to think about that now.

She picks her phone off the bed and messages Mark.

Mum's told me about your mum and Harry's memorial on Saturday. I'm going.

The typing is quick; the planning was not. Viv had spent much of her workday crafting this benign sidestep of a text, making sure it contained no judgement, no drama. No hint that Mark must have known about this party for ages and not mentioned it.

Compartmentalisation, that skill's called. Viv's tried and failed to develop it, but then: Mark's married, and he and Viv are having an affair. Being able to compartmentalise is part of the toolkit. He's even able to compartmentalise away the fact Viv is family. (Only through Harry and Alison's late marriage. There are no memories of toddlers sharing bathtime, no teenage holidays in Cornwall, no shared blood. This isn't an incest situation.)

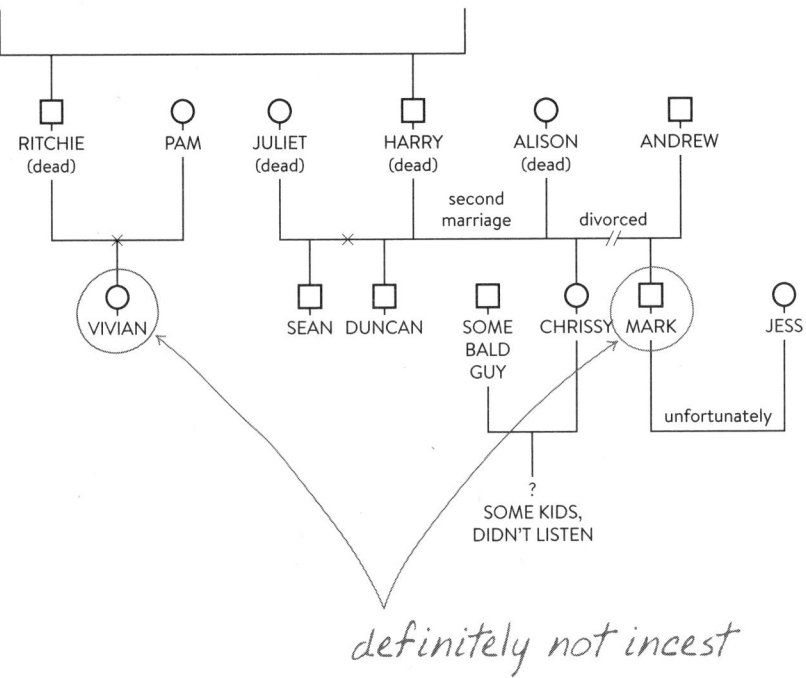

definitely not incest

Three dots appear in the thread with Mark, despite it being only 7 p.m., and not a Pilates night.

Do you really think that's a good idea?

Irritation makes Viv a decisive typer.

Haven't you heard? Nothing I do is a good idea.

She sends another.

I've already RSVP'd to your sister.

Viv drops her phone on the bed and fluffs her hair in the mirror, pulling the front sections down in a way a magazine said *accentuates the cheekbones.*

She glances at the phone.

Mark isn't replying, which is a tactical mistake. He should have said *don't come.* He should have pulled death-rank, told her a mum trumps an uncle, told her that, as son of one of the deceased, his wishes are more important than those of someone invited as an afterthought. He should have told her that, for this one day only, Viv should back off.

But Mark never asks anything of Viv. That way he still gets to feel like the good guy.

Viv slips her feet into her new spike-heeled pumps.

A door opens downstairs. A shout up. '*Did you use the last laundry capsule without putting them on the list?*'

Viv wrinkles her nose. Bethan's question is the very definition of *rhetorical.* She twirls again in front of the mirror.

It's pretty, how this dress nips in at the waist and floats out to knee-length. Twirling like this, her too-high shoes tipping her feet onto Barbie points, Viv could be the doll from a music box. There'll be no accidental pubic flashing on Saturday. She'll never have looked more elegant – or more different.

And Viv won't just *look* different, she'll *be* different. By the end of the day, people will say *Viv? Turned up all smiles, like a TV presenter. So cultured, with her witty-yet-uncontroversial takes on politics. She came, she charmed, she asked after people's kids. She didn't talk too loudly, or minesweep abandoned drinks. She didn't fuck anyone in the toilets.*

There'll be no bad fairy behaviour at this party: Viv won't be showing up with a pin *or* a curse. Of course, she'll still enter to a silent needle scratch, the cobweb sleeves of her dress thin against the sudden chill. You can't change thirty-six years of a villain edit overnight, and Viv's not naïve – she'll never be the hero of their family story.

But, on Saturday, she can at least stop being the villain.

She's never wanted to be a main character anyway.

There's the sound of feet on the stairs. Stomping feet.

'You know what the list is for, right?' Bethan walks in without knocking. 'You know the pen's right there?' She sees Viv's dress. 'Why?'

'A memorial.' Viv fluffs her skirts. 'This weekend.'

'Whose?'

'My uncle.'

Bethan softens her stance. 'Sorry.'

'Thank you.'

Bethan tightens again. 'The uncle who died a year ago?'

'But we're still sad.'

'The laundry capsules are the last straw.' When had Bethan become *this* cold? 'I want you out of my spare room.'

Viv flares her eyes. 'Where do I go?'

'Ask your mum.'

'I never ask Mum for anything, you know that!' There was just that one time Viv broke her lifetime code and spilled her financial trauma to an uncharacteristically silent Mum across the kitchen table. The humiliation was absolute.

36

Viv left Mum's house with no cash, just a heap of parental sorrow and a Tupperware double-portion of under-seasoned tagine, which Viv shame-wolfed in one go, at 1 a.m.

'Can we talk about this later?' Viv says quietly. 'I'm having a tough week.'

'You take the piss.'

'I know, but I can't think about this now. I've got a big weekend.'

Bethan peers at her. 'You're shaking.'

Viv puts one hand over the other. 'As if.'

'Are you OK?'

'You've just asked me to move out of my house.'

'*My* house. I meant other than that.'

'I'm OK.' Viv stands a little straighter. 'I'm always OK.'

Bethan studies Viv for a moment. She walks out of the room, her footsteps softer.

Viv frowns at the softening. If Bethan lets Viv stay because she feels sorry for her, she'd rather sleep in the park.

She twirls slowly again in front of the mirror, holding her own gaze.

She needs to be positive. She's *right* to be positive. Everything's going to change this weekend.

Viv will make things right with her family, somehow. She'll finally feel like she belongs, banish that ever-present jittery buzz in her belly. She'll replace that buzz with the profound inner peace smug twats speak of, and then – finally – stability.

Calm, deep-rooted, stability.

And she won't even find that stability tedious; it'll feel perfect and soothing and *right*. She'll stop trembling for no reason, she'll pay off her debts, and, eventually, she'll buy clothes and cut the labels off. She'll write down when she's used the last washing capsule – no, she'll *buy* new capsules – and she'll remember to eat every few hours. She'll get rid of this antsy feeling she's been doing life wrong; that she woke in her mid-thirties and found she'd fucked everything.

Viv holds her own gaze in the mirror. She grabs her *Top Gun* aviators from the dressing table. She puts them on, looks back at the mirror, and straightens.

Detail. It's all detail.

From this weekend, everything's going to change.

4

Now

It's a long week. Every evening, Viv dulls her pesky thoughts with the soothing white noise of alcohol, and the impact is cumulative: by Friday, she is spent. The kids' voices cut at a pitch that makes her jaw tighten, and it isn't a great afternoon for Sparky, the class hamster, to lunge unexpectedly from his hay and sink his teeth into the fat of her hand.

'*Ouch!*' Viv jerks her hand back. '*You little cunt!*'

She looks up. A sea of five-year-old faces lift from their books.

'Biting the hand that feeds.' Viv tries to smile. 'Who's heard that expression?'

But none of the kids respond, and she's done. The kids might not remember to always put their hands up when they need a piss, but they have perfect grassing antennae: they'll enunciate the words perfectly at the dinner table. There will be outraged parent emails in the head's inbox by morning.

Viv feels another disciplinary coming on.

She's still planning her defence as she walks out of the school at home time – variations on rhyming *cunt* with *runt* – but she's not confident. The job is nearly in the rear-view mirror, and she's realised, now, this is the best job she's ever had.

Far better than cleaning up in a care home, where she'd often left the kitchen to retrieve the washing-up trolley and instead found a different kind of trolley, with a sheeted corpse.

Far better than the call centre, working on a phone that auto-dialled desperate people, asking if they want their debt consolidated, and then listening to them weep. (The kids weep now, too, but the whole thing feels less weighted.)

Far better than that job in the cubicle, where she lasted half a day – she just looked around and thought *nope* – and the receptionist job on the fifteenth floor of a grey tower full of greyer people, where she had to wear a blouse like Thatcher and spent her breaks leaning her forehead on the cold window, looking down at the city, imagining what it was like to fall.

Still, there are loads of jobs out there. *Loads.*

There's selling things that aren't real, like advertising space and extended warranties. She'd make a good HGV driver, even if she'd have to piss in bottles. And learn to drive. The pissing would be possible, she'd just need some kind of funnel and—

'Wait up!'

Mark jogs towards her wearing a short-sleeved shirt and chinos, work lanyard bouncing round his neck.

Viv feels her eyebrows rise. 'I didn't think we did sunlight?'

Mark indicates to keep walking. On the rare occasions they're not huddled like vampires and are actually outside in the daytime, Mark likes to keep moving. He thinks it makes them harder to spot. 'I haven't got long.' He's actively not looking at her, breathing hard, though he's only jogged a few steps from his car.

Viv heads towards the park. 'This *is* a surprise.' Mark looks more ordinary in daylight. His lanyard strap is aggravating a rash on his neck – he's a bad shaver – and he's wearing those inexplicable slip-on shoes he's started wearing with the justification *it's less hassle than laces.*

Viv hasn't told him how much she hates those shoes, just kicks them under her dressing table at the first opportunity, for practical as well as aesthetic reasons. Seeing those things at the key moment would kill the mood as fast as his wife walking in.

They cross the park in the direction of the swings.

'So, I'm not asking you not to come tomorrow.'

Viv glances up.

Mark's raw-looking Adam's apple bobs. 'This definitely isn't that.'

'I'm not coming because of you.' Viv is defensive.

Mark shoves his hands in his pockets.

Viv kicks a branch out of her path. 'This is about my family.'

'You know Jess will be there?'

'Wow.' Viv turns to face him. 'In the tone I use with my reception class.'

From the swings, a toddler yells.

'I know your wife exists, Mark. I don't forget that just because I don't see her.'

Viv wishes she liked Mark less: that he didn't have the hair of a Disney prince; that she didn't feel like he was the last person in the world who found her disarray charming. Or that she had more social options: either one would do. Something's happened in the last few years, something that affected her social life more than any pandemic. The babies came all at once in a mewling plague, and her friends have a new mission: *STAY INDOORS*.

I've still got Bethan. That's what Viv used to tell herself. But that was before shoe-gate, before moisturiser-gate, before washing-capsule-and-*get-out-of-my-house*-gate.

'I'm definitely not asking you not to come.'

'You've said that.' Viv looks into his eyes. 'And it really sounds like it.'

Mark looks away.

Viv and Mark are currently engaged in a game of adult chicken. Viv said she's not continuing this unless something changes, and Mark is distant, 'hurt' by Viv's refusal to understand how delicate the situation is. Which leaves them ... Viv's not sure. With all the sneaking around and guilt of an affair, but little of the sex and companionship.

She never was any good at game theory.

'Tomorrow's about Harry as well as your mum.' She keeps walking. 'If they're having a memorial for Harry, you know I'm going to be there.'

Mark shoves his hands into his trouser pockets and there's a faint tinkling of coins. Mark is the only man under retirement age who still uses cash, and Viv used to think it was a cute throwback, until she realised *cash* meant no paper trail. *Cash* meant Jess wouldn't question why there was a new entry in the joint account for the *Wing Wah* takeaway thirty minutes across town on a night Mark told her he stayed in, watching the snooker.

Viv watches a woman push a squealing toddler on the box swing, a too-big bucket hat obscuring the top half of the kid's face. Will she ever see a tanned baby again, outside of old photos? 'Would you have told me about tomorrow if I hadn't found out?'

Mark pauses. 'I don't think of them when I think of us.'

Viv shakes her head. Compartmentalisation: it's the fucking dream. 'Why are you holding this memorial anyway?'

'It's not me, it's Chrissy,' Mark says. 'I just turn up.'

'But why? She doesn't enjoy parties. She does family stuff like it's jury duty. What's she atoning for?'

Mark says nothing.

'And why the hell does she send me Christmas cards? We've only met a few times.' Viv glances up. 'And on one of those I spilled taramasalata over her suede Mary Janes.'

'I remember.'

'I've seen prisoners looking happier stabbing litter on community service. And *Christmas cards*?'

Mark makes his voice quiet. 'I won't be able to acknowledge you tomorrow.'

'I'm pretty sure she doesn't even *like* me.'

'And you can't mind.'

Viv processes the caveat, mentally adds it to the list. *You can't mind that I can't always pick up the phone. You can't mind that I don't stay the night.* The unwritten contract about what Viv is and isn't allowed to feel gets longer by the day. 'I wasn't expecting to go as your plus one.'

'And you won't be able to avoid seeing Jess.'

'Interesting.' Viv watches the wind rustle the hedge. 'You're the one who made her the promises and you see her every day.'

Mark's brow darkens.

Viv looks away. Sometimes, these things just slip out.

'I've got to get back to work.' He searches her face for something. 'Think about it. You've still got time to change your mind. Though I'm not asking—'

'You're definitely not asking me not to come. No, I've got that.'

'I'd better go.' He leans to kiss Viv on the cheek. In a park. In daylight. When stationary.

The man must be rattled.

Viv watches him walk away. '*You should have told me yourself!*'

Mark turns back.

'About the memorial.' Viv lowers her voice. 'You should have told me.'

He takes a second. 'I didn't think.'

'And as you're definitely not asking me not to come, I'll see you there!'

Mark pauses. This time, he doesn't turn back, just keeps on walking towards his car.

★

Compartmentalisation. How did you get to do that?

At least Viv was pretty sure it was compartmentalisation, not what happened at the last funeral, why Mark hasn't mentioned this memorial.

Because she isn't the only one of them with bad funeral etiquette.

She's been to so many family funerals over the years, you'd think she'd know how to behave by now.

But she doesn't. Clearly.

And she set her stall out, making that pattern clear, from the very first one.

5

Thirty Years Ago
The First Funeral

Two weeks after her sixth birthday, Viv stood in the function room above the pub on a Tuesday afternoon, watching all the adults she'd ever known cry and smoke.

All the adults – except one.

Everyone else was only in this room today because Dad couldn't be, ever again.

Viv pulled at her collar. This dress was scratchy and hot, and it was meant to be her new party dress, but she'd never worn it to a party – and now she never wanted to. She wanted to rip that dress off right there, just stand in the middle of the pub in her tights and vest.

A pair of scissors on the nearby table caught Viv's eye, abandoned and glinting. The scissors were shiny as a birthday balloon – big, and sharp at the tips, nothing like the safety ones at school.

Viv stared at the scissors.

'Hey, champ.'

Viv kept staring, though the voice was Harry's.

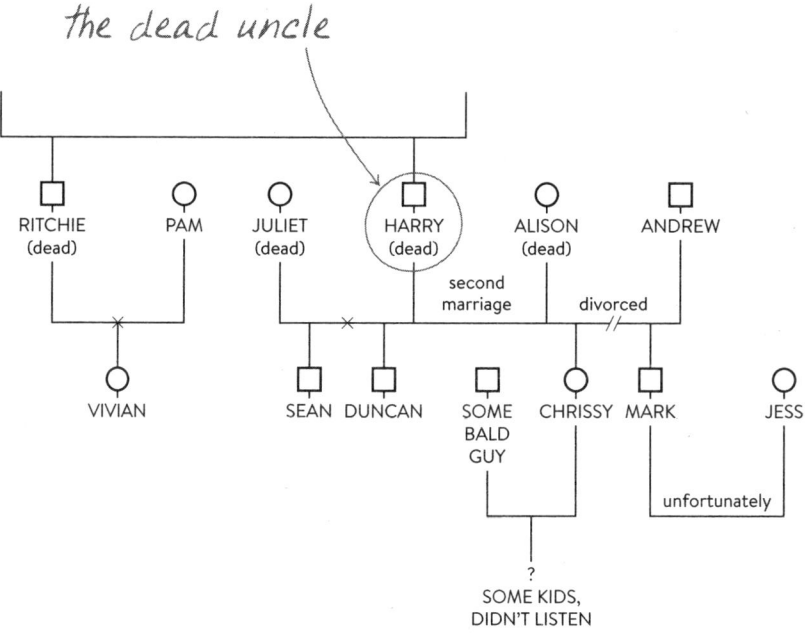

There had been too many adults today, too many conversations. *Champ. Buddy. Monkey.* Turned out, when your dad died, your name died too. And everyone wanted to be your friend.

Most people, anyway. There were some adults here who wouldn't look at Viv. If they accidentally caught her eye, they kept their gaze moving till they found something easier to rest it on. One man – one who had been smiling with screwed-up eyes a second before he caught her gaze – spent a good five minutes looking at a toilet door, rather than have to risk making eye contact again.

Harry pulled one of Viv's plaits. 'I'm so proud of you.'

The plait fell back awkwardly and rested on Viv's shoulder, pulling painfully on her scalp. She didn't flip it back.

Everyone was proud of Viv today. It didn't feel as good as it should.

Harry crouched, balancing with his hand on a nearby table. 'Can I get you anything?' One of his knees made a pattering sound as he lowered, like pinging elastic bands. 'Another Coke?'

Viv had had a Coca-Cola bottle jammed between her palms for two hours, clinging on to it like an oar in a storm, making the glass as warm as a mug of evening milk.

Harry spoke softly. 'You and me are going to take care of your mum. Together.'

A beer mat stuck to the bottom of a nearby man's glass fell to the floor. It hit Viv's ear on the way down. The man didn't notice.

Harry picked up the beer mat. 'Did that hurt?'

Viv shook her head.

Harry placed the mat back on the table. 'I'm going to take care of you too. I promise. I'm going to look after you as well as I look after my own lads. You'll be wanting for nothing.'

Viv lowered her face to the bottle, moving the straw with her mouth.

'You're doing us all proud, Champ.' Harry's voice cracked.

Viv sucked hard at the flat, warm cola. She thought of the

leisure centre – of the verruca footbath moat between the lockers and the pool.

'And your mum's doing brilliantly too.'

Mum was a few metres away, leaning on the fruit machine. People had been queuing for her all afternoon, taking their turn, like she was an ice-cream van. Her eyes had gone wet then dry, wet then dry. The area around them went sooty and black, like a ring-tailed lemur's.

Harry must be thinking the same. 'It was brave of Pam to wear make-up today, but that's your mum. She's got standards.'

Mum saw them looking. She gave Viv a brave smile. 'Harry looking after you?'

'I am,' Harry said.

Mum nodded. She held Viv's gaze, about to say something else, but got pulled into a hard hug by a neighbour. Her face was mashed against the woman's chest, one lemur-eye pressed into the woman's left breast.

Viv sucked the warm footbath-Coke again. The straw gurgled.

Harry's eyes darted to the bottle. 'Shall I get you another?'

Viv watched the woman grip Mum's two hands, pumping up and down like she was working a car on a cartoon railroad.

'Viv?' There was hope in Harry's voice. 'Shall I get you another Coke?'

Viv shook her head, watching her mum rest her forehead on the shoulder of the woman's jacket. The jacket was white, and Mum's black lemur-eyes were touching it, leaving a mark, but the woman didn't push Mum off, just kept stroking her head.

Nothing about today was normal.

There was a long pause.

'What can I do, Viv?' Harry's voice crept upwards. 'Tell me. *Please.*'

Viv looked at the carpet. She sucked, making the straw gurgle.

Outside, a pelican crossing beeped.

Harry stood. His knee pinged like elastic bands again. 'I can get you another Coke.'

Viv looked up. 'I'm not allowed Coke. A lady bought this for me without asking.'

Harry reached for her empty bottle. She tried to hang on.

He pried it from her fingers. 'I'm pretty sure you're allowed Coke today.'

Viv watched Harry walk to the bar. Her hands felt empty without the warmth of her comfort-bottle.

She looked around, at all the adults who were proud of her. None of them were looking.

She glanced at the sharp scissors, left there on the side. She looked down at her best new party dress.

She stretched the hem, and started to cut.

Shiny material was harder to cut than paper, but Viv had still managed to cut up from the bottom of the dress to her vest by the time anyone noticed.

'Viv!' A lady with crinkly eyes crouched in front of her. 'Oh, no, lovely. Let me take those.'

Viv let the woman pull the scissors away. Her hands hurt.

People started to fuss – *Champ, Buddy, Monkey.* The voices blurred into one.

Viv looked down at her cut-up dress.

No one even told her off.

6

Now

Viv gets off the bus in the city centre wearing her new dress and old boots, her tote bag containing her box-fresh heels slung over her shoulder. She passes the fancy shops and the homeless tents in front of the central library. It's a bright day for April and the midday sun has clean-washed the busy streets, erasing the pigeon shit and litter, like an optical trick.

She sits at a bus stop and changes into her heels. She peels the cellophane off a nicotine patch and presses it onto her bare shoulder. She's going to be flawless today. She's not even going to *vape*.

A round-faced young woman, as wholesome as a spaniel, walks towards Viv, smiling. If humans' ears could bounce, hers would.

There's a blond man next to her too. He has the air of a clean-cut boyband member: the sexually unthreatening one put in by the Svengali to attract the mums.

Viv looks at the leaflets in the young people's hands. *Turn Your Face to Jesus.*

She sniffs. She bins the nicotine wrapper.

'Excuse me!' The woman's voice rings out. 'Do you have time to …'

Viv walks away. It's a kindness.

These people definitely don't want her.

She arrives at the museum early and kills time in the ground-floor gift shop, picking up and putting down souvenir tat. She pulls at the tiger-print jacket spread across her shoulders like a cape, self-conscious in her floaty dress and heels.

'Now *that's* cool.' A half-height kid brushes past Viv, his puffy jacket designed for arctic conditions, not a warm day in April. He points at a Minecraft piggy bank. 'I'll ask Mum to get me this.'

Viv wants to say *don't get excited, kid – your mum's not dropping a twenty on shite like that* – but what does she know? Places like this make people unpredictable. It's all the education, it sends parents nuts.

She idly picks up a packet of sandwich bags illustrated with periodic tables and puts them down. She isn't good at being early: she hasn't had much practice. She considers the array of books – *Peppa in Space*, *A Cat's Guide to the Night Sky* – and reaches past the books to a black-and-star-wrapped bar labelled *Space Chocolate*.

She turns the bar over. *Contains popping candy.*

When Harry used to bring her to this museum as a kid, he said *pick anything you want from the gift shop,* but he meant *except chocolate.* Harry needed Viv to want things with instructions: the man was a science teacher, even at weekends. He was diligent in his commitment to parent her. His enthusiasm was the worst thing about him.

'You touch it, you buy it.'

Viv looks up.

'Just me.' Sean smiles, hands in pockets. 'Being a twat.'

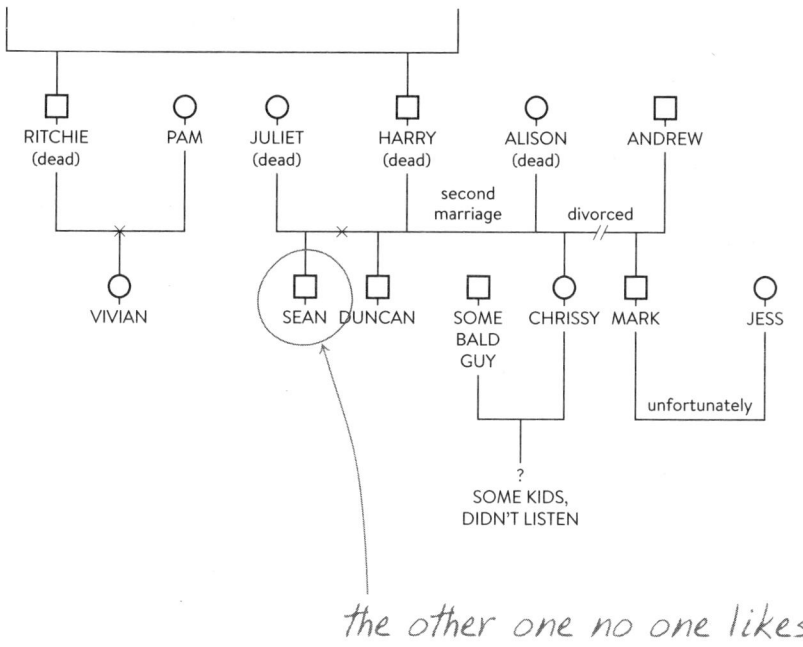

the other one no one likes

'I'm not buying it,' Viv says.

'Not even for me?' Sean doesn't look like Sean today. He's in a suit, and it's not a cheap one. 'You know I'm a stress eater.' His trousers are the perfect length, settling on the lowest eyelets of his conker-shiny shoes. He could be auditioning for a TV talent show.

Viv's not the only one who's come in disguise today. 'Not at two quid a bar.' She drops the chocolate bar into the rack.

'I didn't know you were coming.' Sean leaves a pause. 'They *do* know you're coming?'

Viv nods. The white speckles at Sean's temples are a surprise. There's only a one-year age gap, and Sean will still be Viv's baby cousin in their eighties, though the chances of both making it are slim. Viv's lifestyle isn't exactly one recommended in colour supplements. Sean's a gambler who's sofa-surfed through adulthood and she's pretty sure he doesn't get his five a day either.

'Star maps. Solar systems. Periodic tables.' Viv indicates a shelf of jigsaws. 'You'd think the merch would have moved on in two decades.'

'Look.' Sean indicates out of the shop, to the museum entrance. 'We beat Chrissy.'

Chrissy walks towards the door of the building with her family, the feathers of her coral fascinator quivering. She stops just outside the entrance and gets a tissue out of her pocket, rubbing a mark off her daughter's face.

Viv stares at the girl. *Nope.* 'Do you remember the name of that kid?'

Sean looks amused. 'You're asking me?'

A security guard opens the door for Chrissy. Flustered, she thanks him with a curtsy, bobbing back up self-consciously. She's overthought it.

Viv's cheeks warm on Chrissy's behalf. 'Do we go over?'

Sean takes a moment. 'I don't think she'll be in a rush to see us, do you?'

Viv sniffs. 'It's ironic.' Idly, she picks up a flask illustrated with the solar system. 'Usually, people want me at parties.' She thinks of Francine, of the paddocks she won't be seeing any time soon, and considers the picture on the flask. 'One thing's changed since your dad used to bring us here, at least.' She taps the picture. 'Pluto's gone.'

'If you're not feeling welcome today, that makes two of us.'

'Isn't this your gig?'

'Chrissy's gig. The rest of us just put cash behind the bar.'

Viv stands straighter. 'Good for you.'

'My dad's money. Obviously.' Sean gives a tight smile. 'As I'll be reminded today at every opportunity.'

Viv places the Pluto-less flask back on the shelf. 'How long do you think it takes for a nicotine patch to kick in?'

Sean smiles faintly. 'Whatever happens' – he touches her sleeve – 'just know Dad would have wanted you here.'

Viv stares fiercely at her shoes. She hadn't emotionally prepared for anyone to be nice to her today.

Viv and Sean step out of the gift shop, past the statue of Alan Turing, into the open atrium. Empty air stretches forty metres up, surrounded by art deco balconies with black steel railings.

They get into the lift and out at the top floor.

Chrissy is standing in front of the ramp to the roof terrace, talking to a member of staff. She's a similar age to Viv, but the way she has her hands linked primly in front of her lap makes Viv feel like they were born a century apart.

'We can't be first. We'll ruin her day.' Viv indicates an

empty part of the museum floor and walks under a sign – *The Wonders of Time*. Sean follows. After passing a collection of old grandfather clocks, she stops at the art deco balcony railing and leans over.

A long way down, adults move like exasperated shepherds. One man has an antenna draping a piece of turquoise ribbon, waving it in the air with the seriousness of a rhythmic gymnast. Viv can't tell which kids he's meant to be herding. None are looking.

'That's why it's empty up here.' Sean leans next to her. 'Only Dad ever had the stamina to get kids to the top floor.' He nods at the museum floor. 'Your mum.'

Forty metres below, Mum walks towards the lift, taking careful steps in shoes Viv suspects are new. She looks thinner than last time Viv saw her. Mum will be delighted, unless it's the not-cancer.

No – even if it's the not-cancer, she'll be delighted. She's worked so hard over the years to make herself smaller, all that Nimble bread and cottage cheese, and she just loves a silver lining. Viv can hear her now. *Yes, there were months of lying awake, worrying it might be terminal – but, on the upside, I haven't been able to fit into these leggings since 2016!* The body positivity movement has passed Mum by, and Viv's weight is one thing Mum is consistently proud of, though less so when a hairdresser friend once asked Viv's secret.

I'm anxiety-lean, Viv said. *And I take a shedload of Class As.*

The hairdresser laughed. Mum didn't.

Viv leans further onto the balcony railing, taking the weight off her heels.

She and Sean watch the tiny people cross the floor below.

Around them, the grandfather clocks tick insistently.

'Dad was so happy working here,' Sean says, his voice quiet.

Viv touches his arm. She wonders if Harry would have chosen to meet Alison, all over again, if he'd known they'd get less than a year of marriage. That their time together would end with blue lights and paramedics, and car-cutters, and memorials.

She glances at Sean. She decides she doesn't need to say every thought out loud.

'Come on.' Sean pushes himself upright. 'It's time.'

7

Two Years Ago
The Not-a-Wedding

Viv weaved across the dancefloor towards the bar, coaxing bodies gently to the side to clear her path. It was a hazardous journey, but Viv's drink remained unspilled. The dancers were really going for it at this *not-a-wedding*. Harry's invitation had been clear it was 'just' a party to celebrate their town-hall marriage.

It *felt* like a wedding.

The rugby club was conversation-limitingly loud, the DJ playing 'Don't Leave Me This Way' at a volume that thrummed through Viv's chest. Disco lights roamed the room, bathing dancers in neon spots, casting glowing shadows through the pastel balloon arch.

Viv hadn't imagined Harry going in for balloon arches.

But, then, Viv hadn't imagined Harry going in for a second marriage at all. Especially not so soon after Aunt Juliet died.

The song reached its peak.

'Aaaaaaaaaaaah, BABY!'

The dancers crescendoed in unison, bouncing into the air with the passion of footballers straining for different headers.

Mum didn't bounce. She jigged on the spot, giggling, twirling her arms and pointing, face flushed. Viv smiled.

Next to Mum, Angela made claw-fingers at shoulder height, moving the claws left to right, looking like a werewolf in a dance troupe. Tonight, Viv even smiled at *Angela*. Weddings, even not-a-weddings, especially *no-presents-please* weddings, brought out Viv's goodwill to all men. As a single woman, Viv got head-tilts, but only because people didn't know her. Viv's *happy-ever-after* visions contained more nights of Negronis than slow-death-by-Netflix. One friend once told Viv she and her husband didn't even click *Next Episode* – they just let the seconds count down as one episode turned into the next, like they were already dead.

Over reaching acquaintances and taxi drivers might tell Viv *there's still time*, insisting her biological clock would tick as intensely as any incendiary device, but Viv was pretty sure her clock was broken. Having kids was something she bracketed with skydiving and skiing under *expensive hobbies for other people*. The bombs that blew up Viv's life were strictly non-biological.

There was a voice at her shoulder. 'Your mum's got moves.'

Viv gave Harry a hug. 'You can talk. You dance like an electric spider.'

'I'm going to assume that's a compliment. Where have you been all day?'

'I never want to monopolise the star at a function.'

'But you *have* met Alison?'

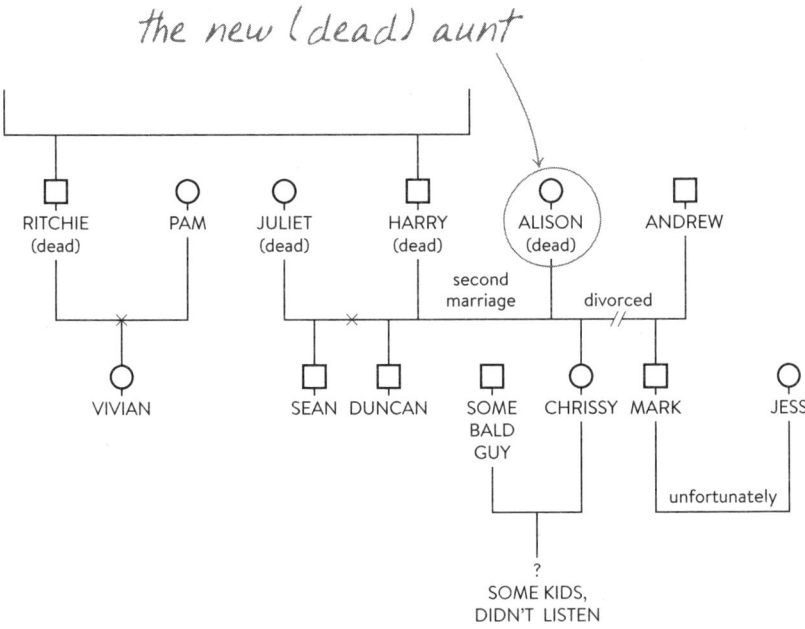

the new (dead) aunt

Viv looked across the room, at the woman with her hair in victory rolls, one hand on the hip of a skirt suit cinched fiercely at the waist. Alison gave off a Second World War vibe – though the angle she held her glass of wine at was more contemporary, dangerously close to horizontal.

Viv shook her head. 'I told you. I'm not a monopoliser.'

'I'll introduce you after I've rescued her from that cousin.' Viv knew that look: she'd disappointed Harry. 'You don't want to hear about his Ring doorbell.'

Viv indicated the balloons behind. 'I didn't have you down as a balloon arch kind of guy.'

Harry tapped his ear and leaned in. 'Say it again. I spent too many years with my head in a bass bin speaker.'

Viv shouted into Harry's proffered ear: *'I said I didn't see you as a balloon arch guy!'*

'Alison's idea.' Harry straightened. 'Instagram.' He watched Alison, smiling, in a way he'd never smiled at Juliet. There was that feeling again, the feeling that had stopped Viv going over to Alison: a sense of betrayal-by-proxy. Viv's Aunt Juliet had made her a lot of sandwiches over the years. She'd been a place of refuge, her chest a reassuring size when she pulled Viv in for a cuddle. Juliet had always smelled of safety: of smoke and apple blossom. Her death by heart disease had prompted much sadness, many platitudes, and a lot of pseudo-scientific conversations between Mum and Angela about the mono- and polyunsaturates in different brands of margarine.

Alison sensed herself being watched. She looked up, and Harry beckoned her.

She came over, smiling, adjusting her glass to vertical.

'Alison, meet Viv.'

'Viv, finally!' Alison looked genuinely pleased. 'I've heard so much!'

Viv felt her smile tighten. 'Oh dear.' She swigged her drink. 'From Angela?'

'Harry only says nice things.'

Viv looked at Harry.

He nodded.

Alison's smile was kind. 'If there was a difference of opinion, I know whose views I'd value most.'

Viv tried not to look pleased. 'Good point. And congratulations.' She took in Alison's hair, crispy with spray. Viv bet those rolls would stay in place when the pins came out. 'You got one of the good ones here.'

'I did, didn't I?' Alison looked at Harry admiringly. 'He even made me a picnic on our first date.'

Viv turned to Harry, one eyebrow raised.

'With flapjacks. And mini-quiches.'

This was unbelievable. 'Homemade?'

Alison beamed. 'Can you believe it?'

'No!'

Was Harry blushing? 'Don't ruin my tough-guy image, Alison. And don't tell Viv anything else she can use to take the piss. She's already told me today I dance like an electric spider.'

'Why haven't you made me mini-quiches, Harry?'

'He hasn't made me them since either.' Alison looped the fingers of both hands through Harry's. 'And electric spider is a perfect description.'

Harry pulled her towards him and kissed her, even though Viv was standing right there. Viv took in the softness on his face and glanced around. What must today be like for Sean and Duncan, seeing their dad so in love, only a year after their mum died? The whole thing was so unlikely. Quick, spontaneous, feet-first declarations of adoration were so un-Viv's-family.

She was pretty sure Harry had spent longer choosing a sofa.

Alison left to request 'Somebody Else's Guy' from the DJ, and Viv watched her go. 'I like her.'

'Good. Now, do me a favour. Talk me up to Alison's kids.' Harry's gaze settled behind her. *'Mark!'*

A guy with good hair and heavy pointed eyebrows walked past without hearing.

'Chrissy, then.' Harry jerked his head at a woman with a ratty orange fascinator perched limply on her head like a flagging bird of paradise. 'Go and meet Chrissy.'

Viv eyed Chrissy. She was in conversation with another woman, their expressions serious. 'What should I know about her?'

'She runs a catering company.' Harry wiped his forehead with the back of his hand. 'She writes birthday cards for the year in January.'

Viv frowned. 'No, she doesn't.'

'And her freezer's stacked and labelled like a serial killer's. Must mingle.' Harry patted Viv's shoulder. 'Make yourself useful. Talk me up to Chrissy.' He shimmied away across the dancefloor, his shirt stuck to the centre of his back with sweat, making alarmingly erratic shapes with his arms.

Viv swigged her drink. Harry was that rare person who, when he asked her to do something, made her want to comply. She walked over to where Chrissy was in conversation and put on a pre-emptive smile.

'I'm pretending I'm delighted, obviously,' Chrissy kept her head close to her friend's. 'But I checked in on Dad earlier. He said he's varnishing a coffee table, then having an M&S meal deal and watching the Grand Prix. He couldn't look me in the eye.'

Viv's smile wavered.

'Every time I ask what he's had for tea, it's toast. Cheese on toast. Beans on toast. *Toast* toast.'

'Not even butter?' the friend asked.

Chrissy baulked. '*Of course* butter.'

Chrissy's friend shook her head. 'Men of that age just can't be on their own.'

'Exactly. Just see how happy *he* looks.' Chrissy gestured at Harry. 'His wife dies, so he gets a new one straight away. Never mind she's already taken.'

Viv's pre-emptive smile felt more forced by the second. Should she ...?

She took a small step back.

'Mum wouldn't tell me too much, *out of respect for your father*, but she did say it was twenty years since Dad had bought her a Valentine's card, let alone ran her a bath. But did Dad know she wanted a bath? Did Mum ever ask him, specifically, to run her a bath?'

'She does look happy,' the friend said tentatively.

'She was happy before. She has grandchildren.' Chrissy noticed Viv and put a warning hand on her friend's arm.

'Hi!' Viv refreshed her smile. 'Don't worry, I wasn't listening.' She looked over Chrissy's shoulder. 'Though I agree that some men can't cope on their own, but Harry's not one of those. He's made me a hundred omelettes over the years. I've heard him book his own doctors' appointments, and I've seen him peg out washing. But, like I said, I wasn't listening.' Viv held out a hand. 'Viv. Harry's niece.'

Chrissy shook her hand. 'The one who stole his car?'

Viv paused. 'Not *stole*. That story's got exaggerated over

the years. I only planned to drive it round the cul-de-sac, and I didn't know how to use a clutch anyway. Harry just came back from work to find me kangarooing on the drive. I was fourteen.'

There was a long silence.

'Harry gave me a right bollocking, but only verbal because, like I said, he's one of the good ones. And I'm sorry if your dad's not dealing with things well, but it sounds like he's making a good fist of it. Varnishing a table is not an act of a man who's given up. And cheese on toast is a great meal.'

Chrissy looked at her friend.

Viv gave a weird salute she regretted instantly. 'How about I leave you to your conversation?'

8

Now

Viv and Sean walk back past the grandfather clocks towards Chrissy, who is standing in front of the ramp to the roof like a supermarket greeter. She's taken her raincoat off, revealing a bright coral dress the same colour as her fascinator.

It's intriguing, how Chrissy can make bright colours look so insipid. Her vibe is the opposite of Viv's, who can make a daisy-patterned tea-dress look like it should be paired with Perspex stripper heels.

Chrissy releases a woman from a hug, beaming. 'Can't wait to catch up! It's just up the ramp.' She turns to the next guests, smiling in anticipation.

Seeing who the next guests are, she falters.

Viv gives her sweetest smile. 'Lovely day for it, Chrissy.'

This woman thinks she's better than Viv, with her fascinator and her mother-of-the-bride coral. But, then, she *is* better than Viv. Chrissy has probably never taken ketamine at a wedding. Never fucked a married man at a wake. Never woken up in a stranger's bed, the pounding dehydration of a sambuca headache battling the pain of something deeper – and *definitely* never been given money by that stranger in the morning because he thought she was a sex worker.

Viv takes a tiny sidestep, putting extra air between her and Sean. It was a mistake to enter together. The least popular people here, they're worse than the sum of their parts. Together, they're bad fairies, squared.

Viv decides, too late, to hug: Chrissy has already turned away.

'Roof terrace is up that ramp.' Chrissy flicks her gaze onto the next guests. 'Oh, Jeanie, *your hair*! I love it! You look like that one off *Countdown*!'

Sean and Viv head up the ramp.

Sean keeps his voice low. 'They *definitely* knew you were coming?'

'I told Chrissy on the phone! And Mum will have RSVP'd for me.' They pass a wide staircase leading down to a mezzanine level and Viv spots a cloakroom. 'One sec.'

She hooks up the tote bag containing her chunky boots and steps onto the roof terrace to a panoramic view, taking in the cathedral spire and cranes, the half-built apartment blocks and glass towers gleaming in the sun.

The terrace is almost as impressive: a garden in the air. Lush foliage trails from planters, and outdoor sofas with hidden feet levitate over Victorian tiles. Strings of filament bulbs line a wooden bar, and waiters circulate with trays of drinks, weaving between groups, not even asking for payment.

For the first time, Viv thinks this day might not be all bad.

Sean looks around. 'This is not what I expected from the science museum.'

Viv's stomach clenches. 'We shouldn't be here.'

Sean nods. He gets it. This place is for people like Francine: the paddock people, the people with the triceps and the time-travel skincare. Viv's family are not paddock people. Viv's family are off-peak, two-for-one, yellow-label-at-the-deli-counter-at-5-p.m. people. They are supermarket-snacks-in-the-cinema people – and those snacks are budget knockoffs, called things like *Twirk Bites* and *Maltegsers*. Chrissy only arranged this memorial here because, apparently, *it's what they would have wanted.* Viv's pretty sure Alison and Harry wouldn't have wanted to have died in a car crash aged sixty-two, after less than a year of marriage, but that's exactly the sort of thing she mustn't say today.

Her stomach flutters. 'What does a person have to do to get a drink round here?'

Sean takes two champagne flutes from a waiter's tray and Viv sips. Champagne and its substitutes are wasted on her, but it's something.

'It suits you, darling. So glam!' A woman in a peacock two-piece fingers the waist-length hair of a younger woman. 'It wasn't so long ago all women were expected to cut their hair off at thirty. Even if it was still thick and glossy.' The peacock woman curls a lock of the other's hair round her finger. 'Can you imagine?'

The younger woman frowns. 'Honestly?'

The peacock woman pauses. 'My mother's generation, not mine.' She drops the hair. 'I'm a cusper. Verging on Generation X. It's a real thing.'

Viv brushes past some greenery in a tall planter, sending out a cloud of sharp scent. She leans over the railing and looks down to the cobbled street, to the parked cars and industrial bins.

At the prickling sensation of being watched, she turns.

Mum stands alone, her dress the colour of fresh blood, fiddling with the gold filigree pendant she bought in Málaga.

Viv goes over immediately, because Viv is a grown-up, and this is how you prove it. 'You look great, Mum. Are you completely recovered from your op?'

'Fit as a flea.' Mum hugs her. 'You look so ladylike!' She pulls away, a strand of her blonde hair sticking to Viv's lipstick.

Viv picks the hair from her lips.

'Sorry,' Mum says.

'No problem.'

They both smile, the pause long. They could be exes at a wedding.

'That's a lovely dress,' Mum says. 'Though grey is an unusual choice of colour.'

'It isn't grey. It's silver.'

'Of course,' Mum says quickly.

Viv's dress is grey. She'd forgotten the *bright colours* direction of the invitation.

A waiter approaches Mum with his tray of glasses. He is late twenties, his cheeks mottled with a rash of scars from long-ago acne.

Mum looks at the tray. 'It's quite early.'

The waiter says nothing. His angular face and pointy chin give him a hard look.

Viv considers his tray. Is it bad form to take another glass when she's still holding a half-full one?

Mum glances up at the waiter. 'Do you have anything soft?'

The waiter studies his tray. 'It seems I only have Prosecco.'

There is something about his tone. Polite, yet not.

Mum feels it. 'But haven't you got anything—'

The waiter moves on.

'No need for soft drinks today, Pam.' Frank loops his arm through Mum's. Mum's ex-partner has clearly got the *bright clothes* memo – his shirt is red, with exaggerated clown spots. 'It's a celebration!'

Frank sees Viv. He nods.

She nods back.

See, they can do this. It's been two decades.

The years (and penchant for solo drinking?) are evident in the broken veins on Frank's nose. The rings under his eyes are darker and baggier than when he lived in Viv's house, but he seems lighter, somehow. He no longer gives off an undertone of restrained aggression, of someone who wishes corporal punishment wasn't frowned on in the twenty-first century.

See, they can all be civil. This is fine.

Viv tips back the contents of her glass.

Mum points at another waiter's tray. 'That waiter's got orange juice.' She leans to get a glass.

But Frank is quicker. 'Allow me.' He lunges, grabbing a drink with a dramatic swipe. 'There, Pam,' he says, triumphant. 'One orange juice.'

Mum smiles. She takes the drink, like over-polite aggressive lunging is normal.

Viv narrows her eyes. She'd forgotten Frank used to do that, act like Mum was some frail princess who needed help to do the most basic things. The worst thing was that Mum seemed to like it.

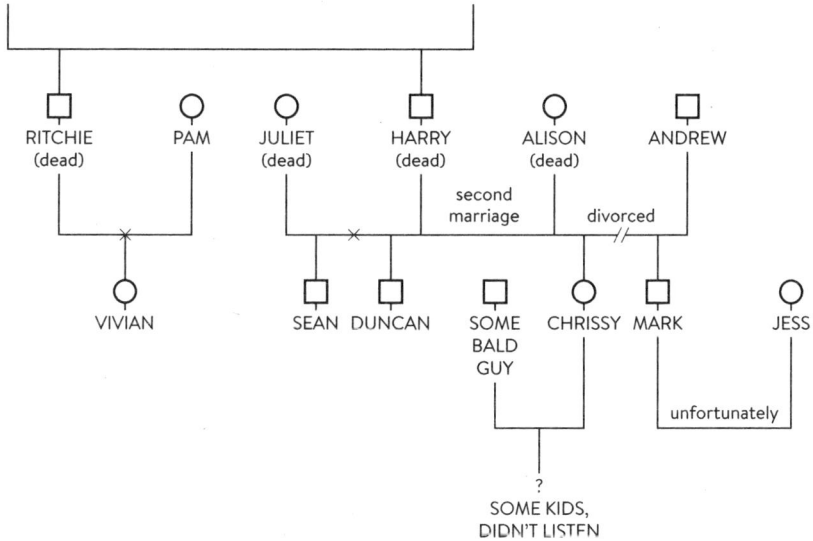

he's not on here – Mum never married him

'Sean.' Frank pats Sean's arm. 'Did your father ever tell you about the pub's pool tournament lock-in?'

Viv pretends to listen to Frank's story. Mum inches her

face closer, her foundation biscuit sweet. Viv tenses.

'Well done for remembering about today,' Mum whispers.

The fibres in Viv's stomach knot tighter. 'You only told me last weekend.'

Mum's breath is hot on Viv's cheek. 'Harry would be pleased you remembered too.'

She pats Viv on the shoulder – *good girl* – and turns to beam at Frank. 'Not that lock-in, *again*, Frankie! We've all heard about it!'

Viv swipes a full drink from a passing waiter's tray. Mum is trying to be nice, with no intention of backhand, but her low expectations have always smarted.

Mum had been expecting Viv to mess up the plans for today.

Viv steps away, pretending to look at the photos on an easel. Sean edges towards her, out of his conversation with Frank.

'I forgot to wear a bright colour.' Viv keeps her voice low. 'I got it wrong before I even walked in. Why are we here?'

Sean shakes his head.

'It's an actual question. Why is Chrissy doing this? *Really?*'

'She thought the whole thing was too messy last year, because Dad and Alison died a month apart. She thought the funerals weren't happy enough.'

Viv shakes her head. She heard about a friend of a friend rehiring a make-up artist and photographer to recreate their wedding photos after deciding the originals weren't hot enough, but at least the couple *paid* the photographer.

Sean holds his hands up. 'Chrissy's view. Not mine.'

Viv spots a streak of teal across the terrace. She narrows

her eyes. 'Christ, of course *she's* here.' Angela is rearranging the contents of her handbag, wearing the party clothes of the week before. 'Can't I catch a break?'

Sean watches Angela bring an orange tube out of her handbag. 'An insulin pen? I didn't know Angela was diabetic.'

'Don't feel sorry for her. She doesn't deserve it.'

Sean studies the easel again. 'Can you believe I'm not in a single photo?'

Viv shades her eyes and looks at the photos. There are raised-to-camera glasses and birthday cakes and patios. Roast turkeys and Christmas hats and conga lines. Sunshine and beaches and ill-judged sombreros. No Sean.

'THAT'S MY ARM!' Sean points to the sleeve of a grey t-shirt. 'They cut me out!'

Viv pats Sean's (real-life) arm.

'The *one* photo I was actually in!' Sean takes an over-large sip of his drink. 'Do they have to make it so obvious?'

Viv leans her elbows on a high bar table, lifting her heels out of each shoe in turn. Fifteen minutes in, and these shoes were a mistake. When Viv bought them, she'd disassociated for a moment, briefly forgetting she wasn't actually the twirling figure from a music box – that she actually had to step and walk and stand.

'I was even going to bring Paula at one point.' Sean's voice is tight. 'And then I thought *why?* So she can see my whole family think I'm a dick?'

'I don't think you're a dick.' Viv's about to add *who's Paula?* but Sean is quicker.

'I've never asked to borrow money off you, have I?'

73

Viv laughs. 'I mean, you could try.'

He gives a small, tense sip.

She takes in the heaviness of Sean's brow. 'Don't let today get to you. Outside of the family, people think you're great.' Viv hears herself, how emphatic she sounds. It's definitely just Sean she's trying to reassure.

'Who thinks I'm great?'

Viv pauses, caught in her friendly lie. She's not seen Sean outside a family situation for two decades and feels solidarity: she never lets people friendly-lie to her either. 'That nurse at Alison's funeral said they all liked you at the hospital. One of them even wanted your number.'

'That the best you can do?' He glances at Viv. 'The nurses only liked me because I brushed Alison's hair. But thanks for trying.'

Viv is about to reply, glancing at the door.

Instead, everyone shrinks back. The noise; the laughter; the people.

She grips her glass harder.

She'd hoped to get several drinks down first. Too late.

Mark and Jess are here.

9

Fourteen Months Ago
The Spark

Viv knew it was fine to be in a bar alone at 5 p.m. on a Wednesday. Everyone knew you weren't a problem drinker as long as you white-knuckled Mondays and Tuesdays sober.

And you were never alone with a scratchcard.

She leaned over the table, her spine aching. Washing thirty paint pots in a child-height sink always fucked her back and Viv needed a different future, hence the scratchcard.

She worked at the card with the coin. £20. £10. £50,000. £50,000.

She slowed down with two boxes to go, eking out the moment of possibility, thinking what she'd spend fifty grand on. She could drink cocktails by a pool in Vegas. Put down a deposit for a house. Get a puppy – two puppies, even. Three. Because why the fuck not?

She scratched the final boxes – *£10. £50* – and blew silver dust from the card.

She screwed the card up and shoved it across the table.

She would only have pissed fifty grand up the wall anyway. Besides, winning anything would fuck up her whole worldview.

She scrolled through her phone contacts, mentally cross-referencing people she might want to see with their likely availability. Now her friends had kids, the phrase *impromptu night out* featured in conversations about as often as *shitfaced* – which was never. The words were as relevant to her friends' lives as *thou* or *betwixt*.

She scrolled through the options.

Tall man from Christmas do
White shirt from Jager Lounge
LRS – Don't Call

She sent a message to Last Resort Steve, looking up as she pressed *send* so she didn't have to see herself do it. She made accidental eye contact with a man across the room.

He was with an after-work crowd, his top shirt button undone in a gesture to the evening. His crowd of men looked office-energised, celebrating something with loud brays – Viv knew the type. Self-conscious men with drab suits and bright socks, men with late-emerging confidence and driveways, men with clever wives who'd done the trad sidestep and now made ceramics with the zeal they used to put into their careers. These were the kind of men who paid for the whole hotel room and wouldn't look you in the eye after, but who gave you a business card, 'just in case'.

But this man seemed different.

He had a small smile at the side of his mouth, like he was just in this bar ironically. He had hair like the *after* section of a dandruff shampoo advert. And she'd seen those eyebrows before: heavy and angled downwards, giving him the air of an Angry Bird.

This was Alison's son. From Harry's not-a-wedding.

And he was looking over too. Holding her gaze.

A *sexy* Angry Bird.

Viv sat up straighter, the ache in her spine gone.

She closed the messaging app on her phone.

Alison's son – Mark – focused on his group, standing slightly away, not laughing as hard as the others, not back-slapping. Viv messed around on Instagram for something to do, sensing his continued awareness of her. She could tell it by the hunch of his shoulders, the way he idled and ordered another wine as the rest of his crowd gradually dispersed.

Eventually, his crowd had all gone.

Mark hadn't.

Viv walked up with her empty glass. She signalled for the barman's attention and leaned on the bar. 'I've worked out where I know you from.'

Mark put his phone down. 'Viv.'

The barman poured her another and Viv smiled her thanks. She turned to Mark. 'Surprised you remember me. I don't think we even said *hello* at the wedding.'

'We didn't.' Mark paused. 'I've heard a lot about you.'

Viv lifted her chin. 'All good, no doubt.'

A beat passed.

'Yeah.' Viv picked up her drink. 'I'm not bad, I'm just drawn that way.'

Mark tweaked his Angry Bird eyebrows. 'Marilyn Monroe?'

'Jessica Rabbit.'

Mark let his attention trail down Viv's body. She felt herself glow. Four gins in was Viv's equivalent of the golden hour. She might be wearing faded black work trousers and a ribbed jumper, but, right then, she *felt* like Jessica Rabbit.

'What have you heard about me?' Mark asked.

'Nothing.' Viv sipped her drink. 'Absolutely fuck-all.'

He was still looking at her.

'What?' She made the word a challenge.

'I like your jumper.'

'It's a piece of shit.'

He raised an Angry Bird eyebrow.

'We ladies are meant to bat away compliments with simpering modesty.' Viv leaned forward. 'What *have* you heard about me?'

'Well.' He sips his drink. 'There was Harry's car.'

Viv flapped a hand. 'Childish high spirits.'

'Duncan's graduation.'

'A decade ago. You can do better.'

Mark studied her. 'If we're going to be serious, Harry makes a point of saying you're good fun, and OK deep down.'

Viv's throat tightened with emotion. 'He really said that?'

Mark nodded. 'All the time.'

'I should call him more.' She stirred her drink. 'I never get *OK deep down.*'

Mark made his voice soft. 'He said you'd been unlucky.'

Viv stared at her drink. 'Bollocks.' She wanted Mark to keep talking, but she didn't know how much more emotion her throat could take.

'You're *not* unlucky?'

Viv shook her head, hard.

'And what about the rest? Is that true?' Mark raised his Angry Bird eyebrows. 'What about *fun, and OK deep down?*'

Viv indicated a free table. 'Why don't we find out?'

Half an hour later, one of Mark's colleagues stood over them, his forehead wrinkled in a question. 'I came back for my coat.'

Viv punctuated the awkward pause by offering the man her hand. 'Viv. Mark's cousin.'

The man pulled on his coat, clearly relieved. He nodded at Mark. 'See you tomorrow.'

Mark watched the man leave. 'Please don't go around saying you're my cousin.'

Viv toyed with her straw. 'What's wrong with saying I'm your cousin?'

Mark paused. 'You know what.'

She looked up.

They held each other's gaze for a long second.

'It must be great, living with a friend.' Mark sat jammed next to Viv at the tiny table in the next bar: a too-large office party were crowding them out, forcing them close. 'Don't you want the whole shebang? The wedding, the joint mortgage, the shared washing baskets?'

'I just don't understand marriage as a concept.' Viv stirred her drink. 'You fancy someone when you're young, so you have to share kitchen drawers till you die?'

'You want freedom?'

Viv nodded.

'I get it.' Mark leaned forward, his face flickering in the glow from the candle. 'I'm in a place right now, I feel the urge to *live*. Mid-thirties, and there's so much I haven't done. I've never been to Glastonbury. Never been to Ibiza. I've never even done MDMA.'

'Ibiza's expensive.' Viv watched people enter the bar. 'But if you're after MDMA, I can give you a number.'

Mark laughed.

'Anyway,' Viv leaned forward, holding his gaze. 'How's your wife?'

Mark stopped smiling.

Viv stopped smiling. It was a punt.

Mark looked down.

Viv moved her leg, so it wasn't touching Mark's anymore. 'Right.' It was shit, being right all the time.

Mark took a long swig of his wine. 'She's OK. I think. We're separating.'

Viv held his gaze. She let her leg fall against his again. This time, she let it stay.

Mark told Viv she was *refreshing* several times that night. He was charmed – of course he was – by Viv, the manic pixie dream slut in going-out underwear, one with the number of a great dealer.

Viv even let Mark pretend he wasn't lying when he said 'this is cool' as he studied her shit bedroom with its bare walls and coffee-stained duvet cover, two hours later.

They swapped details afterwards. Mark didn't save Viv in his phone as *Craig (work)* immediately.

That night, he saved her as *Jessica Rabbit*.

Last Resort Steve messaged back the next day.

Well, helloooooo stranger!

Viv replied.

Hi Steve! Hope all good. Sorry, I'm busy now.

10

Now

Mark and Jess step onto the roof terrace with the ease of Hollywood celebs walking onto a red carpet. One second is all it takes to know: Mark had been right. Viv shouldn't have come.

Mark has one arm draped casually around Jess's waist. He pushes back the jacket of his suit with his other hand, revealing a glimpse of belt.

Viv knows how that belt smells: acidic and warm.

She takes in Jess's elfin haircut, her gold slip dress, her spaghetti straps and flat, pointed shoes. Jess is ethereal. Sexy-healthy. Clean.

A second ago, Viv felt elegant in this try-hard dress and heels. Now, she feels crudely overdressed, like she's drunk-crashed a party dressed as a slutty cat, and it's not even Halloween.

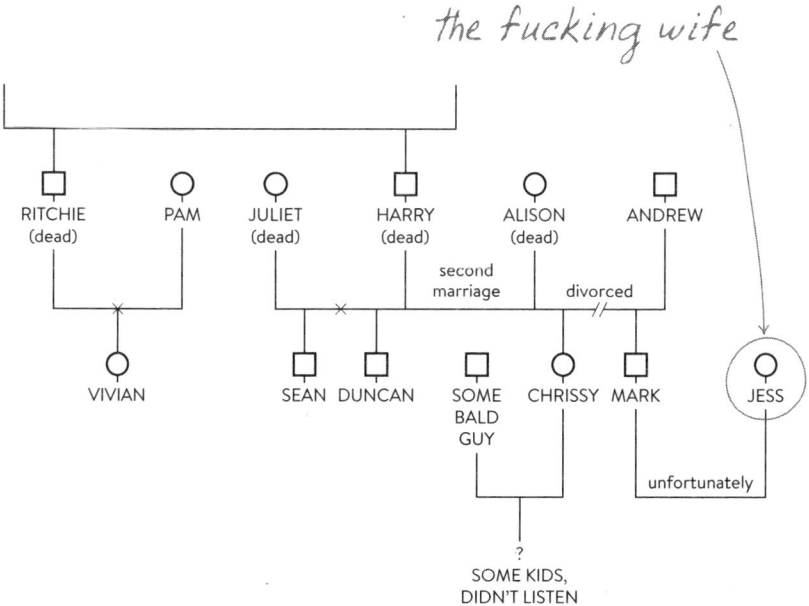

Viv is proving again she is who everyone at this party thinks she is. The one whose social radar is off, the one who ruins things, the one who pushes a joke too far.

Viv puts her hand on a high table, steadying herself.

Mark talks to Chrissy. With his open-necked shirt and the sleeves of his navy suit rolled up, he looks both formal and casual, like a keyboardist from an eighties band. He talks calmly, as if all this is normal, as if there's no emotional landmines on this rooftop that could explode with any misstep. No one whose life he's been taking a little holiday in, no one with whom he's in a fourteen-month game of adult chicken, no one he's told he's leaving his wife 'any day'.

The bright sun is dazzling. Viv lets it hit her, full force.

83

Sean's voice is far away. 'Viv, what the fuck is wrong?'

Next to a grand planter across the terrace, Jess leans forward, placing her hand on the middle of her gold satin dress.

Viv zeroes in on Jess's hand on her belly; her breath stops. Is that a roundness there?

Because this is *Jess*. Jess, of the Strava personal bests, of the three HIIT classes a week, of the artfully mismatched sports bra and leggings, of the *smashed it!* bicep-flexed *this is thirty-five!* posts. Women so disciplined never let themselves put on weight, especially not women who work in beauty, and Jess runs a nail salon, a tasteful place, all huge-fronded plants and soothing pastels. (Viv has studied this woman's social media with a focus she never had at school.)

Viv takes an involuntary step back.

But Jess stands up straighter again, and her stomach is flat, and now she's picking a glass of Prosecco off a tray. Viv's heartbeat pumps in her ears.

She's imagined it.

She has enough trouble sleeping as it is. If she has been having an affair with the husband of a pregnant woman, she would never sleep again. Her vagina would surely snap shut, seal itself as tight as Aladdin's Cave.

'Sean!' Frank turns away from Mum. 'Have you heard about your dad and the raffle for the guide dogs?'

Viv puts her drink on the table. She hurries down the ramp, past the ticking grandfather clocks, into the deserted space of *The Wonders of Time* exhibition. She shoves her stomach into the polished wood railing of the art deco balcony, deliberately taking her own breath away.

She is everything she never wanted to be.

She leans over the railing, staring at the tiny people several flights below.

Sourness swills in her mouth: the thin sharp liquid of self-hate.

She fumbles in her bag for the nut-sized twist of tissue containing the two fake-brand diazepam she'd put in her bag, but was definitely not going to take today.

She presses her clumsy fingers into the bag's corners. *Come on, come on!*

There's a movement behind, and it's unlike anything she's ever felt before. It takes a moment for Viv to realise how wrong it feels.

Hands. On her calves.

Viv can't understand the sensation, and her fingertips keep searching the bag for her diazepam. All she can think is *Hands. Human hands.*

Does this happen? People grab each other's calves from behind?

No. This is not how the world works.

Yet, apparently, it *is* happening. The hands clasping Viv from behind raise her up and force her body weight over the railing.

The world tilts. The ceiling lists sideways. Viv's hair flops in front of her eyes.

She's too confused to make a sound.

Her handbag flies past her face, catching on her shoulder. Her phone, house keys and wallet rain out, her EpiPen falling last, the multicoloured plastic rotating cap-over-tip.

And Viv can't feel polished wood beneath her stomach anymore. She can't see the listing ceiling. There's a rush of blood: her feet are light, her head heavy.

There's a flash of grandfather clocks, and they're gone too. A rush of cool air hits her cheek.

Finally, she gets it.

Terror floods her core.

She takes in one millisecond's glimpse of shocked faces below, and the stone museum floor soars up to meet her.

PART TWO

11

Now

Viv wakes, upright and gasping. Two background images slide into place, a pair of scissors snapping shut.

And she is here. Gripping the stem of a glass in the bright sunshine of a rooftop bar, standing with Sean and Mum and Frank in his clown-spotted shirt, watching Mark step onto the terrace next to Jess in her gold satin dress.

Viv staggers forward. Prosecco sloshes up the glass but doesn't spill.

'That the best you can do?' It's Sean's voice. 'The nurses only liked me because I brushed Alison's hair. But thanks for trying.'

Viv puts both hands to her throat, still holding the Prosecco. She gasps for air.

'Viv, what the fuck is wrong?'

Viv places the glass down on the table, followed by her hand, steadying herself. She tries to work out *what the fuck is wrong*.

'Sean!' Frank turns away from Mum. 'Have you heard about your dad and the raffle for the guide dogs?'

Viv grips the table harder. There are flashing lights all around, her vision pixelating like the broken screen in an arcade.

A waiter with a tray of glasses strides purposefully into her eyeline. 'Come with me.' His voice is just for her. 'Right now.'

Viv glances at Sean.

The waiter puts down his tray of drinks. 'I can explain what's happening.'

Viv clamps the table harder with clawed fingers.

He raises his voice, speaking for an audience. 'Of course I can show you to the bathroom.' He stares at Viv. His focus is so intense, the downy hairs on her arms stand up.

He strides away.

Viv takes a second. She follows him, brushing the bar tables with her fingertips. She cuts through groups of party guests, senses them talking, laughing, drinking. They are normal. There are no scenes scissoring into these people's visions, no glitches in their consciousness.

But this waiter *knows*.

Viv pushes inside and runs down the ramp, instinctively turning away from the grandfather clocks. She follows the art deco railing, towards a metal door that she – somehow – knows is the bathroom.

The waiter is in there, holding a cubicle door open. 'In there. Right now.' He gives her a light shove. 'Otherwise, you piss yourself.' He pulls the door shut behind her.

Viv staggers down to the seat. She lifts the wispy skirts of her dress and tugs down her underwear, just in time.

'Viv, you know you feel like the world just glitched? Something about the world has broken.'

Piss comes out of its own accord.

'You keep dying, and you're living today on repeat, and the only person who remembers is me.' His voice is even. 'And you keep dying because one of your family keeps murdering you.'

12

Eleven Months Ago
The Day of the
Last-But-One Funeral

'I know funerals aren't meant to be all confetti and Pin the Tail on the Donkey,' Viv said, slowly stirring her gin with her straw, 'but this one was particularly shit.'

On the next stool, Bethan glanced at the bar owner, Rob.

It was 6 p.m. on a Monday night in Viv's local, and Viv and Bethan were the only customers.

Rob looked up from polishing glassware. 'Sorry.'

Viv waved a hand. 'Don't be nice to me. I can't take it.'

Bethan's voice was too gentle. 'Harry's funeral was always going to be hard.'

Viv held up a hand. *'Please.'* She brushed imaginary lint from her black dress. 'It wasn't just that it was Harry's. Or that everyone kept checking their phones to see if Alison had died. It was how people were with *me.*' She shakes her head at her glass. 'Looking up to say *hello,* and then seeing who it was. Watching their faces change, like they've ordered a lovely bouquet, and found it's come crawling with maggots.'

Viv rested her hands on her forehead, shielding her eyes.

Bethan glanced at Rob. 'I'm sure your family don't see you as *maggots.*'

'You didn't see them, Beth.'

'*A* maggot, singular, at most.'

Rob turned away to adjust bottles on the shelf. The tea towel wedged in the back pocket of his jeans hung down limply like a cotton tail.

Viv looked up from under her fingers. 'Do you ever get the feeling your family don't like you?'

Bethan and Rob glanced each other.

'It's an emotional day. I'm sure they like you.' Bethan took a second. 'Deep down.'

'Pretty deep then.' Viv pulled her hands apart. 'Deep like the bottom of the ocean, the dark places the freaky fish live.'

Rob and Bethan said nothing.

'Do your family like you?' Viv spun the bar stool round to face Bethan. 'And I don't mean the idea of you, like, *great, we have a daughter,* but *you,* Bethan Kennedy, the actual flesh human?'

Bethan shook her head. She hated it when shit got real; she was a conversational surface skater. She wanted to bitch about reality stars and the price of electric toothbrush heads, why her colleagues would think it's OK to put haddock soup in the microwave. And Viv was the same. It was her philosophy not to read anything into anything: to see no patterns, make no connections, to studiously avoid any recognition of cause-and-effect. Viv had the same approach to her own character development as *Seinfeld*: no hugging, no learning.

Usually.

Until one of those days when reality just smashed her in the face.

'Would your family choose to spend time with you if you didn't share DNA? Would you choose to spend time with them?' If Viv couldn't surface-skate tonight, she wouldn't let Bethan surface-skate either. 'Or would you say *no way, fucking weirdos, you can keep your unsolicited advice and your GB News.*'

'*Viv.*' Bethan looked up at Rob. 'I told you about GB News in confidence.'

Rob shrugged.

'It's a new thing. Dad's a good man in other ways.'

Viv fixed on Bethan. 'So that means you *like* your dad?'

'What kind of question is that?'

Viv waved a frustrated arm. 'Imagine all bets are off. No history. No shared blood.' Bethan was being deliberately obtuse. 'Would you spend time with your family if you weren't related? Do you *like* them? Do they *like* you?'

Bethan was silent.

Viv turned to Rob. 'What about you?'

Rob had been drying a glass. He paused his tea towel, holding Viv's gaze, too sensible to answer.

'I'm saying it doesn't compute as a thought experiment.'

Bethan folded her arms protectively round herself, like the temperature of the room had dropped. 'You can't suddenly be not related. There's no way of testing it.'

'But do your family smile at your jokes?' Viv leaned closer. 'Do they look pleased when you turn up, or does only the dog rush to greet you? Does everyone else give each other snide glances and start muttering about Duncan's graduation?'

Bethan looked up now. 'They still go on about Duncan's graduation?'

Viv raised her voice. 'Do they *like you*?'

'Yes.'

Bethan and Viv looked up.

'*Yes*, they look pleased to see me,' Rob continued slowly. '*Yes*, we would spend time with each other if we weren't related.'

The pause was long.

'Then good for you,' Viv said finally. 'That's lovely.'

'That's because you're so nice, Rob.' Bethan took a second; she turned to Viv. 'You are too. You just hide it better.'

Viv stabbed the lime in her glass with her straw. 'Right.'

'You confuse the situation with more distractions, like a *Where's Wally?* picture. You're more complex.'

'Complex.'

'Complex,' Bethan repeated firmly.

There was the hydraulic hiss of a bus stopping on the street outside. A woman got off wearing *Working Girl* trainers and an office skirt.

Viv was way too drunk for office hours.

'I'm sure your family like you.' Bethan patted Viv's leg.

'Today will have been hard for them, especially if everyone's waiting for your aunt to die.'

Viv stared at her glass. 'She's not my aunt.'

'It's too quiet.' Bethan looked up. 'Shall we have music, Rob?'

'Disco.' Viv looked up from her glass. 'Harry loved his disco.'

Rob tapped at his phone. 'I can do disco.'

The peppy baseline of 'Funkytown' started up, the beats jarring after the silence.

It was still too quiet. Viv could still fucking think.

She reached over the bar and yanked up the dial. Disco beats filled the bar at a Saturday night volume.

'Better.' Viv pulled off her tights and shoved them into her handbag. She drained her glass. 'Now.' She looked up at Rob. 'I think we need another drink.'

13

Now

Viv and the waiter stay either side of the cubicle door, the only sound the catching in-and-out of Viv's breaths.

'In your handbag you have four keys on a shark keyring.' The waiter's voice is soft. 'You have your phone and your EpiPen for your peanut allergy. You have a tissue twist of two dodgy diazepam you got off the internet. You have your wallet with seven cards and a receipt for £2.05 for three packets of instant noodles, bought at 9.54 last night when you were, quote, *jonesing for dirty salt.*'

Viv stares at the toilet brush.

'Check your bag, Viv. We don't have long before your mum comes.'

Viv looks up desperately, for *anything* to make this make sense.

'You know I'm telling the truth. You felt the glitch, Viv.'

In all her moments before this one, Viv *got* time, sensed the seconds of her life beating with the regularity of a metronome. Even when it felt like time speeded or slowed, she knew it didn't, Viv's lost weekends never quite so lost as her stories suggested: *and, next thing, I woke up in Glasgow* making a better anecdote than *I have hazy memories of drunk-cry-dialling, getting a cab to the station, waiting on the cold platform.*

She inhales. The room smells acrid: of floral air freshener, with an undertone of bleach.

'You've told me all your secrets, Viv. I know you can't pour liquid from a carton without spilling, that you consider it an under-researched medical condition. I know about the time you nicked a doorknob from that house party.'

Viv pushes the swing-lid of the sanitary bin. Scent wafts up, earthy and animal. 'Why did I take the doorknob?'

'You were tripping and you thought it was a muffin.'

Viv lets the lid go; it swings back into place with a *shush*.

'I know you turn your mobile phone screen to black and white when you want to look impressive, that you made a salad from three types of crisps.' He pauses. 'There were Monster Munch, Chip Sticks and those other ones, I've forgot the name ...'

Cheese savouries.

'... biscuity ones, they're shaped like the suits from a pack of cards ...'

Cheese savouries.

'You know the ones. You said they made a good base for salad, that they were the lettuce.'

She pulls up her underwear and unlocks the door. 'Who *are* you?'

The waiter is leaning against a sink, one foot crossed over the other. He gives a tight smile. 'Jamie.' His sharp features twist. In contrast with Viv's panic, he is stifling a yawn. Unsuccessfully.

'What is happening?'

'You keep getting murdered, and the world keeps resetting to this point.' The waiter – Jamie – holds her gaze. 'I remember every time, but you don't. No one else notices.' He indicates the recessed fish tank. 'When your mum comes in, tell her I was here to remove this dead body.'

Jamie takes off the tank's lid. Tiny flashes of orange and kingfisher swim back and forth. At the water's surface, a frilly black goldfish floats upside down. Jamie curls his hand into a spoon. 'You won't believe me yet, so just go with it.' He scoops the fish into the paper towel bin. 'Until you're up to speed, I keep everything the same between now and 5.03 by the canal.'

'You're telling me we've had this conversation before?'

He nods. He lets his eyes shut for a long second, like a micro-nap.

'But no one wants to kill me. Lots of people think …'

He opens his eyes. '*No one wants to kill me,*' he says automatically along with her, his timing perfect. He continues, even though she's stopped. '*Loads of people think I'm a twat, but no one wants me dead.*'

Viv grips the cubicle door hard, the plastic tacky in her fingertips.

'Give me your phone.'

To Viv's surprise, she does.

'I have to go. If your mum finds me in here, I get sacked.' Jamie taps in Viv's passcode. 'Your mum will come in and say I have a face like a weasel. Show her the fish, then come back up to the roof when you've decided you're going to prove me wrong. That will take four minutes and seven seconds.' He meets her gaze. 'It will be 4.01.'

Viv swallows.

'At the party, your mum will talk to you about earrings. You'll be rude to Sean, you'll piss off Chrissy, Frank will choke on an olive. At 4.09 you'll realise I'm telling the truth, and you will come and find me on the fire escape.' He pushes himself off the sink. 'Until then' – he makes eye contact – 'don't let your mum wind you up.'

He strides out of the bathroom, leaving the door to close with a swish.

Viv stares in the mirror. *So.*

It has finally happened, like they always said it would. The Class As have finally caught up with her.

Viv smooths her hair straight against her cheeks.

Psychosis isn't ideal, but there'll be doctors. There'll be pills, proper pills, *legal* pills – Viv, of all people, doesn't need any convincing about the power of pharmaceuticals. Admittedly, antipsychotics made Viv's friend Sophie lactate, but this does not feel like a situation where *good things come to those who wait*. Viv is all about the big picture. The odd spurt of breastmilk is by-the-by.

She will do the responsible thing. She will call the emergency services, right now, get herself sectioned.

She lifts her phone. Her screen is open to a new saved contact: *Jamie (Time Loop).*

100

She frowns. This whole thing *feels* real, but so do those dreams where she's running from an orca and the stairs turn to sponge.

Viv pulls the piece of twisted tissue from her bag and looks in the mirror. She holds her own eye contact.

Would diazepam be a good thing here? Or a very – *very* – bad thing?

Mum enters the bathroom, pushing up her sleeves. 'Why was that man in the Ladies?'

Viv drops the tissue into her bag. 'He was removing a dead fish.' She indicates the fish corpse on the discarded paper towels.

'That waiter has a touch of cruelty about him.' Mum shuts herself in a cubicle. 'It's the weaselly face.'

Viv runs the tap, splashing her face, trying not to *think*. Rivulets of mascara seep into the corners of her eyes.

Mum comes out of the cubicle. She stares at Viv.

Viv holds a tissue to one eye. 'Migraine.' Her mascara leaves the tissue stained as black as the dead fish.

Assuming the dead fish exists. Psychosis can be sneaky.

Mum stares at her. 'You're not ... unwell?'

Viv snaps back into the room. She can read Mum's subtext. 'I've only had two glasses.'

'Just be careful, Viv.' Mum pauses. 'I hope I don't need to say—'

'No. You don't,' Viv snaps. How is she managing to get irritated *now?*

Mum holds her gaze in the mirror. 'Chrissy has gone to a lot of trouble.'

'*I said* I've got a migraine.'

Mum gives a small nod. She pushes on the metal door and is gone.

Viv drops the mascara-streaked tissue into the bin. One lifeless bubble eye stares glassily up. The corpse is a Black Moor goldfish: Viv had two as a child, though Ken died a week after arrival. Barbie managed to last most of the summer before turning fins-up and getting flushed to fish heaven. Viv picks up the fish corpse. It is cold. Damp.

She's pretty sure it's real.

And she's pretty sure the waiter was real too. Not *legit* – definitely not legit – but physically real.

Viv wraps the black goldfish in a paper towel and places it in her handbag. She will find that man, right now, make him tell her how he did this conjuring trick. Then she'll throw this stupid fish in his stupid face.

Viv takes one last look in the mirror, refusing to notice the time on the clock above.

Refusing to notice that at 4.01, exactly as Jamie said she would, Viv is heading back to the party.

Viv pushes through the doors to the roof terrace. It's the same.

Still a sea of jewel-bright dresses and men in shiny suits, still the low hum of voices and the sharp smell of foliage. Over the clear railing, the ageing brick spire of the cathedral is still dwarfed by cranes.

Relief swells within. It's not perfect – Viv's still at a party with her family who think she's a shithouse – but, still. It's like waking up from a nightmare to find herself in her own bedroom: comfortingly familiar despite the overflowing washing basket and strewn cups, despite the sound of kick drums from the neighbour's hardstyle playlist making the wall vibrate.

The waiter from her waking nightmare crosses her path with a tray.

She hurries after him. 'Hey!'

He speeds up and pushes through a swing door.

She slows. Now she's back, grounded in reality, she could give this man a slow handclap.

He's a conman. A low-rent Sherlock, using the tools of a cheap psychic to hook his mark. He wants something from Viv – she doesn't know what, but everyone wants something – and he took one look at her try-hard dress, sensed the vibrations of tension at a family event, and knew *Don't let your mum wind you up* was a guaranteed bullseye.

Viv rubs her temples slowly. The aura of her migraine has lessened to celestial twinkling at the edge of her vision. Every second she stands here, it's easier to know she imagined the glitch.

She follows the waiter through the door to find a kitchen, all steam and metal and the sharp smell of raw onions. A chef is piping fillings onto pastry cases, a white-aproned kid loading plates into the hood of a dishwasher.

Viv blinks. The waiter has gone.

The kid glances nervously at the chef.

Viv takes in the other door at the back of the room and makes herself smile. 'Sorry.' She heads back into the bright light of the terrace.

'I'm sorry if I was blunt earlier.' Mum steps in Viv's direction. 'I always seem to say the wrong thing.'

Viv gives a small nod.

Mum is studying her. 'You really do look so pretty today. You have such a lovely figure. And you know what would finish off that outfit nicely?'

'Mum.' Viv holds her breath, urgent. 'Please don't.'

'Some earrings.'

Viv turns, rattled. It's not proof. Mum must have said something about earrings earlier, and the man must have overheard. That'll be it. Conmen are magpies, always alert for useful trinkets.

Someone falls into step beside her. 'Do you want another drink?'

'NO!'

Sean baulks. He backs away, hands in the air.

Viv scans the room. 'Sorry.'

Frank, in his spotted clown shirt, is talking to someone, laughing. Not choking.

The sharp-faced waiter – is his name even Jamie? – cuts a path between sofas. He puts his tray down on a high table and walks back inside. He's not even pretending to serve drinks.

Is he even a fucking waiter?

Viv grabs a passing woman's sleeve. 'Did you see that man?'

The woman frowns.

Viv lets the woman go.

She takes the paper towel parcel out of her handbag. The wetness has soaked through, turned the paper transparent, but when she unwraps it, the fish is still there. Frilly fins. Scales. Glassy eye.

She looks up. She makes eye contact with Chrissy.

Chrissy is watching, the corner of her lip raised in distaste.

Viv shoves the fish back into her bag. She's about to explain – how, she's not sure – when there's a wheeze from behind.

Chrissy focuses over Viv's shoulder; her sneer drops. 'He's choking!'

The coughing gets louder. Wet. Heaving.

Viv takes one step back. And another.

'Hit him on the back, Mark!' Chrissy waves her arm. 'Hit him!'

There's pounding. Gasping. More pounding.

'Harder! Do the Heimlich!'

Reluctantly, Viv turns. She knows what she's going to see.

Frank flails his arms, face red with strain. He bends; he coughs out a flash of black. The flash rolls under a sofa. Frank gasps in air.

There is a ripple of relief across the terrace.

Frank takes another shuddering breath. He holds his palms up to the crowd.

'Excuse me.' Viv strides towards the double doors, speeding as she goes. 'Excuse me.' She doesn't want to hear it.

'Olive,' Frank croaks.

Viv stumbles down the ramp, round the balcony, towards the fire exit. She runs up to Jamie, who is sitting on the last-but-one step at the top of the fire-escape stairs, smoking a roll-up.

Before she even gets to ask, Jamie looks up. 'We think it's because I was holding you when you died.'

14

Today

But Eighty-Three Lives Before

Jamie's day had been going badly even before Viv started dying on him.

He woke up alone, tasting fluff.

He gave an *umf* of disgust and pushed Random Cat's tail off his mouth. Random Cat worked the building hard, meowing outside every flat, waltzing around like a tiny landlord with no respect for tenants' rights. Jamie didn't stand for it, but Imran was made of softer stuff. A few plaintive miaows, and Imran had the door open, shaking a box of Dreamies.

Jamie found Imran in the main room, lying in a foetal position under a blanket on the broken-backed sofa. A pillow suggested he'd slept there.

Another bad sign.

Jamie flicked the kettle on. He didn't get a chance to place down an apology brew.

Imran jerked up to sitting. 'Where were you?'

Jamie dropped two teabags into some – yeah, probably clean – mugs. 'I didn't feel like it.'

Imran threw back his blanket with a jagged energy. He grabbed the ashtray from the coffee table and, not losing eye contact, tipped the butts of Jamie's joints into the bin.

The lid swung shut. A cloud of ash puffed into the air.

Jamie tried to stare the kettle into boiling. 'You know I'm not big on birthdays. What was it, twenty-four? Not even a special one.'

'She'd hired a room, got balloons.' Imran was too angry to smooth his bed hair: it pointed in all directions like unmown grass. He'd slept in Jamie's old gym hoodie, softened from a thousand washes, with the thunder-coloured marl faded to fog. 'I told everyone you'd be there.'

Jamie stared at the contents of Imran's pockets on the carpet: the semi-circle of receipts, phone, vape and keys.

'Everyone kept asking about you and I said *he's definitely coming, he knows it's really important, he wouldn't mug me off.*'

Imran stormed into the bedroom.

Jamie took a large swig of lukewarm water from a nearby glass. The top of the water shimmered with a thin layer of dust.

He put the glass down.

He'd meant to join Imran last night, maybe. But once he'd fired up *Call of Duty* and lit that third joint, he wasn't moving from the sofa. Imran's sister was a dick anyway, with all her talk of *side hustles* and *five-year plans,* always asking about Jamie's *ambitions.* Farah was like a product of another time, twenty-four going on seventy-five-in-the-nineteenth century.

Skipping her party had felt like a good idea. Last night.

'*Miaow.*'

Random Cat sat elegantly at Jamie's feet, paws neatly together, eyes round with expectation.

Jamie pointed to the door. 'Go.'

He got no response, so Jamie picked up the cat and walked it to the front door. He slammed the door after it, ignoring the final, bereft *miaow.* He looked through the open door to the bedroom.

Imran was moving with quick, stampy steps, making an unnecessary amount of getting-ready noise, slamming his underwear drawer, making an impressive bang with a plastic pot of wax on a melamine bedside table. He even managed to clang the door of their wardrobe, getting up a decent momentum, despite the wardrobe being made of canvas.

Jamie turned away. He'd let Imran calm down, then he'd apologise. This was their thing. Jamie always said he'd join Imran later, and Imran would dress up like he was going to an eighties yacht party. He'd kiss Jamie goodbye in a cloud of Dior Sauvage, Jamie would relax into the sofa for a little smoke and fire up the PlayStation, Imran would return home fuming, and Jamie would wheedle and apologise until Imran calmed down. It all worked out in the end.

Imran stalked out of the bedroom, clipping his work tie to his collar. 'You know Becky's boyfriend came to walk her home from the bar?' He arranged the tie under the leaves of his collar, covering the clip. 'He'd just got off a twelve-hour shift. They've been together two weeks.'

Jamie reached for Imran's tie; Imran stepped back.

Even in that cheap security guard uniform, he looked good. The shirt was synthetic, nothing like anything Imran would ever wear in real life, the fabric too thin, but the white collar emphasised his jawline. Jamie liked to pull Imran towards him by his tie.

Jamie reached for the tie again, but Imran didn't let himself be pulled. The tie unclipped, hanging limply from Jamie's hand. 'Aren't you even going to say sorry?'

'I did say sorry.' Jamie caught his arm. 'I *am* sorry.'

Imran shook him off. 'You're a selfish twat. Even your mum says so.'

The hairs on the back of Jamie's neck rose. 'Can we leave my mum out of this?'

Imran swiped the tie. 'Everyone tells me I deserve better.'

Jamie glanced at the cooker clock. He only had half an hour to eat and wash the stale smell of inside weed out of his hair. 'How about we talk tonight?'

Imran just stared. 'Get out.'

Jamie frowned. 'Of where?'

'If you're not gone when I get back, I'll throw your stuff out of the window.'

He bloody would, as well: Imran loved a dramatic gesture. Never mind that they'd both be in the street picking up all Jamie's stuff half an hour later, Imran laughing and apologising.

Jamie rattled through the options.

You can't throw me out, it's both our names on the lease.

You know you always feel better when you calm down.

'Don't make this a deal. Your sister's too thirsty. No one needs a big party at twenty-four!'

'She's twenty-*three*! You'd know if you'd seen the balloons. Get out, now, or I'm putting your stuff on the street.' Imran picked up his coat. 'It'll get wet too, because we don't have bin bags. You never did go to the shops like you said you would.'

Imran strode away, slamming the door behind.

The loose woodwork of the doorframe shivered to a stop.

An hour later, Jamie left another voicemail for Imran as he walked into work. 'I didn't realise how important it was. I would have gone if I'd known.'

He walked down the towpath towards the museum.

Things hadn't been great with the two of them lately. Jamie's level of anxiety was high – life, social media, the usual – and the night thoughts just kept coming, which Jamie dealt with by smoking more weed. He'd always had a problem with intrusive thoughts. He still got flashes of child-sized coffins from a news programme he'd watched years before and, lately, the unwelcome thoughts had taken a new, unnerving tangent. An elderly teacher's face from primary school had started appearing during sex. The more Jamie tried to stop her, the more Mrs Churchill loomed, glasses on a chain bouncing against her bosom as she played the piano, turning the pages of sheet music while singing a jaunty 'Autumn Days When the Grass Is Jewelled'.

Imran didn't understand why Jamie had been less enthusiastic about sex lately, but Jamie couldn't tell him about

Mrs Churchill. Imran would find it hilarious and make jokes, it would become *a thing*, and Jamie would have no chance of Mrs Churchill fucking off then, would he?

Jamie checked his phone. Imran worked in a team of two on the door of the restaurant: he always had time to call Jamie back.

But Imran wasn't calling. Jamie was leaving him messages – and Imran, the man who filled any awkward silence, the man who bought treats for piss-taking cats that weren't even his, the man who was always in a corner at parties with an arm round the too-drunk stranger saying *don't cry, angel, you can do so much better* – Imran wasn't even *trying* to make things right.

Now, Jamie was getting worried.

At work there was a big function starting on the rooftop terrace. A funeral, but not quite.

Jamie circled the roof terrace, the surprisingly fierce April sun searing his back, offering Prosecco to a crowd dressed up for Chester races. People asked him for soft drinks when there was perfectly good alcohol on the tray, and he had no free hand to wipe the perspiration from his eyelashes. The bar manager insisted staff stood in the sun on hot days, leaving the shade for the guests, because Brent was a ruthless customer service machine – and one who never got dizzy, with a perfectly regulated internal temperature, and no sweat glands.

Brent headed toward him now. '*Still* no iron?'

Jamie turned away. 'I lent it to a neighbour. She's got my spare charger too. This is why I don't do people favours.'

Brent looked at Jamie's feet. So, what, Jamie had a hole in his shoe? Brent should pay him more. This place made enough money: just yesterday Jamie had seen an invoice on Brent's desk for a thousand pounds, for hanging baskets.

In his pocket, Jamie's phone buzzed.

He waited till Brent was distracted by a customer, then dumped the tray.

It was Imran.

Call me. Right now.

No kiss, but it was progress. Jamie touched the bag of weed in his pocket for reassurance.

He got in the lift and out at the ground floor, passing groups of kids and adults all looking up at the Space exhibition.

Jamie never looked up. There were only so many times you could see floating dummies dressed as astronauts and replica planets.

Which is why he didn't see her fall.

A metre ahead, the woman hit the floor with a solid bang.

Now, Jamie stared. *A woman. From the sky.*

The woman lay, twisted and unmoving. Red flowed from her head, a blood circle growing in all directions, spreading silently across the stone floor.

From the sky. From the sky, from the sky.

He processed it.

'*Phone an ambulance!*' Jamie dropped to the floor, his phone skittering away and into the Alan Turing statue. '*Someone phone an ambulance now!*'

He crouched, grabbing the woman's limp hand. 'Hey.'

Her eyelids gave a tiny flicker.

Jamie cradled her. 'You're going to be OK.' He pushed strands of hair from her eyes, gleaming with blood. 'Hang on.'

He tried not to sound panicked. It didn't work.

And there was *so much* blood now, pumping through her grey party dress, soaking the fabric black. He could feel the blood seeping through his shirt, still warm from her body. She smelled like the butcher's section of the supermarket.

Jamie glanced at the museum entrance, but there were no blue lights. No paramedics, no ambulance pulling up.

A crowd had formed around. Silent. Not helping.

'Someone take over!' He whirled around desperately. 'Someone with skills!'

No one did.

'Please,' he whispered to the woman. 'Please don't die.'

Her eyelids stayed still. The blood on his shirt started to cool.

Jamie raised his voice to a scream. *'Please!'*

A flash of white blinded him momentarily, and Jamie's arms felt empty. He wasn't crouching anymore.

Instead, he was standing several flights up in dazzling sunshine on the rooftop terrace wearing a dry, clean shirt, holding a tray of glasses. He watched the dead woman – now an *alive* woman – stumble back into a table in shock, wearing heels too high for this party, her grey dress no longer blackened by blood.

His body knew before he did. It vibrated with a primal fear.

Brent looked him up and down with faint disgust. '*Still* no iron?'

Jamie's tray of glasses tumbled to the floor.

15

Now

On the fire escape, Jamie talks. Next to him, on the step, Viv pictures a body, splayed and motionless. A wispy grey dress, soaked black. A pool of red, expanding silently across the stone floor.

Below, beeps of city traffic are softly audible.

'Was there a lot of blood?'

'We've agreed not to talk about your deaths.'

Death-*s*. The word would be disquieting, even if it wasn't a plural. '*I* haven't agreed anything. You're saying I'm going to die again this afternoon?'

'*No.*'

'So, *this time* I'm going to live?' Viv sits forward. 'When you've already told me you say the same things to me every time?'

Jamie takes another drag of his roll-up. He doesn't answer.

Viv sits up, triumphant – but this is the most pyrrhic of victories.

She slumps back. 'Why is this happening?'

Jamie smokes slowly. He looks like a man in his twenties, yet he moves like a much older person. 'We don't know. At first, we wondered if the universe thought you shouldn't have died, but neither of us believe in that woo-woo.' Jamie throws down the butt of his roll-up. 'Then we went through a phase of thinking you're some kind of chosen one, but decided you're the last person the universe would have chosen.'

Viv was about to argue, but decided Jamie and Dead Viv had a point. 'How many times have we done this?'

'Eighty-four.' He glances at her. 'That I know of.'

'That you know of?'

'We don't know what happened before I held you and I got dragged in.'

Viv shivers. The idea of eighty-four times is incomprehensible enough. Yet this could have been going on longer still? Forever? 'How come you remember and I don't?'

'It's not as much fun as you might think.' He's sarcastic for a man who looks this exhausted.

She supposes he's had a chance to practise these lines. 'I remember walking into the party with Sean.'

'You remember everything till the room scissors and Sean talks about the nurses liking him because he brushed Alison's hair.' Jamie stands, casting a shadow over Viv. 'I have to show my face now or my boss comes looking.' He nods at her bag. 'Throw that fish away before it starts to smell. You want to get your money back on that bag, remember?'

He goes inside, clanging the fire door shut behind him.

Viv stretches her legs, taking in the warmth of the sun on her pale shins. She takes the dead fish out of her handbag and considers it. Tiny. Light.

Harmless …?

Probably.

She hurls the fish off the roof.

So. She will die today.

Of course, she's daydreamed about dying. But not *dying* dying, not the bad bit, just the reassuring, painless aftermath. She's visualised the packed crematorium; heard the sobbing, whispered conversations. She's seen her friends who don't reply to messages anymore looking small and frail, in oversized sunglasses hiding eyes red with regret. Viv's like an artist who wasn't appreciated in her own lifetime and, finally, at her funeral, she'll be understood. People will cling to each other for support. They'll say *angels come in many forms.*

Surely?

Surely.

Without Jamie, she's antsy. She reaches under the back of her dress, feeling for the patch. She presses it harder against her skin, trying to coax more nicotine into her bloodstream.

Is this piece-of-shit thing working?

She really could have done with not choosing today to stop vaping. She'd been planning to impress these people. All the while, one of them had been planning to kill her.

Was that irony? Viv had never quite got her head round what was or wasn't irony.

117

Of course, Viv's assuming it's only one of her family who's been planning to kill her. The only thing that could be worse is if this is one of those *Murder on the Orient Express*-type scenarios, and the plan was cooked up, mob-handed, on that family WhatsApp group Viv wasn't invited to.

As Viv finds so often, thinking isn't helping.

She strides to the railing and tries to focus on the city. She will do some of that *living-in-the-moment* guff the soft-voiced bun-haired mansplainers bang on about on Instagram. She will find five things to see, four things to touch, etc.

She takes in the vista, looking for five things she can see. *Railway arch. Crane. Anti-homeless bench. Trolley in canal.*

She is just deciding on the fifth when a metallic ratcheting tells her Jamie is back.

'First thing.' Viv turns away from the railing. 'Have you ever thought we should just leave this party?'

'What do *you* think?' Jamie is surprisingly snippy for someone who has had this conversation before. 'You always reset, whatever I do.'

'*Reset.* What a nice, clean word.'

'You die even if we leave, in different ways. You definitely got run over one time – I heard the car roar up behind. We'd been holed up in your house for safety, but we had to go out for a Chinese. There was nothing of yours in the fridge except an inch of pesto and some milk.' Jamie scratches his stubble. 'And the milk was off.'

Viv's cheeks warm. 'I get busy.'

'There was a label on a shelf saying *Viv, don't eat my stuff.*'

Viv doesn't acknowledge this statement, just rises above it.

'It's someone at this party who wants you dead, so we decided it's better to stay and work it out.'

'I think maybe I want *this* Viv to try leaving.'

'*We* decided, Viv. You agree with me.'

Viv sits down. 'Stop telling me what I think!' She puts her head between her legs. Somewhere, in the universe, there is a fallen army of *her*: a succession of Vivs, toppled like dominos.

She bites the flesh of her cheek. Pain shoots in.

She *feels* real, but Jamie's saying she's not, not properly. She's just the next chocolate bar in the vending machine, the one pushed forward by the wheel of wire.

'It's not what you think,' Jamie says. 'You're still the same you, waking up again and again.'

Having someone anticipate your every question should feel *way* more satisfying than this. 'How do you know?'

'You didn't need directions to the toilets, did you? Or the fire escape?'

'But if my body keeps dying' – she stops herself adding *horrifically* – 'why do I come back intact?'

He holds up his palms. 'Next time you get stuck in a broken universe, try to get stuck with a scientist, not a waiter.'

'And how do you know my death isn't an accident?'

'I thought it was, the first times.'

Death-*s*. Time-*s*. This guy is so casual with his fucking plurals.

'But when I kept you away from the balcony, everything reset anyway. One time someone must have spiked your canapés with satay because you went into anaphylactic shock – and someone had taken your EpiPen from your bag.'

'Really?' Viv raises her brows. 'I can't believe I survived anaphylactic shock without my EpiPen.'

Jamie glances at her.

'Right. You mean you discussed it with a later Viv.' She puts her hands to her throat. 'And now that Viv is dead too.'

She presses her neck, imagines her airways constricting. Another cookie-cutter Viv, pushed out by the vending machine wire and tipped into the abyss.

Jamie is studying her, and she doesn't like it. He's shaking his head with a kind of awe – but not awe like *wow, what an impressive performance of rhythmic gymnastics.* More like *what kind of arsehole lets their dog crap on a station platform and doesn't pick it up?*

'What?' It comes out as a bark.

Jamie sighs. 'It doesn't matter.'

'You've got something to say. Say it.'

He holds her gaze. 'It's just sometimes I can't help wondering what you've done to these people.'

Viv crunches her toes up in her shoes.

She wishes she was able to say *me too.*

16

Three Years Ago
Duncan's Graduation

After some deliberation, Viv decided to go to Duncan's PhD graduation. She wasn't keen – Mum had what she called a *pad of news* by her phone, and a good portion of it was made up of her cousin's achievements. (Duncan's, not Sean's, obviously.) And did Viv imagine it, or did Mum deliberately leave a generous pause afterwards for Viv to compare and self-reflect?

Either way, Viv chose not to use the opportunity. Not unless she was having a really bad day.

And Duncan was a bore, true, but Viv hadn't spoken to him directly for a decade, so maybe he'd got better? She was pretty sure twenty-nine-year-olds didn't still play air piano and insist *I'd be a Ravenclaw.*

And there'd be free food and booze. It might even, at a push ... be fun?

This was all back when, yes, Viv's relationship with her family was awful – but the awfulness was still drawn in pencil.

Before Viv went over the lines of that awfulness in permanent ink.

The day was long: lots of sitting, lots of clapping, lots of speeches about *potential* and *talent* and *future luminaries*, words that made Viv shift in her seat.

The company wasn't great either. A powder-caked face loomed into view on the way into the town-hall-type building.

Viv grabbed Mum's arm. 'Why's Duncan invited Angela?'

'She's a friend of the family.'

Viv let that go. She didn't say *not the whole family*, so that was growth, right there.

The audience clapped hard as Duncan wheeled onto stage to accept his scroll, and Viv clapped hardest of all, showing willing. Duncan looked so proud in his long gown, a tasselled hat on his head, like that meme of the TV owl.

Viv scanned the crowd with every clap. They were here to celebrate *exceptional mathematics* and, while Viv didn't know a lot about the topic, she thought it pretty exceptional, mathematically, that there could be so many people in this room, and not a single one she would want to have sex with.

★

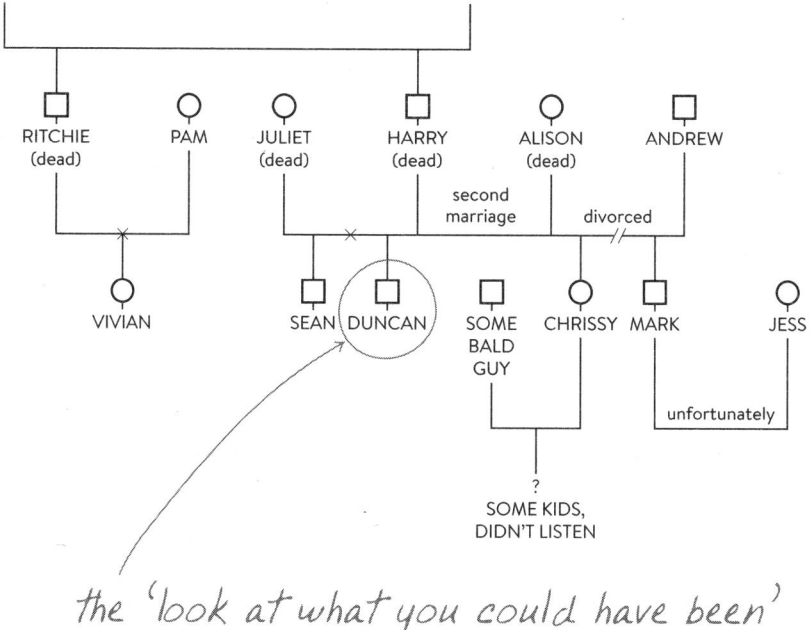

the 'look at what you could have been'

Later Duncan hosted a meal for forty, the occasion an oil-and-water mix of family and friends. Duncan's female friends were all split ends and no make-up, draped in drab, loose Victorian-orphanage layers, talked about food miles and, likely, had kids called *Vulva*. The men were, somehow, worse. They had a way of speaking Viv couldn't get her head round, all *it behoves me to say*, and *I was discombobulated*. They cared about the *impact of capitalism* so much more than they did about coming over as pricks.

There was no behove-ing or capitalism from Viv's family, of course, just giggling and curtseying and *do we call you Doctor now, Duncan?* Viv's family weren't used to academia. Mum, in particular, spent a big chunk of time trying to understand the living arrangements. *Why do you call it a college? Isn't the whole thing the college? How does the servant thing work? Do you have a little bell?*

Inevitably, Mum scooped Viv into the conversation, because no achievement was too random to be celebrated. It wasn't Mum's fault – Viv hadn't given her much to be proud of, so she had to take advantage of pride-by-proxy. 'Did you know Duncan has his own backgammon channel?'

Viv swigged her wine. 'No.'

'Harry says he has over two thousand subscribers on Twitch. Isn't that wonderful!' Mum leaned towards Duncan. 'Now, please tell me what that means.'

Duncan explained, and Mum continued to beam, adjusting the top of her dress as she listened. Her neckline was deliberately low: Mum had no age spots, and saw this as vindication of her dislike of suncream. She once told Viv *it's the parabens that actually cause the cancer.* That was a few years ago: Viv hadn't heard about parabens for a while. Big Paraben conspiracies couldn't compete on Facebook now, not in the age of Fifteen Minute Cities and Big Vax.

'Not like a TV channel, OK.' Mum adjusted the top of her dress again. 'I don't completely understand, but it sounds wonderful.' She turned to Viv. '*You* could play backgammon, Viv.'

'I'm sure,' Viv said.

'Wouldn't it be nice to get a hobby?'

'I've got hobbies' – Viv had a little bag of them in her handbag, right now – 'but you sound interested, Mum. Maybe you should play?' Viv shoved her chair back. 'I need the toilet.'

She walked away, turning her phone screen black and

white as she walked because, while she might not have split ends or a PhD, she could be classy in other ways.

She sent Bethan a message.

Kill me now.

Bethan replied instantly.

Your emergency ket still intact?

Viv smiled.

I told you I wasn't going to take the ket 😇

Viv was still congratulating herself on her self-restraint as she re-buttoned her jumpsuit in the cubicle.

The bathroom door swung open. There was the sound of clicking heels.

A woman's voice wafted under Viv's door. 'You don't think she's pretty?'

'For now.' Viv knew that voice: lemon-sour, and under-cut with salt. 'Cherubic faces only look good on the young. There're no cheekbones.' There was an indicative jangle of bracelets – Angela miming cheekbones. 'No scaffolding.'

There was more clicking of heels.

Viv lifted her feet up silently onto the toilet seat. She tucked her arms round her knees.

The conversation stopped while the women pissed. Inevitably, the flushes came, and there was the metal slide of locks. The creak of opening doors.

'I've told her mother she needs to hurry up.' Angela raised her voice to be heard over the tap. 'Once she doesn't even have looks to offer, *then* what?'

The adverts on the back of the door blurred in Viv's vision.

It was fine. *Call-me-auntie* Angela could be talking about someone else.

'It's such a shame for poor Pam,' the other woman said.

Viv wrinkled her nose. *Arse.*

'Any moment now, it'll happen. The big slide.' Certainty made Angela's voice silky. 'By forty you get the face you deserve.'

'Isn't it fifty?'

'It'll be forty for her.' More jangling of bracelets. 'No scaffolding. And she's done her best to ruin her looks with drugs and alcohol. She gave herself a prison tattoo when I was babysitting, using a school compass and some ink. *A prison tattoo!* On my watch! Why couldn't she just wait and get a Sanskrit dolphin in Turkey?'

Viv felt her heart beat against her thighs.

'I've got a dolphin on my ankle. Got it done for my fortieth in Byron Bay.'

'Exactly! Like a normal person.'

The hand-dryer blasted. There was more clicking of heels on tiles. The door swished open and closed.

Viv waited a minute more before putting her feet to the ground.

She pulled her wrap of emergency ket out of her handbag. She glanced at the star tattoo on her hand, one she'd stupidly hand-poked two decades before.

She placed the wrap on the cistern and fished in her bag for a note.

The courses came. Viv ate nothing, pushing food around her plate, rearranging it like furniture. She went back to the bathroom several times more. She poured herself more wine, even though wine wasn't her drink. She watched Angela talk.

And Angela could *talk*.

About the need for regulation of the Christmas markets – 'spreading like flies'.

About a TV presenter's new haircut – 'I would have said, if you want to look like a sailor, knock yourself out, but …'

About the film *Parasite* – 'it's wonderful – *and* it's Korean!'

About her favourite subject – 'she's counting on us all forgetting Diana when she's trotters-up in the palace, but she doesn't realise some of us have long memories.'

Viv leaned over. 'Angela.'

Angela looked up.

Viv enunciated carefully. 'Why don't you keep your vacuous opinions to yourself' – she slowed further – 'you – *thin – lipped – cunt*.'

The table went quiet.

'You feel sorry for *my* mum?' Viv waved a hand at Angela's daughter. 'Candice is here wearing bows on her shoes, and she's *thirty-eight*.'

Viv got up – and stumbled.

She leaned forward, trying to balance herself.

She pitched head-first at the long wooden table, dislodging one of the legs, sending herself, the table and everything on it to the floor. After the shattering stopped, the restaurant was silent.

Viv stared up at the ceiling, as still as a broken puppet, looking up at the horrified faces of the coffee-and-wine-spattered people. Blood oozed down her vision in the red liquid curtain of the James Bond credits.

Mum cried in the taxi the whole way to A&E.

17

Now

Viv and Jamie walk back to the museum. He tells her to change back into her chunky boots before the speeches start.

She swaps her shoes in the cloakroom with a hint of regret. It's sensible not to be tiptoeing along at a forty-five-degree angle when there's someone out to kill her, but if she'd known she'd wear these shoes for less than two hours, she would have saved herself two hundred quid.

Someone is clanging a spoon against a glass on the terrace. Viv hurries into the crowd.

At the far railing Chrissy stands on a wooden box, holding cue cards. 'It's so wonderful you could all be here today.'

Chrissy's doing a speech, because of course she is. But that doesn't mean Viv's going to listen. Especially with

Chrissy's pile of cue cards being so alarmingly thick.

Viv scans the crowd. *Which of you fuckers is it?*

It won't be that barperson, probably. Or that woman in the sculpted dress and the green heels, the one dressed like a noughties WAG. And it won't be that man with the stoop and the military moustache – he and Viv have only met once, at Harry's funeral, and their whole conversation hinged on the challenge of finding an NHS dentist.

Viv's gaze lands on Mark. Warmth creeps up her neck.

No. Obviously.

Because … no.

'It's great to see so many of you.' The feathers of Chrissy's coral fascinator quiver. 'Thank you all for coming, to this place that meant so much to Mum and Harry.'

Viv scans the room while Chrissy bangs on. Mum beams as she listens, because she's kind like that: she once nodded and smiled her way through a five-minute best man's anecdote about a groom's clumsy encounter with a sex worker in Amsterdam – even after the words *payment was exchanged*, and the top table had long gone still.

Behind Mum, Frank leans against a wall, holding a pint. He takes a swig, leaving a wisp of foam on his top lip. He doesn't wipe it.

Could Frank really hold a grudge for twenty years? Two decades is excessive, surely?

Fingers of cold patter across Viv's back. She could be standing in front of a draughty window in an old, old house.

She doesn't like this. She doesn't like this at all.

Chrissy keeps serving platitudes to the crowd. 'I want today to be all about the joy Mum and Harry gave us.'

Viv spots Duncan in his wheelchair at the back of the terrace. His face is turned to Chrissy but he's wearing sunglasses, so Viv can't see where his attention is focused.

Duncan?

No. No way. Yes, she ruined his graduation dinner, but that was ages ago, and it was an accident. They never got on, even before that – but that was on Aunt Juliet, not Viv. It wasn't Viv's fault Juliet didn't understand how childhood worked, that when the kids got bored and scrappy, the worst thing she could do was look up from her sewing machine and say *Duncan, why don't you play the others something on your flute?*

'I'm sure most of you know this museum is where Mum and Harry met.' Chrissy smiles at the crowd. 'In one of the many quirky synchronicities of their lives, they both got retirement jobs here. Neither were ever happier at work than they were here.'

Did Chrissy's smile get tighter when she mentioned Harry? Because Viv doesn't remember Chrissy thinking of it as a *quirky synchronicity* at the time. Not when Chrissy was outraged about her mother leaving her father in a late-middle-aged purgatory of M&S meal deals.

Viv lowers her gaze to focus on Angela. She's been even more heavy-handed with the face powder than usual, giving her complexion the texture of a well-floured bap. Her eyebrows, always thin, have finally disappeared. She's drawn some on for this occasion.

Angela?

After all, Jamie says it's one of Viv's family trying to kill her, but he means someone here today, not necessarily someone with shared DNA – and no one radiates more hostility than Angela. Viv will stand by *thin-lipped cunt* until she dies.

And Angela plays dirty. She sends Mum links to podcasts about *setting boundaries with adult children*. But even Angela wouldn't want her dead. Surely? Who would she lord it over then when she wanted to feel better about herself?

'Mum and Harry took so much pleasure from their short time together.' Chrissy catches Viv's gaze, and frowns.

Viv frowns back – *rude* – and remembers Chrissy watching her pull a dead fish from her handbag – *fair.*

Viv can't do this. She can't just stand here and watch Chrissy get through that disconcerting number of cue cards, all the while knowing one of these people wants to kill her. She *can't.*

She feels someone touch her sleeve: Jamie.

Indicating the doors with his head.

She follows him out of the room.

Jamie leads Viv through the deserted Time exhibition. The museum is still open, but there's been no one up here all day: only the super-keen make it this far without losing the love of science. 'This is where you fell the first time.'

Viv leans gingerly over the art deco railing. 'Right.' It's like being shown round by a particularly ghoulish estate agent. She's never understood those grisly Jack the Ripper tours, how they're so popular with London tourists – and this tour is *so* much worse. The murderer's still out there, they're going to kill today, and all the dead women are *her.*

Viv leans further over the railing. Have floors always looked so *solid*?

She ignores the sensation of newly iced blood and follows Jamie past a floor-to-ceiling panel of a picture of a man in a long wig.

'Don't be on your own with anyone near balconies or steep drops or roads.' Jamie keeps walking. 'Keep your bag zipped and your EpiPen safe. Reduce your risk of reset.'

Viv can't meet his eyes. '*Reset*, again.'

Jamie glances at her. 'You want to call it something else?'

Viv keeps her gaze ahead. 'No.'

The two sit on an uncomfortable bench by the canal. Jamie gets out his tobacco and starts making a cigarette.

Viv stares at the half-submerged shopping trolley rearing up from the water, its metal bars furred like it's been brought up from the *Titanic*. The illuminated red and yellow sign of the area's last kebab shop glows across the canal.

'What's the plan for when we work it out?' When Jamie doesn't answer, she turns. 'We *do* have a plan?'

'We do.'

'And?'

He keeps rolling. 'You don't like it.'

Viv sighs. How much easier life would be if she was the kind of person who didn't ask. 'Hit me.'

'You start by not dying.'

'Sounds good.'

'Then we work out who is doing this.'

'I like this plan.'

'Then you kill them before they kill you.'

'Jamie! No!' Viv sits straighter. 'I get rid of spiders with a cup and a card! I'm a shitty person, but I'm just entry-level shitty! I don't *kill!* Can't I just get whoever it is arrested?'

'How? If you're still alive, the person hasn't done anything. And you don't believe in the police. You call them *jumped-up Stasis.*'

'But there's a time and a place for jumped-up Stasis, and this is it.'

'*We* think you should kill them.'

'Oh, do *we*? How convenient.'

Jamie stops rolling. He runs a hand through his hair in frustration.

Viv wonders whether she gets more frustrating with every reset. Probably. Very few people have spent time with Viv and said *the thing is, you just need to get to know her.* 'If we have to kill them, *you* do it.'

'Fine. Work out who it is, and I will.'

Despite the late afternoon sun on her head, Viv shivers.

A bucket-sized chunk of meat rotates slowly in the kebab-shop window.

'If we've done this eighty-four times, we must know quite a lot by now.' She glances at Jamie. 'Who was where when I was pushed. Alibis and such.'

Jamie licks his roll-up.

'We do, don't we? Jamie?'

'Remember I'm rarely with you in your moment of dying.' He doesn't look at her as he lights up. 'And you'd already died lots of times before I understood what was happening. And I had to get you to listen, and you're not exactly a good listener.'

'Victim-blaming. Nice.'

'And I used up a lot of lives just trying to get you to

leave the museum. But this is the third time in a row I've managed to get this routine the same. *Look!*' He tilts his phone at Viv in satisfaction. '5.03!'

Viv leaves a polite pause of appreciation. 'So, what *do* we know by now?'

'That you keep letting yourself get killed.'

Viv narrows her eyes. 'And I'm sure you didn't mean that to come out so judgy.'

'And that there are people here who want you dead.'

Viv stretches her legs out, trying to get comfortable on the bench specifically designed to do the opposite. 'No, we know there are some people here who don't like me. Just *one* person wants to kill me.'

Jamie glances at her.

'It's an important distinction.'

'You think it's most likely to be Frank because of what you did to him.' Jamie pauses. 'Of course, your mum wasn't happy he left her either.'

Viv holds up a hand. 'Can we not talk about that, please.' Since Frank left, Mum's been single for twenty years. She walks into funerals alone and drives herself to her own surgical procedures. She buys discounted loaves of bread and freezes them in single slices.

Today is confronting.

Jamie looks tactfully back at the towpath. 'But fortunately there are other people here who don't like you.'

'Surely you must have some leads. You must have done loads of investigating?'

Jamie looks at his feet.

'Jamie?'

'Look, it's hard for me. I follow people and listen in on conversations. But I also have to try not to get sacked, or I can't stay here. So I have to keep serving people. I try to see who's there when you die, but thing is, the person never does it in front of me and you don't always die straight away, so it's hard to be definite about alibis and ...'

'You're telling me you've done fuck-all for eighty-four lives?'

He blinks. 'I am definitely not telling you that.' One of his eyes twitches with tiredness. 'Let's go through the people again. Who wants you dead?'

'Surely we've done this before?'

'Sometimes you say things you don't at other times. You're not always consistent.'

Viv thinks about this. *Story checks out.*

'Jess, maybe?' Viv pulls her sleeves over her hands. 'Except Jess doesn't know' – she takes a second – '*me.*'

She's only met Jess once. It's absolutely, definitely not a lie.

'How about Chrissy? I've seen you have run-ins with Chrissy.'

'Maybe because she saw me take a dead fish from my handbag at her mum's memorial. You couldn't have stopped me? Told me not to take the fish?'

'I can't risk changing anything until you're up to speed. The time I stopped you taking the fish, the conversation with your mum went differently. You move on from the earrings to an argument about a trip to Italy when you missed the plane. When that happens, we waste an extra hour and it puts you in a terrible mood. You're less careful and you die more quickly.'

Viv thinks about this. Not fucking Italy again. 'We'll keep the fish.' She could do without the talk about how Mum had to visit the Trevi fountain alone.

'How about Chrissy's brother? Mark, is it? Have you had any issues with him?'

Viv takes a second. She stares into the kebab-shop window. 'It won't be Mark.'

'Why?'

She watches the meat revolve. 'Because I don't know him either.'

She glances at Jamie, waiting for him to call her out, but he just keeps smoking, leaving Viv's pathetic lie unchallenged.

It's a punch in the tit.

Mark has managed to avoid her *for eighty-four lives.*

18

One Year Ago
The Grains of Sand
Become a Heap

Viv wondered why, in a world full of men, she had to get obsessed with one who was married, and her almost-cousin.

Maybe it was because of his hair: thick and shiny with natural highlights, perfect for running her fingers through.

Maybe it was because he made a change from the younger men who had become Viv's usual type: ones who said *sex isn't everything* and checked for consent, who told Viv they were queer and left a space for her to congratulate them. (She was pretty sure none had touched a penis that wasn't their own.)

Maybe it was because Mark told her he'd stopped Angela slagging her off at a christening.

Maybe it was because Mark laughed at her jokes, and thought it fine for a grown woman to wolf three packets of instant noodles in one sitting.

Or maybe – and this was the bit Viv didn't want to admit – it was the timing. Maybe her life had been a game of hedonistic musical chairs, and he had been the man she'd been dating when the music stopped, at the time she finally saw the appeal of a different kind of life. Lately, Viv had taken to lapsing into brief but alarming fantasies, picturing a future that wasn't hers: of polished shoes, of plants kept alive and 10 p.m. bedtimes, of a kitchen decorated in eggshell, with big tiles giving the effect of little tiles, and bifold doors to a herb garden. (*Herb garden* wasn't even a euphemism for *weed farm*.) In this future, Viv would own inexplicable things, like paprika, and a piping bag. She'd buy celery. With Mark in her life, these things felt suddenly achievable – and, for the first time, desirable – when she was in the right mood.

Which was why it was *such* a shame about his wife.

Viv didn't *know* know Mark was still with Jess for a while. Like a grain of sand can get added to other grains without it becoming clear the exact moment those grains become a heap, Viv learned about Mark's marriage inconclusive fact by inconclusive fact.

Four weeks into the relationship: '*We're still hashing out the practicalities.*'

Six weeks in: '*We're living together while we work out what to do with the house.*'

Eight weeks in: '*We're just finding the right time to tell people.*'

Mark wanted to be respectful, and Viv liked that. Jess would be mourning the kids she might not get to have, dreading the idea of 'getting back out there', kryptonite to men of her own age. Viv had so often arranged to meet men 'in their thirties' on apps, only to find optimistic white-haired chancers stand up from the pub table: men with stents and wild eyebrow hair, ones Viv was pretty sure had been alive for the moon landing.

It made sense Mark didn't want to have Viv to his house. It made less sense that Mark didn't want to go out in public, but even that, he could justify.

'It'll kill her if she heard from someone else,' he said, the two sitting next to each other on Viv's bed, legs straight out.

Viv nodded. She was chill. *So* chill. 'I want to make the process easy for her.' (When Viv reflects on her naivety, she wants to pull out her own hair.)

Mark massaged Viv's knee through the silky fabric of her new jumpsuit. 'Thank you for understanding.'

Viv stared at the hand-tied bouquet Mark had brought. She'd leave a tactful gap before she told Mark to buy booze in future, that flowers are a worthless harbinger of future decay. 'No problem.'

Mark leaned in to kiss her. 'And happy birthday.'

That night, they cancelled Viv's restaurant reservation and phoned for a takeaway. Viv spilled Thai dipping sauce on the leg of that jumpsuit, scrubbing with a nailbrush till the fabric bobbled, but the stain never went fully, and the jumpsuit never felt new again.

★

Part of the reason the grains of sand never quite formed a heap was because Viv was a cynical bastard: everyone said so. Never knowingly optimistic about human behaviour, she never expected insurance to pay out, and she kept scammers on the phone for fun.

Yet this time, inexplicably, Viv was too trusting.

So, Mark kept coming round to Viv's house, wearing the good pants his wife bought. The grains of sand only finally became a heap on the night of the pizzas.

Viv had cooked the pizzas – admittedly, with supermarket sauce and bases. Mark always paying for the takeaways made their relationship feel like it had some kind of transactional element – which, if you took this thought to its natural conclusion, meant Viv was being paid for sex through the currency of chow mein.

A bleak thought, even before you considered Mark usually got early-bird discount.

After they ate her semi-homemade pizzas, Viv washed up the dishes straight away, to stop Bethan bleating.

Mark leaned on the counter watching her. This was the beauty of affairs, Viv decided. She bet Mark never watched when Jess washed up.

'Mum says she and Harry are having a wonderful holiday in Wales.'

Viv rinsed a plate. 'That's good.'

'They took a picnic up Snowdon. They were recreating their New Year's Day first date.'

Viv frowned. 'Didn't they go to Duncan's for New Year?' One of the side-effects of dating Mark was how much more Viv knew about her family.

'This year. I mean New Year's Day the year before.'

'But they can't have been dating then. Harry would have still been married.' She glanced back from washing her glass. 'Juliet didn't die till Valentine's—'

The soapy glass slipped from her hand.

Instinctively, Viv went to catch it. The pain was instant. '*Fuck!*'

Mark jerked forward. 'You OK?'

'No!' Viv pulled out a spiky shard of glass. Blood spurted. 'Shit, shit, *shit*.'

Mark grabbed a tea towel to wrap her hand. Beads of red sprang through the linen.

Viv risked peeling back the tea towel. 'That much blood is bad, right?' She put the fat of her hand in her mouth, tasting metal.

Gushing metal.

Mark grabbed his phone. 'We need to get you to A&E.'

'Oh my God, it's flooding through.' She watched him type. 'Why are you typing?'

'I'm calling you a taxi.'

'But your car's outside!'

Mark looked up. Was that pleading in his eyes?

Viv gripped the tea towel. 'Mark, I need to go to hospital, *right now*!'

It was hard to forgive the second Mark took before reaching for his keys.

They sat side by side in bolted-down A&E chairs, the silence frosty from both sides.

Mark had wanted to drop Viv in the car park.

A few hours in, a man in a hiking jacket walked over. 'Well, hello, hello!'

Mark stumbled to his feet. 'Col!'

'Watering can.' There was marvel in the man's voice. He indicated the child next to him. 'Stuck on his head. Took two docs half an hour to get it off.'

Affably, Mark patted the kid on the shoulder. 'Aaron, mate!'

The man looked expectantly from Mark to Viv.

'No watering can here.' Viv raised her hand in its bloody tea towel. 'Just a knife.'

The man winced.

'Washing up. The kitchen looks like I've gone into labour.'

Mark didn't take a beat. 'The *work* kitchen.'

'We're looking forward to Saturday.' The man turned back to Mark. 'I heard Jess is doing her Sri Lankan curry?'

Viv's skin prickled.

Not looking at Viv, Mark gave a tiny nod.

'I've been practising my Bowie in the shower.' The man turned to Viv. 'Mark's wife always gets the karaoke out. Hope you get seen soon, that hand looks painful.'

Mark and Viv stared straight ahead, long after the man and son had gone.

Mark swallowed. 'Viv—'

'*Vivian Slade!*'

A nurse scanned the waiting room, holding a clipboard.

Viv followed the nurse without looking back.

★

Twenty minutes later, Viv came back to the waiting room with a freshly stitched hand.

Mark was still there.

'You waited? Really?' Viv stalked past him. 'Didn't you want to get home and practise your Bowie in the shower?'

He stood. 'I can explain.'

'Fuck off.' Viv stopped. 'No, give me a lift home, *then* fuck off.'

They sat in Mark's car outside Viv's house, staring at her neighbour's hedge.

Finally, Viv asked: 'How many people will be at your karaoke dinner party?'

'Eight.' His voice was quiet.

'All couples?'

Mark took a second. He nodded.

'How stupid *am I*?'

A neighbour walked past the car, chihuahua straining on a lead.

Viv pulled down the sun visor. 'You've made me *that* person.'

'It's not like that. It's complicated.'

'You can't just do this to me. Or her. And now you're making me think about her, and I don't want to. She's your problem, not mine.' Viv opened the door. 'Sort this.'

'Thank you for understanding.'

Viv leaned down to hold Mark's gaze. 'I didn't say I understood.'

She stopped cradling her hand. She slammed the door, forgetting.

Pain came in a whole-body explosion of light.

She kept her face straight. She didn't look at Mark again, just stared into the distance until the rear lights of his car had gone.

Only then did she let herself look down, at the fresh waves of blood soaking her bandage.

Viv wasn't sure she could feel any more pain than this.

But that was before Harry and Alison crashed their car the next day.

19

Now

Viv gets a gin from the wooden-shuttered bar and edges beneath a busy umbrella for shade, trying not to loom over the seated occupants. Even under half an umbrella, it's too hot on this roof terrace. Sweat beads at the underwire of her bra. She wipes her lip with the back of her hand.

She's never been an elegant perspirer.

Jess walks back out onto the terrace rubbing her hands, clearly one of those people who uses hand cream dispensers. Her legs are similarly well-moisturised, and gleaming. The only clue to the afternoon heat is a gentle sheen on her cheeks, because Jess *is* an elegant perspirer. Everything she does is sophisticated, down to the *slap-slap* sound she makes when she walks, so much classier than the retro *tip-tap* of the shoes Viv wore for the first hour of this party.

Viv would bet other people's good money Jess has never stayed out on a thirty-six-hour bender. Never taken a pill without a prescription. Never woken up in an unfamiliar bedroom and thought *fuck my life*. Viv's friend Kirsty used to say about people like Jess: *they may get their five a day but they'll never have our anecdotes* – but that was before Kirsty joined the ranks herself, got a Labrador, started flossing.

Jess walks up to where Mark stands with a group. She listens to what he's saying and gives a bark of laughter. 'Don't believe him.' She rests one hand on a jutted-out hip and smiles round the group. 'He says he rinses before putting cans in the recycling, but he's never rinsed in his life!'

Mark looks round at the others. 'Jess likes to exaggerate.'

Viv wrinkles her nose at the poor quality of the chat. She's never fathomed why anyone would subscribe to those inexplicably popular *husband and wife squabble cutely* podcasts, feeling an unkind blip of pleasure when the couples put the inevitable *it is with regret that after eight wonderful years* ... posts on Instagram. Couples' low-level bickering about their small-stakes relationship gripes is always excruciating – and that's even when the couple *aren't* Viv's boyfriend and his wife.

Viv stirs her gin with her straw, sending ice cubes clinking.

She's never seen Mark put out recycling. Which is fine, obviously.

She stirs her drink faster.

There are so many normal things she's never seen Mark do. Never seen him hang out washing, never seen him shout at the dog. Never seen him swim or answer the door. She's never even seen him shave: he never stays at Viv's long enough to need a razor.

Still, she doesn't need to see him shave to know he's terrible at it. There they are again, today: those whiskers at the corners of his mouth. Viv teases Mark sometimes, sings *I wish, I wish I was a catfish*, and if his wife wasn't standing right there, the memory would be cute and funny.

Jamie steps beside Viv, pretending to survey the room.

She keeps her gaze ahead. 'I'm not dead yet.'

'So I can see.' Jamie indicates her drink. 'That's just tonic, I presume.'

'Just one, for courage.'

Jamie sighs. 'One time you're going to tell me it's just tonic.'

'Don't worry – I'm a good drunk. A master, in fact.' She pats his arm. 'I've put in the legwork, done my ten thousand hours. Learned anything?'

'I'm trying to eavesdrop on Frank, but that last conversation was all about the benefits of Screwfix versus B&Q. I'll keep trying.' Jamie steps away without looking up. 'Angela's coming.'

Angela watches Jamie go. Close up, her hand-drawn eyebrows are an unnaturally bright chestnut. 'Please tell me you weren't flirting with a waiter, Viv.'

Viv sips her drink. She has a newfound serenity today, because that's what happens in life-and-death situations. She can refuse to engage.

'What unfortunate choices of footwear you make.'

Even though Viv is, of course, still wholly serene, it rankles. She wonders what Angela would do if she saw Viv rescue a child. Viv never *has* rescued a child, but if she ever walked past one struggling in a lake, she'd jump in, no question, whatever the weather – and even Angela would have to clap.

'Speaking of unfortunate footwear,' Viv says, 'you need to loosen the straps on your slingbacks. Don't be shy to punch another hole, Angela. Your ankles have got muffin top.' She throws back most of her gin and heads to the bar before Angela can reply.

The customer in front turns. Mark.

'Shit. Hi.' How did she not see him move? 'Shit.'

'Hello.' Mark glances nervously round. 'It's Viv, isn't it?'

'Yep, Viv.' She gives her sweetest smile. 'Though some people call me *Craig from work*.'

Mark's eyes flare. 'Please ... don't.'

Viv watches him not look her in the eye. He really is a terrible shaver. Today, along with catfish whiskers, Mark has a pocket of hairs in the groove below his nose.

The seconds tick by, Mark looking anywhere but Viv.

Neither speak.

'Well,' Viv says finally. 'It all feels a bit different from your mum's last funeral, doesn't it?'

20

Ten Months Ago
The Disabled Toilet

It's what she would have wanted ...?

Viv gripped Mark tightly, trying not to wince as he rammed into her. She told herself *respect for the dead comes in many different forms.*

The whole thing didn't *feel* hugely respectful.

While other mourners snacked on cheese-and-pickle sandwiches in a room above a pub at Mark's mother's wake, Viv had one foot hooked in a grab rail, being fucked by Mark under the too-bright light in the disabled toilets of the park next door.

The bottom of Mark's trousers had pooled over his kept-on shoes.

But was this, in a way – Viv tried to ignore the cramp in her thigh – the ultimate form of respect? Funerals were about giving comfort to the bereaved, and here was Viv, comforting Alison's son. Maybe, at a big-picture level – if you zoomed back a little, blurred the lens, glossed over the specifics – maybe it really was *what she would have wanted*?

Mark kept grief-thrusting, silent, his severity a new unwelcome turn in their sex life since he got the news about his mum. In the waist-height mirror opposite, Viv watched his half-clad bum thrust back and forth. She normally liked watching them having sex, but this was a mirror in a disabled toilet, one that cut their bodies off mid-torso.

Mark made a gulping noise, and Viv patted his back with encouragement. It was a sound – and it wasn't *definitely* tears. Today wasn't about her, and that was fine. Today was about Mark needing a release.

She wished she'd known he'd need a release at his mum's funeral – she would have brought some lube.

Viv felt Mark speed up. She gripped him tighter, thigh cramping further. She tried to stretch, but couldn't extricate her heel from the grab rail.

It would be a few years before she'd start telling *this* anecdote at parties.

Mark shuddered, and came. 'Oh, God.' His breath was hot in her hair. 'I'm so sorry.'

'Don't say that.' Viv wrinkled her nose. 'It was nice. Being a girlfriend isn't all boxsets and trips to Asda.' Irritated, she dislodged her heel from the grab rail and placed it on the floor. 'Hey.' She made her voice gentle. 'It's OK.'

He rested his cheek on her hair. 'I can't even look at you.'

151

The too-bright light flickered overhead.

Viv lifted his arms from her and placed them by his side. 'No harm done.' Here she was, comforting Mark again – and in a new, shit way.

She waited. Was he going to cry again?

She wriggled her underwear up. 'Maybe we just get back to the wake?'

Mark left the public toilet first. Viv waited a few seconds more, looking around, taking in specifics for the at-least-ten-years-in-the-future anecdotes.

Was this the bleakest place she'd ever had sex? Probably.

Which was a shame, socially speaking. As Viv understood it, there were loads of people into cottaging – surely the council should have better facilities?

With the tip of her shoe, Viv moved the sanitary bin back to its original position, in no rush to get back up to the pub's function room. She'd managed to avoid Mark's wife all day, she didn't fancy her chances of keeping it that way. Viv was caught in affair-grief-stasis. Alison and Harry's deaths had changed things in so many ways, all of them bad. Viv couldn't expect Mark to leave his wife now. His mum's accident had bought him a couple of months' grace, minimum, and Viv couldn't even mind.

Viv left the toilets. She saw a figure in a wheelchair at the bowling green, next to the entrance to the park. Looking right at her.

Duncan.

Viv hurried over. 'Duncan? How long have you been there?'

He held her gaze.

'I can explain.'

'I have no interest in what you do, Viv.'

Viv raised her eyebrows faintly. 'Come on! *Surely* that's not true!' Viv's life was interesting. Not *good*, not anything to be proud of, but *interesting*, surely? She indicated the pub. 'How come you're not inside?'

'It's stifling. All the same people, so soon after Dad's funeral. All repeat conversations. I think I'll go home.'

'You can't leave so soon.'

'And yet here you are, not there yourself.'

Viv paused. 'Extenuating circumstances.' She hoped Duncan hadn't seen who she was having *extenuating circumstances* with. 'And I'm going back in now.'

'Maybe I have extenuating circumstances too. I have complicated feelings about today.' Duncan put his hands on his rims. 'If anyone asks, tell them I didn't feel well.'

Viv watched him wheel away, a sense of unease fluttering within.

She took one look back at the pub – and took out her phone. She practised her sad blank smile in her front-facing camera, trying to get the expression just right for meeting her boyfriend's wife at her mother-in-law's funeral.

21

Now

At the roof terrace bar, Mark and Viv stare at each other.

'We have to greet each other, or it looks suss.' Viv leans to hug him, inhaling his familiar ocean smell. In February, when she was proving a point to Mark about double standards, she took a man home from a bar purely because he smelled of that shaving foam.

To distract herself from her disquiet, Viv takes two canapés from a passing waiter's tray. Of the many pointless 'truths' Mum shared with Viv growing up – *make sure the bowl's scrupulously clean for a soufflé; the own-brand cornflakes are made by Kellogg's too; never buy the big towels* – Mum said *you should always eat delicately in front of a man.* Like most of Mum's advice, Viv would have ignored it even if it hadn't turned out to be bollocks. Mark once watched Viv tip her head back to get the right angle of entry for a sloppy pizza, and told her *your appetite is impressive*. Viv had wiped marinara sauce from her mouth and replied *and after this I'm going to go at the family-sized Dairy Milk in the fridge.*

Mark looks over Viv's shoulder. 'Angela!' The shape of his face changes. 'So nice to see you. You know Viv?'

Viv shoves a canapé in her mouth.

'I do.' Angela raises her bright eyebrows. 'Oh, I do.'

Viv wipes pastry flakes from the bodice of her dress. She swallows too early; the canapé jams, making a rock in her throat.

Angela looks up at Mark. 'Free food is Viv's favourite.'

Viv holds up a finger – *wait*. She feels every step the rock travels of its slow, painful journey. She gulps the rest of her drink.

'Can I get you a canapé, Angela?' It is an effort to speak so soon, but Viv makes her voice sweet. 'Are you allowed to eat pastry with your diabetes?'

'*Type one* diabetes.' Angela beams at Mark. 'And I don't eat ultra-processed food.'

'Because of your diabetes?'

'It's nothing to do with my *type one* diabetes.'

It's not even fun. 'Excuse me.' Today might be a multi-level headfuck, but Viv is operating on the highest, most existential plane.

'She rents a room in a house, you know.' Even from her higher plane, Viv can hear Angela's voice as she walks away. 'Living like a student and she's thirty-six. Her mum cried when we looked the house up on Street View.'

155

Viv looks around, trying not to let that land.

Across the room, Jamie is tidying up glasses near Frank, and he's doing a good job. Only Viv would know he's there eavesdropping on the conversation between Frank and a man Viv doesn't know. A man who looks like a bore.

Viv doesn't envy Jamie, having to listen to these conversations again, and again, and again. She's the one who keeps dying, but at least she gets to forget.

Maybe she's actually the one getting the better end of this deal?

Past Jamie, Chrissy stands alone on the outside of her party, and Viv feels a flicker of empathy for this woman who has either forgotten how to have fun, or never knew how. Of course, it's not great to know how to have too much fun, waking to find items in unexpected places: a stranger in your bed, a kebab in your handbag, a doorknob-not-a-muffin on your dressing table. Yet Chrissy's way of being looks worse. She needs to learn to live for today, because the menopause is coming fast, and that shit looks bleak.

Viv strides up to her. 'I'm sorry about bringing out that goldfish, Chrissy. It's a long story. A funny story.'

Viv tries to mentally generate that long story. Turns out a dead goldfish in a handbag is harder to explain than a kebab.

She is saved by Jamie approaching with a tray of drinks. Chrissy places her empty glass on the tray and takes another. 'Thanks.'

Viv's about to take a glass too, but Jamie moves the tray out of reach. He walks away.

Viv drops her hand. *Dick.* 'How are you, Chrissy?' She

laughs lightly. 'Sorry.' She puts her hand on Chrissy's arm. 'That's a cunt's question, isn't it?'

Chrissy looks up.

'And I use that word in the British, general sense, not the American sexist one,' Viv adds hurriedly. With the whole imminent-death thing, it's getting harder to remember she started out today planning to impress these people.

Chrissy doesn't look hugely impressed. 'A cunt's question?'

Viv flaps a hand. 'People ask, but they don't want the answer.'

Chrissy doesn't *not* smile.

'So, when people ask *how are you?*, I punish them by telling them.' Viv goes to drink from her glass – it's still empty. 'I say, *oh, you know – jittery. Scared for no reason. Full of basic human despair.*'

Chrissy is considering her. 'I can do that too. I'm doing better since they've upped my SSRIs.' Her voice is even. 'Still making those dinners, still driving to ballet, still washing those uniforms.'

Viv beams. 'See? Isn't this better than *I'm fine, and how are you?*' She scans the terrace for a waiter with a tray who isn't Jamie.

'It's just the nights that are a problem. When did nights get so long?' A broken feather hangs from Chrissy's fascinator. 'That's when my brain throws up the dark questions.'

'Mine too.' Viv has never liked Chrissy more. '*What will happen first – the water running out, or a nuclear war? When the sea levels rise and civilisation breaks down, will it be because I didn't recycle that frozen yoghurt carton?*'

Viv waits for Chrissy to make her excuses and move on.

She doesn't. 'I think all night, sometimes. Just *think*.'

Viv pats her arm. 'Unlucky.' If Chrissy keeps talking like this, Viv could almost forgive her for her Instagram profile: *Winging it at motherhood, one lentil at a time.*

Across the room, Sean is eating canapés at quite a rate. Viv smiles fondly. He wasn't lying. He *is* still a stress eater.

She catches his eye. He takes a step away from the plate.

'I obsess about Mum's accident,' Chrissy continues. 'Not sleeping drives me crazy.'

'I hear you.' Viv shelters her eyes from the sun. 'I once saw faces coming out of the wallpaper.'

'The maddest thoughts came at 3 a.m.'

'I wasn't even high.'

'For a few weeks there, I even convinced myself car accidents can be arranged.'

Viv processes this. She stares.

'Yeah.' Chrissy nods, her broken fascinator feather quivering. 'I even started researching the detail of the accident. Can you believe that?'

Still staring, with the smallest possible movement, Viv reaches behind and presses the nicotine patch into her shoulder.

'I decided Mum and Harry had been run off the road.' Chrissy gives a joyless smile. 'I looked into where people were and found Sean had been caught speeding at that *exact – same – time.*'

'In Wales?'

'In Essex.'

'But the accident was in Wales.'

Chrissy flaps a hand, jingling her bangles. 'I decided Sean

deliberately let himself get caught speeding for an alibi. He was in forty grand of debt, and he'd just been sacked from his forklift job.'

The heat of the sun is full on Viv's neck, so it's impossible she can feel *this* cold.

She looks across the room. Sean glances over at them again, not eating anymore.

'Sean's car was going forty-eight in a thirty past a static camera that everyone local knows gives an automatic ticket. And you couldn't see the driver in the photo.'

'You saw the photo?' Sean can't know what they're talking about from across the room but, still, Viv's face warms. 'How?'

Chrissy sips her drink jaggedly. 'Sean's emails. Dark web.' She sees Viv's face and pulls her eyebrows together, like she's suddenly realised what she's saying – and to who. She flushes. 'Viv, I—'

'Chrissy!' A woman with a flame-haired bob grabs her arm. 'Remember me – Sandra? From your mum's choir? You spent a day with us once on a barge. Alison wore the most incredible poncho.'

Chrissy takes a moment. 'I remember it well. The dog liked to sleep on it.'

Sandra-from-choir tells a long anecdote about the Horseshoe Falls on the Llangollen canal, and Chrissy's smiles politely, but keeps looking at Viv. Viv makes a subtle mouth-zip gesture and leaves Chrissy to Sandra's story.

She brushes past Jamie deliberately on her way to the fire escape – her head so full, she doesn't even think to grab a drink from his tray.

★

Five minutes later, Jamie's eyes shine. 'This is *it*!' He bangs the fire-escape step. 'Finally!'

Viv shakes her head. 'This isn't it.'

'You're getting murdered because *they* got murdered!'

Viv stares into the sun for a beat too long, colours popping. 'Nope.' She'd been excited to tell Jamie what Chrissy said too … right up till the moment she actually heard herself.

He stands. 'This is *it*!'

'*It* is just that grief sent Chrissy nuts. And it's not like she was fine to start with. You look at those spreadsheets too long, you buy too many drawer dividers, this shit can happen.'

The extractor fan in its metal cage whirrs, wafting out grease.

Jamie sits back down. 'Harry and Alison were on a walking holiday in Snowdonia?'

'We're not doing this.'

'Humour me.'

Viv sighs. 'They were driving back through North Wales when they crashed.' The extractor fan judders, one of the flaps catching with every rotation. 'I get why you want this to be true, Jamie, I really do.'

'How would you feel if it wasn't Sean she was accusing?'

'She's not accusing anyone, not anymore. She knows it was mad. She admits she wasn't sleeping properly.'

'We never questioned whether those deaths were accidental.' Jamie jumps to his feet again. This is the first time today he's moved like a man of his own age. 'What are the chances of there being two murderers at the same party?'

'Maybe' – Viv can't keep the sarcasm from her voice

– 'higher than the chance of the universe breaking and us getting caught in a time loop?' She watches Jamie pace. 'You're way too hyped. I told you she's batshit, right? I told you about the keypad tones and writing all the birthday cards? Birthday cards for the year. In *January*. She uses a calligraphy pen.'

The extractor fan wafts out more grease.

'And even if we say someone killed Harry and Alison,' Viv tries to sound patient, 'that has nothing to do with me.'

'It suggests there's a murderer here.'

'No, I get it – thanks.' Viv can do condescending too.

'And Sean needed the money.'

'Sean's a gambler and a flake. He's not a murderer.'

Jamie rustles his tobacco pouch.

'He's not a bad person.' Viv sets her jaw. 'And just because everyone loves to write people off, that doesn't mean they're responsible for everything bad that happens in this *fucking family*.'

Jamie stops rustling.

Viv's face warms. She takes a beat. 'Besides, Sean didn't even know he was in Harry's will.'

Jamie turns. 'Are you sure?'

'Yes.' Viv leans forward, triumphant. 'I was there when Harry told Sean he was out.'

22

Two Years Ago
The Not-a-Wedding

By 9 p.m. at Harry and Alison's not-a-wedding, an impromptu piggy-back competition was taking place on the rugby club dancefloor. Round-bellied men jumped on the backs of women in high heels in some kind of *winner-stays-on* arrangement.

Mum, always cautious, kept her distance at the farthest edge of the floor, bobbing up and down to 'We Are Family' with self-conscious enthusiasm. Piggy-backers and dancers all got out of the way as Harry twirled a giggling Alison past. One of Alison's false eyelashes was coming loose at the edge.

Viv watched with Sean at the bar. 'I heard your dad made Alison a mix tape.'

'Stop it.' Sean swigged his pint. 'Think there'll be evening food coming out? A bacon sandwich, at least?'

'How can you still be hungry?'

'I'm not. Can I have yours?'

Viv smiled. 'Tough night for you then.'

'Tell me about it.' Sean watched Harry scissor Alison's arm up and down. 'Think you'll ever get married?'

Viv sniffed into her drink. 'If I want to get involved in a twenty-year pass-agg argument, I can just phone Mum.'

A woman in a tasselled dress stumbled past, her jaw set with concentration. The man on her back made joyous lassoing gestures to the appreciative crowd.

Viv studied the man. He looked familiar. Had she slept with him? Or had she just slept with someone *like* him?

It was a depressing fact about getting older: that many of the men she'd had casual sex with were hitting early middle age, losing their hair, starting to look increasingly homogenous. Sometimes, trying to figure out whether she'd slept with a particular man was like trying to identify a specific egg in a catering-size box.

Alison's son Mark walked into her eyeline and Viv took in his thick hair. Now, *that* man was someone she'd remember fucking.

'Dad wants me to make an effort today.' Sean looked past Viv. '*Chrissy!*'

Chrissy, who was walking past, stopped and turned.

Sean looked at Viv. 'You two know each other?'

Viv paused. 'We've met.'

Chrissy walked up. The silence was awkward.

Viv looked around for something to say. 'After a certain

age, don't men all look the same?' She indicated the room, indicating egg men. 'Bald guy. Bald guy. Bald guy.'

Chrissy held her gaze. 'That's Paul.'

Viv, unsure of the relevance, shrugged.

'My husband.'

'And baldness suits him,' Viv continued quickly. 'Such a nice-shaped head.'

Eyes wide with social awkwardness, Sean turned to Chrissy. 'When Dad first told me he was getting married again, I asked if your mum was pregnant.'

'Ha.' Chrissy walked off. 'Excuse me.'

Viv patted Sean's arm. 'Thanks for trying.'

Sean watched Chrissy go. 'She *did* get I was making a joke?'

'She said *ha*.'

'She said it dismissively.'

Viv patted his arm. 'I'm guessing she's having a weird day too.'

'I'm pleased I've got you alone.' Sean's voice was low. 'I need a favour.'

Viv didn't react immediately. It was *this*, why people in the family were wary of Sean.

(And Viv.)

'You know I follow the snooker?'

Viv shook her head.

'I follow the tour, keep an eye on the players, find the small betting edges. By rights I should be coining it in, but the betting sites keep shutting down my accounts.'

'Because it's illegal?'

'Because they're arseholes. You start consistently winning,

164

they don't let you play. You have to get clever if you're going to beat the system.'

Viv fluttered her fingers against her glass. She didn't know *exactly* where this conversation was going, but she sensed the general direction.

'If you'd let me set up an account in your name, I'll be able to work it for a bit before we get shut down.'

Viv watched the (familiar?) egg man dance. *Had she …?* She wished there was a one-night-stand equivalent of IMDb. She could ask him, of course. But then he might think she'd want to do it again. And Viv wasn't *that* drunk. Not yet, anyway.

'It's not fair to have a skill and not be able to use it,' Sean continued. 'Did they stop Pelé playing football? This is kosher.'

'Kosher.'

'Kosher-*ish*,' Sean said easily. 'Five minutes of admin, max, with everything linked to my bank account. It would just mean you couldn't use the betting site in your own name later. You'd be banned.'

Viv thought for a second. 'I've got all the vices I need.'

'That's a yes?'

'If you *promise* there's no catch.'

Sean hugged her. 'Don't listen to what anyone says, Viv, you're a great person.' He'd called her some variation of *great person* three times now, which was three times more than any of the rest of her family had.

Viv savoured the inner glow. Maybe she *was* a great person. Maybe she just had layers? People just needed to make the effort, peel them back.

She gave Sean her admin details.

He slipped his phone back into his pocket. 'You're the best.'

'You can tell Mum that later, maybe?' Viv indicated Mum, who was still bopping on the dancefloor. 'Though maybe best to imply I helped you set up a charity whist drive or something.'

Sean's attention caught on something on the dancefloor. His smile faded.

Viv looked.

Harry had grabbed Alison's waist and was giving her a long, youthful kiss. Viv saw hunger in there. And – definitely – tongue.

Sean looked away. 'I want him to be happy, of course.' He swigged his beer. 'But did he have to be *so* much happier than he was with Mum?'

'It's new, that's all.' Viv patted his arm. 'Don't think about them fucking.'

His eyes flared.

A man strode up to Harry looking severe. Harry released Alison from his grip and took a step toward the serious-looking man as he listened.

Alison spun towards another group, unbothered. She was a lithe dancer. Her moves were definitely from another era, but they were more controlled than Harry's. She moved her smooth hips with ease, and less flailing. She raised her forearms in front of her face, in her own world, mouthing the words of the eighties song Viv didn't know. She saw Viv watching and grinned.

Viv grinned back.

Maybe this was a relative she could actually get behind?

Meanwhile, Harry had stopped smiling. His face had gone redder as he listened to the other man. He turned and stared in their direction, hostility evident.

Viv's stomach flipped. 'What have I done now?'

Harry strode over, his face hollow with anger.

Viv flushed with guilt. 'Harry, I ...'

'Get out.'

It took a second for Viv to realise Harry was talking to Sean, not her.

Sean swallowed.

Harry turned to Viv. 'He's been asking you for money too?'

'I haven't asked anyone for money!'

'You've no respect. You come to my wedding and ask my guests to gamble for you.'

'Not *for me*. I don't need anyone to gamble *for* me.'

Duncan wheeled up, his face a question.

Sean didn't even look down. 'Go away.'

'Well?' Harry turned to Viv. 'Has he asked you?'

Viv made her face blank. 'Asked me what?'

'You expect me to believe *you're* the only person he didn't ask?'

'Leave her alone!' Sean said.

Viv took a second. 'By stopping me opening any gambling accounts in future, he's saving me from myself.'

Harry's face was going redder by the second. 'Stop covering for him!'

Duncan let out a long sigh.

Sean spun to face him. 'Why haven't you gone away?'

167

'You had to do this *today*,' Harry said. 'Your mother would be so disappointed.'

'You think *I'm* what would disappoint Mum today?' Sean's voice climbed, nasal. 'Tell me, how long had she been gone when you first asked Alison for a drink? One month? Two?'

Harry didn't look like he was breathing. *'Get out.'*

'Hey.' Viv put her hand on Harry's arm. 'Why don't I get us all a friendly sambuca?'

'Everything's always been about money for you.' Harry didn't take his gaze off Sean. 'Your mother never wanted to believe it, but it was always money.'

'I haven't asked anyone for money.' Sean's voice was quiet.

'The position you have put Viv in is unforgivable!'

Viv felt her eyebrows rise. It was unfamiliar, featuring in a family argument as the victim not the villain. It wasn't even *that* much more comfortable. 'Shall I get those sambucas, or—'

'If you want to be part of this family' – Harry carried on talking to Sean like she hadn't spoken – 'you do it knowing there will never be another penny in it for you. No more fake gambling accounts, no hand-outs – you won't even be in my will!'

'You think I'm here because of money? You think that's why I'm watching you paw at another woman? I'm here because I'm being nice! I'm being fucking nice!'

Roaming neon lights shadowed the contours of Harry's face. 'Get out.'

Sean looked from Harry to Duncan. He looked like he wanted to say something.

168

He walked towards the exit, taking a bacon sandwich from a passing buffet trolley without breaking stride.

23

Now

Jamie swivels on the fire-escape step to face Viv. 'But we know Sean definitely inherited. He told you earlier today. Which means Harry must have put him back in the will.'

'Yes, but I'm sure Sean didn't know.'

'Either way, we've got a focus finally.' Jamie glances at her. 'Please stop drinking.'

Viv presses her face into the metal fire-escape pole. 'I'm a good drunk.'

Jamie side-eyes her. 'Want me to tell you what happened the times you kept drinking?'

Viv pulls away from the pole. 'A master, remember. I put in my ten thousand hours.'

'One time you went around making people look in your

eyes, telling them *no one in this family appreciates nuance.*
That was the time you kept badgering the staff for more
canapés. *Or, if you can point me in the right direction, I can
microwave them myself. Or cheese? Have you got any cheese and
biscuits?'*

Viv screws up her eyes.

'Then there was that time you kept sneaking behind the
bar to put a song on repeat. "Anti-Hero". You told everyone
Taylor gets me. Chrissy ended up calling security.'

Viv, eyes tighter still, squints over the balcony.

'There was also that time your mum asked you to leave.
And that time she saw us whispering and asked if we were
sleeping together.'

'I hope I died quickly that time.'

The humour drops from Jamie's voice. 'You need to look
into Sean.'

'It won't be him.'

'We need you to ask questions about money. Find out who
inherited what.'

'What a ridiculous idea.'

'Let's divide and conquer. I'll follow Sean when I get back
inside. You ask people about money.'

The door to the fire escape opens. A tiny waiter with box
braids in a bun comes out and looks from Jamie to Viv.

Viv jumps up.

'It's no problem.' Jamie is smooth, changing gear. 'But
guests have their own smoking area.'

'Sorry.' Viv nods theatrically. 'I'll find it.'

She goes in, pulling the fire door shut and heads round
the balcony.

Ask questions about money. Find out who inherited what. Jamie says it like it's so easy.

Like she isn't already less welcome at this party than Pepé Le Pew.

Jamie thinks he's helping, of course. But there's helping and there's *helping*. She'll ask around a little, humour him, but that's it.

But where to start?

Viv looks up the ramp, in the direction of the roof terrace.

Deciding who to ask questions to is like Sophie's choice – admittedly, with fewer Nazis. Or like asking Viv to pick a door that might have a car or a goat behind, except there are no cars, and the goats are all leopards.

No, Viv's not choosing. She will leave it to fate to decide whose day she's about to ruin. She will pick off the first family member who comes along, one isolated and vulnerable, away from the herd.

She stands at the lifts, watching the ramp to the roof terrace.

She can't believe Jamie wants her to ask about money.

Harry and Alison weren't murdered over money: they weren't the type. Viv doesn't know who the type are, but they'd definitely have more top hats and tailcoats, with Coutts bank accounts and grand jewelled necklaces called names like *Star of Venice*. Or there's the other kind of person who gets murdered for money, of course: the kind of death that comes with bags of skag, with blue lights, with kids circling high-rise estates with bikes.

But people in the middle? People who are saving for plastic double glazing and buy M&S jeans – people who travel off-peak, and get tubs of Celebrations at Christmas?

No way.

Chrissy is the first to head down the ramp towards the bathroom. She's chatting to someone Viv doesn't know – an alert-looking woman who's either had a bad facelift, or has an unfortunate Startled Resting Face.

Chrissy spots Viv. They hold eye contact for the briefest moment. Chrissy looks away.

Viv sniffs. It will be *this*, Chrissy's embarrassment from over-sharing today, that will finally stop her sending Viv those calligraphy-ed Christmas cards.

Now Mum is heading down the ramp towards the bathroom. It's not ideal, but Viv made a deal with herself. The first person.

'Mum!' Viv raises her voice. 'Wait up!'

She messages Jamie.

I'm going to ask Mum about the wills.

Mum waits at the balcony.

'What a day.' Viv steps up. 'As if this family needed another funeral.'

'I know.' Mum turns to lean on the railing. 'I don't know why people want to focus so much on death. Enjoy being young, when you get invited to more weddings than funerals.'

Viv nods, even though she doesn't get invited to a whole load of weddings – and prefers the funerals. It's hard to be self-satisfied when you're dead, however sincere people are in their eulogies, however much they describe you as a cross between Isaac Newton, Mother Theresa and Lassie.

Mum sighs. 'You've been to far too many funerals. I still wonder whether I was right to have taken you to Dad's when you were so young. Whether it scarred you.'

Viv's eyelid twitches. Mum at least stopped herself before saying *and whether that's where it all went wrong.*

'Today is making me think life is short.' Viv concentrates on the gold chain resting between Mum's collarbones. 'Had you written a will by the time you were my age?'

'By your age, I was widowed with a twelve-year-old.'

Viv's face warms as the implication unrolls in the silence. Viv is thirty-six: no house, no car, no kids. She still scrapes Bethan's sofas for change, and her once-close friend has morphed into a frosty landlord with a penchant for pass-agg fridge notes. Viv's here at a party in a 'borrowed' dress, its still-attached price tag spiking her armpit, her illegal benzos stashed in a handbag she's also planning to return in the morning. She doesn't even have a pot of moisturiser to call her own, she never did get round to being able to drive, and seven out of her last ten meals have been cereal.

'Who would get my things if I die without a will?' Today is a hellscape, and Viv has no choice but to walk face-first into the flames. 'You would, I'm guessing.'

Mum looks round for a waiter.

'I do have *some* nice stuff.' Viv goes hot. 'I've got a four-year-old laptop. I've got my Stella McCartney jacket. I've got this ring.' Viv splays her hand, showing Mum the chunk of silver twisted to a pleasing flourish – at least, Viv *thinks* it's silver. It's an art ring. Art doesn't need labels.

Mum frowns. 'You have a Stella McCartney jacket?'

'Charity shop,' Viv says quickly. Mum would not

understand the concept of *finders keepers* about a coat she found in a bar. 'Have you made a will?'

The air between them shifts.

'Christ.' Mum's voice is strained. 'I'm only sixty-one.'

'Of course. I'm just thinking about wills in general.' Viv pauses. 'Not yours. I want you to live forever, obviously.'

'I haven't got very much money, Viv. If that's what you're asking.'

'This isn't that.' Viv pauses. 'No, this definitely isn't that.'

Mum shakes her head, a gesture managing to convey that, while her expectations of Viv were low, Viv has still managed to slouch under them. 'I'm going to speak to Chrissy,' she says quietly.

Viv turns in the opposite direction, towards the Time exhibition, itching her arms through her cobweb sleeves.

Thirty-six years, she's had, of being misunderstood. And she's *still* surprised.

She strides along the balcony, past the grandfather clocks.

Mum *has to* think the worst of Viv – every time. And, worse, Mum is a positive person. It's only Viv she makes that face for, only Viv who makes her go quiet. Why won't she give Viv the benefit of the doubt, like she does everyone else? Why can't Mum—

Viv's body slams into the railing. Her hip flares with pain.

The hands on her flesh are urgent, lifting her.

Viv claws her fingers. '*NO!*'

She scrabbles uselessly in the empty air and hurtles down to the museum floor.

PART THREE

24

Now

Viv wakes, upright and gasping. Two background images slide into place, a pair of scissors snapping shut.

The force on Viv's chest lifts. She staggers forward.

'That the best you can do?' It's Sean's voice. 'The nurses only liked me because I brushed Alison's hair. But thanks for trying.'

Viv puts both hands to her throat. She gasps for air.

'Viv, what the fuck is wrong?'

'Sean!' Frank turns from Mum. 'Have you heard about your dad and the raffle for the guide dogs?'

A waiter with a tray of glasses strides purposefully into her eyeline. 'Come with me. Right now.'

★

By 5.03, Jamie has briefed Viv about the previous eighty-four lives, and the two sit next to each other on the canal bench.

'One final point – stay away from your mum today. For me. *Please*.' Jamie shakes his head as he exhales smoke. 'You and your mum' – he bumps his fists at the knuckles – 'it's Shakespearean.'

'That's not what Shakespearean means.' Viv doesn't know what Shakepearean means.

Jamie throws the end of the burning roll-up onto the towpath. 'This life, we need to focus on what Chrissy said.'

Viv takes a second. 'Harry and Alison weren't murdered.'

Jamie puts one finger and thumb on his closed eyelids.

'Do I annoy you?'

'We went through all this last time.'

'I didn't believe it then either?' Viv feels a burst of solidarity with a self she doesn't remember. Her life might be fracturing into afternoon-sized portions, but she's a consistently stubborn twat across lifetimes.

'Ask someone – not your mum – who inherited what.'

'First, tell me how I died last time.'

Jamie looks like he's going to dismiss the question, but sees her expression. Clearly, he's experienced a lot of stubborn-twat-ness.

He leans onto trouser knees shiny with wear. 'It was 6.13.'

Viv glances at her phone. 'But that's less than an hour away!'

Jamie leaves a meaningful pause.

Viv refuses to interpret it. 'Go on.'

'Last time I checked, you were standing with your mum

at the balcony by the lifts. I went back outside, looking for Sean. A minute later, your mum came out to the terrace, alone.' He side-eyes Viv. 'I headed for the doors to look for you but, before I got there, the screaming started.'

'I went over the railing again?'

'So I assume.'

'Didn't you look?'

'I don't always.'

'That's cold.' Viv hugs herself. 'My death gets samey after a while?'

'You must have died immediately this time because it was less than a second later I was back in the main room, holding that tray.'

Viv's neck prickles. 'I always die immediately, don't I?'

Jamie doesn't reply.

The prickles patter downward. 'They're tall flights.'

Jamie stares at the *Titanic*-wisped trolley in the canal. 'It's always immediate.'

He's lying, and Viv can't bear to think why. It's *imperative* she doesn't let a single one of those thoughts in. She fidgets aggressively with her whole body, shifting her weight between sitting bones. 'Was anyone missing from the roof terrace when the screaming started?'

'I don't know. I didn't see Sean.' Jamie pauses. 'Mark was near the lifts when I last checked on you.'

She flinches.

'What?'

Viv shakes her head. Jamie wouldn't be so matter of fact if he knew *quite* how unwelcome that information was. 'And who else?'

'What do you mean, who else?' Jamie baulks. 'There are over *a hundred* people at this party. Do you know how tired I am? I'm the only one outside the time loop! I've been awake for days! Everyone else resets when you die but I don't. My body doesn't get a break, and nor does my mind. I've been awake continuously, no sleep, for I don't know how long!' His words run into each other in his vehemence to spit them at Viv. 'They deprive people of sleep as a form of torture! And yet you expect me to follow everything? Do you know how many different people I'm trying to watch at once? How I'm trying to follow all these conversations, and also trying to keep serving drinks so I don't get sacked, to keep you safe?'

'No need to get defensive.'

'I'm *not* getting defensive.'

Viv sighs. The more she thinks about it, the more she feels exhausted for him. 'It's just … all these lives. It feels like it should be easier.'

'It really does.'

At the edge in his voice, Viv turns.

'You had one job. Not to be alone near the balcony.'

'Right.' Viv screws up her eyes. 'And *I've said* I'm sorry.' She isn't sure she had. 'How long was Mum back in the main room before I fell?'

'At least twenty seconds.' He glances at Viv. 'She can't have pushed you.'

Viv nods casually, her throat closing with emotion. She makes herself focus on the meat rotating in the kebab-shop window.

Jamie studies her. 'Wow.'

Viv waves a hand over her throat. 'It's just good to know,' she swallows, 'that's all.'

Back on the roof terrace, it's hot. Viv gets a glass of water and walks up to Duncan, who is alone next to an outdoor sofa.

'Hi.' She casts a shadow over his face. 'Long time.'

She wavers, and sits. She never kisses Duncan hello, and early middle age feels too late to take a new approach. There's always been a layer of frost between them, a legacy from their childhood, from Aunt Juliet's terrible approach to school holidays – *Duncan, why don't you play the others something on your flute?*

Duncan raises a performative eyebrow. 'I didn't know you were coming.'

'I'm like a gift you weren't expecting.' Viv sits opposite him. 'Didn't you want to do a speech today?'

'Chrissy did ask.' Duncan brushes something invisible from his rumpled shirt. 'I declined.'

Viv watches Sean stride across the terrace, Jamie following a discreet distance behind. She's struck again by how slow Jamie moves.

'Does Sean mind you're always asked to do the important stuff, even though he's older?' Viv lifts her hair off the back of her neck and flaps it in a weak attempt to circulate some air. 'You were even the executor of Harry's will, weren't you?'

The pause is long. The back of Viv's knees feel tacky with sweat.

It's getting hotter still under Duncan's critical gaze, but

she keeps going. 'Did … did your dad leave anyone else money? Or was it just the two of you?'

The silence swells.

Duncan looks at her like she's a clump of hair in the plughole. 'The probate was settled a long time ago.'

'I know. Of course.' Viv widens her eyes. 'No, this isn't that, I'm not after … I'm just thinking it must be a comfort to Sean that Harry never took him out of the will. I'm so happy they made up before he died.'

Jamie trails Sean to the bar. His spying looks obvious to Viv – but probably only because she's looking for it.

'They didn't make up. Sean didn't know he was still in the will until afterwards.'

Viv pulls her brows together.

Duncan nods. 'And if you'd been there when I told him, you'd know what a shock that was.'

25

One Year Ago
The Halfway Café

Two weeks after his dad died, Duncan sat in a café off the
A1 in Lincolnshire, a cup of gritty coffee on his table. He
stared at a plastic display on the counter containing two
age-deflated pastries, their icing sweating, mendaciously
labelled *Fresh Donuts*.

Duncan picked up the laminated stand-up menu. All
breakfast foods, most American, none nutritious. The only
vegetable was a grilled tomato, and there was nothing green
– unless the food came with a cress garnish and, looking at
the 'fresh doughnuts', that felt unlikely. (Duncan actively
thought out the extra letters in his head. *Donuts* was an
abomination of a word.)

Through the rain-streaked window, he saw Sean pull up.

Immediately, he took a sugar sachet from the pot and twisted it between his fingers.

The door of the café opened with an electronic chime.

'Nice venue.' Sean slipped into the hard red chair opposite. 'Find it in a tourist brochure?'

'A halfway website.' Duncan crunched the sugar. 'Though it isn't perfectly equidistant. It was two hours for me, and two hours and seven for you, but the next place was at least—'

'I can live with seven minutes.'

Sean's voice had that tone it had when Duncan tried to explain anything enthusiastically as a child – how a potato clock worked; how you converted pounds to Euros in your head; why, mathematically, you should never split eights in Blackjack. Duncan only ever explained things he thought Sean would find interesting (hence the Blackjack), but apparently even gambling could be boring when Duncan did it.

'A halfway website.' Sean ordered a coffee and turned back. 'Tell me, when you share a tube of Smarties now, do you still count them out exactly?'

'You're the only person I've ever shared Smarties with.' Duncan watched the waitress walk away. 'The coffee here is bad.'

Sean sat back. 'But we're not here for the coffee.'

'Probably best.'

'So why are we here?'

Duncan looked at his cup. 'How are you doing?'

'We're not here for that either.'

Duncan took a second. 'I spoke to Chrissy this morning.' He made himself put down his support-sachet. 'There's no change with Alison, they're just waiting.'

Sean stared at the table. 'I only ever met her at the wedding.'

'We all assumed there'd be plenty of time.'

'Did she make Dad happy?'

'Very. Except when she filled in his crossword without asking.'

Sean thanked the waitress for his coffee. Duncan nudged the pot of sugar towards him.

Sean half-smiled. 'Gave up fifteen years ago.' He glanced up. 'So how does it work? Do we wait for Alison to die to have Dad's funeral?'

Duncan stared out of the grimy window. 'When I suggested that to Chrissy, she made a kind of yowl. She's still hoping for some kind of divine intervention. She says you have to *believe* – though I'm not sure what you're meant to believe in.' Duncan paused. 'Definitely not doctors or science. I think we should go ahead with the funeral. Otherwise we don't know how long we'll be waiting, and I don't want to risk making Chrissy yowl again.'

Sean nodded. 'Agree.'

'Will you want to do a speech?'

Sean blew on his coffee. 'People will want you to do the speaking.'

'We could *both* speak.'

'We all know you'll do it better than me. You're the pro.'

'Not at this.'

There was a long pause.

''Scuse me!' Sean got the waitress's attention. 'Turns out I'm going to need one of those doughnuts.'

'They look awful.'

'You know I'm a stress eater.'

Duncan nodded. 'Do you have any views on music?'

'Not my area.' Sean placed his cup down. 'I didn't actually see Dad, as you know. He didn't like me.'

'It's only this last year you haven't seen him.'

Sean concentrated on his coffee. 'But what a year.'

Duncan didn't like self-pity. Self-flagellation achieved nothing. 'Why would he have left you half of everything if he didn't like you?'

Sean raised his head. 'You know he cut me out of the will.'

'Not true. I'm his executor and I can tell you it's there, in black and white.'

Sean stared. 'He didn't get round to taking me out?'

'It wasn't that. He loved you.' Duncan held Sean's eye contact. 'What Dad said to you at the wedding ... he never meant it.'

Sean blanched. 'Serious?'

Duncan nodded.

Sean shoved his chair back. 'I can't take this.'

He strode out of the café and into the car park.

Duncan picked up the sugar sachet and started crunching it again.

Minutes later, Sean was back. 'I find this out *now*? Now it's too late to fix things with Dad?'

Duncan stared fiercely at the table.

'I'm different now. I could have made him proud.' Sean

sat down. He got out his phone and started tapping the screen. 'Look.'

But Duncan was getting out his folder of papers to show Sean. 'Alison had half the house, plus about forty grand in savings.' Duncan passed him papers, grateful for the prop. 'There are also death benefits with his pension. These are the calculations for now, and I will give you more detail after the valuation.'

Sean pushed his phone back into his pocket. 'What are we doing with Dad's personal things?'

'They're all mixed up with Alison's stuff. I haven't dared raise it with Chrissy. Do you want to come and—'

'*NO.*'

The waitress walked past, shoes squeaking on the lino. She placed Sean's doughnut down.

He was so shocked, he didn't even touch it. '*Money. Actual money.*' Sean sat back. 'We'll be able to buy a proper home.' He glanced up, his voice fierce. 'But I never would have wanted it like this.'

Duncan nodded. He went to say something – something that could show he understood the scale of his brother's loss. Something to show they were in it together, that they could learn from this, that they could do better, *be* better, grow closer.

The two sat in silence.

Sean reached for the elderly doughnut.

'Sean.'

Sean looked up.

Duncan picked up the sugar sachet again. 'There's something else.'

26

Now

'Why are you asking about wills, Viv?' Duncan frowns. 'Do you think that's appropriate today?'

Viv wipes the sweat from the back of her knees instead of answering. It will be easy for Duncan to believe she's being inappropriate. People used to speculate whether she was *on the spectrum* all the time, until more progressive types realised how tasteless that speculation was, and the others decided she was just a cunt.

'I need to be ... somewhere else.' Duncan knocks a drinks menu off the table with his elbow as he wheels away. He slows, not even pretending he had an end in mind. He may not think her *appropriate*, but at least if Viv makes an excuse, she gives a half-hearted pretence of follow-through. It's only polite.

'Canapé?'

She looks up at Jamie, who has a tray of pastries in one hand.

'You heard me asking Duncan about wills?'

Jamie nods.

'Then you'll know what I actually need is alcohol.' Still, she stands, taking a napkin from his tray.

The two stand, each scanning the area behind the other. Viv keeps accidentally catching people's eyes. She would make a terrible spy.

Jamie makes his voice low. 'Sean seems tense. He's just been very short with one of Harry's friends who tried to talk to him about the United line-up for tomorrow.'

'How many pastries has he eaten?'

'About twelve.'

Viv nods. Clearly, Sean is as uncomfortable here today as she is.

Which is why Jamie should cut him a break. 'He might have been lying to Duncan about not knowing he was still in the will.'

Viv shakes her head. 'It's not Sean.' There's a thought twisting, *twisting*, nearly in reach. She stands up straighter. 'In fact, it can't possibly be him killing me.' She tries to control the triumph in her voice. 'We were leaning on the balcony just before the glitch – with no one around. Sean had loads of opportunity to push me then, and he didn't. It can't be him, can it?'

Jamie keeps scanning the room, his expression unchanging. His shoulders sink.

'Everyone here just has it in for him,' Viv says quietly.

'Do Mark next, then. Ask him about Alison's will.'

'Give me a minute.'

'Viv, come on.' Jamie jabs with his tray for emphasis. 'Trust me.'

'Why? Because you know what's best for me?' Viv tries to keep her voice down. 'Then how come I still keep dying?'

Angrily, she shoves a canapé she didn't want into her mouth.

Jamie smiles behind her. 'They're mushroom.' He offers his tray to an elderly lady.

The woman chooses a pastry with excessive care and leaves.

Jamie snaps to face Viv. 'Do you know how hard I've been working on this? Do you know what it's like to be so tired the room's started to wobble? The least you can do is ask Mark about Alison's will.'

He walks away.

Viv stays where she is, not wanting to make eye contact with anyone, not wanting to see any more faint reactions of disgust. She stares over the edge of the terrace, pretending to be one of those people who can get entranced by a skyline.

She has absolutely no intention of talking to Mark today.

She watches Jamie offer Jess a canapé but, of course, Jess doesn't take one, not even by accident. Pastry is a long way from sushi, which is Jess's favourite food, assuming Jess puts the truth on her Instagram, which she obviously doesn't.

It's disquieting: Jess will not have a clue what Viv's favourite food is, will never have thought to care. Jess will never have thought to look Viv up, or block her – or have an

192

opinion on her teeth, or the transparency of her humble-brags, or her skincare game.

Having a rival who doesn't know you exist is terrible for the self-esteem.

Jess glances up – and catches Viv looking.

Viv, with no option, gives a faint smile back.

Jess takes a second, her face blank. She steps closer. 'Have we met before?'

Viv's ears roar with blood. 'Maybe. At Harry's funeral?'

There's a long pause.

Viv presses sweaty palms against her dress. She makes fists to hide her nails. 'That's it. We met in the toilets at Harry's funeral.'

The silence is too long. It's broken by the click-click of kitten heels, as Chrissy hurries past.

Jess turns. 'Chrissy! One sec!' She follows Chrissy, leaving a wisp of woody perfume in the air.

Viv leans against the wall. She watches the two sisters-in-law chat easily as they head inside. There should be a word for this feeling – a word like *nostalgia*, but for something you've never experienced and definitely don't want. Being a sister-in-law must be an arse, all thoughtful gifts and coordinating calendars and working out how big to get the turkey.

It's a fantasy – and a mistake. Being a sister-in-law wouldn't suit Viv; it only looks good because she hasn't actually tried it on, like when she buys sunglasses online.

'Mark's *right* there.' The voice at Viv's shoulder is low. 'Ask him now.'

It's all Viv can do not to shout at Jamie to *fuck off.*

But, then, Jamie has a point – Mark's right there, alone, looking fine in his suit, more handsome than usual. (Granted, every time she's seen him in a suit before, he's been crying.) And they haven't spoken all day, and Jess is out of the room and …

She walks up. 'Mark.'

He turns, his smile blank.

'She went inside with Chrissy.'

His shoulders relax a millimetre. 'You know we can't talk. Though you look beautiful today.'

Something smoulders in Viv's belly. Sometimes, on long nights, she worries she and Mark aren't going to work. That he is taking too long; that she's no prize. After all, she has no money, she doesn't have a cool job, she's not elegant or clever. Thirty-six years old, and she's just found out she's been saying *mischievous* wrong.

She's itching to run a hand through his hair but she can't, obviously, and she can't let him off the hook quite yet, she's still cross about … everything.

She's still smouldering when Jamie leans to pluck a napkin from the floor by her foot.

The smouldering stops, instantly. Viv could have been sprayed with a garden hose.

Jamie needs to *get out of her face.*

A man with slick red cheeks strides up. 'Mark.'

Mark looks up. 'Dad.'

Mark's dad doesn't look at Viv. 'Have you seen your sister?'

Viv gives a disarming, *yes, officer?* smile. 'I saw her go inside.' She waits for Mark to introduce his dad.

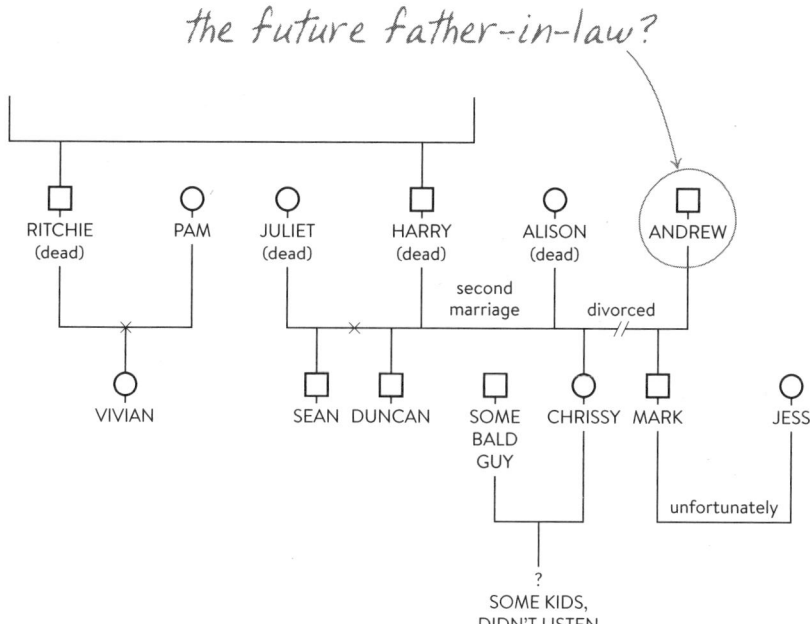

the future father-in-law?

RITCHIE (dead) — PAM — JULIET (dead) — HARRY (dead) — ALISON (dead) — ANDREW

second marriage   divorced

VIVIAN   SEAN DUNCAN   SOME BALD GUY   CHRISSY MARK   JESS

unfortunately

?
SOME KIDS, DIDN'T LISTEN

Mark doesn't.

'Thanks.' Mark's dad walks away.

Viv takes a beat. 'It's nice your dad's here today.' Her gaze catches on the rows of caramel bottles behind the bar, gleaming temptingly. 'I thought when people divorced, they fell out forever.'

'Not Mum and Dad. They still got together to watch Eurovision every year. Mum would make her special sangria.'

'But didn't they fall out about money? *Everyone* falls out over money.'

'Mum never cared about money. She let Dad keep the house. She didn't have a bean.'

Viv makes herself keep going. 'So you didn't get rich off her inheritance?'

'I bought myself a whole coffee grinder. I can't stand here today, Viv. You understand.'

Viv watches him go, rubbing her upper arms softly. The upside of Mark being so keen to get away was he didn't notice the tastelessness of that conversation.

Jamie steps into Viv's eyeline.

'Oh.' She focuses. 'Mark had to talk to someone else.'

Jamie gives her a look she can't decipher. He turns for the kitchen.

No, she *can* decipher that look.

Disdain.

'Jamie?' Viv pushes through the door into the steamy room, ignoring the other staff. 'It's not Mark. None of this is anything to do with Mark.'

Jamie says something under his breath, his voice barely audible.

'What?'

'*Fire escape.*'

There is no shade on the fire-escape platform. The heat bounces back at Viv from every surface as she waits for Jamie, the sun's reflection on the metal pole gleaming white in the sunlight.

There's a bang; Jamie shoves the fire door into the wall. 'You can't just follow me into the kitchen.'

Viv watches him sit on the step and yank his rolling papers out of his packet. 'Sorry.' For the first time today, he looks energised. She wants to sit, but he's left no space. 'Alison had no money.'

He shakes his head in disbelief.

'And it's definitely not Mark.'

'Why.' Jamie's question has no question mark.

'I can just tell.'

'Right.' He arranges tobacco with jerky fingers. 'I listened to most of your conversation, so help me with the gaps. Who did Mark say was the executor of Alison's will?'

Viv takes a second. 'Have you tried working these things into conversation? How did it go for you?'

Jamie neatens his tobacco. 'But you *did* ask who else was in Alison's will.'

'He said he didn't get much. Just enough for a coffee grinder.'

'And the money only went to him and Chrissy?'

Viv tries to wind the conversation back in her head. Problem is, Mark can be so distracting, with his ocean foam smell and his Disney prince hair. 'I can't remember the specifics.'

'Right. Because it isn't important, is it?' Jamie mis-rolls his cigarette; he lets it unfurl and re-rolls, with jerky hands.

Viv watches, saying nothing.

'So that's that.'

Uncertainly, she nods.

'And Mark would have no motive to want you out of the way. None *at all*.'

In the heat of the sun, Viv's neck prickles.

'Tell me.' He jerks his head up. 'If you don't give a shit that you're going to die, why should I keep risking this job for you? This job that I really need to hang on to if we're going to survive, by the way.' Jamie lurches to standing. 'So why bother? Why shouldn't I look after my own life for once? Why would I help you when you don't bother helping yourself?' He turns at the door. 'Viv, that man's a *goon*!'

Viv stares.

'Eighty-five lives and never a hint of him leaving his wife. He's married and he's staying married! He reads books about billionaires, and he tells anecdotes about cars! Do you know how much I've had to yawn-listen to him today? He's never said one thing that's interesting! You only want him because you can't have him! If you spent more time with him, you wouldn't even like him! Sort your fucking head out.'

Viv sinks down onto the metal step, understanding hitting in a clammy wave.

Jamie strides inside. 'You're on your own. I'm going to sort something for me, for once.' He slammed the door with a clang.

27

Six Months Ago
The Unprecedented Pie

'Welcome home!' Viv greeted Bethan at the door. 'I've made a pie.'

Bethan placed her quilted bag on the kitchen counter. 'In what way?'

Viv frowned: there was no other way to say it, so she said it again. 'I've made a pie.' She indicated the apron she was wearing. 'A *pie* pie.' She'd been given this apron covered in tiny, illustrated strawberries by her mum, on one of those birthdays when Mum forgot who Viv was. 'You're free tonight, according to the calendar.'

Bethan had instituted the 'shared phone calendar' policy when Viv moved in, because they only had one bathroom and needed to stagger overnight guests.

That was before Mark, of course. Mark never stayed over.

Bethan pulled her loafers off. 'A *pie*?'

'To eat! I don't know what's so hard to understand.' Viv opened the fridge door. 'I've even made pastry leaves.'

They both studied the pie. It was clumsy and misshapen, but it was the taste that counted. Viv was pretty sure there was no such thing as *bad pie*.

'It's going to be a great evening.' Viv pulled a bottle of *Tesco Finest* Gavi from the fridge. 'Join us for pie.'

Bethan stopped smiling.

Viv lined up the corkscrew, deliberately not looking up, making her voice even. 'Mark's coming for tea.'

Bethan pulled slipper-boots over her work tights. 'His wife on a yoga retreat?'

Viv pulled out the cork. 'Don't be all …' She indicated Bethan's new stiffness with the corkscrew.

'I don't know how you want me to be.'

'Yes, you do.' Viv threw the cork into the bin. 'You smile when he comes in. You say *nice to see you again, Mark, great shirt.* You fake polite interest and goodwill, please, like I did with Big Ted.'

'Big Ted wasn't the same and you know it.'

Bethan's boss at the fulfilment centre was called Adam, not Ted, but he had tiny black close-together eyes and was furry all over. Viv had observed him leaving the bathroom in Bethan's dressing gown, and said *it's like you got him from the Build-A-Bear workshop.*

'Big Ted was *actually* separated.' It was one of the things Viv liked least about Bethan: so finickity about details. 'You know what I think about Mark.'

Viv took the pie out of the fridge. 'You know it's ...' – she didn't say *not like your dad* – '... different.'

Bethan had a particularly tiresome origin story: her dad had an affair and left when she was tiny, and her mum never got over it. As a pigtailed kid, Bethan had sat on the doorstep for hours with her overnight bag and fluffy hedgehog, sitting until long after dark, refusing to believe her dad had forgotten to pick her up.

Viv swatted the air. 'I've brushed milk on the top and everything! What more do you want from me?'

'I can't believe you, of all people, are putting up with this, Viv! And cooking him *pie*! You've turned into a people pleaser!'

Viv sucked in her breath. *'How dare you!'*

Bethan was silent.

'I've never pleased any people in my life, and you know it!' Viv slid the pie in the oven. 'And it's not an affair, it's a crossover. He's going to tell her this week.' She switched the oven on. 'He might even be telling her right now.'

Bethan watched Viv, her gaze steady. 'You putting that in a cold oven?'

Viv leaned back against the (cold) oven door. 'Please, Bethan. I was so nice about Big Ted. And I was so understanding when you sacked me.'

'What was I meant to do when everyone knew you phoned a fake sickie from *my house*?'

'Some people would have still held a grudge.' Viv brushed flour from her jumper cuff. 'Not me.'

Both had started in the fulfilment centre in their twenties and Bethan was now Logistics Manager, complete with annual bonus and ten days' extra holiday. Viv had lasted just long enough for Bethan to get promoted to Team Leader and be given her first 'in-job management development opportunity' – managing Viv's disciplinary exit process.

Bethan picked up her quilted bag. 'What time are we eating?'

'Seven thirty.' Viv made her voice quieter. 'Thank you.'

By 7.45, Viv and Bethan had eaten all the crisps. The pie had browned, and Viv moved it into the top oven to keep warm.

'Is he close?'

Viv refilled Bethan's wine glass, then her own. 'I'm sure he is.'

'Maybe he's telling her right now. Like you said.'

Viv stopped herself saying *fuck off, Bethan*. She tapped Mark another message.

You get held up?

'Pie always tastes better when it's had time to settle.'

With her finger, Bethan dabbed at the last scraps of crisps.

Jess came back from her work thing early. Sorry.

Bethan watched Viv put her phone down. 'Oh.'

Viv wouldn't meet her eye. 'He's not coming.' She pulled the pie from the top oven. 'He always said it might be a struggle tonight.'

'You OK?' Bethan's voice was soft.

Viv stabbed the pastry crust with a knife. 'Fine.'

Steam rose up, burning her hand. She carved out a slice, her hand on fire.

Bethan watched. 'Does that hurt?'

'No.'

'It looks like it does.'

'Well, it doesn't. Clearly. Or I would have said. Now.' She made herself smile at Bethan. 'How about we open the next bottle?'

28

Now

Viv sits on the steps, the fire door reverberating from Jamie's slam. *The cunt.*

Problem is, she suspects *she* might be the cunt. This man would apparently rather be stuck in a time loop forever than spend another second with a lying arsehole like her.

Ahead, a glass apartment block glows the sterile green of hospital scrubs.

Viv doesn't usually lie, not about important things. Frank might have called her a *little psychopath* when she was a kid, but the adult Viv only lies about things that don't matter, like why she's phoning in sick, or her feelings.

This time was different: this was a positive lie, for morale. She wants the man working so hard to save her, a man so tired his eyes kept flickering, to think she's worth saving.

Still, now she's alone, without Jamie looking out for her, which means she's definitely going to die in the next few hours.

There's no way she's dying sober. Not with a free bar.

She stands, about to head up to the roof. Reflecting.

Actually, if she's going to die, she doesn't *need* a free bar.

Viv scans the menu. 'The scallops with marigold to start.' The cardboard menu is unnecessarily large for something outlining only a handful of dishes. 'Then the oysters with truffle foam.' She looks at the sides. She doesn't know what *cavolo nero* is, but it doesn't sound like chips. 'Do I need chips?'

The waiter pauses.

'And chips.' Viv hands back the menu. 'Thanks.'

She watches the waiter walk away. She expected a Michelin-starred restaurant to be dim with dark wood, like those gentleman's clubs in TV dramas where they bring in women to get sexually assaulted, but this restaurant is brightly lit, with white plastic furniture. It must be that kind of high fashion Viv's too basic to understand, like when actors in magazines wear dresses made of scuba-diving fabric or sheet metal: dresses all spiky zigzags, that cost more than gold, and don't show legs, arse *or* tits.

Viv sips her wine. It was the most expensive bottle on the menu, so it felt right to order it on death-day, but it just tastes like a headache. Yet again, Viv has forgotten herself.

'Hi.' She stops the waiter. 'Can you bring me a glass of your cheapest gin? It doesn't have to *be* cheap.' She pushes the half-drunk wine away. 'It just has to *taste* cheap.'

Two drinks later, Viv picks at a scallop. It's coming back to her now, who she actually *is*: a woman who drunkenly dislocated her thumb trying to light the hob when she was so desperate for her instant noodles; a woman who uses ketchup as pasta sauce; a woman who survived for four days on just Haribo. It's like Viv's body refuses to be classy. It's not her fault kombucha tastes like sour pop, and wheatgrass shots don't create the same sense of well-being as tequila.

Viv should have gone somewhere else for her perfect death-row meal – this is like the soil-and-leather cocktails all over again. Has she learned nothing from her night with the paddock people?

The waiter indicates her still-full plate. 'Are you ...?'

She pushes the plate away. 'God, yes.'

The paddock people probably like scallops. *Jess* probably likes scallops.

And Mark?

Viv rubs her arms, restless. She doesn't know what he'd choose to eat if they went out for dinner. When they meet, they've been eating Chinese, Thai or pizza takeways. That's been their social life. For fourteen months.

Viv makes a noise in her throat.

In a second, the waiter is there.

'False alarm,' Viv says.

The waiter leaves.

Jamie can act like he knows everything, spouting off like he's the god of relationships, but he's only seen what she and Mark are like on one day – *this* day. To understand relationships, you need more wraparound. You need *context*.

And Jamie said Mark *reads books about billionaires, and he tells anecdotes about cars* – and, yes, those things are shit, clearly. But relationships are about shared connections, not shared interests, and if Jamie's too shallow to get that, Viv feels sorry for him.

If you spent more time with him, you wouldn't even like him. Viv shakes her head for an invisible audience.

Jamie talks rubbish. It's true she's at that point in life where she's ready to experiment with early nights and wall-papering, willing to try living in a house with no fridge notes and a full set of working lamps and bifold doors. But she and Mark are about *more*. They have a connection Jamie doesn't understand, and it's the kind of connection people sing songs about, which is why love songs are always so painful and fucked up and sometimes even stalky. Viv isn't destined for pure level-headed happiness – it's too bland for someone like her. Jamie hasn't even *tried* to understand.

Her phone buzzes.

I'm sorry. Come back. We need to focus.

Viv looks at Jamie's message for a moment. The waiter arrives with her gin.

'Thank you.' She accepts the drink with a smile and turns her phone face-down. 'Now, is there anything I'd recognise on your cocktail menu?'

By the time Viv has drunk two (off-menu) Pornstar Martinis in the Michelin-starred restaurant, Jamie has sent several more messages.

I've been watching Chrissy and just heard her ask someone where
you were

Interesting she noticed you missing

She doesn't like you, it seems

She told Jess you call her Captain Clipboard

Please come back

I can't do this without you

'Another drink?'

Viv sighs and looks up at the waiter. 'Apparently, I just want the bill.'

She strides back towards the museum, past the tall glass-fronted shops and the homeless tents in front of the central library.

A woman's warm voice rings out. 'Hello, again!'

It takes a minute for Viv to place the faces. The enthusi-astic rosy-cheeked woman and the man with boyband hair, both with wholesome, spaniel vibes. They wear *Lambs of God* badges and hold *Turn Your Face to Jesus* leaflets.

'You've been out here all day in this heat?' Viv shakes her head. 'I hope they pay well.'

'We don't get paid.' The woman keeps smiling. 'You were wearing different shoes earlier.'

'I was. And I was also *much* less drunk.'

The two young people beam wider. Viv frowns. Why hasn't she put them off talking to her? Maybe that's the point – maybe Viv's a challenge. Like people who run desert marathons don't bother tying up their laces for a 5K park run, maybe when it comes to catching fish, the bigger the twat you hook, the more high-fiving goes on back at God-base. These people must *dream* of bringing in someone like Viv as their personal Everest, their *Best in Show*.

The man's nose has reddened from a day in this sun. 'Do you have time to talk?'

'I've got somewhere to be.' Viv smiles. 'But I promise, if I ever get to find God, I'll come and join the team.'

'We're around the rest of the day. And we're back again next week.'

Viv turns to walk. 'Make sure you get paid!'

'Jesus is on your side,' the man calls.

She throws a wave behind. 'Good to know!'

The ground floor of the museum is quiet, the building closed to the public by the time Viv heads back in. The party attendees are the only guests left, and Viv's footsteps echo. Her voice cuts through an eerie silence as she explains to the security guard she was there earlier.

He lets her past and she stumbles into the lift. Ideally, she wouldn't be looking into a whole wall of mirrored glass right now: her reflection isn't ideal. Her eyeliner always smudges as she drinks, and she's drunk a lot. The area around her eyeline has blackened considerably, her smoky eyes turned sooty. She's got something (scallop juice?) on the bodice of her dress, which she wipes semi-successfully.

She's about to head up to the terrace, but spots a pair of black trainers attached to black-trousered legs sticking out along the floor next to the grandfather clocks. The left trainer has a hole in the toe.

Viv walks over.

Jamie has his back to the glass display case of grandfather clocks, head tipped back, eyes closed.

Viv stands over him. 'Hi.'

His eyes flick open. 'I wasn't asleep.'

'Really.' She shakes her head. 'And to think, you're the one they sent to save me.'

He pushes himself up, sitting straighter. 'Thanks for coming back.'

Viv sits next to him. 'Did you sort out your thing? Your own life thing?'

'Not even close.'

'I'm sorry to hear that.' She stares at the art deco railing. 'And I'm sorry for not telling you about Mark. I just didn't want you to think less of me.' She pauses. 'For morale, you know?'

'You told me you barely know him.'

'I know.'

'Again and again.'

Viv stares across the Time exhibition. The lights must be on motion sensors because only the area they sit in is lit up, the rest all shadows. 'In my defence, I only remember lying today.'

'I listened in on Chrissy's conversations. She doesn't like you, you know. She's nervous that she can't see you anywhere.'

'I'm like a spider in the bedroom. You don't want to see it, but you definitely don't want it to scuttle out of sight.'

'What have you done to her?'

'Nothing!' Viv thinks. 'I didn't think she knew I called her Captain Clipboard.'

'Think harder.'

'I've maybe taken the piss out of her calligraphy.'

'Come on, Viv.'

'I'm trying!' Viv frowns. 'Maybe there was that thing at Alison's funeral, but I thought I'd imagined it. I ...'

Before she can finish the thought, a man in a suit rounds the corner. '*Jamie?*'

Jamie scrabbles to his feet. 'I had an emergency, Brent. A customer emergency.'

'It's true.' Viv gets to standing. 'I'm the emergency.' She brushes down her skirt, about to come up with a story about having a breakdown and threatening people with cutlery – but Brent clearly decides, as so many people do, that it's better to pretend Viv isn't there.

He turns to Jamie. 'You're needed in the kitchen.'

Jamie touches Viv's sleeve, and follows Brent round the corner.

On the terrace, the sun is low. Hundreds of fairy lights twinkle faintly in bay trees and mesh nets.

Viv scans the terrace, antsy. She can't see Chrissy, but she does see Jess, standing alone next to a high table.

And with this much gin inside her, something about seeing Jess makes Viv walk up. 'Is your favourite food really sushi?'

Jess raises her head from her phone.

'Be honest. Is it? Have you even *tried* crisps?'

Jess blinks.

'It's a simple, normal question.'

'No, it isn't normal.' Jess puts her phone down. 'It isn't normal at all.'

211

Viv stares at her. 'You're beautiful.' And Jess is, but in a different way than Viv had imagined, real and flawed, not doll-smooth and perfect. Without social media filters, Jess's forehead shows faint brown patches of melasma. The skin around her eyes is crinkled and make-up has settled in the creases, lines of foundation leading out from the corners of her eyes like spokes on a wheel.

It was so much easier to dismiss Jess when she wasn't real.

Jess folds her arms.

Viv runs her hand through her hair self-consciously. 'Sorry.'

Jess is too well-brought-up to point out how weird Viv is being.

Viv runs her hand through her hair again.

Jess watches the movement – and stares.

Viv frowns. 'What?'

Jess grabs Viv's hand and turns it over, revealing Viv's decades-old, compass-stabbed star tattoo. She looks up in shock.

Viv stares at her own hand – and realises. She struggles, trying to get away.

'You came into my salon?' Jess tightens her grip on Viv's hand, nails digging in. 'You came into *my fucking salon*?'

29

Five Months Ago
The Salon

Jess smiled goodbye to her client and sterilised her cuticle pusher and scissors. She laid a fresh towel on her station and fanned out the display ring of nail colours, even though her next client, Elaine, had only ever alternated between *Vampy Berry* and *Hollywood* in three years of appointments.

Jess's phone buzzed with a message.

Not going to make it, so sorry. Don't hate me. My life! 😭 It's so crazy! xx

Jess made a noise in the back of her throat. She typed back OK with sharp taps. She stared past the living plant wall, actively not making eye contact with the woman looking in from the rainy street, hood pulled forward.

Jess had no interest in asking what was so crazy about Elaine's life this time – and why Elaine had only become aware of the craziness three seconds before she was due. It was late November and Christmas party season had started. Elaine was taking the piss.

Not for the first time, Jess wished she worked in an office. At least when Mark went to work, he knew he'd always get paid.

She decided to use her free time to clean the door of fingerprints left there by customers (and nail technicians) who didn't know how to use a handle.

She carried her glass cloth and spray to the salon door. The woman with the hood was still lingering.

Jess went out with a smile. 'Can I help?'

The woman flinched. 'I was just looking at your nail prices.' She pulled her hood forward, covering her short black hair, shadowing her face. 'I've got time to kill. That's definitely what' – the woman indicated herself – '*this* is.'

'Then it's fate.' Jess beamed. 'You've got time to kill, and I've had a cancellation!' She backed into the door, pushing it open.

The woman swallowed.

Jess walked the door further back. 'I can do you half price. Eighteen quid for a full set of gels.' She felt like a market trader. 'That includes coming back for removal.' She walked the door even wider. 'I'm Jess.'

The woman paused. 'Sarah.' She walked past Jess into the salon.

Jess stared at the back of her hood. She was good at reading auras, and this woman's was off.

Jess let the door close behind them, already starting to regret her decision.

'You've always bitten?' Jess asked, filing the bits of nail she could.

The woman nodded, hood still up. She had a migraine that day, apparently, and found bright light painful.

'Gels will help you break that habit.' Jess wiped the woman's nails with a pad. 'Have you had gels before?'

'I borrowed my friend's machine once. Made a right mess.'

'Home gels can be dangerous.' Jess wiped the dust from the woman's nails and shook her bottle of base coat. 'Methacrylates can leak into the skin if you don't know what you're doing. You have tender cuticles, you know.'

The woman glanced up. 'Right.'

Jess started applying the base coat. 'So why are you killing time? What are you doing after this?'

The woman paused. 'Dentist.'

'Ugh. Unlucky. At least you'll have a fresh set of gels for it.' Jess indicated the UV light with a jerk of her head. 'Under.'

When the woman didn't move, Jess indicated the UV light again. 'I mean, put your hand under there.'

Finally, the woman did.

Under the table, Jess's phone buzzed. 'It's my husband. One sec.'

The woman stared fiercely at the table.

Jess answered the phone. 'I'm with a client.' Mark and Jess had been together too long for *hello*s in work time.

'Dad said those dates are fine.'

'And he's OK if we drop her in the night before?'

'Yep.'

'Great.' Jess ended the call and shook the bottle of black polish the woman had chosen. 'We're about to book Gran Canaria. I needed to check my father-in-law could take the dog.'

The woman raised her head. 'You're going on holiday?'

Was it *such* a strange turn of events? 'I know it's winter, but it'll still be warm. Warmish anyway.'

The woman looked back at the table. 'What date are you going?'

'February. It's good Mark's dad can take her.' Jess finished painting the bitten nails. 'Last time we had to put Bonnie in kennels. She wasn't right for a month. Under.'

When the woman didn't move, *again*, Jess mimed swapping hands under the UV lamp.

After a long moment, the woman did.

Jess applied two coats of black varnish and topcoat. She rubbed in cuticle oil. 'All set.' The effect was slightly ruined by the woman's home-stabbed star tattoo, but Jess wasn't responsible for her clients' unfortunate life choices. 'You'll be surprised how quickly they grow.'

The woman stumbled to standing. 'Thank you.'

Jess stood. 'Half price is eighteen—'

'*Don't do me half price!*' The woman sounded surprisingly fierce.

Jess frowned.

'I'll pay full price. Please.'

Jess blinked at her. 'You're the customer.' She tapped the price into the card machine.

The woman shaded her card from Jess as she paid.

'Removal's included.' Jess tore off the receipt. 'You just book a slot online.'

The woman turned. 'Thanks.' In her hurry to leave, she caught her thigh on the sharp corner of another station. She didn't slow, just let out a staccato *fuck!*

Jess watched her go. The woman hadn't removed her hood, all session.

Yes, Jess could read auras.

And she was pretty sure this woman wasn't coming back for removal.

30

Now

Jess is still staring at Viv's amateur hand tattoo. 'I wasn't going to do this today' – a fleck of Jess's spittle hits Viv's cheek – 'I promised myself I wasn't, but then I realise *you came into my salon?*'

Viv takes a step back. She reaches for the high table behind. 'You know.'

'That you fucked my husband and now you won't leave him alone?' Jess stares at Viv. 'Of course. But I didn't know you'd *made me do your gels!*'

Viv must hold eye contact, out of respect for Jess, because Jess is right to be furious. Going to the salon was *unhinged.* Viv had just been planning to peer through the windows, see if Jess looked sad at all, if there was any hint she looked like a woman having crisis conversations with her husband.

Viv's visit to that salon is the single most shameful thing she's ever done – in an extremely busy category. Yet it's the thing her mind whispers to her about, taunts her most about being a piece of shit about, when Viv's brain is skewering her with self-hate at 3 a.m.

'You're pathetic.' Jess leans forward. *'Pathetic.'*

'I know.' Viv nods. 'And a shithouse.'

'No, not like that. You don't get to *allow* me to be angry.' Jess raises her voice further. *'No.'*

Around them, everyone is looking.

'I do not need your permission to be angry!' Jess shouts.

Viv takes in the bitten skin at the side of her fingernails – Jess was right, she *does* have tender cuticles – and looks up at the other guests. Chrissy. Frank. Mum. All standing nearby, frozen and quiet, drinks in hand. Viv wants to say something to Mum, something to make this better, something to explain—

'She fucked my husband then made me do her gels!'

Mum puts her hand on Frank's arm. Frank puts his hand over hers.

Viv stares into the middle distance, concentrating on her breathing. *In two three. Out two three.* She tries that grounding exercise from Instagram, looks around and tries to focus on five things she can see. *Hanging basket. Angry face. View of the cathedral. Angry face—*

Where the fuck is Mark?

Not that it would be better if he was here – it would be even worse, in fact – but he deserves to share this moment. This shitshow is the very *definition* of his problem.

Jess holds up a palm. 'Sorry, Chrissy.' She walks away, banging into a hanging basket. She puts a hand out to steady it and keeps walking.

Viv doesn't bother moving on to the 'four things she can touch' part of the grounding exercise, just gives a single, regal nod to the crowd, and follows Jess inside.

Her mind reels.

Jess knew?

She was going to say nothing all day, just hold it all in? She must have a level of self-control Viv could only dream of.

Though – not quite. She has just screamed at Viv in front of the whole party.

Viv runs down the ramp. Jess is nowhere to be seen.

Probably for the best. Because what can Viv even say? *Yes, I fucked your husband and, yes, I'm going to do it again.*

Viv considers doing the grounding technique again, now she's out of the vicinity of the angry faces, but she hasn't a clue how you ground yourself out of *this*.

It's situations like this, why drugs were invented.

Viv hurries past the grandfather clocks towards the railing, increasingly panicked. Why's she even resisting dying? What about this life is she trying to save?

She has broken this life. And Viv is lucky, if you look at it from a particular way up. She has been given the gift of being able to take an eraser to her history. She's been given the gift of *redo*.

There's smashing crockery behind. Viv turns.

Jamie stands in front of the lift, tray in hand, surrounded by smashed plates.

Brent stares at him, red-faced. 'Go home. I *knew* you were high.'

'No. I'm just tired.' Jamie's voice is urgent. 'I need to stay.' He glances at Viv and back. '*Please.*'

'I'm not meant to tell anyone *you're fired* until I've spoken to HR. They will confirm it formally.' Brent pauses. '*If* you're fired.'

Jamie stares at Viv. 'Keep going without me.'

'What are you *on*?' Brent shouts.

Viv shakes her head. 'I'll just let this one end. I've fucked it anyway. And you said you couldn't risk being sacked.'

'No!' Jamie stands straighter. '*It might not work like that!*'

Brent pulls Jamie roughly towards the lift. Jamie lets himself be herded in, still twisting to look at Viv. 'It might not work if you *let* it! *Please!*'

The lift doors close between them.

Viv hurries to the railing and watches Jamie be walked out of the lift on the ground floor.

He looks up – and starts resisting Brent. '*Get away from that railing!*'

Brent and a security guard wrestle a still-shouting Jamie out of the front doors.

Viv shakes her head, surprised he can be so naïve. She's been disappointing her allies all her life, and Jamie's known her for eighty-five of those. If he's shocked, he hasn't been concentrating.

She leans further over the railing and waits.

The good thing is, with the museum closed, there are no kids on the atrium floor forty metres below. The worst damage she can do on the way down is hit some plastic planets and cases of moon rock.

She lifts her heels, moving her bodyweight further over the railing. A calm comes over her – a kind of drunk peace. This is where today has been heading to: a shit, shit outcome. Viv knows how to deal with a shit outcome.

It is time. She is ready.

Her bag is vibrating, and it'll be Jamie on the phone, but she can talk to him in the next life. She'll be better in that one, it'll be easier to concentrate. She will have *eternal sunshined* her mind by then, cleansed it spotless. In that life, Viv won't know quite how badly she's fucked everything up.

She grips the railing. She stares at the deserted museum floor.

And she waits.

31

Four Months Ago
The Christmas Meal

Bethan had been weird with Viv since the night of the pie, and Mark wasn't around much: Jess had hurt her leg hill-running, so was at home more in the evenings, and Mark had Christmas parties, and was really busy at work and Viv didn't understand why these things were Viv's problem, but there were a lot of things Viv didn't understand, like why she also only found out he was going on holiday from Jess. Viv was no etiquette guru, but if you only find out your boyfriend's booked a holiday because you've inveigled your way into his wife's salon pretending to be someone else, something's gone wrong.

And it wasn't just Bethan and Mark who were unavailable

this time of year. The rest of Viv's friends were tedious in their enthusiasm to brandish their social *Get Out of Jail Free* cards of babysitter challenges. So it was a culmination of things, basically everyone's fault but hers, that meant Viv was sitting across from an old colleague, Zoe, in a Pizza Express, eating a Sloppy Giuseppe garnished with holly.

Zoe was inexplicably delighted Viv had said *yes*. 'Seeing you is my Christmas party!' Zoe's deeley-bopper antlers bobbed as she ate. 'This is my big night out of the year!'

Viv smiled, patting Zoe's hand. *Poor bastard.* Still, she was pleased Zoe had got in touch. She wasn't sure if the antlers were meant to be ironic, but she'd cut Zoe some slack. She worked from home and had three under-fives. It was impressive she was wearing anything at all.

'Have you got your tree up yet?'

Viv tried not to sigh. 'Bethan's put an old fibre-optic one up on the kitchen table.' She pried black gel up from a bitten fingernail. Jess had said Viv wouldn't be able to bite through the gel, but Jess had underestimated her client's determination to ruin a good thing. 'Bethan goes to her family in Glasgow for the week so she can't be arsed with a proper tree.'

The wine bottle was near-empty, and Viv looked for the waiter with the moustache curled like a Victorian strongman's, though they were three weeks out of Movember.

'And what are your plans for Christmas?'

There it was, the worst December question of all. No one cared about the answer, *surely*?

'I've got a few things in.' Christmas was usually mince pies and *Die Hard* with Mum – Mum relaxed her *no carbs after 6 p.m.* rule significantly at Christmas, and Viv did the same with her own rules about diazepam – but it wasn't happening this year. In a pass-agg act of genius, Angela had invited Mum to hers. Mum asked Viv if she should turn it down and Viv said *it's fine, as long as I don't have to go.* 'It's a non-event, really. Christmas is about kids and families.'

That had better not be pity in Zoe's eyes. 'I read an article about people like you.'

Viv tried again to get the waiter's attention. 'People like me?' It was fine for Zoe: she still had half a glass left. Amateurs made nights out tedious in December, all the shouting and crying and bar queues. Viv had even seen a clearly-out-of-practice-at-drinking man drop his trousers and shuffle across the restaurant area in a Bella Italia, his belt trailing loosely on the floor.

'People like you.' There was that note in Zoe's voice again. 'The article said it can be a hard time for people without families.'

Viv was about to say *I have a mum* – and then got it.

Zoe tilted her head.

Viv kept looking for the waiter. It was December, that was the problem: she should have let Zoe order that Diet Coke.

'Like you said, Christmas is about kids.' Zoe studied Viv. 'I'll have to check with Kev, but would you like to come and spend Christmas with us?'

That, finally, got Viv's attention.

'I'd like you to experience a proper Christmas, with children.' Zoe paused. 'Not Christmas Day, obviously.'

Viv stared at Zoe's quivering antlers. 'Obviously.'

'Or Boxing Day. But the day after? It's really not a problem.'

Viv made eye contact with the waiter with the twirling moustache.

Zoe got in first. 'Just the bill.'

Viv slumped.

'Kev's got a big meeting tomorrow, I said I'd help him with his slides.' Zoe adjusted her antlers. 'But you'll come on the twenty-seventh?'

'I have plans.' Viv made herself smile. 'But thank you.'

'She felt sorry for me, Steve. *Sorry for me.*'

Last Resort Steve pushed the bag of gummies across his coffee table. 'I'm so pleased you called.'

'I don't do weed.' Still, Viv ate a gummy anyway. There was no washing on the radiators, but Viv could smell it had been there – the hint of Tropical Breeze, the undercurrent of armpit. Steve had tidied up for her arrival, though she'd only given him five minutes' warning. 'You can't even be angry with someone if they're trying to do you a favour, can you? Still, I'm fuming. Do I look sad to you, Steve?'

Steve frowned, like the idea was unfathomable.

'Thanks.' Viv took another edible. 'I should call you more.'

'I would have got something else in if I'd known you were coming round.'

Viv glanced at Steve's schnauzer, asleep on a chair, four legs raised with casually impressive core strength. 'Does Trixie still have anxiety?'

'Sorry, Viv, I can't give you any more of her benzos. The vet monitors the numbers.'

Viv tried not to sigh. 'Of course.' Dogs got good meds with so much less hassle, and Viv couldn't help being jealous that Trixie's uppers and downers came from a lab, clinically tested and in blister packs. Whereas Viv's meds came from …

She tried not to think about it.

But Viv had never drunk from a puddle (that she remembered, anyway), so … swings and roundabouts. 'You don't feel sorry for me, do you, Steve?'

'Why would I? Look at you! You're great!'

'And you're great too.' Viv reached for another gummy. 'You not having any?'

'I'm on shift in a bit,' Steve said.

'Sorry. I'll get a taxi in five.' Viv looked up. 'It's just Christmas, you know?' She tapped her head. 'Gets me every time.'

Steve nodded.

'One sec.' Viv reached for her phone. She sent the message before she could think.

I accidentally went to see your wife at her salon.
Which I think we can both agree means something has to change.

She put her phone down and reached for another gummy.

32

Now

Viv has waited for minutes now, eyes closed, waiting to be thrown over the balcony. Eventually, her ears stop beating with the pump of her own blood.

They're not coming.

Every other time, someone's killed her when she didn't want them to. Now, she's standing here, giving them a deliberate opportunity – and they're not even fucking coming.

Now this had to be irony, *surely*?

She heads for the bathroom, the motion-sensor lights coming on around her. She uses the toilet, running her fingers over the puppy-shaped dimples on the toilet roll, ignoring her constantly vibrating handbag.

She washes her hands and wipes them on her dress. She

leaves the bathroom, walking into the empty museum.

So, *this* is her life now.

She passes the lift and looks up the ramp to the doors to the roof terrace. She can't go back up there, not yet.

She follows the railing round in the direction of the grandfather clocks.

Eighty-five lives, and *this* is the one she's going to have to live.

The one where Viv knows that Jess knows about the affair. The one where *everyone* knows about the affair. The one where she downed several Pornstar Martinis and racked up a four-hundred-pound bill at a Michelin star restaurant.

The one where, because of her, Jamie's been sacked.

Viv pulls her vibrating phone out of her handbag. Jamie hasn't stopped hassling her this whole time.

She answers the call. 'I know, Jamie, don't say it. I know, I'm a fucking dickhe—'

She's shoved into the railing. Her phone tumbles out of her hand.

Air rushes past her face, and the museum floor comes up to meet her.

PART FOUR

33

Now

Viv wakes, upright and gasping. Two background images slide into place, a pair of scissors snapping shut.

The force on Viv's chest lifts. She staggers forward.

'That the best you can do?' It's Sean's voice. 'The nurses only liked me because I brushed Alison's hair. But thanks for trying.'

Viv puts both hands to her throat. She gasps for air.

'Viv, what the fuck is wrong?'

'Sean!' Frank turns from Mum. 'Have you heard about your dad and the raffle for the guide dogs?'

A waiter with a tray of glasses strides purposefully into her eyeline. 'Come with me. *Now.*' He puts his tray down with a clatter.

She doesn't move immediately; the waiter wrenches her arm. *'NOW!'*

He yanks her off the terrace, down the landing. 'How could you do that?' His stride is rigid. 'Why wouldn't you *listen?*' He shoves open a door to a bathroom. 'How could you be so *stupid?*'

He pushes Viv into the room; she stumbles. Her vision is honeycombing; she can barely see. 'Who *are* you?'

The man's manner changes. He places his hands on the sink and closes his eyes.

A long moment passes.

When he opens his eyes again, he is calmer. 'So, I'm Jamie.'

They stare at each other.

His eyes flare. 'Shit.' He pushes Viv towards a cubicle. 'You need to piss, *right now.*'

This waiter tells her things about her life – mad things he can't possibly know, like what's in her handbag, and that she chain-ate instant noodles last night. He knows she's made a salad out of crisps, knows she stole a muffin/doorknob from a party, and Viv doesn't understand how he's coming up with this stuff but it's scary and weird and she's getting more pissed off by the second.

'Viv!' The man slams his hand against the cubicle door. 'Stop getting distracted!'

'Distracted?' She throws the door open, the skirts of her dress caught in her underwear. Today is … something else. *'Distracted?'* She rearranges her dress. 'Some guy I've never met drags me to the toilets, tells me he's been stalking me,

234

orders me to piss. And I'm meant to think that's OK?'

The waiter makes a throat-noise of frustration. 'You felt the glitch! I'm *helping* you!'

'I know we're all meant to be cool about fetish shit now, but call me old-fashioned.' She strides past him to wash her hands. 'Get some therapy.'

'Oh, God,' the man says.

Viv marches out of the bathroom.

The stalker hurries into the lift after her. 'Viv.'

'Get out.'

He doesn't.

'Fine.' Viv presses the button for the ground floor.

'*You* told me those things! And I only told you to piss so you didn't wet yourself! You're usually terrified!'

The lift doors open.

Viv walks out. 'Well, this was fun.'

'*Viv!*'

She holds up a hand and keeps walking, past the statue of Alan Turing towards the museum exit.

The waiter makes the throat-noise of frustration again. 'Wait for me!'

The man won't leave Viv alone. He hurries after her, listing dates and times and feelings, telling her everything she's ever known and ever done.

'Sit.' He is breathing heavily. 'Please. *Sit.* Let me try again.'

It's getting harder to understand how he can possibly know all this so, finally, she sits next to him on the bench by the canal. He tells her what he wants her to know, going through it all again, more slowly this time.

★

'And you drag me to the toilet like that every time? Don't I mind?'

He twists his mouth.

'I would have thought I'd mind.'

'I'm not usually like that.'

'And do you have to be so *shouty?*'

'I got my routine wrong this time.' He has a tiny whorl at his crown, hairs pointing in every direction like the bristles of a hoover attachment. 'And my timing's all off now. I was frustrated because of what you did last time.'

'What did I do?' She holds up a palm. 'Actually, no, don't tell me. You can't blame me when I don't remember. You can't hold resentment over different lives; it doesn't work that way.'

Viv doesn't have a clue how this works.

'I'm just scared!' He raises his voice. 'I don't know how to keep you safe!'

With shaking hands, Viv pulls the twist of tissue from her handbag.

Jamie makes a revving noise in his throat. *'Really?'*

He lunges up to bat the tissue away. Two pills bounce out onto the towpath.

'Hey!' Viv falls to her hands and knees, scrabbling on the gritty path for the pills.

Jamie dives for the closest pill. Viv retrieves the other from a puddle and shakes the water off. Jamie knocks it out of her hand. 'You absolute twat. You think that'll help?'

'It's just a couple of benzos, to take the edge off.'

'Viv, I know I've messed up, but *please*. You can't be taking benzos today.'

'It feels like the perfect day to me.' She picks the other pill up off the floor. 'You wouldn't believe how anxious I am.'

'Please. Can't you just *care*?'

'Of course I care!' Viv stares at the pills in her hands, imagines the chalky feeling on her tongue. She glances up to meet Jamie's eyes: they're pleading, vulnerable. 'Fine.' She wraps the pills back up in a tissue. 'But I'm still keeping these for emergencies.'

It's shaming, the level of relief on his face. 'Thank you.' He sits. He looks like he could sleep for a week.

'Do I really make you that frustrated?'

Jamie turns his gaze to the towpath. 'It's just getting harder to believe we're going to make it.'

Viv takes that in. 'Did we find out anything last time?'

'I found out Chrissy really doesn't like you. You thought you might know the reason why.'

Viv thinks about this. Her face warms. 'I've no idea.'

'Then why do you look like you know?'

'I'm just formulating a thought,' Viv lies. 'I'll get there.' She stares at the water. 'What else don't we know yet?'

Jamie closes his eyes for a long minute. Viv thinks he might be asleep.

'Loads.' Jamie flicks his eyes open. 'Someone might have engineered the car crash, but why? Are we sure Harry only got together with Alison after your aunt died?'

Viv is about to say *obviously*. Except what did Mark say that one time? *They took a picnic up Snowdon. They were recreating their New Year's Day first date.*

Which didn't make sense; Juliet didn't die until February.

'Harry wouldn't … Harry was a better person than me.'

237

Despite the heat of the day, Viv shivers. She needs it to be true.

'How did Mark's dad feel about the divorce? We need to find that out.'

'Great.' Viv closes her eyes. '*We.*'

If you'd asked a few hours ago how Viv planned to meet Mark's dad, it would be by making wry, memorial-appropriate jokes. By being funny but not *too* funny, not too edgy, not too loud. Ideally, she'd drop in the charity work she's always intended to get round to.

'I don't even know which one he is!' Viv wails.

'Red cheeks and purple polka-dot tie. Lots of opinions about cyclists running red lights and Low Traffic Neighbourhoods. Doesn't understand why women today are so open about the menopause. Name's Andrew Gilmore. Same big bread forehead as Mark.'

Viv looks up.

Jamie indicates with a finger. 'Goes out at the top, like a piece of bread.' The lid of his left eye droops like a half-closed blind.

'What's up with your eye?'

He turns away. 'It's been doing that the last few lives.' He glances at the clock on his phone. 'We're running late this time.'

'That's on you, angry man.'

'When we go back in, you have to avoid your mum for ten minutes.'

At the casualness in his voice, Viv looks up. 'Should I ask?'

Jamie scrunches his nose.

Viv lets out a long breath. 'Right.'

★

The man Jamie described stands with a group of late-middle-aged women on the roof terrace, the women all dressed similarly in low-heeled slingbacks, with bright shawls hanging from elbows. Mum and Angela are with them, so Viv can't go over, not after what Jamie just said.

Instead, she studies Andrew Gilmore.

His forehead *is* like Mark's.

It *does* look like a slice of bread.

She knows him, of course. She's never met him, but she's seen him before.

He's the one the nurse was talking about at Alison's wake.

34

Ten Months Ago
The Last Funeral

Viv circled the room over the pub with a child's-sized plate, feeling the secret frisson of mild discomfort, both psychological and physical, after fucking Mark in the disabled toilets.

It was better to think of the feeling as a *secret frisson*, rather than just *sore*.

Viv put some pitta and taramasalata onto a plate, though she couldn't stomach food. The smell-echo of stale urine had stayed in her nose, and that would dampen any kind of appetite.

Which must have been why the sex was so bad. The worst

sexual experience she'd ever had – a pretty big call, when Viv worked through the mental Rolodex.

This was worse than the time that student's cat walked in and mewl-watched Viv fuck its owner with an air of neutral study, like it was planning to flip up a scorecard with its paw.

Worse than the time Viv gave an external decorator a hand-job so he'd take the rap for the vape-smell in a work meeting room (an experience that had left her staring in the work bathroom mirror for a very long time).

It was worse, because it was Mark.

Sex with Mark didn't have to involve *I love you*s, of course. It didn't have to come with crashing waves on a deserted beach, or a stirring soundtrack. She didn't even mind if they kept the TV on. But it was at least meant to be *pleasant.*

The stench of stale urine would have been bleak enough, even if she'd had the foresight to bring lube and – crucially – the man she'd been fucking hadn't cried.

Viv watched Sean at the other end of the buffet, piling his plate with mini burgers. He took his time peeling the buns off, discarding them on the serving platter, just taking the meat.

Viv was impressed with his practicality. This wasn't his first time stress-eating of course. He didn't want to take a risk with all the carbs.

Sean dissected the last two burgers and Viv looked round for a stranger to talk to. One who didn't look well connected; one who wouldn't respond to the name *Viv* with a top lip primed to curl upwards with faint distaste.

She spotted a wide-eyed woman in nurse's scrubs. Viv has always found nurses good value at social occasions – they were often unshockable, with a stark line in gallows humour. As healthcare professionals on a night out, nurses were way more fun than doctors, much less insecure. The only downside was that they were less likely to offer you a line.

'Hi!' Viv carried over her plate of pitta and taramasalata. 'Did you know Alison from … the end?'

The nurse nodded.

'It's kind of you to come.'

'I wanted to. When you spend time with someone in their final days, you feel like you know them, even if they're not talking. It's been lovely to hear all the stories about Alison today.'

The nurse looked at Viv expectantly.

'We weren't close, though I liked her. She adored my uncle Harry, you could just tell.' Viv paused. 'I was impressed at the angle she held her glass at, at her wedding.' She mimed a nearly horizontal glass. 'Not a drop spilled. A true pro. And a great dancer.'

The nurse smiled politely.

Viv scanned the room, her gaze hooking on Sean. Two years younger than Viv, he looked *old* today. That had better be grief-aging, not real aging: Viv, as his older cousin, wasn't ready. *'Sean!'*

He looked up from his pile of burger patties.

That was a lot of wasted bread. Chrissy wouldn't be happy. 'We're sharing stories about Alison.'

Sean put his plate down. 'Siobhan's heard all mine. Have you seen Duncan?'

Viv thought. 'I think I saw him outside.' She was a lot of things, but never a grass.

Sean frowned. 'He hasn't left already?'

Viv paused again. 'He did say he wasn't very well.'

Sean's face clouded. 'I said I'd be home by five, but now I can't. There'll be no one to represent Dad.'

'I can represent your dad.'

Sean was tactful enough to pretend Viv hadn't spoken. 'I'd best make a call.'

He walked towards the bathroom, putting his phone to his ear.

Viv watched him go. 'He's a sweetheart, really. Even if he did eat all Chrissy's mini burgers.'

The nurse smiled. 'We know. He brushed Alison's hair when he visited; he was very gentle. My colleague Rach said it was a shame he was married.'

Viv didn't bother correcting the nurse. She indicated Mark. 'Did her son visit often?'

'Mark? Of course. We saw a lot of him.'

Viv felt a warmth within.

'And his wife.'

Viv's inner warmth racheted down.

'She was lovely. Very kind. Offered me a free mani-pedi as a thank you. Though none of the family visited Alison as much as Andrew.'

Viv turned to look at the man the nurse was indicating. He was older, serious-looking, his shirt tucked into a too-high waist. 'That's Mark's dad?'

'He was there all the time.'

Viv considered Andrew. 'But he and Alison split up ages ago.' He must be in his sixties, but he had a good head of wavy hair, giving him the look of a silvery ... if not *fox*, then a woodland mammal just a couple of acorns down the scale. 'He must have been very sad.'

The nurse looked at Viv and looked away, something in her expression.

'What?'

The nurse sipped her orange juice. 'He *was* very attentive. He kept playing Alison albums from her heyday, apparently she loved Blondie and Madonna. But one time I went in, he was raising his voice. We don't often get that in our ward.'

'Did you hear what he said?'

The nurse lowered her voice. 'He shouted *why did you have to ruin everything?* He put his arms around her and started to sob. I had to ask him to leave. I even had to wipe her face – he'd got tears all over her.'

The nurse said it in a critical voice but there was something nice about it, Viv thought. Someone caring enough to cry actual tears on your unresponsive, dying face.

Chrissy stepped up. 'Siobhan, we all really appreciate you coming today.'

The nurse's face reddened immediately.

'Some people have given cash donations.' Chrissy didn't notice, just continued talking. 'Should I give the money to you?'

Chrissy and the nurse talked some more while Viv, on the edge of the conversation, dug a piece of pitta into some taramasalata.

Chrissy trailed off, staring at the buffet table. 'What kind of monster has wasted all the bread from my mini burgers?'

Someone nudged Viv's arm. Taramasalata splatted onto Chrissy's shoe.

Viv grabbed a napkin. 'Sorry.' She dropped to the floor and rubbed Chrissy's Mary Jane. 'I've got it.'

Chrissy said nothing.

'And it definitely wasn't me,' Viv added quickly. 'The mini burgers.'

'I spilled that dip too earlier.'

Viv paused her rubbing.

The voice was Mark's.

Viv tried to catch his eye, but he was focused on Chrissy. 'It's a thinner consistency than you'd expect. Not one of yours, sis. I can tell. You make much better dips.'

Viv stood up slowly.

Mark wouldn't let her catch his gaze, just walked away quickly.

'That was gentlemanly of him,' Viv said.

Chrissy turned to Viv, her face unreadable.

No, not unreadable: impassive. Very, very cold.

'He's devastated right now.' Chrissy seemed to be choosing words carefully. 'Not himself at all.' She was looking past Viv. 'I saw him leaving for a breath of air earlier. I went after him. He'd gone for a walk across the park.'

Viv felt her face redden. Had Chrissy seen?

'Not himself at all,' Chrissy repeated.

'I'm sure none of you are feeling great.'

'Have you met Mark's wife?' Chrissy's voice was quiet, even.

Viv shook her head. She said nothing.

'Jess is nice.' Chrissy folded her arms, not making eye contact. 'You should meet her.'

Viv watched Chrissy walk away. Did she know? Either

way, Viv was the bad fairy at this funeral, like she was at every social event.

She hadn't even wanted to fuck Mark in the toilets.

Even when she did a nice thing, it always got misconstrued.

35

Now

Viv, still waiting for the few minutes Jamie has said to let pass before she goes over to Mum's group, examines the photos on the easels.

All relationships have patterns, of course. But she hadn't realised till now that Mark ignoring her at funerals was one of them.

''Scuse me!'

The waiter hears and comes over with a tray.

'Thank you.' Viv lifts a glass from the tray, thinks, then lifts another. 'This one's for my friend in the toilets.'

She looks back at the easel. A twenty-year-younger version of Andrew smiles with Alison and the teenage Mark and Chrissy on a pedalo, their four wet life jackets shining lip-gloss red in the sun.

Viv considers the teenage Chrissy. As a child, her teeth stuck out more. She must have got braces.

Viv convinced herself after Alison's funeral that she was being paranoid, that Chrissy didn't see Viv and Mark meet at the park toilet. But Jamie says Chrissy *really* doesn't like Viv.

Could it be Chrissy knew all this time? And does she blame Viv alone, because Mark was grieving? Or because of some sexist medieval views about women being temptresses, about men not having agency?

If she blames Viv, that is unfair. Viv is single: Mark is the one who is married.

Viv finds Chrissy and beckons her over. 'Tell me about these photos.'

Chrissy steps up and looks. 'That's Crete. 1998. I was stung by a jellyfish within half an hour. No one had fun at the taverna *that* night.'

They both stare at the photos, quiet.

'Chrissy, I'm sorry.'

Chrissy looks at Viv in a question.

'For anything I've ever done that upset you.'

Chrissy moves her mouth to the side. 'I'm going to speak to Jess.'

Viv turns back to the photos, rattled. She spends a few more minutes studying them, killing time, trying to distract herself by drawing conclusions from the photos.

That Alison mustn't have liked her teeth, because she always smiled close-lipped.

That the bread-head thing runs down the whole Gilmore male line.

That there isn't a single photo of Viv.

Viv's sure she must have left it Jamie's specified ten minutes. She heads over to Andrew, Mum and the group.

Angela is there, her back to Viv. 'Can you imagine? A teaching assistant? I thought Pam was joking when she told me.'

Viv slows.

'I said *are you sure she should even be around children?*'

Viv fixes on the back of Mum's neck: the tiny hairs; the light sweep of freckles; the thin gold strands of her filigree chain. She wills Mum to speak.

And she does. 'Stop now, Angela. That's not funny.'

'It's you I'm thinking of, Pam.' Angela shakes her head. 'On Tuesdays and Thursdays, when I've had Polly's girls since 8 a.m. and I'm exhausted from playing peekaboo and chaining *Bluey* and it's not even lunchtime, I think of you and I'm grateful.'

'Maybe you'll get lucky,' a canary-shawled woman says. 'Maybe Viv will have an accident.' She adjusts her shawl. 'I meant, get pregnant.'

Mum stares. 'I know what you meant.' She walks away from the group.

There's a tug at Viv's sleeve.

Jamie holds a tray of canapés. 'Pastry?'

'*This* is why you told me to stay away from Mum for ten minutes.'

He wrinkles his nose. 'Oh.'

'They say this every time?'

'Of course not.' He makes his voice firmer. '*No.*'

'You're lying. You lie to me on a day like today?' Viv's voice is a bark. 'Am I a joke to you?'

Jamie heads for a discreet table and puts his tray down. He fills a napkin with pastries. 'Let's go.'

'My own mother not telling Angela to fuck off when she says I shouldn't be around children.'

Viv and Jamie both rest against the display case of grandfather clocks, their feet sticking out.

'Like I chop out coke and watch porn under the big caterpillar in the reading corner.'

'She doesn't think that.' Jamie holds out his napkin. 'Here, have a canapé.'

Viv pushes his hand away. 'I don't want a canapé!'

A second passes.

Viv indicates for him to pass the pastry back. 'I can't do this.'

'You have to.'

'Not now. Let's get out of here. We can go anywhere, you choose. Can we just get away?'

'We can't. If I get caught then I'll *definitely* be sacked.'

'Just for half an hour. Please. I can't do this.' She looks up. 'And I've got something to tell you, but I don't want to do it here.'

He looks at her face and sighs. 'OK. Just half an hour, and just this one time. You're lucky I live right round the corner.'

Jamie lets Viv into his flat, clearly unsettled. He jerks his attention around without letting it land, like he doesn't want to focus on anything.

Viv considers the emptied ashtray, the dirty kitchenette. The cup on the side, the broken microwave.

Jamie puts his hand on Viv's arm. 'Smell that.'

Viv inhales, taking in a smoky, detergent, candle scent.

'That's our flat smell.' Jamie's voice is full of wonder. 'I only usually smell it if I've been away for a while.'

Viv glances at him. 'You OK?' She told Jamie to take her anywhere, but she should have said *except anywhere you have an emotional connection to.* She's in bits right now. At least one of them needs to be on their game.

'*Miaow.*'

Jamie shuts his eyes. 'Already?'

Viv looks at the closed door. 'You have a cat?'

'No. She is just one roaming entitled prick.'

Viv wants to ask why Jamie's opening the door anyway. Why he's looking softly at the tortoiseshell bundle with soft feet placed neatly together, its gaze raised expectantly to Jamie, eyes round with manipulation.

'Hi.' His voice is gentle. He picks up the cat and buries his nose in her fur.

The cat gives a surprised mewl.

'Warm dust and Dreamies. The smells are hammering me today.'

'You're *sure* that's not your cat?'

'No.' He glances at Viv. 'For the record, I hate this twat.'

He tries to sniff the cat again, but she scrabbles too much. He lets her jump out of his arms. She gives Jamie a suspicious side-eye and stalks into the bedroom, her high tail wisping.

'This isn't your flat!' Jamie shouts after her.

Viv watches. 'It's weird being here, I guess.'

'Yeah.' Jamie picks up a grey marl hoodie. 'This is mine, but my partner always borrowed it. No matter how many times I washed it, it smelled of him.' Jamie starts lifting the hoodie to his face: he changes his mind, and drops it like it's hot. 'We need to get out of here.'

'Five minutes.' Viv looks around. 'It's just hit me you know everything about me, and I know nothing about you.' Viv indicates the game controller on the floor. 'You're a gamer?'

'We need to get back.'

'Five more minutes,' Viv repeats. 'I'm learning.' She picks up a cardboard-framed photo of Jamie and another man riding a looping rollercoaster, the other man's shoulder-bag suspended in the air. 'Like now I know who buys these photos.'

Jamie glances at the picture. 'They always get Imran with the overpriced souvenirs. Twenty-five and he's still obsessed with Disney. He's always the first to dance at weddings. He puts a reindeer nose and antlers on his car in November.'

'He sounds great. Well done.'

'He dumped me this morning. Eighty-five lifetimes ago.'

Viv puts the picture down. She sits next to him. 'I'm sorry. Did you deserve it?'

Jamie nods. He tells her about Imran, about his sister's birthday, about making an excuse. About how he wishes *he*, not Viv, could have a do-over. 'We can't waste time,' Jamie says quietly. 'We don't know the world will always work like this, and I'm exhausted. I don't know how long I'm going to be able to keep helping you. We need to go back, right now.'

'I can't believe this, Jamie. I can't believe this is happening to' – she's about to say *me* – 'us.' At least she's only been trapped here for a few hours. He's been living this for so much longer, and the physical impact looks huge. She lifts her gaze. 'Are we friends, Jamie?'

'We need to get back.'

'Mates, at least? Will we see each other after all this is over?'

His lack of a response tells Viv all she needs to know. She stares at this man, with his hole in his shoe and his broken microwave door and a hot-and-cold codependent relationship with a cat. He's the only person who knows who she is right now, and what today means. He's the only person helping her.

And he doesn't even like her.

'What were you going to tell me?' Jamie says finally.

Viv can't put it off anymore. 'You asked about Chrissy earlier, if there's a reason she doesn't like me. And I think maybe … maybe she knows something bad about me. That I slept with her brother at her mother's funeral.'

Jamie stares at her.

'Because I've avoided telling you this today. I'm sleeping with Mark.'

Jamic docsn't say anything.

'Mark, at the party. Thick hair, slip-on shoes, bad shaver. The married one.'

When Jamie doesn't respond, she sits back.

'You know. *Of course* you know.' She stares at the wall. 'I've told you before.'

'No, you've never actually told me.'

'Right.' The humiliation is *real*.

'But you've told me now. And this is the first time.'

They sit in silence.

'I thought he was leaving Jess. You knew that part, right?'

Jamie makes eye contact. 'Yes.' He scratches his chin. 'Though I didn't know you slept with him at Alison's funeral. That's so fucked up.'

'Not at the *funeral* funeral. In the disabled toilets in the park.' She stares at the games console rather than look at Jamie. 'And it was as sexy as that sounds.'

'You haven't slept with him today, have you? Please tell me you haven't slept with him today.'

Viv shakes her head. 'He's never going to leave her, is he?'

Jamie doesn't answer.

Viv throws a cushion onto her foot, so she can kick it away. She misses. 'I don't understand how I've become this person.'

Jamie turns to her. 'Thanks for telling me.'

Viv nods briskly.

'Maybe we wouldn't be friends outside of this, but I've got used to you. I don't think you're as bad as you think you are. But I don't recognise you when you're with him. You really fucked him at a funeral?'

Viv sniffs. 'With no foreplay or lube.' She kicks the cushion, connecting this time. 'He barely acknowledged me afterwards.'

Jamie puts his face in his hands in a gesture of utter despair.

'You know what? Fuck him.' Viv stands. 'I'm going to end it. Right now.'

'There's no point. It'll just waste time. You won't even remember you did it next time.'

'Then you can remind me.'

Jamie flares his eyes. 'No way.'

'Either way, we need to get back. You can't risk getting sacked.'

Jamie nods.

Viv watches him head for the door. 'Don't you need to get that cat out of your bedroom?'

Jamie changes direction. A second later he comes out of the bedroom, the cat scrabbling in his arms. 'Off you pop,' his voice is soft, 'you little arsehole.'

'I'm going to do it. I'm going to end it with Mark, whether I remember it or not.' Viv follows him to the door. 'The thing with your partner. Is it recoverable?'

Jamie dumps the cat outside the door. 'No.' The cat walks down the corridor, its tail giving a regal curl.

'Why don't you take some time off, see if things are fixable? I'm sure they can't be that bad.'

'They are that bad.' Jamie gives a faint smile and pulls the door shut. 'Trust me. I checked last time.'

36

Today
But One Life Before

'He reads books about billionaires, and he tells anecdotes about cars!' Jamie shouted at Viv with eighty-five lives' worth of fury. 'Do you know how much I've had to yawn-listen to him today? He's never said one thing that's interesting! You only want him because you can't have him! If you spent more time with him, you wouldn't even like him! Sort your fucking head out.'

Jamie strode inside. 'You're on your own. I'm going to sort something for me, for once,' he said, before clanging the fire-escape door behind him. *Fuck it.*

He headed for the lift. *Fuck it, fuck this, fuck HER.*

He jabbed the lift button.

If Viv was going to lie, not even bother trying to save herself, why should he?

He strode out of the museum, trying to ignore the bugs marching up and down his arms. He rubbed them hard.

Still, he could feel the scuttling legs. The pincers tweaking his skin.

These bugs had started to appear these last few lives. Tiredness was making him feel things that weren't there.

He passed Viv's 'auntie' Angela, who was walking back towards the museum with Andrew Gilmore, but Jamie didn't have the headspace to think about where they'd been or why they were together.

He sat at a bus stop and got his phone out of his pocket. His screentime report once told him he was practically fused to this thing, but it felt as relevant to his life today as an abacus.

He typed into the search engine: *How long can humans cope without sleep?*

The record for the longest time a human has gone without sleep is 264 hours and twenty-five minutes, set by seventeen-year-old Randy Gardner in 1963. He stayed awake for just over eleven days. Afterwards, he slept for fourteen hours before needing to use the bathroom.

There is no official longest time a human can go without sleep, but it isn't long before the effects of sleep deprivation start to show. Symptoms include irritability, paranoia, difficulties with speech, mood changes, and cognitive rigidity. After only three or four nights without sleep, you can start to hallucinate.

Jamie put the phone back in his pocket. He'd worked out that last bit for himself.

He'd tried not to show Viv his despair, but it was getting harder. His pessimism was growing with his need for sleep. The whole thing didn't seem to be affecting Viv in the same way – she'd never mentioned hallucinations, and she didn't have to drag her legs up the stairs like he did. Viv reset every time in a way he didn't. She didn't understand that they might not be able to do this forever. That at some point …

Jamie couldn't think about this now.

He'd never left the hotel before this life. Not since the beginning anyway, not since he'd realised he couldn't outrun this. But if he was going to fail, be stuck here for eternity, he was going to make things right.

He had to apologise to Imran.

He weaved through stationary traffic and roadworks and, with tired steps, reached the restaurant.

And there he was: Imran. For the first time in eighty-five lives. Tall and straight-backed in his security uniform, listening to a dapper elderly gentleman in a fedora talk.

Imran smiled patiently, nodding. The dapper man's anecdote was long, and no doubt shit, but Imran was kind. He was always the first to stand on a packed bus – too keen, sometimes, to indicate someone who was barely past middle age and was probably able to do more press-ups than Jamie, and say *Imagine that was your nana, J. Offer up your seat.*

The dapper elderly man adjusted his fedora and walked away.

Jamie stepped forward. 'Hi.'

Imran raised his head. 'No.'

258

'I get it. I get it all.' Jamie tried not to see the ice in Imran's eyes. 'I'm sorry.'

'If you were sorry, you wouldn't mug me off. You can't be here, I'm working.'

'I've changed. I'm listening. I've given up weed.'

Imran's gaze hardened further. 'Since this morning?'

Jamie screwed up his eyes. Admittedly, it wasn't as impressive from Imran's side.

'It isn't fair, coming to my work. I can't walk away.'

'I wish I'd gone to Farah's birthday last night,' Jamie said quietly. If only the time loop had started twenty-four hours earlier. He couldn't say that to Imran, of course. Imran would think he had lost it, but there was nothing Jamie would like to do more than chain-live Imran's sister's birthday. He'd choose her a present, again and again – wrap it and everything. He'd happily put on Imran's favourite shirt, the one that brought Jamie's neck out in a bumpy rash. He'd stride into the bar, arms outstretched – *Farah! Congratulations!* – and cheerily answer her questions about his ambitions – *be fucked if I know.* He'd put his arm around Imran's sister, kiss the top of her head, and say *it's so good to see you.*

'What can I do?' Jamie reached to straighten Imran's tie. 'To prove I'm different?'

'Nothing.' Imran stepped back. 'And go back to work. You can't afford to lose your job. Being single's expensive.'

Jamie dropped the tie.

'I deserve better. Everyone says so.'

Jamie swallowed. 'If I'd called as soon as I got that message, would it have made a difference? I couldn't call. Someone was dying at the museum.'

'Dying.' Imran's voice was normally so animated, but he sounded dull. 'If I call the museum, they'll tell me someone died there?'

Jamie paused. 'I *thought* they were dying. Turns out ...'

Imran strode into the restaurant.

Jamie turned, vision blurring. He stepped into the road.

A horn blared. *'Hey! Dickhead!'*

Jamie held up a hand in apology.

He was so tired, he couldn't even do normal stuff, like remembering roads and cars were a thing.

He heard a faint noise, getting louder. He frowned.

It was kids singing. The plink-plonk of a jaunty piano.

No.

'Autumn days when the grass is jewelled—'

In the entrance of an alley littered with industrial bins, Mrs Churchill, Jamie's old primary school teacher and star of his intrusive sex-thoughts, sat bobbing away at the keys on a piano stool. Her glasses on a chain bounced against her chest, a chip wrapper floating down the cobbles next to her.

Jamie went cold. Even in his clearest of intrusive mind-generated movies, Mrs Churchill had only flashed and gone. Now, she was *here*. On the cobbles, between the bins and the chip wrapper. Playing the piano.

He ran towards her. *She isn't real. She isn't real.*

And then, she wasn't. As suddenly as she'd come, Mrs Churchill had disappeared.

Jamie slowed. He watched the chip wrapper waft down the cobbles.

This was getting serious.

They couldn't waste a single moment more.

He sent Viv a message.

I'm sorry. Come back. We need to focus.

He'd worked so hard. *So hard.* He'd used up so much energy, eavesdropping and following people, trying to remember everything he'd learned in eighty-five lives. And it wasn't enough.

He tried to ignore the scuttling on his arms as he hurried back towards the museum.

He tried to remember traffic existed.

And he tried not to let the despair take over.

37

Now

Viv follows Jamie out of the lift at the top of the science museum. 'I'm going to be less of an arsehole from here.' She presses *send* on her message.

Come and meet me at the Time exhibition.

'Poor Mark.' Viv puts her phone in her bag. 'Getting messages from *Craig from work* on a weekend.'

'When you're with him, stay away from the balcony.' Jamie heads up the ramp to the roof terrace.

Viv, disquieted, straightens her dress. She heads in the other direction, past the grandfather clocks. She'd passed people downstairs on the way back from Jamie's, because the museum doesn't close for another hour, but the Time exhibition is, as always, empty. The only movement is sand running down the person-height hourglass.

She walks idly round the exhibition, taking in sundials and water clocks. She lingers at a boxy-silver collection of the world's first digital watches, as retro-futuristic as *Barbarella*.

Her phone buzzes – but it's not Mark. It's an email from a company she once bought a replacement fridge shelf from.

Treat yourself! 15% off this weekend only!

Viv reaches the end of the Time exhibition. She looks ahead to *History of Technology*, but it doesn't look any more interesting there, just wordy panels and old computers. One display, headed *Cables*, is literally just a glass box containing pieces of cable.

It's like this museum doesn't want visitors.

She walks back into *The Wonders of Time*, past a panel titled *The Atomic Clock – A Revelation in Timekeeping Accuracy*.

If this murder's too hard to solve, maybe there's another way of getting out of this?

Maybe a Time exhibition is just what she needs right now? Maybe she can … get smart? Actually *understand*?

She reads the panels, one after another, but it's no good. Viv has a problem with time today, but there's nothing here that can help her – nothing practical-educational, nothing helpfully headed *Whoopsie! You got caught in a time loop!* The exhibition is mainly names and dates and pictures of men in wigs, all with a comical self-importance and surprisingly child-like faces.

Viv leans against a panel. She types multiple lives into Google.

Eleven signs you may have had previous lives
Past life regression
Signs you were royalty in a past life
Many worlds: the weirdest idea in quantum physics

She clicks that heading.

Ever wondered what would have happened if you applied to that different school? Turned down that job? Asked that pretty girl from the coffee shop on a date?

According to an analysis of quantum mechanics known as the 'Many Worlds Interpretation', there may be endless universes, each with a different version of you. Every individual event has multiple possible outcomes. Even the way a particle of light hits the Eiffel Tower, or the way a raindrop falls into the South Pacific – even the tiniest event might split the world into alternate realities. Subatomic splits are—

Viv isn't ready for *subatomic splits*. She scrolls past more entries.

Will life repeat?

It's a blog post.

Space is curved and so is time. Our finite timeline exists as a tiny fraction of a limitless arc. Extend our timeline forward infinitely and it will ultimately reach the same point from which it is extended.

Every atom in the atmosphere is in a relationship with any other atom at any given moment. Each change in relationship is another event. Since there are not an infinite number of atoms, there can't be an infinite number of changes in possible relationships. Therefore—

Viv looks up. She homes in on a swinging pendulum in a silent video: how a clock works.

What did she expect? Half an hour of reading and she'd suddenly have become smart enough to solve a broken universe using science?

A wisp of cool air dances over the back of her neck. It is hot outside, but the inside of the building is cold.

She checks her message with Mark. Two blue ticks: he's read it.

Viv flicks back to her search. She clicks the next entry.

AnyoneMe has asked a question on a discussion forum.

Do we live the same life over and over again?

I can't sleep since hearing about the theory of temporary loops. Have other people heard of this? I wish I hadn't.

My aunt's a scientist and she explained it. She said at the big bang everything was formed and, over time, the universe expanded as far as it could. And then, because it was finished, it had to start going backwards and reversing itself until it went boom – and then it all happened again. The theory is everything you've ever done and thought will happen again. And life is going to repeat itself the same way, over and over, forever.

It can't be true. Can it? I can't be doing all this, again and again, forever?

Viv looks at a grandfather clock face. She's been here, in the dullest place in the world, for forty whole minutes.

She sends another message.

Mark? Did you see my message?

Viv flicks back onto the forum.

Do we live the same life over and over again?

The first reply is: I believe it.

The second: There is a philosophical element to this. 'Those who cannot remember the past are condemned to repeat it.' That's George Santayana's *The Life of Reason*. Life teaches you the same thing over and over. If you don't learn from your past, you will live the same life, again and again.

Viv looks at the grandfather clock face again. She lets her phone hand fall against her leg.

She wanted a chance to tell Mark. For her own peace of mind, her own self-respect, her own need to let off a bit of steam with a man who thought it was apparently fine to keep their relationship on battery-saver mode, keeping it just alive enough to stop it shutting down.

But telling Mark wasn't just about herself, or about settling scores. It would have been about, finally, doing something *right*.

But he's not going to let her.

Because it doesn't matter what she wants. It doesn't matter how long she waits here, how many messages she sends.

Mark won't meet her, not even less-than-halfway – not today, not ever.

Mark isn't coming.

38

Three Months Ago
The Stag

Mark wasn't enjoying the stag weekend. Not because of the bunkhouse, with its child-sized bunk beds and insole-thin mattresses. (Mark never understood why, if all the wives and girlfriends were staying at home, the men couldn't pay an extra twenty quid for adjustable thermostats and bathrooms with doors, not cubicles.) Nor was it because Mark had a supplier crisis that Friday afternoon, meaning he was the last to arrive, leaving the only remaining bunk above Gammo and his sleep apnoea.

The worst thing wasn't the accommodation. It wasn't even the fact that Mark wasn't much of a drinker these days, finding hangovers hitting so much harder.

The worst thing about the stag do was the conversation.

Two decades after leaving school, Mark and seven old friends sat round the orangey pine table in the bunkhouse kitchen, eating the lamb bhuna Wrighty's wife had sent, along with homemade chutney and raita. Mark occasionally ate these meals and daydreamed about Jess giving up work, but, then, Jess wasn't really a raita-from-scratch kind of woman.

Mark scooped up bhuna with a piece of naan. 'Why isn't Pete here?'

'No money.' Daniel gave a meaningful look round the group. 'Jules kicked him out. He'd been having a thing with a woman at work, the fucking idiot.'

Around the table, others started gesturing emphatically with naan.

'*Stupid cunt.*'

'*How does anyone have the time?*'

'*No, how does anyone have the energy? Can you fucking imagine?*'

Mark took in the eye-rolls and shaking heads. He focused hard on his bhuna, trying not to let the thoughts enter his head, willing them, instead, to flutter peacefully around him like harmless feathers and – with any luck – land lightly, far away and out of sight.

But his thoughts didn't float like harmless feathers. Something about the vehemence of the *stupid cunt*s and the *can you fucking imagine?*s.

Mark lay in bed that night, listening to Gammo snore like an irregular motorbike: going silent then choking back to life with a soul-gasp. He pictured the incredulity in his mates' eyes as they jabbed those naans.

Being reminded Viv existed made Mark's brain fuzz like a badly tuned TV. He didn't like cross-contamination. Thoughts of Viv had no place here. Mark's job was analytics: he understood the importance of applying rules to keep data separate. He aimed to box off his own difficult thoughts, hiding the irrelevant ones from his mind's algorithms.

If, occasionally, the rules of Mark's mind's data engine got breached – *mayday* – he distracted himself until those thoughts went away.

But distractions were hard to come by in the rural middle of the Peak District with no phone signal, at 3 a.m.

It was disquieting, that Viv had been to see Jess.

Mark lay there on the insole-mattress, taking in every stop-start of Gammo's motorbike-breathing, feeling a hangover come on in real time.

The morning brought outdoor paintballing – because, when you'd been on this many stag weekends, sometimes you ran out of activity inspiration and had to start again. Hence Mark found himself in a *The Last of Us*-style apocalypse that he was at least a decade too old for, one that smelled of wet wood and drains.

He stood with Daniel, their backs to a fence, breathing heavily. There was something about waiting for zombies with guns to show up that didn't help with hangxiety.

Daniel lunged forward. '*Run!*'

The two sprinted to the abandoned ice-cream van. They crouched behind the counter and peeked through the serving hatch.

Mark's heart beat in his ears.

Daniel sat back onto a bench. 'There's one behind the taxi.' He took off his goggles, inspecting the lenses.

Mark sat next to Daniel, faint from nausea, his blood sugar low. He'd grabbed some mints from the car, but it wasn't enough. That was the other paradox about all-male trips: little planning coordination. It meant people brought enough booze to generate raging hangovers, but no one brought breakfast.

'Can you believe that about Pete?' Daniel wiped his goggles. 'Stupid twat.'

Mark surveyed the perimeter. 'I don't even know why flesh-eating zombies *need* guns.'

'How can he even be arsed?' Daniel shook his head in disbelief. 'That's before you even think … doesn't he feel bad? He had a diamond in Jules, and he knows it. Why would you cheat on a wife you really like? What kind of imbecile *is* he?'

Mark stared out of the hatch, scanning the wasteland. Where were the gun-toting zombies when you needed them?

'You're humming.'

Mark stood up, his gun slack.

'No!' Daniel tried to pull him down. 'What are you doing?'

Mark took the shot, right in the chest.

Later, Mark and his friends sat round the table in a terrifying parochial pub, one decorated by a landlord who *really* liked animals dead. Unmoving old men sat hunched on individually distanced stools, and groups of alarming young men exuded aggression. Mark deliberately hadn't gone to the bathroom, not wanting to risk being the lone gazelle separated from the pack. They clearly didn't like outsiders round here and he wouldn't put it past one of these men to start on him when he was taking a piss.

Daniel glanced at Gammo. 'So, where's Pete living now?'

'He's back at his mum's. She's fuming. She won't take his wedding picture down from next to the telly.'

Mark's other mates leaned forward.

'It makes me think less of us, you know? Men. I sometimes think the women are right. We're actual morons.'

'How are we so fucking small?'

'Why would he risk it?'

Mark straightened his beer mat. Jess complained that girls' nights' chat always ended up with catchment areas, but Mark would kill for some catchment-area chat right now.

'He's never going to be able to afford a place on his own.'

Mark's future unravelled in his mind, in one continuous, ugly carpet. Asking Dad if he could move in, seeing the disappointment on Dad's face. Eating divorced father-and-son baked potatoes in front of *Match of the Day*. Jess would get custody of their friends because she was the victim, plus she was the one who'd always put the effort in. And Mark wouldn't want to see his friends anyway because, clearly, they'd be calling him a *stupid twat*.

'Mark's humming again.' Daniel lifted his glass to Mark, as if in a toast. 'He did this at paintballing.'

Mark pushed his chair back with a jerk. 'I'm going for a piss.'

Why would he risk it?

In the fleeting moments Mark let himself remember he was having an affair, he wondered about that.

It was about Viv, of course. With her Class As and her lie-ins and her refreshing lack of financial planning, she was interesting. He'd not been single since he was twenty-two, and women like Viv – sharp, abrasive, women you had to be on your toes for – would have never been interested in him then. There was a spark to Viv, and a different kind of reality. She'd never once shown him bathroom brochures or mentioned defrosting the freezer. She'd never think less of him if he said he didn't fancy going up a ladder to unclog the gutters in this wind.

Mark thought a lot about ladders lately – about roof ladders, and mortality ladders.

Because since Mark's mum had died, he sensed himself one rung higher up. The Facebook cancer updates had started – tragically early, yes, but somehow not unthinkable. Mark didn't know who was top of the music charts anymore – did they even *have* charts? – and the last time he went to a club, a young lad wearing a woman's blouse raised his eyebrows at him in amusement. *'Alright, shirt boy, come straight from the office?'*

This was a wake-up call: Mark needed to get a grip. While technically he could still go to Burning Man, he probably wouldn't. He'd never be an astronaut, and never play right wing for City, or even a semi-professional football team. It was time to recognise he'd never do an ultramarathon, and 10Ks were fine.

There was no shame in a 10K.

Mark would end it with Viv. He'd tell Jess, make a clean

breast, and they'd start trying for a kid. On Saturday nights they'd eat Pad Thai on separate sofas in front of shiny-floor game shows. When Jess was out and the dog was asleep, Mark would treat himself to some porn – the nostalgic kind, no spitting or choking – and he'd know, while life wasn't exciting, it was fine. He'd know he was a good man, one who'd made the right choices, and not, in any way, a *small* man.

And Viv would be fine too. She didn't want shiny-floor TV shows or kids. Viv was Friday nights, not Tuesday mornings. She talked about the future, but she didn't really want this. It was just part of the dance, and part of the danger.

This weekend was a wake-up call. There would be no *stupid cunt*s for Mark. No mates jabbing their naans over his bad decisions, no father-and-son baked potatoes.

Mark would sort this. Soon.

39

Now

Viv sits with Jamie on the steps of the fire escape. 'I suppose Mark didn't try to kill me.' She makes her voice light. 'So that's something.'

Jamie doesn't answer.

'And apparently it's fifteen per cent off fridge parts today.' Viv watches the sky turn to dusk. '*Plus*, the killer didn't come and find me in the exhibition. And I was alone for ages! Perhaps—'

'Eighty-five lives, Viv.' His voice is flat. 'They killed you every single time.'

Viv slumps back against the step. 'And in those eighty-five lives were you always such an Eeyore?'

Jamie puts his fingertips to his eyelids, stretching the skin of his forehead. 'It's getting much harder.'

'A thought experiment for you.' Viv stares out over the cathedral. 'If you've tried to end a relationship but the prick stands you up, does it still count?'

Jamie jerks upright, scratching his arms. 'Can you see the bugs on me?' He sees Viv's face. He stops scratching.

'Look, take some time off. Leave this one loop to me.'

He shakes his head. 'All those chances.' His jerky energy has gone. 'And I still wasn't smart enough.'

'Oh, my God! *Jamie!*' Viv pushes him. 'Maybe I *deliberately* blocked out the last eighty-five lives. Keep going like this, I'm going to start throwing *myself* off that balcony.'

'We're just going in circles.'

'We need to *focus*. And I can't die now, can I? I've dumped Mark, sort of. I've stopped lying to you. I'm finally worth saving!'

When Jamie doesn't look up, Viv adds: 'I know I've not solved climate change or saved a village, but it's still growth.'

Below, the city streets are silent.

'You always come back at the same time.' Jamie gets a yellow disposable lighter from his pocket. 'What happens at that exact point in this day?'

Viv shakes her head. It's like he doesn't even *appreciate* her growth.

'Viv ...? What happens right before the glitch?'

Viv thinks. 'I'm staring at Mark and Jess, feeling sick because I think Jess might be pregnant. Not that he'd have cared if it was the other way round.' Viv smooths her skirt, self-soothing. 'Unless it was his baby. Now *that*'d shit him up.'

'Wind back a bit. You come up in the lift. What happens next?'

Viv is still imagining Mark's face if she broke news of a pregnancy: his leeching of colour, his collapsing face. He'd stand there, all passive panic. Viv bet she'd be the one to have to say the word *abortion*.

Jamie is waiting.

She snaps back. 'I get stressed and run through the Time exhibition. Sean waits with me by the balcony, then we walk in together.'

Jamie nods.

'Mum and I compliment each other's dresses, it's all super-polite, super-awkward, as we both try not to say the wrong thing. We both agree my grey dress is silver.'

Viv and Jamie both take in Viv's dress, as grey as a raincloud.

'You come over with a tray of Prosecco. Mum asks if you have any soft drinks instead, and you make a snide comment.'

Jamie wrinkles his forehead.

'Don't you remember?'

'It's a long time ago!'

Viv makes her voice airy. 'Rubbish not remembering, isn't it?' She smiles. 'Frank comes over and Mum tells me not to ruin everything. Sean said everyone hates him and I tell him the nurses from Alison's hospital said he was nice. He says, "That the best you can do?"'

'It *is* pretty bad.'

'Then Frank starts telling a story about Harry and a pub raffle, and Jess and Mark arrive, and that's when the world scissors. Then you come along with your tray and start shouting like a psycho.'

'Not like a psycho. Like a man under extreme stress.' Jamie thumbs the wheel of his lighter back and forth, making a metallic *scritch*. 'And I told you, I don't usually shout.'

'So you say.'

Jamie rolls the lighter wheel some more.

Scritch, scritch, scritch.

Viv holds out her palm. 'Give that over.'

'I'm struggling, Viv.' Jamie hands her the lighter. 'I normally investigate too, listen in to conversations, but I can't this time.'

Viv looks at him, takes in the obvious effort to keep his eyes open. 'Clearly.'

'So you need to step everything up from here. Provoke conversations. Fuck the future.'

Viv narrows her eyes. 'Fuck *whose* future though?'

'You need to go up to people and say *I know you killed Harry and Alison.*'

'I certainly do *not*.'

Jamie nods encouragingly, like she said *fine by me*. 'Start with the first person you see, and keep going till they kick you out.'

Viv throws the lighter up in the air in frustration. '*Fuck!*'

Viv doesn't even need to reach the roof terrace to find her first target. Sean is there on the landing, heading back from the guest smoking area.

Viv considers him. While it's not Sean, obviously, it's always best to make enemies with no allies.

She walks up, indicating the Time exhibition. 'Let's do a

tour of the museum, for old times' sake. There's a video of a pendulum, it's great.'

She sends Jamie a message.

If I die now, it's Sean.

She sends another.

Though it's not Sean.

She gets a message back immediately.

Please don't die.

Viv glances at Sean. She suspects she might be about to make him stress-eat. 'One sec.' She puts money in the vending machine by the lift and takes out a pack of Mini Cheddars. She leads Sean past the grandfather clocks.

'I've been meaning to get you alone.' Sean follows her. 'Why did you freak out on the terrace when we got here?'

Viv is about to deny it – but why? It's easier to tell the truth. 'I freaked out because Mark and Jess walked in. Mark and I have been having a thing.' She leans on the balcony, looking over. 'I've done the maths and we're not actual blood cousins, so it's not proper incest.'

'Mark? As in … *Mark*?'

'Yep. Slip-on shoes, face like a loaf of bread, dressed like he's in Huey Lewis and the News. He said he was going to leave Jess.' Viv screws up her eyes. 'I just tried to dump him, but he didn't even turn up. You having a better day than me?'

'Christ, no. I'd have more fun at my *own* memorial.'

'Yeah.' Viv pictures her own. The crowds, the tears and regrets. The hushed snippets. *We never even tried to understand her, and that makes it a double tragedy.*

'Mark, really?' Sean leans on the railing. An eyebrow hair like a single antennae twangs up his forehead. '*Mark?*'

Viv takes a breath. 'Sean, did you murder your dad?'

Sean stares. Just stares.

Around them, many clocks tick.

He puts both hands over his mouth and nose, breathing deeply. He pulls his hands away. 'Did I murder *my dad?*'

Viv holds his gaze.

'Wait.' He holds up a palm. 'Did I hear that correctly?' Sean keeps his palm up, his face inscrutable. 'No, there's no other way to take that.' He recoils from the railing. '*Have you lost your actual mind?*'

'Depends.' Viv puts her hands on her hips, taking up as much space as she can. 'Have I?'

'*Why would you even say that?*'

Viv shrinks. She puts her hand on his arm. 'I'm sorry.'

'I don't understand!'

Viv opens the bag of Mini Cheddars and holds them out. 'Nor do I.'

'I knew you were being strange today. I knew it!' Sean doesn't take the packet. 'You think I killed my dad?'

'I can explain.'

'And you think it's OK to ask that? What made you even think it?'

Viv proffers the Mini Cheddars again. 'Instinct.'

'*You think I killed my dad!*'

279

'Of course I don't. Not really.' This is so easy for *fucking Jamie*, directing her like a bloody puppet, his only job having to slap a few imaginary bugs away and bleat *I'm so tired*. 'I was just trying to see your reaction after Chrissy said something.'

Sean grabs the Mini Cheddars. There is a flash of gold on his ring finger. 'What, *exactly*, did Chrissy say?'

'That she thought someone caused your dad and Alison's accident.'

'Me?' Sean grabs a handful of Cheddars. 'Wow.'

'I never believed it!'

The silence is long. Sean chews hard.

'This is why I told Paula not to come today.' Sean grabs more Cheddars. 'Though not exactly *this*.'

'Can we forget I said anything?'

'*How?*' Sean says through a mouthful of biscuits.

Viv pats his arm. 'Yeah.'

'Chrissy thinks Dad was murdered?' Sean finishes the packet. 'Why?'

'There was a car on the scene and the driver didn't come forward. Chrissy said you got a speeding ticket.' Viv screws up her eyes. 'Giving you a perfect alibi.'

There is silence.

'Wow.' Sean screws up the empty packet and shoves it into his pocket. 'And I just told Paula my family thought I was a grifter. Where was my imagination?'

'Who's Paula?'

'Paula.' He raises his hand, showing a gold band on his finger. 'The reason I was speeding that night.'

40

One Year Ago
The Speeding Ticket

'The first ones are always late.' That's what Sean's friends had said, sharing wry looks with the wisdom of tribal elders. 'Get your hospital bag ready, sure, but you've time to make a Thermos.'

Sean hunched over the steering wheel, knuckles white. *'The liars!'*

A stationary bus indicated to pull out into Sean's lane. Sean didn't let it, raising his hand in a not-sorry apology.

His engine whined. Sean went up a gear. *Nope.* He dropped back down.

They hadn't even bought a changing mat. *'Why haven't we even bought a changing mat?'*

He glanced in the rear-view mirror.

Paula was turning over on the back seat, eyes wide with fear. She whimpered.

The sound sliced him open. 'I know.' He made himself sound as calm as he could, for a man taking a suburban Chelmsford street with the speed of a rally driver. 'We'll make it.' He gripped the wheel tighter. 'And we've got a car seat, at least.'

He glanced at the glove compartment. He had some honey-roasted cashews in there.

But even he knew this was not the time to be sourcing honey-roasted cashews.

An ambling old Toyota came into sight ahead. Sean, a lifelong atheist, closed his eyes in prayer.

He overtook the Toyota, eyes closed. The horn blared.

This was a mistake – a *massive* mistake.

Why did Sean ever think he could do this? What could he give a child, except an awful lot of information about betting on snooker and a genetic predisposition to asthma?

He shouldn't have been allowed to do this. Why did they let you just *make* a baby, without proper checks? Not even taking into account the risks of childbirth to both parties? (Sean had recently read Paula was at even more risk of complications than most: people with diabetes have bigger babies. How had he been allowed to get her pregnant without knowing that? To get her pregnant, without even doing the most basic research?)

At the side of the road, a light flashed.

He almost laughed. Like he cared about a speeding ticket *now*.

Paula made a huffing noise – like breathing, but not.

'You'll be brilliant.' He tried to sound calm, his grip sweaty on the steering wheel. She had enough to focus on, what with the panting and the turning. Sean was the support act here.

Unless he killed them all through dangerous driving. That would bump him up to *headliner*.

Paula took a huge gasp. 'Sean …'

'Nearly there.' Sean tried to smile in the rear-view mirror. 'Nearly there.'

Four hours later, everything had changed.

The universe, the world. Life itself.

In the ward, Sean smiled at Paula. 'You were brilliant.' It wasn't enough.

He sat as close as he could without being annoying – Paula had already told him to *stop looming*. He traced the tiny red fingers peeking out of a too-long baby grow.

It was incredible that Sean would sacrifice his life for this little guy, right now, and he'd only known Archie an hour. The depth of feeling was scary. What would he be willing to do once he'd known him for *a day*? 'You're amazing.'

Paula glanced up. 'Me or him?'

'Both.'

Paula's eyes fluttered.

'Here.' Sean reached for Archie. 'I've got him.' He lifted his son gently. 'Just rest. You're my hero.'

Sean studied Archie's fingernails. How could something that came from Sean be this magical?

He made himself inch his face back. Archie deserved better than Sean's coffee breath.

283

Paula's eyelids fluttered. 'Is he still perfect?'

'Still perfect.'

Paula smiled, eyes closed.

He wiggled Archie's (perfect) fingers in wonder. He kissed the top of Archie's (perfect) head, feeling his (perfect) warmth in the crook of his arm.

Sean took all of Archie in. The eyelashes. The chubby limbs. The slight scalp-crust. Never mind Jesus or the Venus de Milo – they should build statues of *this guy*.

He felt a buzz in his pocket.

He pulled out his phone and wanted to laugh. Of all people, it was his stepsister, Chrissy. A person he'd met just once. A person who had never phoned Sean, not ever, and had chosen right this second to change that.

It was a sign. Family mattered.

'Chrissy! What timing!' He felt the smile crack his cheeks. 'You'll be the first to hear my news!'

On the other end of the phone, there was silence.

The sobbing started.

41

Now

Viv steps back from the railing, trying to take it all in.

Sean hands her his phone. 'This is Paula.'

The home screen shows a picture of Sean with a wavy-haired woman in a park, both crouching by a wooden donkey on a spring, supporting a baby.

'I didn't know you had a child.'

'That's because I never told anyone. I wanted to keep my new family completely away from my old one because my old family think so little of me. Didn't that turn out to be a good decision?'

Viv keeps her gaze fiercely on the picture.

'Archie had been alive barely an hour when Chrissy rang.' Sean jerks the phone out of Viv's hand and swipes through a

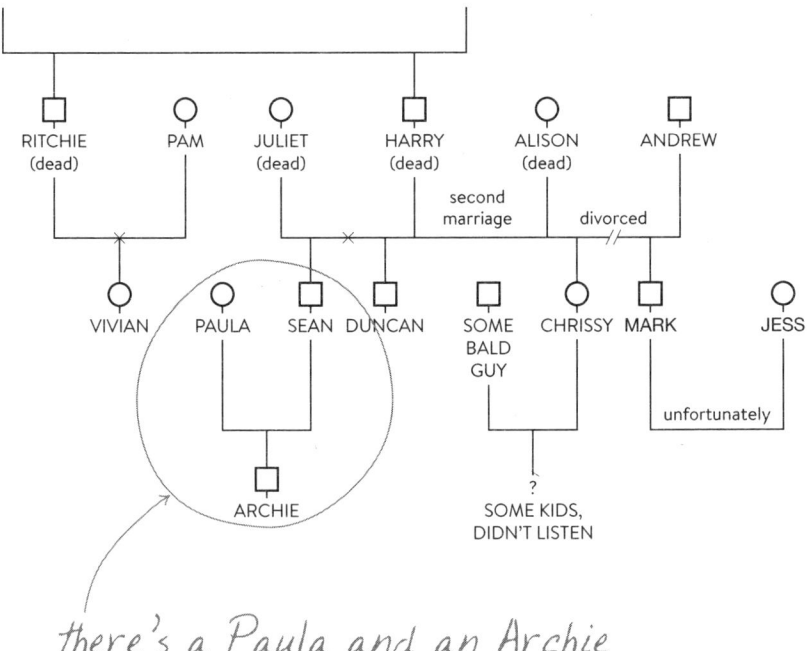

there's a Paula and an Archie

carousel of photographs. 'Here, this is his birth certificate.' He studies the photo. 'It doesn't say the time of birth. You'll just have to trust I didn't kill my dad while my wife was in labour.'

Sean makes Viv look at the screen. She looks away.

'Come on, Poirot. You need more, surely?' He swipes again, and thrusts a photo of Paula in a gown, holding a newborn in a blanket, Sean beaming next to them. 'This will be minutes before I got the news about Dad. If you click the picture, it'll tell you the time.'

Viv shakes her head.

'*Click it.*'

Viv whirls around, looking for someone, *anyone*, to push her off this balcony.

Sean clicks the photo himself. '10.55 p.m. on the first of April. No doubt I could have altered the phone's time settings, of course.' He stares at the screen. 'But if it's an alibi you want, I can find you hospital porters, midwives, nurses. That'll be about when I was watching a doctor stitch up Paula's vagina.'

Viv puts a hand on his arm and speaks quietly. 'I'm sorry.'

'I didn't even know I was getting any money until I got the solicitor's letter, if that's what you were thinking.' Sean shakes his head in astonishment. 'Dad told me he wrote me out of the will at his wedding. Have you forgotten that? You were *there*.'

Sean's expression changes. He puts his hands over his face and starts to sob.

Viv wants to rub his shaking back, but doesn't. 'Can we start again?'

He looks up in despair. '*How?*'

'You're right.' Viv loosens the grip on the balcony. 'I'll go.'

She heads back to the roof terrace and looks up at the sun, making her vision pop with painful colour, neon lights crossing over.

'Hi.'

Viv's so distracted, she doesn't even turn at Mark's voice.

'I know we need to talk.' Jess can't be on the terrace, because he's looking at Viv properly. 'But today's a particularly bad—'

Viv swats the air. 'Mark, do *you* think your mum was murdered?'

Mark's brow knits.

So *this* is how it feels to have his full attention.

'Chrissy said she once thought the crash wasn't an accident.'

Mark just stares.

A flash of gold satin streaks through the crowd towards them.

Viv makes a noise of frustration and glances back. 'What do you think when you hear me say that?' The gold streak is in touching distance. '*Quickly.*'

But Jess is there. 'This looks intense.' Her gaze is flint.

Mark takes a step back. 'Not intense.' He tinkles the coins in his pocket softly. 'Not at all.'

Viv glances from one to another. 'I'm not gonna lie, it was *a bit* intense.'

More tinkling coins. '*She* approached me.'

Viv stares at Mark, not delighted by the tone of that *she*. *She* is the woman on the tram muttering to herself and holding a can of Red Stripe. *She* is the person who wears flipflops to the park in December and waves her fist at the pigeons.

Mark blinks excessively. 'It's not what you think, Jess.'

Viv takes him in, any remnants of affection for him draining. There's something fundamentally unsexy about watching a man panic-blink at his wife.

Jamie is right: Mark *does* look like a slice of bread.

Mark's expression as he looks at Jess is pleading. 'Viv says Chrissy thinks Mum was murdered.'

Viv stands taller, placing her hands on her hips in a power pose. This is how it's going to be today. The more humiliating things get, the more powerfully Viv's going to stand. By the end of the day, she'll be a towering sweetcorn giant, shading houses from the sun, biting watermelons like apples.

Jess turns to Mark. 'I'll handle this.'

Mark takes a second and hurries into the building. Viv frowns.

'Really, Viv?' Jess turns to Viv. *'Really?'*

Viv refreshes her power stance. She gives a small nod.

'If we have to talk about Chrissy's mental blip, we can't do it here.' Jess's voice is low with anger. *'Inside.'*

'What?' Viv blinks. 'You *knew?*'

42

Two Months Ago
'We Need to Talk'

The sentence *we need to talk* had always caused Jess anxiety. It never ended with ... *because you've won a holiday!*

It always ended with the other kind of information. *There's water coming through the fitting. The gearbox needs replacing. A buyer's pulled out down the chain.* From an ex-boyfriend on one particularly life-changing occasion, after paying the suppliers for the wedding in full: *I don't want this anymore.*

Jess read Chrissy's *we need to talk* message at her station in the salon, with five minutes between clients.

She replied carefully.

I'm working till six. All good?

I'll call you at six.

Jess was apprehensive about that call all day. Last week, Chrissy had fed her daughter marshmallows instead of a meal. She'd walked to the shops in no coat or tights when there was snow on the ground. She'd spontaneously broken into gulping tears in a café when 'Both Sides Now' by Joni Mitchell came on the radio.

No. Jess was pretty sure things were not *all good*.

At 5.59 p.m., Jess's phone started flashing.

She tucked it under her ear and flicked all the salon lights off, leaving only the gloam of the emergency lights. 'I'm just locking up.'

'Mum was murdered.'

Jess stopped reaching for her coat.

'Mum and Harry's car accident. Sean caused it. I *know it*, Jess.'

Jess switched the lights on again. She sat.

'Jess? Did you hear me?'

Jess rotated her chair, walking her feet slowly to the left. She looked through the glass to the black damp of the street.

'*Jess?*'

'I'll just ring Mark and tell him I'll be late back.'

You didn't just marry the man, you married the family. This was what they meant by *for better, for worse*, Jess thought, walking from the salon to the car, listening to Chrissy's torrent of 'evidence', batting the words back with the rationalisations which, if Chrissy had been in a normal state of mind, would have been fucking obvious.

People don't murder people in real life.

The police don't think it's anything but an accident.

Why Sean? You barely know him.

If it's not nonsense, why are you whispering?

Jess had called it: no good ever came from the phrase *we need to talk.*

'And I can prove it!' Chrissy hadn't sounded this sure of herself since the time Jess phoned for advice about food processors.

'Prove it *how?*'

'They take photos, don't they, when people are caught speeding? How do we get hold of the photos?'

Jess sat on the bonnet of her car. 'We don't.'

'Someone needs to get set up at a temp agency, apply for jobs at the DVLA. I'll arrange a memorial party, make him feel guilty, smoke him out. Then—'

'*Chrissy.*'

Chrissy went quiet.

'This is not OK.' Jess fiddled in her bag for her car keys. 'Have you spoken to anyone about this?'

'You're not listening!'

'I'm listening, I promise. I'll keep listening.' Jess stared up at the black insects dotting the glass of the streetlamp above. 'But you have to promise to never say any of this to anyone.'

An hour later, Jess let herself into the house. Bonnie danced around in the usual frenzy, her four spaniel feet going like oscillating floor mops, greeting Jess as if she'd returned from a five-year tour of military duty.

Jess threw her keys into the bowl. 'Your sister can *talk*.'
She let Bonnie dance around her until she wore herself out.
'She's struggling.' Jess took in the glass of wine on the coffee
table. 'Really? On a Tuesday?'

Mark stared at his glass. 'We're all struggling.'

Jess took in his puffy eyes. 'OK.' They'd had several rows
lately in which Mark had implied Jess needed to 'lighten up'.
Jess hadn't appreciated the implication she was a killjoy, just
for pointing out he'd left the milk on the side.

'We need to talk.'

Jess sank slowly onto the sofa. 'Please, God, no.'

Twice in one day? If she just ran away, could she make
this stop?

Mark stared at his glass. 'I've done something bad, Jess.'

Jess frowned, too exhausted for this. Bonnie had all four
paws to the floor now. Jess scratched behind Bonnie's ears,
making her back leg twitch vigorously.

'I slept with someone else.'

Jess stopped scratching.

Mark tipped down the rest of his wine.

Jess walked out of the room.

Mark left it several minutes before padding up the stairs to
find Jess.

'It was grief. The madness of grief.'

Jess sat on the bed, her knees pulled to her chest, the heat
of her breath bouncing back onto her face. 'When my mum
died, I did a marathon for charity.'

'I wasn't in my right mind.'

'Who?'

'You don't know her.'

'But she's not a killjoy, I guess?'

Mark placed his hands on Jess's knees.

Jess pushed his hands off. '*Who?*'

'Nobody.'

'How many times did it happen?'

'I've told her it will never happen again.'

She raised her head slowly. 'You told *me* I was the only one you ever wanted.'

Mark's face crumpled. Disgust made Jess's eyes narrow. 'No. You don't get to be the one to fall apart here. Why have you told me? Were you about to get found out?'

'I didn't want this hanging over us.'

'Right.' Jess stood. 'Fuck you.'

Mark blinked at her.

'Did telling me help with your conscience? You feel better now?'

Jess shoved him out of the way and shut herself in the bathroom.

Mark left it a few more cowardly/sensible minutes before his voice came softly through the bathroom door. 'Are you saying I shouldn't have told you?'

Jess leaned against the other side of the door, legs out on the tiles. 'I'm saying you shouldn't have *slept with her.*'

There was a scuffle of paws behind. Bonnie whined.

Jess unbolted the door and let Bonnie into the room before locking it again. She stayed in that bathroom for two hours, stroking the dog, sitting bones growing numb from the cold tiles.

How quickly her life had exploded.

Everything was different now – in both her future and her past. All Jess's memories of the last decade, everything she knew about their wedding, of their holidays, their *life*, now carried a disclaimer, like those posts on social media. *This source is unreliable.*

Jess could see a different future, the images kaleidoscoping fast and hard. The friends' head-tilts. The *for sale* sign sticking out of her daffodil patch. The grey-suited solicitors and tiny rooms in shared houses. The letter reminding her that business rates on the salon go up in April. The *swipe-swipe-ghost* of Tinder.

Jess got up and opened the bathroom door.

Mark scrambled up from sitting on the carpet.

Jess held up a palm. 'No closer.'

'Please tell me I haven't ruined everything.'

Jess looked him up and down. 'The only way we might get through this is if you tell me *everything*.'

He reached for her.

She shook her head. 'I said *might*.'

At how pathetically grateful he looked, she tasted bile. He was a different man now. Before this, he was a man who couldn't fit a dog-flap, a man who was crap at washing up, a man who had never bought insurance, who walked past his own Post-it reminders on the kitchen table – but those faults were tolerable. They came within the package of a decent man.

But that was before.

'Tell me everything, right now, or it's over.' Jess felt a tiny flicker of the person she had been.

Mark looked terrified. 'I don't think it will help.'

'Maybe not. But in case it's not clear,' Jess wrapped her arms round herself, 'I'm going to have to see *all* the messages.'

43

Now

Viv follows Jess into the building.

'When Chrissy said her mum and Harry were murdered, she wasn't well.' Jess folds her arms over her slippery dress. 'She knows that now. I just hope to *God* Sean hasn't heard.'

Viv looks down at her boots, face warming.

'There was nothing dodgy about the accident, the police knew that. Chrissy was just looking for someone to blame. You know she even wanted to sue the hospital for negligence?' Jess shakes her head. 'Alison was braindead at the crash with huge internal injuries. She was on a ventilator. What did Chrissy think the hospital were meant to do?' She hardens her gaze. 'Don't repeat what Chrissy said to anyone.'

Viv finds her voice. 'I won't.'

'Especially not Sean.'

Viv swallows. 'Goes without saying.'

Jess turns to walk away. 'He'd be so hurt.'

'Absolutely.' Viv watches Jess walk away. 'I'm truly sorry. I regret a lot of things, Jess.'

Jess pauses. She looks like she's going to say something, but keeps walking.

A gunmetal cloud sits over the city, shading the fire escape. The air is tight, pressing in like the start of a tension headache.

Next to Viv on the step, Jamie is motionless. 'So what you're saying is Sean isn't the one.'

Viv is about to say *and I told you that all along* but, at the look on his face, doesn't. She's growing today, and that's a good thing, maybe. As long as she doesn't start doing mad shit, like jigsaws, or meditating.

'And the police say Harry and Alison weren't murdered.' Jamie sounds broken.

The tall building ahead fires a thin red laser from its roof, like a tiny bat signal.

Jamie's still talking. 'Not a single person wants you here—'

'That's blunt.'

'—and everyone at this party hates you *so much*—'

'Not *so much*, not *everyone* – there are degrees.'

'—but none of them want you dead.'

Viv's heart flickers. 'So maybe I'm not going to be killed this time?'

'Eighty-sixth time lucky?' Jamie slams his hand into the wall. 'FUCK!'

Viv grabs his hand. 'Don't.'

'We've got *nothing.*'

A pigeon flies down and lands on the platform, pecking at the tarmac. They both watch it, unspeaking.

Jamie's head lolls.

'Hey.' She nudges him. 'You're falling asleep, mate.'

He doesn't react, so she shoves him – hard.

He flicks his eyes open. 'I can't do this anymore, Viv.'

'I know.' Viv stands. 'Let's get you somewhere safe.'

Viv gets her jacket from the cloakroom. She helps Jamie to the *History of Technology* section, down to a patch of floor obscured by the display headed *Cables.*

'No one will ever come here,' Viv folds the jacket into a makeshift pillow.

Jamie closes his eyes. 'If you call me, I'll leap up.'

'I reckon you're safe here.' Viv tucks the jacket/pillow under his head. 'Worst-case scenario, some kid draws a cock and balls on your forehead.'

'The museum's closing now anyway.' Jamie's voice is slow, slurring.

'Really? It's just the party guests in the building?'

There's no answer. Somehow, Jamie's already asleep.

Viv folds his arms across his chest, but he looks like a vampire, so she re-lays them flat by his side. She watches his breathing lengthen. It's comforting – until it isn't.

Without Jamie, she's completely on her own in a world with new rules she doesn't understand.

'Jamie,' she whispers.

He doesn't answer.

A bit louder. 'Jamie.'

She looks down at her trembling hands.

She shakes herself off, hard, like a dog after a rain shower. She runs back up to the roof terrace as fast as she can, only slowing when she reaches the top.

Viv would rather be in the bosom of her hostile family than be alone in a broken universe.

By now, there are fewer people milling on the terrace. The guests who remain sit mainly on sofas, with sleeves rolled up and party shoes cast aside. Make-up is patchy, melted by sweat.

Viv puts her arms round herself in a one-woman hug.

Until today, she's aimed low: just tried to get through every day without anyone confiscating her pharmaceuticals, without kicking any underdogs, without getting anything poky or stingy in the eye.

And *now* ...?

If this is her last viable life to solve this, if Jamie can't help her from here, she can't just keep going up to people and accusing them of murder. What if she ends up saving herself against all the odds? Having accused everyone she knows of murder would surely be an obstacle to any kind of future.

'Viv?'

Duncan wheels in front of her, his face a question. There is a faint pink patch on his crown where he has caught the sun. 'Are things ... all right?'

'Why wouldn't they be?'

'You're shaking.'

'As if.' Viv clamps her arms by her sides. 'It's just been a long day.'

'So it appears.' Duncan's attention is steady. 'And yet we haven't spoken at all.'

Viv studies him. 'The museum's closed. Want to sneak down and look round, for old times' sake?'

She expects him to say *that's against the rules.* To her surprise, he says, 'Let's go.'

Duncan and Viv sit next to each other in the museum's 3D cinema, wearing the glasses provided. On the screen ahead, the track falls away in front of the rollercoaster.

Duncan stares at the screen. 'I get the sense you're having a bad day.'

Viv watches the track loop. Her stomach lifts. 'Don't be nice to me.'

He doesn't look. 'Why not?'

'Oh, come on! You're *that guy*.' The rollercoaster chug-chugs its way to another crest, tipping over with a whine. 'Mum's pad-of-news-by-the-phone guy. *The university are holding a dinner in Duncan's honour. Duncan has a Norwegian princess in his tutorial group.*'

On screen, passengers scream as the rollercoaster roars down. Viv's stomach lurches, easily manipulated.

'Interesting. The meal wasn't actually in my honour. And she was a Swedish princess, though she dropped out after a term.' Duncan's voice is even. 'I'm your *that guy*?'

'And Sean's.'

'Interesting,' Duncan says again. 'I've got a *that guy* too.

301

He's called Simon Bostock. I don't know how in God's name he has time to churn out so many papers – and he's barely required to submit changes!' He shakes his head. 'Infuriating.'

'Every time they talk about you, it's like, *this is what you could have been.*'

'I'm sure they don't think like that.'

'They call me Amy Winehouse.'

Duncan has the decency to look away. 'Do they?'

'In the WhatsApp group you're definitely in.'

The rollercoaster slows to a halt. Viv and Duncan leave the cinema.

'Credit where credit's due. I hear you're doing better now.' Duncan slots his glasses back in the holster at the exit. 'You've got a proper job and everything.'

Viv thinks of her upcoming disciplinary and says nothing.

'And Sean's sorted his life out too. His little lad looked adorable when he showed me the picture.' Duncan indicates a sign to the World of Mathematics. 'Shall we?'

Motion sensors flick the lights on as they walk through. Duncan stops at a display case with an old book inside: *Polygraphic paper coder/decoder by D'Montfort.* He sees her looking. 'It's a cipher machine.'

'Don't *educate* me, Duncan.' Viv leans against the wall, pushing her nicotine patch more firmly into her shoulder. *Is this thing on?*

'Surely there's *some* branch of science that interests you as an adult?'

Viv stops banging her shoulder into the wall. She raises her head. 'Do you know anything about quantum theory?'

'My area is applied mathematics. Quantum theory is more what you'd understand to be physics.'

Viv takes a step closer. 'But you do know something?'

'It's the study of matter and energy. On the atomic or subatomic levels.'

Viv nods, like she's following. 'And that includes time?'

'Of course.' He indicates the display cases. 'Anything you want to see through there?'

'No way.' Viv's heart beats distractingly quickly, like she's on hour twenty of a hangover. 'How does it work when time is broken?'

Duncan moves on to the next case, looking at an object like a misshapen piano. 'Are you questioning the hypothesis of time as a linear constant?'

Viv clenches her jaw. She doesn't know how to reply to that.

'You're asking if there are alternatives to the block universe idea?'

'Maybe?'

'There's the concept of multiverses, of course.' He wheels towards the next case. 'You'll have seen *Doctor Who*.'

Viv follows him. 'Never.'

He stops wheeling. '*How?*'

'Busy.'

That gets him. He takes a second to process this. 'Marvel, then. You'll have seen Marvel films. There's the concept there are different versions of us, living different lives, across multiple universes.'

'You believe it?'

'Not exactly. I don't *not* believe it. You can't prove a

negative hypothesis.' Duncan indicates a sign for the Robotics exhibition. 'Shall we take a tiny peek?'

Viv shakes her head and makes for the lift. 'If time can repeat, would it repeat for the same version of a person?' She presses the lift button. 'Or would there be other versions lined up and ready, like chocolate bars in a vending machine?'

Duncan has the gall to smile.

'Don't be proud of me! Duncan, *listen*! If there can be different versions of us' – she sends spittle flying with agitation – 'how do we know we're the main one? *Stop smiling!*'

'I've never heard you curious about science before.'

She follows him out of the lift at the top. '*Wait!*'

Duncan pauses, hands on his rims.

'Duncan.' Viv makes her voice firm, indicating the vending machine where she got the Mini Cheddars for Sean. 'Are we chocolate bars in one of these or not?'

His smile flickers. 'What's up, Viv?'

Her throat closes with emotion. 'I just want to know if I'm real.'

He looks wary. 'Define *real*.'

'How can I know that *I*' – Viv thumps her chest – '*this* one, standing here in this museum, right now – how can I know I'm the main Viv?'

He doesn't answer. The air has changed. Something about her curiosity has moved from *wonderful* to *alarming*.

She thinks fast. 'I had a bad trip once. Got me mulling.'

His shoulders relax. This, of course, makes sense. 'Then why not look at the situation from a different way up?' He wheels towards the ramp to the roof. 'Even if we're to assume time works in a linear fashion, there are eight billion people on this earth, each with their own consciousness.' He glances up. 'We're making assumptions there, of course, about the nature of individuality and ...'

Viv holds up her palm.

He sees her face. 'Let's take that as a given. Eight billion of us and we're only *real* to ourselves. The only inner world we all have access to is our own. You think *I* think you're the planet's main character, Viv? What about the other eight billion people, and the just over a hundred billion who came before? You are a speck of consciousness in a limitless ocean, and that's before we even get onto the idea there might be multiple timelines.'

Viv puts her hand on the banister, dizzy.

'Fascinating, isn't it?'

'I can't believe you can come up with that off the top of your head.'

'I've had practice.'

'Maybe we should have spent more time together.' Viv turns back to Duncan. 'I blame your mum. And that flute,' she adds, as an afterthought.

'I know you don't like me, Viv.' Duncan stops at the ramp. 'But I never thought you were that bad. I always looked up to you, and Sean too.'

'He's not that bad either.'

'I agree.'

'He visited Alison in hospital.'

Duncan raises his eyebrows. 'I didn't know that.'

'Did you visit her?'

Duncan shakes his head.

'Yet you knew her so much better than Sean did. Why didn't you visit?'

Duncan rubs his fingers and thumbs against each other.

'*And* you left Alison's funeral early.' Viv considers him. 'You didn't want to be there.'

He looks wholly uncomfortable.

'You didn't like Alison.'

'Not true.'

'Is it because you think the relationship started before your mum died?'

Duncan doesn't wheel immediately away, so it's something.

'Duncan?'

'I don't know when it started. Don't make me think about that, please.'

Viv frowns. 'But Harry wouldn't have an affair. He wasn't the type.'

Duncan is looking at her strangely.

'What?'

'It's just ...' Duncan shakes his head. 'How do you forget the stuff you don't want to know? Viv, don't you *remember*?'

44

Twenty-Two Years Ago
The Summer Viv was Fourteen

Viv had done something bad. Something worse than usual, something bad enough for Viv to have to spend the whole summer holidays at their house.

One afternoon, when Duncan was making jam tarts in the kitchen and Viv was there *again*, he turned to Mum. 'You'd trust me alone in the house at fourteen, wouldn't you?'

'Apples and oranges.' Mum ruffled his hair affectionately. 'How many cars have you stolen, my lovely boy?'

Duncan reflected on this conversation as he watched Viv mooch around – '*I'm bored shitless!*'

He reflected as he watched her punch herself in the leg, just to see if she bruised.

He reflected as he saw her sniffing at a permanent marker

– hopefully, then angrily, finally throwing it across the room.

And he thought about the word he'd recently learned – *nemesis*.

Bad things happened to Viv all the time. Because she was her own nemesis.

When the bad things happened, you just needed to follow the breadcrumb trail through the forest, right back to the start, to find Viv in a clearing, the only person for miles, and the one holding the loaf.

One sticky afternoon, the three cousins sat in the garage facing the dartboard Dad had set up low on a patch of brick wall. Sean and Viv sat on the bench Dad had adjusted with bricks, making it the same height as Duncan's wheelchair.

Sean threw a dart, aiming for a double nineteen, but hit a single three instead.

His next dart didn't even make the board, just bounced off the edge onto the ground.

Duncan knew it was because Dad had put the board so low. 'Sorry.' He always over-apologised if adjustments inconvenienced other people.

Sean ran his hand through his hair. 'Don't say sorry.' Since the start of summer, he'd been wearing his hair long, darkening it into crispy pieces with gel. What with that and his wispy fluff-moustache, Sean looked like a baby pirate, and not in a good way. 'I can't throw straight today.'

Duncan beamed. 'You don't ever throw straight.'

Sean turned to Duncan, jaw set.

'And neither do I.' Duncan reached for his darts. 'We all throw in a parabolic curve.'

Dad had been walking past the open garage door. He stopped and leaned on his garden rake. 'Say that again, son.'

Duncan looked up. 'Parabolic curve?'

Dad looked from Duncan to Sean to Viv, joyous. 'He's bloody Einstein!'

Viv looked quickly away. She never liked to look at Dad when he was gardening. He'd cut an old pair of jeans into shorts, and Viv said he'd cut them *way* too close to the crotch.

Sean stood. 'Let's go for a swim.'

Duncan looked down at his darts.

Viv glanced at Duncan. 'Not swimming, Sean. Something else. Raps?'

Duncan sighed. He'd once seen Sean and Viv's knuckles after they'd been playing raps, red-raw and sometimes even bleeding, and said to Mum and Dad, '*Why do they do such stupid things?*' Dad had looked up sharply. '*They're not stupid. They just play in different ways.*'

'OK,' Duncan said. 'Raps.'

Sean dropped the darts on the workbench. 'I'll get the cards.'

Duncan waited for Sean with Viv at the table in the back garden, watching Mum hang up washing.

A fly buzzed up the bottom of Duncan's jeans. He pulled on the material at his knee, letting the fly out.

Viv frowned. 'Show me those socks.'

Duncan lifted his jeans higher.

On the left foot: *Never trust an atom.* On the right foot: *They make up everything.*

'That you, Juliet?' Viv looked up at Mum, who was hanging out washing. 'From the science museum? You know you shouldn't buy him these things.'

Mum took the pegs out of her mouth. 'He likes them.'

'Weren't you ever a kid?'

'What a question!' Mum pegged a sheet to the line. 'You think I got hatched at forty, Vivian?'

Viv paused. 'I'm starting to, yes.'

'They're his favourites.'

'My second favourites,' Duncan said.

'He's got some special socks from the market he's going to wear for his recital.' Mum beamed at Duncan. 'They've got flutes on them.'

Duncan beamed back.

Viv raised her head. 'Recital?'

'Mr Cole says Duncan can play in assembly in the first week of term.'

Viv didn't react immediately. Duncan wasn't sure she'd heard.

'NO!' Viv slammed her hands on the table. 'You can't let him play the flute in assembly! The kids will rip him to pieces!'

Mum frowned. 'They won't.' She turned to smile at Duncan. 'They'll be really impressed.'

Duncan nodded.

Viv jerked her head towards the kitchen. 'Juliet.' She stood. 'A word.'

Duncan watched Viv go inside with Mum, feeling his smile wobble.

It was true kids could be mean, but surely not about something as cool as a flute recital?

Still, Viv was defending him – admittedly, from the wrong way up – but she wanted good things for Duncan. Viv was his older cousin, complete with ear piercings, a hand tattoo and cigarettes – all things that were clearly stupid, but also great. Duncan had recently looked up the word for thinking two things at once, and found the expression *cognitive dissonance*, which was surprisingly pleasing. He liked both the concept and the sound of the hiss.

Come to think of it, Viv had also told him to never say the words *cognitive dissonance* in school.

He watched her argue with Mum through the kitchen window, getting more irate on Duncan's behalf. She shook her head and stormed away, further into the house.

Viv didn't know everything. If she did, she wouldn't have to spend her whole summer here after doing something worse than stealing a car.

Duncan went to find Dad. Dad would know if a flute recital was a good thing.

He found him in the garage, hunched over the cordless phone.

Dad's voice was quiet. 'You can't call me at home.'

Duncan stopped.

'I told you.' Dad sounded harsh, like when he found Viv shaving her legs with his razor. 'Never, ever call me at home.'

Dad clicked the phone off. He looked up and saw Duncan.

He took a second. 'Someone selling insurance.' He gave Duncan a tight smile.

Duncan nodded slowly.

Dad stood. He ruffled Duncan's hair. 'Good lad.'

Duncan watched Dad walk round the side of the house. Viv was standing by the front door.

Duncan swallowed. 'Did you hear that?'

Viv nodded.

'He said it was someone selling insurance.'

Viv put her unlit cigarette back in her bag. 'Then that's who it was.'

'It sounded like—'

'Someone selling insurance,' Viv said firmly.

Duncan held her gaze. Did she believe that? Or was she saying that for him?

Sean threw the garage door open. 'I've found the cards!' He mimed scraping the pack along his fingers. 'Time for rappity-raps!'

Duncan looked down at his knuckles – at the perfect, vulnerable flesh – and sighed.

He wheeled himself slowly after Viv and Sean, trying to convince himself Viv was right, that he hadn't heard what he thought he'd just heard.

45

Now

Viv walks up the ramp, reeling. 'I don't remember that day.'

Duncan wheels next to her, saying nothing.

'No, no, you must have imagined it. Harry was ...'

She wants to say *perfect*, but she's not a child.

'We'll never know.' Duncan's voice is even. 'Change the subject?'

They reach the terrace.

'Anyway.' Viv rubs her pricked-up arm hairs. 'Did you listen to me about not doing the flute recital?'

Duncan shakes his head. 'Still get called *Mr Tumnus* when I go in the local to this day.'

Viv pats his shoulder.

'The kids used to bleat when I passed them in the corridor.

Viv' – he turns – 'what you just said, you've got it wrong. I never hated Alison.'

Viv looks out across the city, taking in the Victorian railway arches. 'Then why didn't you visit her in hospital?'

'Why would I? She wasn't awake. It wasn't my place.'

'Why leave her funeral early?'

'I'd been willing her to die, Viv! And when she did, honestly, I felt so much relief. Then the guilt I felt was huge. The whole situation caused me so much cognitive dissonance.'

Viv raises her top lip in distaste.

'What?'

'Still at it with the cognitive dissonance.'

'I'd just seen all the same people at Dad's funeral, and I was there to celebrate the life of the woman I'd been wanting to die. I couldn't take all the feelings. I just wanted to get out of there.'

'We all wanted Alison put out of her misery. If it had been a different universe, and the car crash had gone differently, if she hadn't been braindead—'

Duncan holds up his hand. 'Viv, I know you've got a thing about multiple universes right now, but remember that was just a bad trip.'

Viv pauses. 'Of course.'

'I didn't like how I felt at that funeral. I didn't like who I was.' Duncan pauses. 'Never felt like that? Like you just want to shut your brain down, get away from your thoughts?'

Viv sniffs. 'Never.' She pats Duncan's shoulder. 'Though if you ever feel like that again, I recommend narcotics.'

Duncan gives a faint smile. He wheels to the bar.

Sean walks past.

Viv grabs his sleeve. 'I'm sorry. I'm sorry, I'm sorry, I'm sorry.'

Sean shakes her off.

'I've just been saying nice things about you to Duncan.'

'I'm not going to forgive you, Viv. Ever.'

'Me and Duncan were talking about alternative universes.' Viv brushes something from her dress. 'Can you please imagine we're in an alternative one where I didn't just accuse you of murder?'

Sean shakes his head.

Mark walks past them, adjusting his cuffs, not looking at her. He quickly engages in a conversation with his dad.

Viv watches him go.

Infinite Marks, with infinite wives, in infinite universes.

All cunts.

There's a flicker across Sean's expression. 'You really went there? *Mark?* Why?'

Viv shrugs. 'Bored.'

'Seriously.'

'Because I thought he was someone else. Because I thought *I* was someone else.'

'Is that why you were talking to Duncan about alternative universes?'

'Maybe. You know, Duncan's all right, in adulthood. At least he didn't bring his flute.'

Sean almost smiles. He's softening – she can feel it. Reading a room is one of Viv's best life skills.

She pretends she hasn't noticed. 'I was asking Duncan

315

whether he believed there were multiple versions of us in different universes.'

'Does he?'

'Not sure. He said something about not being able to prove a negative hypothesis.'

Sean sniffs. 'Viv, you *think* you want to be mates with Duncan, but I've had thirty years of this. And I'm not as smart as him, but if you want to know whether we live multiple lives, this is it, Viv. This is the only one we've got.'

Viv looks at her feet.

'So, if you're making a shit job of yours, do better. I'm sorry.' He turns for the door. 'I don't want to talk to you anymore.'

Viv watches him go inside. She looks around.

She's learned today that she will put up with any amount of hostility over being alone.

Though ... there's one thing she's still not faced.

She searches the crowd, and there he is. Frank. Standing apart from the rest of the crowd, looking down, concertinaing his neck, giving himself extra chins.

The hairs on Viv's arms stand up.

He looks so unmenacing today: a plasticine-nosed, late-middle-aged clown-man, his bright shirt flecked with red spots. He's dabbing his shirt with a tissue, apparently having jostled lager on himself.

But he must hate her more than anyone.

If Viv really admits it to herself, this can be the only way today has been leading.

She thinks about the diazepam in her handbag but – no, she's going to do this, properly. White-knuckle it, without the warm embrace of pharmaceuticals.

316

She walks up. 'Frank. I know it's you. It's always been you. I know you're the one who wants to kill me.'

46

Twenty-Two Years Ago
The Summer Viv Was Fourteen

Long before Frank broke Mum's heart, he'd been their neighbour, wafting in and out like a farmyard smell: mildly annoying initially, but hard to ignore, until one day you thought, *am I expected to put up with this shit forever?*

Frank had been there at Dad's funeral, comforting Mum by the fruit machine, while Viv stood in her party dress with the itchy Peter Pan collar and her bottle of warm Coca-Cola.

He'd been there the summer after Dad died, putting together a swing for Viv, patting the seat hopefully – *'come on, darlin'* – hoping now Viv had a swing, she wouldn't notice she didn't have a dad.

He'd been there when Viv was eleven, lingering at the

doorway to drop off a plant cutting, making Mum way too smiley and appreciative for what was, actually, just a couple of leaves in a jam jar.

And now Viv was fourteen, and Frank had been living with them for four months – first, by not quite going home, and then by not ever going home. His toothbrush arrived, followed by his work shirts, his screwdrivers, his whisky collection.

Everything changed.

He moved where they kept the Sellotape. He moved where they kept the kitchen roll.

He put too many coats on the hooks in the hall, so Viv couldn't always hook hers up properly, and it slithered off into a heap.

He left Mum *I love you* notes by the kettle. He pinched her bum while she was cooking.

He woke Viv up with a morning *hack hack hack* cough like he was bringing up his insides.

He took ages in the bathroom, just when Viv needed it, then opened the door and wafted out *evil*. Viv learned to wee fast, without breathing in.

She got a break from him at school, when Frank was at his job at the council, but he always came back eventually, bringing his noises and smells with him.

He was there when they ate. He was there when they slept. He was there when Viv needed Tampax.

And he was always, *always* watching TV.

One evening, Viv sat on the sofa. Frank had decided to move the reclining chair closer to the TV, blocking some of the screen with his big back, even though that chair had been fine at the edge of the room for Viv's whole life.

Frank was watching the news, so Viv was watching too. To make the point – this was her TV, not his.

On screen, the newsreader looked serious. *'As a precaution, the World Health Organization advises against all travel to SARS-affected countries ...'*

Idly, Viv picked up Mum's glasses case. She stretched open the spring-loaded jaws and let the case snap shut on her knuckles. It hurt, but only for a second.

She did it again. And again.

Just when she was about to give up the whole thing, Frank jerked round. 'Stop it.'

Viv held his gaze. She pulled the jaws of the case back, snapping it on her knuckles again. *Ow.*

'Viv' – Frank's voice was low, dangerous – 'don't make me come over.'

Mum glanced up.

Frank caught her eye. 'She'll damage your glasses!'

'I'm wearing my glasses.'

'She'll damage the case!'

Viv stretched the jaws of the case open, poising theatrically.

'Viv.' Mum's voice was quiet.

'Other countries affected by the potentially fatal illness include Vietnam, Singapore, Canada and Thailand ...'

Viv stared at the back of Frank's head.

She snapped the case.

Frank jerked round, like the noise was a gunshot.

Mum turned to Viv. 'Why are you doing that anyway? It looks painful.'

Viv looked at her knuckles. The skin was glowing red. She *really* didn't feel like doing it again.

She did anyway.

Frank sprang to his feet and stomped over. Viv held the case out of reach.

'Don't, Frank.' Mum stood. 'Viv, give me that.'

Viv let Mum take the case.

Mum pocketed it and turned to Frank. 'Let's go in the kitchen.'

Later, at bedtime, Mum closed Viv's door. 'You could be nicer to him, you know.' Her voice was quiet.

Viv pulled back the duvet. '*He* could be nicer to *me*.'

'Go easy. He doesn't have any practice with kids.'

Viv pulled her duvet up to her chin.

'You don't have to like him all the time, just please stop poking him. For me.'

Viv turned the bedside light out. 'I liked living here so much better when it was just us.'

Mum's silhouette was still. 'I know.'

Two days later, Frank stormed into the lounge and threw his keys and phone down on the coffee table. 'I heard she stole Harry's car!' he shouted.

Mum wasn't even in the room.

'I didn't *steal* it.' Viv's heart beat faster. She pretended to keep watching *The Simpsons*. 'Harry's keys were right there.'

She turned up the volume.

Frank switched the TV off at the wall. 'If I was your uncle, I'd press charges.'

'Frank!' Mum entered, pulling her apron off. 'A word.'

He strode out of the room, Mum following.

Viv switched the TV back on.

'She's turning into a little psychopath!'

Viv turned the volume up.

'Are you happy bringing up a car thief? She needs to be in a borstal.'

'Can we please talk about this later.'

'She's a nightmare! I can't take this anymore!'

Viv heard the back door slam. There was no more noise from the kitchen.

She didn't know what a *borstal* was, but she got the general idea.

She looked at the table, where Frank had left his keys and work phone. She picked the phone up and turned it over. She glanced at the kitchen door.

She sent the message to every one of the two hundred people in Frank's contacts list.

I'm a fourteen-year-old girl and Frank abuses me.

That night, Viv won.

Kind of.

If you didn't count Frank's tears, *Mum's* tears, the grounding, Harry coming over, the police arriving, and all the feelings.

But there would be no more *get your boots off the coffee table, lady*. No more *you said you'd be back by nine, your mother's been going frantic*.

Viv had won. She'd beaten him.

Within a day, Frank was gone.

47

Now

Viv stares at Frank. 'I know you're the one who wants to kill me.'

Frank stops dabbing his shirt. He raises his head. 'Sorry?' He wasn't concentrating.

Viv shifts her weight between her feet. Ideally she wouldn't have to repeat this stuff. 'I said I know you want to kill me.'

Frank stares. She has put him into some kind of shock-trance.

After everything she's done to him, Viv *still* has the capacity to surprise.

'And fair's fair, almost?' Viv raises her palms. 'It's a little over-the-top to hold a grudge for so long, but I know how bad it was.' She steps forward. 'I'm deeply sorry.'

Frank breaks from his trance. He whirls around. '*Pam!*'

'Please.' Viv's eyes flare. 'Don't.'

'Pam!'

'I'm *saying* I'm deeply sorry. I'm *saying* I understand.' Viv pauses. 'Please don't get my mum.'

'*Pam!*'

Mum ambles over, adjusting her necklace. 'Where's the fire?'

Frank raises a shaky finger – in the Salem witness box, accusing Goody Slade. 'Viv's just said ...'

Mum looks from Frank to Viv.

Viv stands straighter. 'I just made a bad joke.'

Frank shakes his head. 'Angela said this would happen.'

'Angela said *this* would happen?' Viv barks.

Mum looks at Viv. She looks at Frank. She looks back at Viv. 'What exactly did you say?'

Viv holds her gaze. 'I apologised for the phone thing.'

Mum makes a whirr in her throat.

'And' – Frank's finger is up again, still accusing Goody Slade – 'she said I'm trying to kill her!'

Viv turns to Mum. 'I said he *wants* to kill me. Plus, he's missing the nuance. This is a very context-specific situation.'

'Are you *high*?' Mum's voice climbs. 'Have you come to this party *high*?'

From the left, there's an exclamation.

'Viv! You *liar*!' Chrissy is there in a furious rush of coral and feathers. 'What have you been saying about Mum's car accident?'

Mum puts her hand over her mouth. She makes an involuntary, not-totally-human squeak.

Viv can't look at Mum right now. 'I just said something to Mark. In passing.'

'*In passing?*' Chrissy stumbles into a hanging basket. 'You tell people I think Mum was murdered *in passing?*'

Viv looks at her feet. 'I know you told me that in confidence. Sorry.'

'I never told you that *at all.*'

Viv takes a moment. 'Of course.' She's getting her lives crossed. 'Let me rephrase.' She tries to work out whether *nuance* and *context-specific* would be more helpful the second time round.

Chrissy untangles her fascinator feathers from the ivy in the hanging basket. 'You know, nobody actually wanted you here today.'

Viv tsks. '*Of course* I know that.'

'And yet here you are.'

'Yes.' What does Chrissy want from her? 'Here I am.'

Chrissy wrenches herself away from the ivy. 'I'm getting security.'

Jess strides up. 'No, leave it.' She links her arm through Chrissy's. 'She's not worth it.'

Chrissy lets herself be dragged away. 'Why would Viv *say* that?'

'Don't give her a second thought,' Jess replies. 'No one else does.'

'Exactly, Chrissy!' Viv raises her voice. 'I'm a piece of shit! Everyone knows it!'

Jess puts an arm around Chrissy and escorts her inside.

Viv sinks into a seat, her vision blurring. Out of the corner of her eye, she sees Duncan heading over.

She holds up her hand. 'Don't be nice again. I can't take it.'

'I won't.'

Still, he doesn't go away.

'I want one of those different universes.' Viv knows she sounds broken. 'I don't mean the same one again and again, I mean a fresh one. One that's nice and clean and sparkling new, one I haven't ruined.' She looks up. 'How do I jump to one of those?'

Duncan gives a faint smile.

'You're not *that* smart then.'

'We can all change, Viv.'

She rubs the space between her eyes. 'What a tedious response.'

'Sean's a different man now he's responsible for Archie.'

Viv looks up. 'How can you tell?'

Duncan shrugs. 'Maybe I'm projecting. But I think I'm right.'

'I think you're right too.' Viv studies Duncan. 'Have you met Archie?'

'No, but Sean showed me a picture last year. We met for coffee shortly after the accident.'

'An emotional support coffee?'

Duncan frowns. 'Not quite. I had to tell Sean he was still in the will.'

There's a prickle of cold on Viv's neck.

Sean told Viv he found out he was still in the will *from a solicitor.*

'You told Sean he was in the will' – she holds his gaze – 'but only *after* your dad died?'

'Of course.' He frowns deeper. 'Viv, what are you—'

But Viv is already moving. 'I need to go.'

In the *History of Technology* exhibition, Viv's coat is still there, still folded in a pillow shape behind the *Cables* display.

Jamie is not.

She spins round. '*Jamie?*' Her voice echoes round the empty museum.

How hard can it be to find a sleepy man?

She calls his number. There's no answer.

'Jamie, where the fuck are you?' Viv says into the voicemail.

There's a soft noise: the slow trundle of wheels across a hard floor.

Viv runs towards it.

A woman wheeling a cleaning cart comes out from behind a display of old computers, her curly hair sticking out of a top-of-the-head scrunchie.

'There was a man there.' Viv waves towards the *Cables* display. 'Asleep.'

'He wasn't asleep, hon, he'd collapsed.' The woman leans on her cart. 'I didn't know what to do!'

Viv's stomach is liquid. 'So, what *did* you do?'

'What *could* I do?'

Viv clenches her hands, waiting.

'I got Brent.' The woman moves her mop out of her way, resting her forearms on the cart. 'Brent was so angry that the man was asleep on the job, and then the man started resisting, and—'

'*And?*' Viv's voice is a bark.

'Brent told him he was sacked. Probably. Not definitely.'

'And?'

The cleaner takes an affronted few seconds.

'And we got Ralph from security.'

Viv runs up to the security desk.

The guard has his feet up on the desk, sipping from a can of Irn-Bru. *Strictly Come Dancing* plays on a propped-up tablet in front of him. For a second, Viv is distracted by his huge feet. 'Where did the sleepy waiter go?'

The guard pauses the screen. 'I put him in a taxi home.'

Viv hurries into the Space exhibition, past a replica moon buggy.

'Party guests are meant to stay on the roof!' the guard shouts after her.

Viv dials Jamie's number. She gets voicemail again. 'Jamie, pick up, I'm going nuts.' She watches a lit-up replica earth rotate, its continents turning from light to dark. 'Duncan said he told Sean about inheriting Harry's money face-to-face, but Sean said he found out from a solicitor's letter. Why would one of them lie?'

Viv glances back at the security desk. The guard is getting up.

'What's even the point? It doesn't even change anything. If Sean killed his dad for the money, what use was learning he was inheriting *after* the accident? What's that about, Jamie? What the fuck's that about?'

There's the sound of large footsteps. 'You can't be here.'

'Can you tell me Jamie's address?'

The man shakes his head.

Viv mentally remaps the taxi journey she took to Jamie's

home, hours before. The back streets, the Green Quarter, a Bargain Booze. A grey apartment block next to an overflowing bin.

'I'm a friend. I've been to his flat. He's got a broken microwave, and a cat that's not his cat.' Viv holds the security guard's gaze. 'I *definitely* didn't just meet him today.'

'What's Jamie's surname?'

Viv flicks to the contacts app in her phone.

Jamie (Time Loop).

Viv looks up. 'I forgot.'

'You have to go back up to the roof.' The security guard folds his arms. 'Or else you have to leave.'

Viv gets out of the lift at the top to find Duncan waiting for her.

'Why did you ask me about wills?' He wheels forward. 'What are you implying?'

Viv stares at the vein on his forehead. 'I don't know.'

'I told Sean. He's looking for you downstairs. Viv—'

Viv pushes open the nearest door. It's a staff room and, in the centre of the table, someone has abandoned a meal. Buds of broccoli in congealed gravy peek out from under a discarded napkin.

'Chrissy said something mad earlier.' Viv lets the weighted door swing shut after Duncan and sits. 'That she once thought your dad's accident was murder.'

It's a long minute before Duncan reacts.

'Chrissy is irrational.' He doesn't take his gaze from Viv's face. 'I have tried to be patient. I know she's grieving. I let this strange memorial go ahead against my better judgement. But when she says upsetting things or starts talking about the negligence of hardworking people, I lose sympathy.'

'Hardworking people?'

'Chrissy wanted to sue the hospital. She thought Alison's care wasn't adequate. But the truth is, even before the seizure caused cardiac arrest, Alison's chances of any kind of recovery were precisely zero.'

It's hard to hold Duncan's gaze. 'Why didn't you tell Sean about the will on the phone?'

'Would you tell someone something that delicate over the phone?'

'But why was it delicate? He was inheriting money.'

Duncan shakes his head. 'This is nothing to do with you, Viv.'

'Please, Duncan.' Viv sits forward, shoving the tray of discarded food away. 'Tell me what was delicate, then I promise I'll leave you alone.'

'And leave the party?'

Viv nods. 'And leave the party.'

48

One Year Ago
The Halfway Café

Duncan had just told Sean he was still in Dad's will. He looked from the margarine-yellow café walls to the plastic display of elderly doughnuts on the counter, taking in the sweating icing.

This service station café felt like an apt venue for the bleakest conversation in the world.

'*Money*. Actual *money*.' Sean sat back. 'We'll be able to buy a proper home.' He made his voice fierce. 'But I never would have wanted it like this.'

Sean reached for the doughnut.

'Sean.' Duncan picked up the sugar sachet again. 'There's

something else.' He twisted the sachet. 'A complication with Dad's will.'

Slowly, Sean raised his head.

'A technicality.' Duncan crunched the sachet again. 'It probably won't be relevant.' He worked the paper between his fingers. 'Dad left everything to Alison in the first instance.'

Sean put the doughnut down. 'But Alison's going to die,' he said slowly.

'Yes.' Duncan dropped the sachet. 'But if Alison survives Dad by thirty days, then, technically, it will be the terms of her will that count, not Dad's.'

The silence stretched.

'You mean' – Sean was barely audible – 'if she doesn't die in the next two weeks, Dad's money will go to them, not us?'

Duncan nodded. All these years, everyone said he was the smart brother, but Sean got this so much more quickly than he had. It had taken several minutes of the solicitor's *to all intents and purposes*-s and *if we consider this clause*-s for Duncan to catch up.

But, then, the solicitor was on an hourly rate.

'But it's Dad's money!' Confusion made Sean's expression glassy. 'And Mark and Chrissy are fine! Compared to us. Me, anyway. They don't even need it!'

Duncan stared fiercely at the service station car park.

'Dad and Alison were *both* in that car accident! They've *both* died, in every way that matters!'

Duncan reached for his emotional support sachet. 'I know.'

'And you're telling me money that should be going

332

to *Archie*, his chance at a decent future, could be going to people who don't need it just because of a stupid technicality?'

Duncan looked up. 'Archie?'

'Dad wouldn't have wanted that.'

Duncan moved the sugar crystals between his fingers.

'They've both got houses. Mark's car's got heated seats and Chrissy's got an Apple watch.' Sean took a breath. 'She told me she's got a multi-temperature-controlled wine fridge, and she barely drinks!'

Duncan stared at the sachet.

'Do Mark and Chrissy know?'

'I doubt it.'

'But—'

The waitress approached. 'Another coffee?'

They both shook their heads and waited for the waitress to walk away.

Duncan looked at Sean. 'Who's Archie?'

'My son. He's two weeks old. The one I can't buy a home for.'

Duncan blinked, about to ask more, but Sean spoke first. '*How* ill is Alison exactly?'

'Dying.'

'You know what I mean.' Sean sniffed. 'Imagine I'm the most selfish bastard in the world.'

Duncan shook his head. 'Days. Weeks at most.'

Sean let out a long breath.

'I know,' Duncan said.

'And now I'm hoping the woman Dad loved will hurry up and die quickly. Like this isn't messed up enough.' Sean pushed back his chair. 'I need the toilet. Your halfway website didn't plan for traffic.'

Duncan watched his brother cross the café.

He'd thought the will would be some comfort to Sean. Duncan believed in *the truth, the whole truth, and nothing but the truth*. Sharing this information was only fair.

Except nothing about this whole thing was fair.

Telling Sean was a misstep. Duncan shouldn't have told Sean he *might* inherit, he should have waited until he had a definite answer.

Duncan had to face it. He might have an IQ of a hundred and forty.

But sometimes his judgement was wrong.

49

Now

In the museum staff room, Duncan and Viv are silent. The only sound is the faint ticking of the wall clock.

'The point ended up being moot, as expected.' Duncan holds his voice steady. If Viv doesn't focus on his undertone, she can pretend he doesn't hate her. 'Alison died twenty-eight days after Dad did, so the clause wasn't invoked.'

'That's why you felt so guilty at Alison's funeral. It was different for you than it was for the rest of us. You were *willing* her to die.'

'I wanted Alison to be out of pain, like everyone. But, yes, knowing there was also a selfish element made me feel uncomfortable.' He puts his hands on the rims of his wheels. 'Don't come back to the party, Viv. You're not welcome.' He manoeuvres to the door. 'I can safely say it will be better for everyone when this day is over.'

Viv gets up to open the door. 'Amen.'

She sinks back into the seat.

She dials Jamie's number.

'It's Sean.' The ticking clock blurs in her vision as she leaves a voicemail. 'I don't know why he's killing me, but he killed Alison. He needed her to die within thirty days, or Alison's family would get Harry's money. That's why Sean drove three hours from Essex to go and see Alison in hospital. He did something to give her a seizure.'

Viv stares at the second hand of the clock. *Tick, tick, tick.*

'I still don't get what that's got to do with me.'

Tick, tick, tick.

'I can't do this alone, Jamie. Where are you?'

Viv clicks the phone off. Slowly, she stands up.

The blonde police officer keeps her face neutral, studying Viv across the table in the interview room. 'Let me see if I've got this right.' She glances at her colleague. 'You suspect this man of wanting to throw you off a balcony.'

'Or push me into traffic. Or poison me with nuts.'

'And this man has done nothing to indicate he wants to kill you.'

Viv shifts under the woman's scrutiny. She nods.

'And you don't know why he would.'

Viv gives a long sigh.

'Plus you've been drinking.' The woman looks at her notes. 'Since 3 p.m.'

'*I know!*' Viv jumps up. 'I *know* how it sounds!'

336

The blonde police officer raises her eyebrows.

The police officer with the half-forehead fringe leans forward. 'You seem anxious.' Her eyes are small and wide set. 'Do you have a history of anxiety?'

'Of course I fucking do. Don't you? But, also, I'm fine.' Viv puts her hands on the table, her attempts at calm failing. 'And you *have to listen*!'

At the looming Viv, the half-fringe police officer leans back. 'When is the last time you took a controlled substance?'

Viv sits back down. She straightens her hair on her cheeks. 'You're missing the point entirely.'

The two officers glance at each other.

'Which is that Sean murdered Alison.'

'Alison.' The blonde one looks at her notes. 'The mother-in-law.'

'Yes.'

'What was her cause of death?'

Viv pauses. 'Car accident. But don't look into that, it wasn't suspicious. Sean killed her after the accident. Why else would he visit her in the hospital? He'd only met her once and he lived at the other end of the country!'

'How did he kill her in hospital?'

'He did something to give her a seizure, messed with her blood or something.'

The blonde officer looks at the other. 'Messed ... with her blood?'

'I don't know, I'm not a doctor!' *This day.*

The blonde checks her notes. 'And has this man, this *Sean*, ever said anything threatening to you? Been physically aggressive?'

'It's not what he's done.' Viv shuffles onto the lip of her chair. 'It's what he's *going* to do.'

'And you say he killed her for money.'

Viv nods, hard.

'Do you think he's after your money too?'

Viv laughs. The sound is too loud; too long. 'No.'

'Then why does he want to kill you?'

'*I don't know!*' She grips the table. 'But he lied, which must mean he killed her, and now I'm being killed too, so it has to be him! And actually, I'd really appreciate it if you could work out how he caused the seizure, because you're the experts. And can you also explain why he didn't kill me when we spent all that time together before the glitch? I'm not smart enough for this.'

The blonde woman glances at her colleague. 'The glitch?'

Viv pauses. 'Ignore that bit.'

The half-fringe woman leans forward. 'You're ... being killed?'

'Ignore that too. Let's concentrate on Alison.'

The quiet in the room is audible.

Viv takes in the looks on their faces. 'You're not even going to *try* to help.'

The blonde police officer makes her voice gentle. 'No, we're definitely going to try to help you.'

Viv stands. 'Don't bother.'

She pulls her phone from her bag, catching the tissue twist of diazepam.

The tissue hits the floor. Two small pills bounce out.

Viv and the two police officers watch the pills bounce softly in parallel journeys, coming to stop next to a dust ball.

338

The officers look at each other. They look at the pills.

Viv nods. 'Thank you for your time.' She knew it was a long shot, but she had to try.

The blonde woman gets up. She crouches for a pill.

Viv hurries out and into the waiting taxi. 'Drive. *Now!*'

In the back of the taxi, Viv leaves Jamie another voicemail.

'This is why everyone hates the police.' She takes in the glossy billboards flanking the flyover. 'At the end of the day, they're just jumped-up Stasis.' Even a silent Jamie makes Viv feel less alone. 'I know what you think, but I'm not going to kill him.'

The taxi driver makes eye contact with Viv in the rear-view mirror.

Viv pauses. 'One sec.' She leans forward. 'This partition isn't soundproof?'

'Not unless I press the button.'

'I wasn't being literal.'

The driver looks back at the road. He indicates to change lanes.

'Can you press the button now, please.'

The driver does.

Viv sits back, raising her phone again. 'It's like the police don't *want* to help.' She stares at a glossy advert for apartments with a young couple laughing in a place no one could afford. 'I'm not killing him, Jamie. You can't make me.'

Viv leaves a moment. Jamie's voicemail doesn't argue.

'And how can I even be sure it's him? He had a great opportunity to kill me before the glitch, but he didn't.'

Viv watches road signs fly by. Thinking.

339

'Which must mean something happened at the glitch,' she says carefully, testing the thought. 'Something that made him want to kill me.'

They turn off the flyover. The taxi drives more slowly into the city and Viv takes in the buildings around.

She taps the driver's screen. 'Can you drop me at that corner shop, please?'

Five minutes later, Viv sits by the canal, smoothing down the first page of her fresh pad. She takes the lid off her new biro and writes a heading:

The Glitch – Rewind.

50

The Glitch - Rewind

I go into the museum.

I meet Sean in the gift shop. 'You touch it, you buy it.'

He is surprised to see me. 'They *do* know you're coming?'

We have small talk about science museum merchandise.

Sean says he put money behind the bar. 'My dad's money. Obviously.'

We go up in the lift and see Chrissy. 'We can't be first. We'll ruin her day.'

We go into The Wonders of Time.

We lean over the railing and see my mum down below. 'Dad was so happy working here.'

Sean doesn't even show a hint of wanting to push me off the balcony.

We greet Chrissy, coral feathers and all.

We walk onto the roof garden. I hang up my jacket.

My anxiety spikes. 'What does a person have to do to get a drink round here?'

Mum tells me I'm wearing the wrong dress. 'Grey is an unusual choice of colour.'

We both agree my dress is silver.

Frank comes up. 'Sean, did your father ever tell you about the pub's pool tournament lock-in?'

Mum inches her face closer. 'Well done for remembering about today.'

Despair. 'Why is Chrissy doing this? *Really?*'

Sean is scornful. 'She thought the whole thing was too messy last year, because Dad and Alison died a month apart.'

Sean comments as Angela rearranges her handbag. 'An insulin pen? I didn't know Angela was diabetic.'

Sean isn't in any of the photos. 'THAT'S MY ARM!'

I try to help. 'Outside of the family, people think you're great … That nurse at Alison's funeral said they all liked you at the hospital.'

Mark and Jess step onto the roof terrace.

The world scissors.

I stagger forward.

Sean keeps talking. 'The nurses only liked me because I brushed Alison's hair.'

I keep staggering.

Sean notices. 'Viv, what the fuck is wrong?'

I don't answer.

I run away.

★

We talked about Sean inheriting money from his dad's will.

We talked about Harry and Alison dying a month apart.

I told Sean the nurses liked him at the hospital.

I went strange. I wouldn't speak to Sean, and I ran away.

Sean noticed I went strange.

Sean thought I'd just put all those facts together.

Sean thought I'd worked out he killed Alison.

51

Now

Viv swings her legs back and forth, agitated, knocking her heels against the fountain surround. 'Sean didn't try to push me before we went into the party because that was *before* the conversation about wills and nurses!' Viv raises her voice to be heard over the running water. '*Before* he thought I'd worked it out!'

The two young spaniel people nod, smiling, their leaflets held to their chests.

Viv swigs from her bottle of supermarket vodka. 'And he didn't try to push me when we were alone on the balcony again this time, because I was accusing him of the wrong murder!' She wipes her mouth. 'He realised I didn't know after all!'

The spaniel people's smiles falter.

'And that should be a good thing! Except now Duncan's told Sean I've been asking people the right fucking questions after all, so I'm in danger again.' Viv swings her legs more violently. 'Why do I have to ruin everything, every time? *Why?*'

She offers the young people her bottle. They both shake their heads.

It's hit Viv today, quite how bad she is at being alone. 'What would you do, if you were me?'

The round-faced woman beams. 'I'd trust in the Lord.'

'Thanks.' Viv takes another swig. 'Not massively helpful, but still better than the police.'

Spray mists Viv's back. She shuffles forward on the fountain and pulls her dress away from her shoulders.

The young woman looks to the man. 'We have to go soon. We need to bake for church tomorrow.'

'You guys really earn your money, don't you?'

'We don't get paid,' the woman says.

'Wow.' Viv puts her bottle down. 'You two are *adorable.*' She looks at the man. 'Make sure you get some moisturiser on that nose; it'll peel.'

The man touches his nose self-consciously.

Viv picks up her bottle. 'And fucking Jamie's not even here to save me!'

The woman smiles. 'Jesus will save you.'

'I know. Thanks. But he's not answering his phone!' Viv pauses. 'Jamie. One sec.'

Viv dials Jamie's number again. It goes to voicemail.

Viv lets her hand fall into her lap. 'I'm completely alone.'

The woman puts her hand on Viv's arm. 'You're never alone.'

Viv holds up one finger, in case the woman's about to bang on about there being only one set of footsteps in the sand. 'Jamie thinks I should kill Sean. But I shouldn't. Should I?'

The woman's smile falters.

'I'm not going to kill anyone, obviously,' Viv says quickly. 'But what can I do? I could let this life end and start again, but what if Jamie hasn't picked up his messages? Then we won't know what I've learned!' The young people are perfect listeners: supportive, friendly, not actually *listening*. 'And what if Jamie's too sleepy to tell me next time? We could get stuck forever.' Viv rests her bottle against her leg. 'As far as I can see, there's only one option.'

The young people wait.

'And it's hideous.'

Darkness is falling, the sky turning the colour of grapes. 'Thanks for listening.' She pushes herself down from the fountain. 'Take care.'

'The Lord will take care of us all,' the woman says.

Viv turns. 'Does that mean you two don't have pensions either?'

The woman shakes her head.

'You know' – Viv raises her bottle in a goodbye – 'I'm starting to really like you guys.' She plucks at the mist-soaked back of her dress and heads towards the homeless tents.

She holds out the vodka to a man sitting cross-legged in an unzipped doorway. 'Any good without the lid?'

The man nods. He takes the bottle.

'Cool. Enjoy.'

Viv plucks at the soaked back of her dress, presses the nicotine patch firmly in and, reluctantly, turns towards the museum.

It's getting late, and the roof terrace is emptier still. The remaining guests sprawl on sofas, drinking spirits, while others are pulling on their coats. The panoramic view looks different in the dark: the glass apartments no longer gleam, the façades opaque and scattered with lights.

Across the terrace, Chrissy hugs Angela goodbye.

Viv marches over. 'Today *can't* be over! Chrissy!'

A waiter leans past Viv for an empty champagne flute.

Viv widens her eyes. 'No! Stop tidying!'

The waiter takes the smallest of pauses. She puts the glass on her tray.

'I'm sure you're resourceful enough to find drinks else-where, Viv.' Angela side-eyes Chrissy. 'Even if they won't be free.'

'Today can't end *yet*!' Viv grabs Chrissy's arm. 'Let's celebrate your mum and Harry with an afterparty!'

'Afterparty? Oh, no, Chrissy, love!' A woman in a palm print walks up. 'I've got the long drive back to Buxton.'

Chrissy holds Viv's gaze. 'So I'm going to keep saying goodbye to other guests.'

'Bye, Viv.' Angela doesn't even bother to hide the curl of her lip. 'It's been a delight.'

'Come on, Angela! Angie. *Ange*.' Viv grips both of Angela's hands. 'It's ages since we caught up! Don't you want to hear about my upcoming disciplinary!'

347

Angela raises her palms.

'It's gross misconduct.'

Angela turns to go.

Viv swallows. *'Please.'*

Angela and Chrissy walk away.

'Viv.'

Viv starts. Mark is standing next to her.

'Chrissy really *did* say that, didn't she?' He jiggles the change in his pocket. 'She said she thought Mum was murdered?'

Viv looks past him. A woman in flamingo is leaving. Frank is leaving. The woman in the palm print is getting out her car keys, ready for her long drive back to Buxton.

'EVERYONE!' A band of tension closes round Viv's chest. 'PLEASE STOP LEAVING!'

Mark takes a deep breath. 'Viv …'

Viv looks past him. 'Oh, God, even *Mum* is leaving!'

'What's going on?'

'I don't have time for this now!'

Mark frowns.

Viv considers him. Those Angry Bird eyebrows. The long eyelashes, framing dark eyes she could never read. 'Did you ever mean to leave Jess? When you said it, did *you* believe you?'

Mark is still.

'Actually, I don't care. But if *Craig from work* gets one more late-night message, he's gonna forward it straight to your wife.'

Mark's Adam's apple bobs. 'I'll call you.'

Viv swipes the air with irritation. 'No! Don't call me!'

She hurries away.

348

Mum walks up, her best grey jacket hooked over her shoulders. 'Why would Mark call you?'

Viv shakes her head.

People are leaving.

She's not *ready*.

'Viv.' Duncan wheels up, his face clouded. 'I can't tell you how disappointed I am to see you back here.'

'Sorry.'

'After I asked you to leave.'

'I did leave. I came back.'

Duncan takes a moment. 'Please leave properly.'

Around, the terrace is emptying. The window of possibility is shrinking by the second. Viv makes a throat-noise of frustration.

Duncan wheels closer. 'Viv—'

Angela is looking for something in her handbag, pulling out a card wallet, a phone, then the orange tube Viv saw her with earlier. Viv stares. She hadn't known what that orange tube was at the time, but Sean did. *An insulin pen? I didn't know Angela was diabetic.*

Sean had recognised that pen, from way across the room. Does that mean he knows someone who injects themselves?

Does that mean he has access to insulin?

Because Viv has watched enough true crime documentaries to know health professionals murder patients by injecting insulin into IV bags.

And Viv knows. She *knows*.

She claps her hands. 'Everyone, listen!' She steps onto a chair, then a table. She glances down at Angela. 'Can you ching your glass?'

Angela shakes her head.

'Fine.' Viv smooths her skirt. 'I've got people's attention.'

Chrissy looks on, her look of distaste unmissable.

Mark has his eyebrows hunched, jangling change in visibly moving pockets.

Mum has that sorrowful expression Viv knows so well, like she thought they'd reached the bottom of the barrel, only to find it was a false bottom, and Viv is getting out her scraper.

Viv looks for Sean. The muttering starts.

'What's she doing? Is she drunk?'

'Is that Pam's daughter?'

'I think that's the table with the dodgy leg.'

That comment catches Viv's attention. She looks down.

'Viv!' Chrissy waves an angry arm. 'Get off that table, right now!'

'Two secs.' Viv spots Sean near the cloakroom. 'Sean! Stay there!' She addresses the crowd. 'Hi, everyone. I have a quick announcement.' She points. 'Sean's trying to kill me.'

The muttering stops.

'I'm hoping he won't manage it, but just in case he does.' Viv looks from one startled face to another. 'If I die of anything but natural causes, then Sean did it. Sean,' Viv points again, 'by the planter. New suit, good shoes. Long eyebrow hair like an antenna. *Sean.*'

'She's drunk.'

'No, not drunk.' Viv can't identify the speaker. 'I'm just wobbling because it's a wobbly table. And I don't expect anyone to believe me, but consider this speech my insurance. If I fall off a building, or go under a bus, or eat peanuts without my EpiPen, then remember it was Sean.' She points at him. '*Sean* Sean.'

The audience is silent.

'Good.' Viv scratches her cheek. 'That was the first thing.' She focuses on a planter and makes herself say it. 'Second thing is, we need to exhume Alison.'

Chrissy spins to the barman. 'Phone security!'

The barman puts the phone down. 'Already on their way.'

'Frank.' Angela strides over. 'Help me do a citizen's arrest.'

A voice came from somewhere. 'Wasn't Alison cremated?'

Viv takes a second. 'Shit.'

'You're psychotic.' Angela grabs Viv's arm and starts pulling. 'Actually psychotic.'

The security guard from downstairs strides through the crowd.

Viv looks around the crowd in desperation. 'Sean killed Alison because if she didn't die quickly enough, she'd inherit Harry's money! He knows what an insulin pen looks like! He injected her with an overdose, that's why he went to the hospital! Why would he visit her otherwise?'

She whirls around, looking for Duncan. The faces blur.

'Duncan!' She finds him. 'It's because of Paula and Archie. That's why he did it. *You* know. *You* know what they mean to him.' Duncan flinches. He is still.

Chrissy strides towards her. 'Get out of my memorial, Viv.'

'Sean killed her!' Viv widens her eyes. 'He felt guilty, look at him! He's a stress eater, look how much he's eaten today! That's why he stress-ate all the mini burgers at her funeral!' She turns to Duncan again. '*Duncan!*'

But Duncan is just staring at her, unfocused, looking through her.

The security guard is getting closer. Viv holds up her palms in surrender. 'Don't worry, I'm done.' She gets off the table.

But Chrissy is frowning at Sean.

Viv feels a blip of hope. 'Chrissy ...'

'*Sean* was the one who ate all the burgers at Mum's funeral?' Chrissy's voice is a bark.

Viv glances around, uncertain. The security guard twists her arm up her back.

Chrissy's gaze on Sean is as cold as when she looks at Viv. 'You were the one who took all the buns off and left them in a heap?'

'He didn't want the carbs – *ow!*' Viv glares at the guard. 'Too rough! I'm not resisting, look!'

She turns back to Chrissy, but Chrissy is ignoring her. 'Sean, did you take off all my carefully handmade brioche buns and dump them in a pile, so no one got to enjoy my mini burgers?' Her voice climbs. 'At my own mother's funeral?'

Sean says nothing, just blinks.

There are tuts in the crowd. Mutters.

'*Selfish.*'

'*That's really disappointing, Sean.*'

'*If your father could see you now.*'

'*And* he said the buns weren't fresh!' Viv shouts over her shoulder as she lets herself be scuttled towards the doors. A lie, admittedly, but Viv is going to hammer a nail into Sean's coffin.

352

'Not fresh?' Chrissy shouts, outraged. 'They were perfect! I made them that morning! While I was *grieving*!'

The mutters of disgust grow louder.

Viv glances at Duncan. He still hasn't moved from the spot, staring at Sean, his face unreadable.

The last words Viv hears as the security guard wrestles her off the terrace is Chrissy saying, 'And you can throw Sean out next, please. I never want to see either of them again.'

52

Eleven Months Ago
After the Last-But-One Funeral

On the Monday evening of Harry's funeral, Viv sat on a stool next to Bethan, the disco synths of Donna Summer's 'I Feel Love' pumping across the empty bar.

From the other side of the bar, Rob looked at Bethan and back to Viv. 'You don't think we should turn it down?'

Viv shook her head. She pushed her empty gin glass towards Rob.

He looked at Bethan again.

'Don't look at *her*.' Viv raised her voice. *'I'm* the one who asked for a drink.'

Rob turned the music down anyway. 'No one wants full volume Donna Summer after work on a Monday.'

'Unless they've been at a funeral,' Viv said stubbornly. 'Turn it up, please. For Harry.'

'It isn't for Harry. It's for you.' Bethan patted Viv's knee. 'And you're not dead.'

'But now I can hear my own thoughts!'

Viv pictured her extended family as she walked into that crematorium. A sea of people, all keeping their faces to the front, all hoping Viv wouldn't choose to sit at their pew.

Including Mark.

Especially Mark.

'We can celebrate Harry at a normal volume.' Rob looked about to say something else. 'I was about to say *it's what he would have wanted.* But obviously I never met him.'

'Clearly. He would have wanted it loud.'

'He would have wanted a struggling bar owner to suffer, all because his niece scared away the few people who like a drink at 5 p.m. on a Monday?'

'I'll drink enough to make up for them.'

'Look, Viv,' Bethan turned to her. 'I know it's been a horrible day.'

'Harry's the only one who liked me.'

'That's not true,' Bethan said.

Viv stared at her glass. 'Maybe Alison liked me a little. Briefly. But only because Harry did.'

'*We* like you,' Bethan said.

Viv pushed her empty glass away.

Rob got the bottle of gin from the shelf. He filled a fresh glass with ice.

'I Feel Love' ended and 'Super Freak' kicked in.

'Harry liked this one.' Viv glanced up at Rob. 'Now you *have* to turn it up.'

Bethan stirred her drink with a straw. 'The thing about family is they'll always be there for you in the end.'

'But what if they're not?' Viv stared at her glass. 'What if, when you need them most, you look round and they're not there?'

Rob put a fresh drink in front of Viv. He held a moment of eye contact with Bethan.

He turned up the volume again.

Viv nodded with satisfaction as the baseline of 'Super Freak' filled the bar. She moved the stool with her hips, twisting it along to the beat. She reached for her drink.

The drink and the music flooded in over her thoughts, pushing them into stasis until morning, at least.

53

Now

The taxi crawls along the narrow street of the Green Quarter. The driver slowly turns to Viv.

'Not this one.' She peers out of the back window. 'It had a bin outside.'

The driver holds her gaze in the rear-view mirror. 'A grey apartment block.' He speaks slowly. 'With a bin outside.'

'Exactly.' Viv pretends not to understand sarcasm. 'Maybe it's on the next street.'

The taxi driver sets off again. 'It's your coin.'

Viv smiles. 'Not a problem.' She stops smiling. Sean has no incentive to murder her now he knows she isn't believed: there's a good chance she might actually survive this loop.

She taps the plastic window. 'Actually, money *is* a problem, so I'll tip double if we find it before the meter hits twenty quid.'

Ten minutes later, Viv recognises a bin and gets out of the cab. She looks at the panel of buzzers next to the door, and presses the one at the bottom right, the opposite one than people would usually go for. For an arsehole, Viv is scrupulously fair.

There's a rustle and a click.

'Hi!' She makes her voice bright. 'I'm here to see Jamie.' She still doesn't know his surname. 'Hair like a hoover brush, hole in his shoe. Can you let—'

The rustling stops.

'Twat.' Viv presses the last-but-one buzzer.

A few minutes and lots of hang-ups later, Viv tailgates a Deliveroo cyclist up four flights of stairs. She knocks on the door she hopes is Jamie's and a man opens it wearing jogging pants. It's the man from the rollercoaster photo.

'*Imran!*' She wants to hug him. 'You look taller in the flesh.'

Imran narrows his eyes.

Viv looks down, taking herself in. A stranger, in an elegant grey dress and old boots.

'Jamie's here, right?' Viv feels her smile fade. 'You wouldn't have kicked out a sleepy man?'

'Who even are you?'

'Viv. I need to talk to Jamie.'

'He's asleep.'

'I know.' Viv steps towards Imran. 'He'll want me to wake him up.'

Imran doesn't move. 'He's never mentioned a Viv.'

'I only became important to him today.' Viv takes in Imran's expression. 'He brought me here and I can prove it. You've got a broken microwave door. You've got a photo of the two on you on a rollercoaster. You've got a cat that's not your cat, one Jamie has a weird codependent relationship with.'

'Jamie hates that cat.'

'Not today. Today he likes the smell of warm dust and Dreamies. I can prove we're friends.' Viv pulls her phone out of her bag. 'He gave me his phone number.'

She flicks to her contacts, shielding part of the screen from Imran, so he can't see she has Jamie's surname as *Time Loop*. 'He'd want you to let me in. We're bonded. He saved my life today.'

Standing in the doorway, arms folded, Imran looks too solid to barge past. He's lean, with visible arm muscles and ropey bits of vein.

She gives up. 'Can you tell him to call Viv when he wakes up?'

Imran nods.

Viv turns to go – and stops. 'He told me he's sad about your sister's birthday.' She turns back. 'He really wishes he'd gone last night. He said it was a wake-up call, and now he knows what really matters. He's going to apologise to Farah.'

Imran is quiet.

'*Now* can I come in?'

'No.'

A wave of tiredness washes over her. 'Can I just sit here and wait?'

Imran shakes his head.

Viv's bus chugs slowly along the underpass, past a well-tagged wall with graffiti of a cat smoking a spliff, along with some impressive but unreadable pop-art writing and a small but legible *Fuck the Tories*.

'Anyway, it's done,' Viv says to Jamie's voicemail. 'Not how you wanted.' She screws up her eyes. 'Not how I wanted either.'

She turns over the tiger-print fabric of her jacket cuff. The silky jade lining is perfectly stitched. She strokes it, nostalgic already, for something that's still here.

She's never owned anything like this jacket in her life. It's the kind of thing you'd get from a London shop with only a handful of items spaced out on heavy white hangers. The kind of place Viv has never been in. She's never had her Julia-Roberts-in-*Pretty-Woman* moment, never got to say *big mistake, huge*. The one time she got (mistakenly) assumed to be a sex worker, she didn't get taken on a shopping spree by a man in a Lotus Esprit, just got left forty notes on the bedside table, along with some chewed gum in an old Metrolink receipt.

This jacket is the nicest thing she owns. But she doesn't actually own it.

And why this is feeling like a problem today, Viv doesn't know.

She gets up and presses the button to stop the bus.

Viv enters the bar, the stripes of neon light from the sign strobing her dress.

Rob looks up from scooping ice. 'Fancy.'

'Always.' Viv sits on a stool. 'Can you stop me being able to think, please?'

Rob reaches behind for Viv's favourite gin. He has his tea towel tucked in his back pocket, his usual drooping linen tail. 'Wedding?'

'Funeral.'

He pours her a drink. 'Sorry. Family?'

'My uncle.'

He looks up. *'Another* uncle?'

'Same one. Disco guy from last year.' Viv takes off her jacket. 'Rob, someone left this jacket here at the end of the night six months ago. I promise I didn't steal it.' She holds it out. 'I didn't try *that* hard to find out whose it was.'

Rob studies her. 'If the person left their number, I'll still have it.'

Viv nods.

'Shame. I always thought that coat suited you.'

Viv wrinkles her nose. 'Nah.' She hands Rob the jacket. 'I'm an ASOS girl.'

She gets her phone out to pay, noticing her bag's still-attached price tag.

She rips the tag off, shaking her head.

Personal growth can be so fucking inconvenient.

Viv drinks at her stool. She chats to Rob. She texts Last Resort Steve.

I owe you cash for those gummies last Christmas.

He messages back.

361

Don't worry about it.

A minute later:

Up to much?

Viv replies.

Busy. And, Steve, back yourself. You deserve to be with people who message you sober.

Viv stirs her third gin idly with her straw. She hunches, putting her mouth down the glass, drinking without lifting. Turns out it's quite tiring, being caught in a time loop. She's not surprised Jamie needed a long nap.

The voice at her shoulder is low. 'Don't freak out.'

Viv freezes, absolutely freaking out, her mouth still on the rim of the glass.

Rob glances up from cutting a lime. He makes eye contact with the person. 'Be with you in a second, mate.'

'It's not bad.' Sean's breath is hot on Viv's ear. 'I just want to talk.'

Viv senses him back away. She spins on her stool.

Sean takes a seat at the table in the window. He sits awkwardly, his palms flat to the table, his chair pushed back, communicating *I'm not here to kill you.*

'Rob,' Viv whispers. 'That guy by the window.' She doesn't take her gaze from Sean. 'I'm scared of him.'

'Want me to get him to leave?'

'Maybe.' Viv's armpits spring with sweat. 'For now, just keep an eye on us.'

Viv heads over to Sean. 'How did you find me?'

'I looked at bars you were tagged in on Instagram. Took two whole seconds.'

Viv folds her arms.

'I'm not a threat, Viv. Look around, there are fifty people in here. What do you think I'm going to do, overpower everyone with my superhuman strength?'

'If you even give a hint of standing up' – Viv puts her hands on the back of the chair opposite – 'I'm going to get you with this chair.'

Viv shoves the chair aggressively, making it squeak. She could herd him backwards, like a lion tamer. Surely you don't need much upper-body strength if it's a life-or-death survival situation? That's how Waitrose mums flip Vauxhall Astras off trapped babies.

Sean raises his palms.

'Keep your hands where I can see them.'

He keeps them in the air. 'Why did you accuse me of wanting to kill you?'

Viv sighs.

'Because I have to tell you' – his hands sag – 'it upset me.'

'Yes, yes.' Viv gives a dismissive wave. 'But don't you think the polite thing, after everything you've done today, is not to also act like I'm nuts? Don't add gaslighting to murder. We both know you wanted me dead to stop me telling people about Alison.' Viv shakes her head. 'Which I didn't even know – not at the beginning. You are the first person in this family to give me *way* too much credit, so more fool you. And no one believed me anyway.'

'You say that' – Sean keeps his hands in the air – 'but Duncan won't answer my calls.'

Viv looks up.

'He wouldn't talk to me before I left. He won't answer my messages. And you and he are the only people in my birth family I care about.'

Viv grips the chair harder. 'You care about me? How do you square that with the fact you were going to kill me?'

'How can you *say* that?'

This is an impossible conversation. Technically, Sean hasn't done anything to Viv – if you ignore the other eighty-five lives, which Viv is finding quite hard to do.

'I *never* would have hurt you!' Sean looks pathetic – hangdog. Like he's watching a dog hanging, and it's his own puppy being led by the tiny lead, up the scaffold. Is Sean genuinely hurt?

Does he not know what he's capable of?

Viv looks at him, and realises maybe he doesn't. Maybe he thinks he was just fantasising about killing Viv. He doesn't know he followed through on every previous occasion. He doesn't have a Jamie around, bleating in his ear about all the shit decisions he's made in eighty-five lives.

Sean's the lucky one. Not having Jamie around would be *so much* better for the self-esteem.

Viv sighs. 'I'm not clever enough to have this conversation.'

Sean's voice is gentle. 'How much have you had to drink?'

'Don't fuck with me. Sean. You haven't tried to kill me yet – fine. But you still killed Alison. We both know it.'

Viv just holds Sean's gaze.

'Alison was braindead. She was going to die any day.' Sean looks at the table. 'That's the only reason I did it.'

'*You're admitting it?*' Viv blinks. 'What the fuck? *You did it?*'

'You said you knew!' Sean's eyes widen in panic. 'You said not to lie!'

'Yes, but *I'm right*?' Viv screeches back the chair she's holding. 'Fucking hell, Sean!'

'I know.' He holds up his palms. 'I know.'

Viv stares. 'But I'm never right!'

'You need to know, I never would have done it for me. I only ever would have done it for Archie.'

54

One Year Ago
After the Halfway Café

Sean let himself into his home, his legs stiff after a four-hour round trip for a short conversation with his brother.

The air in the flat felt damp.

He put his keys down on the table, next to Paula's insulin pen and a half-eaten ham sandwich, one he'd made for her that morning and left for her in the fridge. She rarely finished food these days.

He went over to Paula and Archie on the sofa. 'Why is the heating not on?'

Paula looked up. 'It's April.'

'But it's like February in here.' Their flat was a miracle of science, having both draughts and black mould: both too much air, and not enough.

'You didn't pick up the phone.' Paula re-supported Archie's head. 'I was worried.'

He pushed her fringe away from her forehead and kissed her. 'I was driving.'

That wasn't why.

'That reminds me – we got a speeding ticket on Archie's birthday. Outrageous.' Paula looked up. 'Think they caught me on camera on all fours in the back?'

Sean frowned.

Paula handed him Archie. 'They didn't. It's a joke.'

'Sorry.' Sean cradled his son. 'I'm just slow at the moment, that's all.' He sniffed his son's head, taking in his fresh-bread smell. For a millisecond, everything felt calmer, lighter.

Then thoughts of Dad slammed back, and Sean's chest felt like it would break.

'Did Duncan want to meet to make plans for the funeral? Or did he want to *talk* talk? I know it's horrible to speak of silver linings at a time like this but—'

'Stop.' Paula had always been an optimist. He didn't know what had happened in her life to make her so positive.

It will definitely come to less than fifty quid, we've only bought basic stuff.

I can definitely put up a straight shelf without a spirit level.

We're going to be OK, Sean. We're going to be OK.

'When we go to the funeral' – Paula spoke like life was so simple – 'you can introduce me to Duncan.'

'But I don't want you to go to the funeral.'

Paula hunched her brows.

'There's no one left I want you to meet. You and Archie are too precious. This is my new start.'

Archie started to mewl, and Paula indicated to take him. She unhooked her nursing bra and flipped down a cup.

Sean sank next to her. The sofa sagged. He braced to stop rolling into her. This flat took every opportunity to remind him it wasn't good enough. *Fully furnished to a high spec*, the advert had said, because landlords got to say that now, as long as the place had a roof, and a door, and no cockroaches dropping through the light fitting to the floor in a sinister *pat, pat, pat.*

The day the landlord showed them round, he'd parked up in a Tesla. Sean had said that to Paula, and she'd told him bitterness didn't suit him. And Sean didn't have the heart to point out it did. When he was with Paula, he acted like the kind of person she thought she'd met. Maybe, in time, Sean could become that person.

Maybe, in time, he'd think he could put up a shelf without needing a spirit level too?

Paula looked up from Archie. 'What did Duncan want?'

'To tell me Dad forgave me before he died.'

'Oh, Sean.' Paula leaned in, making the sofa sag more. She held him with her free arm.

Sean breathed in the lemongrass smell of her neck. 'He never held it against me, what happened at the wedding. He was just hurt. It was just words.'

Paula pulled back. 'He left you money?'

'Yes.' Sean paused. 'Maybe no. Half a house, potentially. Some savings. But, Paula, the whole thing's so messy. It's—'

'Oh, my God.' Paula's eyes filmed with tears. 'You mean we get to move out of this shithole?' She moved slowly to standing, holding Archie. 'Bye bye, window mould? Bye bye, Tesla cunt?'

Sean was saying this in the wrong order. 'Maybe. But—'

'I can use a credit card?' Paula's voice went higher. 'I can get rid of this six-way-hand-me-down buggy with beetroot stains, one that wheels like a broken shopping trolley?'

Tears streamed down her face. One dripped from her chin onto Archie's scalp. Archie stopped feeding.

'Give him to me.' Sean took Archie and turned away. 'It's not that simple.'

Paula put her hands to her face, shaking.

And he couldn't quite say it. Not what he needed to say. Not with the shaking.

'We might not be able to sell Dad's house.' *Say it.* 'And I don't know how long probate takes.' *Say it, say it, say it.* 'And ...'

'I'm so sorry about your dad, Sean!' Paula was sobbing: ugly, chest-racking sobs. 'I'm so, so sorry!'

Sean held Archie tighter. 'I know.'

'But this means we're going to be OK?' Paula walked into his eyeline, tears still streaming. '*Actually* OK, like magic? I'm so sorry, Sean!'

Sean watched his wife ugly-cry, emoting and apologising, months of fear coming out with the liquid noises.

If he'd been a better man, they would have had a home in the first place.

Paula sob-said something, her communication jolting and liquid.

Sean handed her a tissue. 'Can you say that again?'

Paula blew her nose. She gathered herself.

'I said I'm going to order a buggy. On a credit card.' She said it like a statement, but looked up in a question.

Sean stared at Archie. This was his job now: protecting this guy.

Alison would die in time. She *had* to.

'Yes,' Sean said finally. 'Why don't you order that buggy.'

Paula put her face in her hands. She sobbed again.

'*Do it*,' Sean repeated, his voice stronger. 'Order it today.'

He picked up the rest of Paula's abandoned ham sandwich, despite its curling, hardened crusts, and shoved it into his mouth in one go.

55

Now

'I was even right about the insulin?' Viv can't believe this. 'I was right about *everything*? I *can't* be.' She raises her hands to her hair. 'I'm *never* right.'

Sean stares, eyes wide. 'Then can we rewind ...?'

'How?'

'The small print of the will wasn't meant for situations like this. Alison was already dead, in all the ways that matter.' In his panic, Sean's gabbling. 'Mark and Chrissy had Alison's money, they didn't even know about Dad's. Archie had *nothing.*'

'If you'd given Mark and Chrissy the chance, they might have given you the money.'

Sean looks up. 'For such a fuckup, how are you so naïve?'

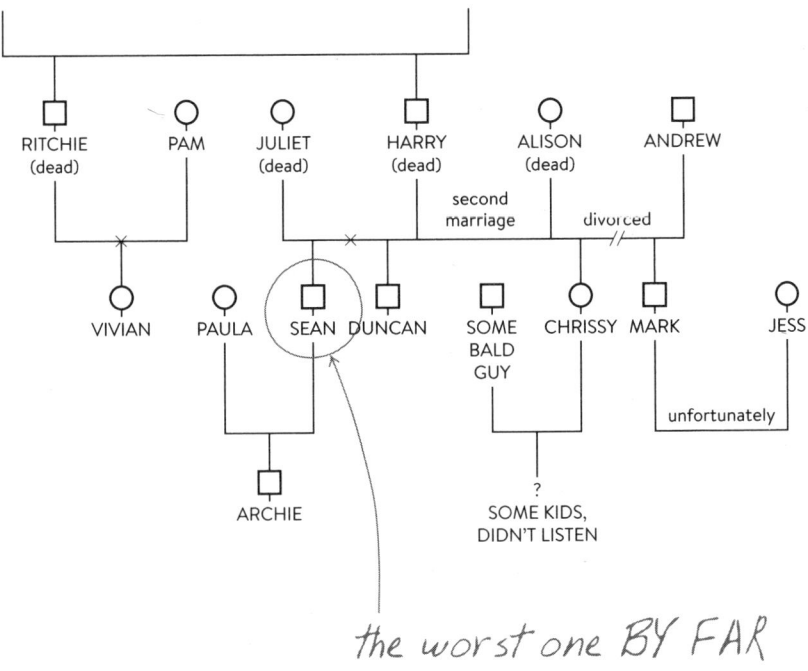

the worst one BY FAR

'And there was me, thinking you liked me. *You're* the fuckup Sean. How many people have *I* killed?'

She needs to *Minority Report* this guy – fast. Get him sent down for thought crimes.

'Mark and Chrissy would have kept the money.' Sean's voice is low. 'Anyone would.'

'People are better than that.' But Viv can't be sure. Didn't Mark tell himself he was leaving Jess, just so he could stay the good guy in his head? Most people don't have a realistic amount of self-loathing, not like Viv. They can walk the earth thinking they are adequate, able to look in the mirror without pharmaceutical help.

'Vets put animals out of their misery every day.'

'And did I need putting out of my misery too?'

And there it is. She sees it in his eyes. The flash of guilt. He is lying. 'You're wrong. I never would have ever ...'

Viv doesn't comment. 'But you didn't even have to kill me, don't you see now? You should have known no one would believe me! I told the truth and they kicked me out anyway. How can you have got this so wrong?'

'They kicked me out too!'

Viv stares. 'They believed me?'

'About the burger buns. Chrissy was furious.' His voice gets quieter. 'But Duncan won't speak to me.' He holds her gaze. 'I didn't actually do it, Viv. I didn't actually push you. That's the thing to remember.'

Viv blinks. 'Get out.' She raises her lion-taming chair. 'Get the fuck out of my bar!'

Sean picks up his coat. 'Take care, Viv. See you in the next life.'

At the choice of words, Viv flinches.

He holds up his hands. 'I promise I won't contact you again.'

Viv follows him to the door. She watches him head down the road, hunched and slow. She doesn't take her gaze off him until he's out of sight.

Half an hour later, Viv's had two more gins and Sean still hasn't come back. She finishes her drink and leaves the bar, walking out into the chill of the cloudless night. Overhead, a streetlamp buzzes.

She takes in this world: the world in which she is going to survive.

The world in which she is *right*.

The world in which she's the good guy? Maybe?

Viv decides not to dwell on that thought. She's never been good with change.

A fox sniffs around some bins, its eyes flashing white in the glare from the streetlamp. It snouts a discarded packet of crisps, turning the packet, trying to get in.

The fox sees Viv. It freezes.

'Evening.' Viv crouches. She opens the packet, ripping it down the middle. She lays the crisps on the pavement between herself and the fox, spreading the foil in the manner of someone laying out crisps to share at a pub table.

The fox just looks at her, not moving.

'Go on.' Viv frowns. 'For you, mate.' She steps back. 'I don't share bin crips.'

The fox approaches the crisps tentatively, moving with elegant, nearly weightless steps. Viv watches it for a moment.

She hitches her tote bag of shoes onto her shoulder, shivering, wondering why she didn't leave it till tomorrow to give back the jacket. Her head light from gin, she starts to trudge the three miles home, conscious of being alive, her arms and legs goosepimpling under the clear night sky.

56

Twenty-Two Years Ago
The Summer Viv Was Fourteen

The night Viv sort-of stole Harry's car – *sort-of* stole it, or *tried to* steal it, or *pretended to* steal it (Pam was never great at reading her daughter) – Pam sat motionless in the front room after she sent Viv to bed.

The timer on the table lamp clicked the light off, leaving her in darkness. She still didn't move.

Pam had always been someone who looked for the positives in any situation. She had had many nights in her life worse than this, and probably would again. She could find several small mercies.

That Harry's car was a manual. That Viv didn't know how to find the biting point.

That she said she only planned to drive it to the end of the cul-de-sac, that she never intended to go on the main road.

And that the night it all happened, Frank was away at a work conference.

The next day, Pam and Harry sat across from each other at the kitchen table.

Pam blew on her cup of tea.

'I give up.' Harry looked up. 'God knows what we do.'

Pam appreciated the *we*. 'I've given her a bollocking.'

'So have I.'

'It's not enough.'

'Mine was pretty brutal.' Harry gave a faint smile. 'Lots of threats. Repeated, aggressive use of the word *lady*.'

'I'm so sorry.'

'Pam.' Harry sighed the sigh of the weary. 'You don't have to say that to me. She's my problem too.' He paused. 'I don't mean *problem*.'

'You do, but it's fine.' Pam lifted her mug to her lips, the tea sloshing and threatening to spill.

Harry sighed. 'She's a little idiot, but she's our idiot.'

Pam nodded. 'And she apologised. She sounded like she meant it.'

Pam blew on her tea again.

'You know what she's like when she's bored. She finds life hard with ... that personality. And she lost her dad so young.'

'You always make excuses for her.'

'I'm not saying she wasn't a dick, Pam. I'm definitely not saying that.'

'Do I tell the school?'

'Why? So they can go harder on her? She knows what she's done. She'll be good for a while.'

'She set the table last night without being asked.'

'There you go,' Harry said.

'So what do we do?'

'We do what we always do.'

Pam sipped her tea.

'We make her life hell. And we deal with the next thing when it happens.'

Pam was stirring homemade squash soup that evening when the front door slammed.

Frank didn't even make it into the kitchen. *'I heard she stole Harry's car!'*

Pam closed her eyes and did the mental news chain. Juliet must have told Angela, and Angela must have told the woman who worked on Frank's reception.

Of course, Angela was on Pam's side, aggressively so. That didn't mean she was helpful.

Pam stirred her soup for a minute longer. She went into the front room to coax Frank into the kitchen.

'She's turning into a little psychopath!'

Pam glanced at the door to the lounge. Viv was *right there*.

'Are you happy bringing up a car thief? She needs to be in a borstal.'

'Can we please talk about this later.'

'She's a nightmare! I can't take this anymore!'

Pam watched Frank storm out of the back door. She straightened the sleeves of her shirt.

It was time.

She waited, mindlessly watching TV, knowing Frank would stay at the pub until closing time.

He'd left his work mobile on the table, and it wouldn't stop pinging, even though it didn't usually go in the evening at all. Eventually, Pam switched it off.

At eleven-thirty, there was a sound of the key in the door.

She met him in the hallway and made her voice low. 'Don't take your shoes off.'

She pulled her coat off the hook and beckoned him towards the back door.

The two sat across from each other at Pam's rickety garden table, under the weak beam of the security light. A bat flapped out from the neighbour's oak tree.

'Pam,' Frank had that sweet, smoky smell of pub. 'Look at me.' He leaned on his forearms. 'Everyone agrees she's a nightmare. *Everyone!*'

'Everyone? You told people at the pub?'

'Just two. I needed to let off steam.' Even from the other side of the table, his beer breath smelled sweet. 'We have to do something.'

It was so different, Pam thought, when that *we* came from Frank rather than Harry.

'She's dangerous.'

Pam leaned forward. 'Frank, this isn't working.'

The frown lines in Frank's forehead deepened.

'You and me. I can't see how this can work.'

Frank grabbed Pam's hand in both of his. 'Of course it can.'

'You have to leave.'

'You don't mean that.'

Pam said nothing.

'Don't do this, Pam. You make me so happy! And I make you happy too! I feel so lucky to come home to you, despite—'

He swallowed.

Pam let out a long breath.

Frank held her hand tighter. 'Not *despite*.'

Pam held his gaze.

'She'll move out in a few years. I can cope till then.' Frank pulled Pam's hand closer. 'It's just a bad week.'

Pam pulled her hand away. 'I'll pay for the hotel. You can pick up the rest of your stuff at the weekend.' She stood. 'And I know this isn't the time, but your work phone is going crazy.'

She walked out of the garden gate.

She perched on the seat of a bus shelter, putting her arms around herself, shivering in the dark.

It was done. The right thing, for her daughter. The person that drove her mad, that she worried about constantly, that she couldn't say the right thing to.

The person she had to put first.

The person she loved more than anyone in the world.

57

Now

Viv wakes to a door being thrown open. Angry steps. '*Please tell me you haven't got my moisturiser.*'

'Shit.' Viv stretches to the bedside table, something sharp digging into her side. She grabs Bethan's pot. 'Take it.'

'I will. Because it's mine.' Bethan snatches it. 'Nice PJs.'

Viv looks down at her grey floaty dress. She slept in it, and now it smells of beer with an undercurrent of sleep-musk. The sharp thing digging into her side is the price tag. 'I'm sorry about your moisturiser. I'll never take it again.'

'Why aren't you saying *it's just moisturiser, don't be so uptight?*'

'I think' – Viv sits up straighter – 'I think I've *grown*, Bethan.'

Bethan narrows her eyes.

'And I want to make things up to you.' Viv glances at her tote bag. 'So have some shoes.'

'I don't want your shoes.'

'They're pretty. Expensive.'

'Stolen?'

'Paid for in full, with my own personal overdraft.' Viv reaches for the bag. '*And* I'm gonna clean the oven.'

Bethan frowns.

'And make you another pie. And buy laundry capsules.'

'I don't want your shitty pie. I only ever wanted you not to be a twat.'

Viv pulls her spike heels from the tote bag. 'Worn once, worth two hundred quid. They even come with a box.'

Bethan doesn't take the shoes. 'What's the catch, then?'

'No catch.'

Not taking her eyes off Viv, Bethan reaches for the shoes.

'Do I get to stay in the house if I tell you I dumped Mark yesterday?' At the surprise on Bethan's face, Viv nods. 'Looks like *Craig from work* will be buying those early-bird chow meins for one from now on.'

Does the hard line of Bethan's mouth soften a little?

She walks out of the room, shoes in one hand, moisturiser in the other.

'Actually, there *is* a catch.' Viv raises her voice. 'Those shoes hurt like hell!'

Bethan's door slams.

This is good. It's the most positive conversation she's had with Bethan in a long time.

Viv picks up her phone. She has several missed calls from Duncan. And a message from Mum.

And the message from Mum is … really odd.

I believe you.

Viv frowns. She must be misunderstanding somehow. She's half-asleep still, of course: it'll make sense when she's fully awake.

She pulls the duvet up round her ears and lets her eyes close.

She wakes to the burst of hardstyle music through the wall. A brightness peeks round the edges of her curtains.

Bethan pushes the door open gently. 'It's 5 p.m.' She tucks her silky blouse into faux-leather trousers. 'You've really ended things with Mark?'

'Yeah.' Viv leans up onto her elbows. 'It's time to make some different mistakes. I can find new exciting ways to set my life on fire.' She nods at her shoes, on Bethan's feet. 'Those look great.'

'I'm off to Francine's gender reveal.'

'She's really milking these pre-baby parties, isn't she?' Viv looks at the shoes again. 'I hope it's not a standing one.'

'She's having a cake with a colour reveal inside. Five tiers.'

Viv raises her chin. 'Was I invited to this party?'

'Francine said specifically not.'

'Her cocktails were shit anyway.' Viv shuffles down the bed. 'And I'm not one for paddocks.'

Bethan leaves. Viv closes her eyes again.

★

A car purrs outside the window, the engine throaty and irregular.

Viv presses her face into the pillow.

Outside, the voice is forceful. 'Honestly, go. I'll be fine.'

'I'll wait, check she's there first.'

Viv shakes her head into the pillow.

The doorbell goes, and she doesn't move. She hasn't ordered any parcels, and, yes, it's six in the afternoon, but she's *sleeping*.

The doorbell goes again. And again.

On the fourth ring, Viv throws back the duvet.

Jamie stands at the door, holding a white supermarket bag.

He barrels at her. 'You did it!'

The force of the hug makes Viv stumble back. 'You're awake!'

'I woke up in my own bed! *Tomorrow!* Which is today now, obviously.' Jamie smells of stale smoke and Fanta. 'One sec.' He turns to the blue hatchback waiting at the kerb.

The car's driver, Imran, looks Viv up and down. 'So you *do* know Jamie.'

'I told you I did. You shouldn't go around being so suspicious, it's not attractive.'

'Is that dress the only thing you own?'

Viv pulls it down self-consciously. 'Jamie's not the only one who's tired.'

Imran flicks on the indicator. 'He's still exhausted. Look after him.'

Viv nods. 'I'll make sure he doesn't operate any heavy machinery.'

Viv and Jamie watch Imran drive away.

'I told him I'm ill. I said I'd explain the rest when he's back from work.' Jamie glances at Viv. 'But where do I start? I don't want to lie.'

'You *definitely* can't tell the truth.'

Jamie sighs.

Viv pats his shoulder. 'We've got hours to work on a story.'

'I brought gifts.' Jamie pulls a packet of instant noodles from the plastic bag. 'Three gifts. Three packs at once sounds like a dangerous amount of salt to me, but it's your blood pressure.'

Viv steps back to let him in. 'Best gifts ever.'

'And I brought milk, too.'

'I've got milk, though.'

'Yours is off. I'm not having you nicking Bethan's.' He walks into the kitchen. 'You have to respect the sign.' He opens the fridge and indicates the shelf – *Viv, don't eat my stuff.*

Viv sits at the table. 'You know, your fancy party trick is going to wear off soon.'

He puts the milk in the fridge. 'I can't believe you killed Sean! I know I told you I'd convinced you, but I never did manage it.'

Viv widens her eyes. 'You gaslit me? We were time loop buddies! I trusted you!'

He has the good grace to look guilty.

'And I didn't kill Sean.' Viv stares at the table. 'I just went back to the memorial and announced to the whole place he was trying to kill me.'

Jamie blinks.

'Angela tried to stage a citizen's arrest, I got thrown out by the security guard. He saw everyone thought I had lost it, that I was no threat.'

Jamie lowers himself into a chair.

'All those lives, I can't believe you didn't think of that.'

'Did *no one* believe you?'

'No. Except … hang on. I got one weird message.' Viv gets her phone. She shows Jamie the message from Mum.

I believe you.

'Think it's some kind of trick?'

Jamie just stares. 'I think you and your mum should go to couples' therapy. Can you go to the police?'

'I went already. They thought I was very strange.'

'So Sean's just going to get away with everything?'

Viv thinks about Duncan's expression. About how smart he is. About how she has several missed calls from him. 'Not everything.'

Jamie is beaming, and Viv should be happy, and she is happy, it's just …

Viv sighs. 'I just wish I'd known I had to live this life. I wouldn't have spent all my money on taxis.'

Jamie stops smiling. 'I got taxis too.'

'*And* you got sacked,' Viv says. 'Isn't this just the worst day ever?'

'Imran's taken me back. So I've had worse.' Jamie looks up. 'You've *definitely* had worse.'

Viv raises her head.

'Life forty-seven. The blood wouldn't stop, it just kept

gushing out.' Jamie indicates her head. 'You were alive, sort of, able to blink. How could there be so much blood in one skull? I could barely look at you.'

Viv makes her voice even. 'How awful that must have been for you.'

'Why us, Viv? Of all people.' Jamie shakes his head. 'That's what I haven't been able to stop thinking, now it's over. What did we do to make this happen to us?'

Viv picks up the salt cellar. She's been thinking about this too. 'I talked to Duncan yesterday. He's watched a lot of *Doctor Who*.'

'I bet.'

'He made me realise how random everything is. How unlikely it is that we were even born in the first place. It's billions to one all our ancestors survived to have children, that's before you factor in that each egg had to be fertilised by the particular sperm that made us. Even before the time loop thing happened, it's official. You and I are bona-fide miracles.'

Jamie takes a beat. 'I'm not sure anyone has ever described me as a miracle.'

Viv nods. 'But they've not thought of it that way, have they?'

'I'm pretty sure no one has described you like that either.'

'That's the point I'm making. You ask, *why us? We're nothing special.* But shouldn't the question be, *why not us?* If freaky things happen, aren't they as likely to happen to us as anyone else?'

Jamie says nothing.

'Maybe things like this happen to people all the time and

we just don't know it. After all, we're not exactly going to tell. You don't even know what to say to Imran.'

Jamie sits back. 'This whole thing hurts my head.'

Viv lets out a sigh. 'Agree. We solved my murder, so let's let ourselves off the hook here. The secrets of time and the universe might be beyond even the two of us.'

'There's so much I don't understand.'

'Tell me about it.'

'But you can fill in some. Like what happened when I was asleep. Come on.' Jamie stands. 'I'll put the noodles on, you can tell me everything that happened after you left me at the *Cables* display.'

Viv nods. 'The pans are in—'

'I know.' Jamie opens the pan drawer. 'So let me enjoy it one more time, because my predictive genius act's going to expire any second now.'

Harry and Alison's Memorial (New) WhatsApp Group

Angela

It was lovely to see you all despite … well. How are you holding up, Pam?

Angela

Everyone knows it's nothing to do with you. Sometimes the apple falls far from the tree.

Angela

And sometimes the apple is rotten.

Angela

https://podcasts.apple.co/gb/podcast/letting-go-of-toxic-people/id2694852003/?i=648354-6

Angela

Pam?

Frank

Let her be, Angela.

Angela

I'm being supportive.

Pam is typing

Angela

There you are, my lovely! How are you feeling? We're all here for you.

Angela

https://podcasts.apple.co/gb/podcast/grieving-when-theyre-not-dead/id269403/?i=6483385-3

Angela

Pam?

Angela

Pam, please don't be a stranger, just because you're ashamed. You have NOTHING to be ashamed of. Not personally.

Angela

Pam?

Angela

Pam?

Pam

Oh do shut the fuck up, Angela, I have no interest in you until you leave my daughter alone.

Pam has left the group

Acknowledgements

Getting a book onto shelves is hard when that book doesn't fit into a clear publishing category, and I want to thank my editor, Charlotte Greenwood, for taking the risk with Viv, and for delivering such a strong, fun vision for the book.

A big thanks to everyone else at Viper, particularly Miranda Jewess, Sarah Kennedy, Drew Jerrison, Sophie Pitches, Robert Loyko-Greer, Emily Jarman, Steve Coventry-Panton, and (externally) Victoria Denne and Rhian McKay. I have been so impressed by the enthusiasm and expertise of everyone throughout this process.

I want to thank my agent, Hellie Ogden, for her guidance and strategic thinking, and for pivoting when this book came out totally differently to the one we planned. *'You said you weren't going to make it funny this time'* – yes, I absolutely did say that; please take this as my public apology. Thanks so much also to Ma'suma Amiri, and to everyone at WME.

Thanks to Siobhan O'Cealliagh for the medical input. All mistakes are mine, obviously – she knows what she's doing.

A huge thanks to everyone who enjoys or reviews or talks about my books, and apologies for my liberal use of the word 'cunt'.

Writers often get asked how much of our books are taken from life, and it's generally not the big stuff. I have never, for example, got stuck in a time loop or had any kind of sex at a funeral. But where I do take from life is by stealing anecdotes, so thank you Rhea Kujawa (aloe vera plant), Kate Taft (noodles), Deana Lynch (more noodles), Helen Cain (kebab in handbag), me (smashed restaurant table), Mum ('don't buy the big towels'), Tim Muir ('shirt boy'), Stu Moffat (specific explicit dialogue).

I am constantly buoyed in this batshit industry by the lovely writer friends who tolerate me despite my woeful use of social media and the fact I'm forever saying *'please can we stop talking about fucking publishing?'* Special thanks to Nicola Mostyn for being my first industry reader: a great champion and a brutal editor. One of those roles is more fun than the other, but I value both.

To my first actual reader: thank you John Fletcher, and apologies you have to read under such heavy surveillance. Yes, I'm aware reading is meant to be a relaxing activity. I know it's not ideal that the merest sniff from you provokes an owl-head-swivel and a series of barked questions, but you know the drill by now. Thanks for not falling asleep during this one.

And, finally, to the rest of my friends and family ... I think I'm meant to thank you too, yet I can't help noticing you did fuck all. Let's just say that if you did anything towards this book (unlikely), thank you – and if you didn't do anything (it's this one), I love you anyway. x